"SO, NICKOLAI, HOW DO YOU FEEL WORKING WITH A BUNCH OF HUMANS?"

"Mosasa isn't human."

"Yeah, you mentioned that, didn't you? Mind expounding on that little tidbit?"

Nickolai pondered his options for a moment. The fact he carried a rather large secret with him made him reluctant, but Kugara was the only other member of the team he would feel comfortable having as an "ally." He also thought she had a point that they both needed one. This mission was going to take them far outside the grip of the BMU, the only law recognized by their nominal comrades. And would he want to trust his life to humans like Wahid or Parvi, or even Fitzpatrick?

Nickolai finished his pitcher and told Kugara what he could about Mosasa. "Our employer," Nickolai said, "doesn't just *work* with AIs. He doesn't *own* them."

"Meaning?"

"He *is* them."

Kugara lowered her mug. The glass hit the table with a slightly liquid squeak. A similar sound seemed to come from her throat. After a moment she said, "Shit."

"Tjaele Mosasa is a construct controlled by a salvaged Race AI device. The 'man' who briefed us is no more real than my right arm. . . ."

**Other fine DAW science fiction and fantasy from
S. ANDREW SWANN**

PROPHETS

Apotheosis: Book One

S. ANDREW SWANN

DAW BOOKS, INC.
DONALD A. WOLLHEIM, FOUNDER
375 Hudson Street, New York, NY 10014

ELIZABETH R. WOLLHEIM
SHEILA E. GILBERT
PUBLISHERS
www.dawbooks.com

First Printing March 2009
1 2 3 4 5 6 7 8 9

 **DAW TRADEMARK REGISTERED
U.S. PAT. AND TM. OFF. AND FOREIGN COUNTRIES
—MARCA REGISTRADA
HECHO EN U.S.A.**

PRINTED IN THE U.S.A.

This is for Michelle,
for putting up with all my crap.

DRAMATIS PERSONAE

Bakunin

Father Francis Xavier Mallory—Roman Catholic Priest and veteran of the Occisis Marines.

Nickolai Rajasthan—Exiled scion of the House of Rajasthan. Descendant of genetically engineered tigers.

Vijayanagara Parvi—Mercenary pilot from Rubai.

Tjaele Mosasa—Proprietor of Mosasa Salvage, owner of the *Eclipse*.

Jusuf Wahid—Mercenary from Davado Poli.

Julia Kugara—Mercenary from Dakota. Descendant of genetically engineered humans. Former member of the DPS (Dakota Planetary Security).

Eclipse

"Bill"—Paralian expert in physics.

Dr. Sharon Dörner—Xenobiologist from Acheron.

Dr. Samson Brody—Cultural anthropologist from Bulawayo.

Dr. Leon Pak—Linguist from Terra.

Rebecca Tsoravitch—Data analyst from Jokul.

Earth

Cardinal Jacob Anderson—Bishop of Ostia, Dean of the College of Cardinals, Vatican Secretary of State.

Yousef Al-Hamadi—Eridani Caliphate Minister-at-Large in Charge of External Relations.

Khamsin

Admiral Muhammad Hussein al Khamsiti—Commander of the *Prophet's Voice* and battlegroup.

Admiral Naji Bitar—Commander of the *Prophet's Sword* and battlegroup.

Salmagundi

Flynn Jorgenson—Forestry surveyor.

Alexander Shane—Senior member of the Grand Triad.

CONTENTS

FIRST PROLOGUE

Signs

The no-mind not-thinks no-thoughts about no-things.
—SIDDHARTHA GAUTAMA BUDDHA
(563–483 BCE)

CHAPTER ONE

The Music of the Spheres

Blaming Fate, God, or Destiny is an admission that you
don't have a clue what's going on.
—*The Cynic's Book of Wisdom*

The only good is knowledge and the only evil is ignorance.
—SOCRATES
(470–390 BCE)

Date: 2502.12.09 (Standard)
5.48 ly from Xi Virginis

The egg moves at half light speed through the vacuum, its surface a deep blackness absorbing every stray photon, emitting
nothing. Particles with small masses—from stray protons up to
grains of interstellar dust—slide around it, nanometers from its
surface, following the ovoid perimeter until they find their original track on the opposite side, where they resume their motion
as if the egg had not crossed their path. The only sign that something exists beneath its event-horizon skin is the resonance in
the fabric of space-time as it ripples gravity in its wake.

The egg has traveled for over two centuries, 228.326 years
standard to be exact. Viewed from the perspective of those
who built it, its journey has barely begun. The Protean outpost on the lawless planet Bakunin, the origin of the egg, had
secluded itself from the persecution of the rest of human civilization and looked far beyond the limits of that civilization
to propagate itself. The egg's destination is removed from its
builders by thousands of light-years in space, and a million
years in time. Packed within it is the combined resources and
knowledge of the entire Protean civilization.

Within the egg sleep the minds of a quarter million people.

One mind is awake. An artificial mind devoid of boredom or emotion. A mind that can observe the egg's travels over the course of an aeon and not go insane.

A mind that sees with an almost omniscient eye.

The egg itself is a collector of every scrap of radiant energy; it touches every ripple in the fabric of space, hears the twist of momentum of the particles slipping close to its skin, and smells the quantum foam of virtual particles that break across it as it moves through the vacuum. The mind is as aware as any sentient being can possibly be.

For all that, the mind's job is simple. Watch, and ensure that the egg does not move through anything that could damage it or its contents. That is the directive, the mind's sole reason for being.

The mind cannot feel pride, but it knows that it is good at its job. It knows in a concrete fashion that it has saved the egg from danger 1,568 times in the past 200 years standard.

Dust will slide by the dent the egg makes in the universe around it, but a stone any larger would not be so easily dissuaded at these velocities. While the egg could withstand the occasional grain of interstellar matter colliding with its surface, the mind knows the distance they are traveling. Even sand grains could cause an unacceptable wear on the egg's resources over the course of their long journey. And, of course, a rock of any size larger than a pea might prove crippling. Fortunately, the egg is forward-looking enough to maneuver around large obstacles, from dark patches dense with interstellar matter to a variable star whose motion would carry it into the egg's path 2,856 years standard from now.

The mind does not feel curiosity. The mind does not sense that as a weakness, since it has a defined procedure for assigning priority to stimuli. Threats receive its full attention. Nonthreats are discarded as irrelevant. Unclassifiable phenomena are stored pending the mind's ability to determine if they are threats or not.

For the past five years, the mind has struggled with its first dilemma. It has observed spectral anomalies around the star Xi Virginis that it cannot classify, and since first detecting it, the mind has returned to consider it every one to five seconds.

Each time, the datum refuses to fit into the mind's model of the universe.

Despite its lack of curiosity, after reviewing the same item for the two hundred millionth time without being able to arrive at any conclusion, the mind decides that it is unable to properly classify the event.

Xi Virginis is now too close in time and space to ignore. Without deceleration, the egg will pass within three light-years of the star. However, decelerating the egg enough to avoid it would radically alter the path of the egg and, therefore, its mission.

The mind of the egg concludes that it requires consultation with its passengers in order to proceed. With its decision, a quarter million minds held in stasis are freed.

There is chaos as the population of the egg wakes. A quarter million thinking individuals suddenly occupy the single body of the egg, each one seizing its share of its processing and sensory abilities. All have a last common memory of donating the contents of their mind to the egg. All have the common shock that they are the result of that copy, and the person they remember is centuries and light-years removed from them now. All suffer disappointment in not finding themselves at their destination. All look out in wonder with the sense array of the egg, once the sole province of the mind.

All hear the mind's message.

"There is something requiring your attention."

The mind is surrounded by a sphere of attention as the population focuses on it. Emotionless, the mind does not flinch from stating that it is unable to decide how to respond to the anomaly. It offers the choice of proceeding as planned, or decelerating and radically altering either their ultimate destination, or near doubling their travel time. To the mind, velocity is too precious a commodity to dispense with without a communal decision.

Almost at once, the populace wonders, "Why?"

The mind shows them the anomaly around Xi Virginis.

Light speed thoughts ripple across the mental sphere inside the egg. Individuals cluster and debate the meaning of the mind's observations. Most of the population study the phenomenon with the egg's own eyes. Camps develop in the debate, first thousands, then hundreds, then a few dozen as points of view converge and communal differences are ironed out.

In the end, there are three camps of belief.

The first, smallest group maintains that the anomaly is non-threatening and should be ignored. The mind should not adjust the course of the egg.

The second group, almost five times the size of the first, preaches caution. Their mission to seed another world should not be endangered by a cavalier attitude. The mind should start maneuvering; decelerating the egg to ensure that the egg comes no closer than ten light-years of the phenomenon, whatever it is.

The last group, and a majority, urges a course of action that the mind hadn't even considered. They should maneuver slightly to take the egg even closer, within a light-year of Xi Virginis. Their mission should not just be a journey of space and time, but one of knowledge. They should, in fact, be studying this anomaly, not running away or ignoring it.

Consensus is long in coming, but the egg eventually maneuvers to come as close as possible to Xi Virginis.

The decision is a mistake, and when the egg is within two light-years of Xi Virginis, it is too late for the mind to correct it.

CHAPTER TWO

Vocation

Everyone is vulnerable to their past.
>—*The Cynic's Book of Wisdom*

I would far rather be ignorant, than wise in the foreboding of evil.

>—AESCHYLUS
>(525–456 BCE)

Date: 2525.09.14 (Standard)
Occisis–Alpha Centauri

Father Mallory was two weeks into his xenoarchaeology class before one of his students finally asked him "the question." The questioner was a kid, barely eighteen standard, with a complexion and height that tagged him as having come from off-planet. Most of Mallory's class were squat fair-skinned Occisian stock who had already done their tour in the Marines. Judging by age, many had put in more rotations than Mallory had.

"Master Gideon," Mallory read the student's name off of the holo display and used his most scholarly voice, "That question is always asked when I give this class." Mallory smiled and faced the ranks of almost-solid holos showing students scattered all over Occisis. Even the classroom was a projection, as Father Mallory actually stood in a small room in the administrative offices of St. Marbury University.

"Can anyone identify the flaw in Master Gideon's question?"

The question was in large part rhetorical. Rarely did anyone ever answer; rarer still did they answer correctly. Mallory paced the two square meters that represented actual floor. Behind him, a display that was virtual to a second level of abstraction showed digital models of artifacts on the Martian surface overlaid by wireframe models of what the original structures might have looked like.

"He is asking if we know why the race we have named the Dolbrians died out a hundred million years ago. As I said, it's a question I am always asked in this class in one form or another. Every person who has ever studied them asks why. A race that left artifacts on planets across of all of explored space, who terraformed planets in dozens, if not hundreds or thousands of systems, a race that spread so widely and evidenced technology and engineering skill barely on the cusp of our comprehension. Why would they die out so completely?"

He had their attention.

"Anyone see a flaw in my premise?"

One of the student holos raised his hand. A Master Bartholomew whose image showed digital pixilation and a slight jerkiness that indicated his signal was bouncing off a commsat or three.

"Master Bartholomew?"

There was a full second delay before Master Bartholomew answered. His skin was weathered, and he still wore his hair cut in military style. He had unit tattoos on his neck that left Mallory subliminally aware of his own, under his collar. *Someday I should have the tats removed,* he thought. *The implants, too.*

"Do we know they died out?"

"Exactly." Mallory pointed at the display behind them. "This is a ruin, Mars is a ruin. For all we know this entire part of the galaxy is a ruin. But the presence of a ruin no more proves the extinction of the Dolbrians than the ruins of Athens prove the extinction of the Greeks. Just because I cannot point to some being somewhere and say, 'This, I know, is a Dolbrian,' does not mean they ceased to exist. Over a time-scale of millions of years we have very little certainty. It is quite possible that the race of Dolbrians evolved into something else, the Paralians, the Volerans, maybe even us . . ."

Bartholomew frowned. "Father, that seems an odd assertion from a priest."

"How so?"

"Doesn't evolution contradict—"

Mallory held up his hand, "Stop right there." Inside, he sighed. This was an undergraduate elective course and generally had an even split between humanities and science majors. Sometimes the students in the humanities had strange ideas about evolution. "So we don't get sidetracked here. Evolution is a scientific description of how species change over time, neither it, nor any other scientific theory, make assertions about faith, Church doctrine, or the nature of God."

"But . . ."

"If you wish, after class I can direct you to Papal rulings on the matter, some of which are over five hundred years old."

Bartholomew looked crestfallen, and Mallory opened his mouth to add something about how Church doctrine upheld the sacred nature of all intelligent life when his holographic classroom abruptly vanished.

He stared a moment at the blank white walls, frowning. After a moment, when his class didn't reappear, he picked up the small comm unit mounted next to the holo controls set in the wall.

"Maintenance," Mallory told the interface as he looked at the small readout showing the status of his classroom.

Mallory didn't know why he looked at the display; he had no idea what the columns of numbers meant. Maintenance probably wouldn't even ask him about the display, assuming—in his case, correctly—the technical ineptitude of the faculty.

"University maintenance, O'Brien here."

"Hello, I have a problem with my classroom."

"Room number, please."

"One-oh-six-five."

"Father Mallory?"

"Yes, my classroom disappeared in the middle of a lecture."

"I'm calling you up on my screen right now—hmm."

"Yes?"

"This isn't a technical issue."

"Mr. O'Brien, I have thirty-five students that just vanished—"

"I can see that. Your class was subjected to an administrative reschedule."

"What? I'm in the middle of a lecture. It's two weeks into the term. This has to be some sort of mistake."

"I can't help you there. You'll have to talk to the administration about it."

"Who authorized it?" Mallory felt a hot spark of anger.

"Only the university president has that authority."

"Thank you."

Father Mallory slowly placed the comm unit back in its cradle.

Why would the administration, the president, cancel his class assignment? Anger was giving way to serious apprehension. This kind of thing was almost always followed by leave or dismissal. In his own university days, he remembered having a mathematics instructor, Father Reynolds, disappear in the middle of the semester. The day after a new instructor appeared to teach the class, Father Reynolds' name was dropped from the faculty directory. He never knew for certain what the gnomelike calculus professor had done, but he had read rumors of some financial indiscretions involving university funds and a gambling addiction.

But for the life of him, Father Mallory couldn't think of anything done on his part that merited that kind of sanction.

"Father Mallory?"

Mallory turned to face a dark-haired woman standing in the doorway of his classroom. She was Vice-Chancellor Marie Murphy, the highest-ranking member of the laity in the university administration.

"Dr. Murphy?"

"Forgive me for interrupting your class, there is a meeting you must attend."

"This couldn't have waited?"

"No, I am afraid not."

Dr. Murphy didn't lead him up to the administrative offices as he had expected. Mallory followed her into, of all things, a freight elevator.

"What's going on?" he asked, as he followed her into the brushed-metal cube of the elevator.

"It will be explained at the meeting."

Mallory shook his head, more confused than anything else now. All the meeting rooms were in the upper floors of the building, above the classroom areas. However, Dr. Murphy keyed for the third sublevel. The only thing down there would be environmental controls for the building, maybe some storage. Mallory was surprised that the keypad accepted Dr. Murphy's input. The biometric systems in the elevator shouldn't allow either of them access to the systems areas; they weren't maintenance or security personnel.

That could be overridden by the administration, too.

Mallory became very aware of the fight-or-flight response happening in his own body. Stress and uncertainty were elevating his adrenaline levels and his old Marine implants were responding. He felt his reflexes quickening, and felt events around him slowing down.

He wiped his palms on the legs of his pants very deliberately. Habit and training, not implants, made him contemplate escape scenarios.

He closed his eyes and started running through the rosary in his mind to rein in the biological and technological panic impulses. He couldn't help but remember recent history, before the overthrow of the junta. Back when the Revolutionary Council was burning monasteries and assassinating priests and nuns in the basements of churches.

When the doors chimed and slid aside, Mallory chided himself for being surprised not to see a death squad.

She led him down a concrete corridor. The hall was unadorned, lit by a diffuse white light that seemed to erase any character from the cold gray walls. Something made him ask, "Where were you during the revolution?"

"Pardon?"

"Do you remember the purges?"

"My father told me stories, but I was only three when the junta fell . . ."

"Oh." Mallory felt too old.

Their footsteps echoed as they passed ranks of large metal doors. Utilitarian plaques identified doors in some machine-readable code that looked more cryptic than any of the alien languages Mallory had studied.

Dr. Murphy stopped in front of one door that, to Mallory, didn't look any different than any of the others. She stood in front of the door, and it slid aside with a pneumatic hiss. She stepped aside and looked at Mallory.

"He's waiting for you."

"Who?"

Dr. Murphy shook her head and started back toward the elevator, leaving Mallory standing in front of the open door. He called after her, "Who?"

She didn't respond.

Mallory turned back to the open door. It was a storeroom lined with ranks of free-standing shelves. He couldn't see too deeply into the room through the shelving, but he sensed the presence of people back there somewhere.

"Hello?"

"Father Mallory," came an unfamiliar voice, "please come in."

Mallory squinted as he walked into the dark storeroom. He tensed when the door hissed shut behind him. It brought an ugly memory; the smell of burned flesh.

Mallory walked slowly down the aisle between the shelves, toward an open space at one end of the storeroom. He reached the end of the aisle and turned to face the pair of men waiting for him. He said, "So what is this . . . ?"

His voice trailed off as he realized whom he was addressing. Each of the two men wore the black-and-red cassock of a cardinal. The cardinal to the right was very familiar to Mallory; Cardinal Harris, who was normally the highest ranking member of the Catholic Church on Occisis.

At the moment, though, he wasn't.

To his right was Cardinal Jacob Anderson, Bishop of Ostia, Dean of the Sacred College of Cardinals, Secretary of State of His Holiness the Pope, arguably the highest ranking and most powerful member of the Roman Catholic Church outside of His Holiness Pope Stephen XII himself.

Father Mallory crossed himself and genuflected. "Forgive my outburst, Your Eminence."

Cardinal Anderson shook his head and gestured for Father Mallory to stand.

"You want to know why you are here. And why I am here."

Mallory nodded. "I didn't know you were on this planet."

"My son, that is because I am not officially here. His Holiness has a favor to ask of you, Father Mallory."

Cardinal Jacob Anderson explained their purpose here, all the time watching Father Mallory's reactions.

From the man's file, he was a perfect recruit for clandestine activity. Despite his age, he had the most sophisticated military training of all the recruits he had seen lately. And, as someone who fought against the Occisian Junta at a time when most of the Occisis Marines had backed the secularist revolutionary movement, Mallory was someone whose loyalty to Mother Church was unquestionable.

That would be important, because what the Church would ask of him would place him on his own, out of contact, for an extended period. There were also indications that what he would face would be spiritually threatening. Cardinal Anderson hoped that the man's grounding as a Jesuit academic, as well at the practical training of an Occisis Marine, would help him face what might be happening by Xi Virginis, seventy-five light-years past the edge of human space.

He looked at Mallory, who patiently waited for him to continue. He could tell the import of a direct papal request was sinking in. Physics rendered simultaneity meaningless for reference frames separated by light-years, making it impossible to interact with people across such distances. A personal envoy was required for any sort of dialogue, but that envoy didn't have to be Cardinal Anderson.

The fact that he had come here to personally talk to Father Mallory had made as much of an impression as if the pope himself had come here. Which was the point, as Cardinal Anderson believed that the Church sat at the cusp of a historical change that could shift the balance of power in the human universe over the course of centuries.

"The Church has received disturbing transmissions," he told Mallory, "originating from the vicinity of Xi Virginis."

Cardinal Anderson saw puzzlement cross Mallory's face. "But, there's nothing out toward Virgo," he said. "There hasn't been any human expansion past Helminth. Has there?"

"None that has made the official histories." Cardinal Anderson took a small handheld holo unit out of his robes. He aimed the device at Mallory and a star map about two meters in diameter unfolded between them. Centered in the display, a large and lumpy dumbbell-shaped cluster of stars was outlined in bright yellow, marking the confines of human space.

Yellow marked the systems that humanity colonized, while red marked the systems that were home to alien species. The greatest concentration of those were clustered on the other side of human space from Beta Pictoris and the tiny airless rock named Kathiwar that orbited it.

Kathiwar had been founded at a time when power between the political arms of the Confederacy was measured, at its base, in the number of planets controlled, giving a strong political impetus to colonize new worlds, even when the economics didn't make sense. One of the arms of the Confederacy, the People's Protectorate of Epsilon Indi, had been the most aggressive in spreading outward, placing colonies on planets solely as launchpads to reach farther out. Kathiwar was built to serve as one of those way stations, scanning the stars around and sending probes, and eventually, colony ships.

Shortly after Kathiwar was established, its observation platforms found a planet orbiting Tau Puppis. The discovery, Tau Puppis IV, seemed an obvious Dolbrian remnant, as no reasonably habitable planet should have evolved around that star. Its history might have ended there, as it was close to five times the maximum distance the Indi ships could reasonably supply a new colony, over 120 light-years away.

But when someone discovered that Tau Puppis was emitting faint EM radiation of demonstrably intelligent origin, the planet was moved to the front of Indi's priority list. First contact with an alien race was important in and of itself, but also in the front of the mind of every Indi decision maker was the fact that the accidental contact between the Centauri arm and the delphinine natives of Paralia had resulted in the development of the first tach drives and Centauri dominance in the new Confederacy. So Indi routed money, people, and Paralian-designed tach-ships down a corridor from Beta Pictoris toward Tau Puppis.

The aliens from Tau Puppis met them more than halfway.

There was a lot of diplomatic dancing, as it became very clear that the birdlike aliens were the rulers of an interstellar empire as large or larger than man's, an empire that claimed much of the 120 light-years of space between Beta Pictoris and Tau Puppis, a volume as great as the whole of the Confederacy at the time.

The end result was to deform the yellow dumbbell of human colonization, pushing it away from the galactic center and away from the red-outlined systems of the Voleran Empire.

None of the other red-outlined systems represented such an interstellar empire. Procyon, within the core of human space, was highlighted red. Familiar to any Occisian as the home system of the Race, the losers of mankind's first, and so far only, interstellar war with another species.

Two remaining systems were outlined red. One embedded in the other lobe of the dumbbell on the opposite side of Sol from the Volerans. That was Paralia, home of the aquatic creatures that designed humanity's first tach-drives.

The last red outline other marked Helminth, home to an enigmatic wormlike race that had cities, and a civilization, but with whom human scientists were barely able to communicate.

Like the Volerans, Helminth marked the edge of the human expansion toward the galactic center. But for a different reason.

The Voleran side of human space had been expanding for two centuries, and the presence of Voleran colonies simply forced the drift of mankind off in a different direction.

Helminth marked the edge of human space by coincidence. That end of human space stopped expanding for political and economic reasons. A hundred and seventy-five years ago, when the Confederacy fell, the planets of the old Sirius-Eridani Economic Community had fared the worst. Where the other arms of the old Confederacy managed to hold on to some sort of political identity, the SEEC began a decades-long inward collapse along ancient fault lines. The dual capitals of Cynos and Khamsin were untenable without the Confederacy to support it, and what was left after the breakup didn't have the resources to move outward.

However, on Cardinal Anderson's map, there were blue-outlined stars flung out beyond Helminth in a pattern that had never appeared in any publicly available chart or catalog; a pattern of half a dozen stars over a hundred light-years from Sol and over seventy light-years beyond the edge of human space.

"A decade ago, a Jesuit observatory discovered those colonies you see there in blue." He adjusted the display and the view zoomed in on the blue systems so names on the stars were visible.

89 Leonis, HD 98354, HD 101534, Xi Virginis . . .

Mallory stared at the cluster of blue-outlined systems.

It was bizarre. Lost colonies were the stuff of tabloid holocasts. Too much time, resources, and people went into establishing a colony—especially one so distant—for the history of it to be lost in the short time that man had been traveling among the stars.

Father Mallory looked up at Cardinal Anderson. "These are alien outposts, some new species?"

"No," Cardinal Anderson said quietly. "These are human colonies, at least six of them, founded as the Confederacy was collapsing. A hundred and seventy-five years ago."

"Six? Why hasn't this been made public? Six established colonies . . ."

"Possibly more," the cardinal said. "These colonies were founded in secret. We believe by people escaping the rise of the Eridani Caliphate. Can you see why we would keep this secret?"

Father Mallory nodded. The Eridani Caliphate, successor to something more than half of the old SEEC, had never had good relations with the Vatican. Often open warfare was only avoided by the fact that the Roman Catholic Church wasn't a nation, as such. However, the pope had many allies in the secular world as the only part of the body of Christ with an interstellar reach. There had been dozens of proxy battles over the past century, fighting the reach of the Caliphate into the remains of the SEEC.

However, the Caliphate currently controlled the area between the rest of human space and these newly discovered colonies. The Caliphate's official position on the ascension of the Islamic government was that it was the rise of an oppressed people into power. The revelation of secular—or worse, Christian or Jewish—refugees from that ascension forming breakaway colonies would be a diplomatic embarrassment to the Caliphate.

Both the location of these colonies, and their possible historical ties to the planets of the Caliphate, made it almost inevitable that the Eridani Caliphate would claim them as part of their sphere of influence, growing by 50 percent almost instantly; expanding into a space that would, given the limits of current tach-drives, have very limited access to the rest of human space. From the point of view of Mother Church, that would be unacceptable.

Father Mallory shook his head. "Forgive me, Your Eminence. I understand the Church's interest in these worlds. What is the interest in me?"

"These worlds were discovered by accident," said the cardinal. "A chance interception of a tach-comm transmission. We've been secretly monitoring ever since. Unfortunately, these are low power signals. Over such distances they degrade. We can only obtain a few hours' worth of comprehensible intelligence over the course of a year. And, of course, a listening post by Helminth, or anywhere near there, risks alerting the Caliphate. We've been using Vatican property on Cynos."

"You said 'disturbing' transmissions, Your Eminence."

Cardinal Anderson thumbed a control on his holo-projector, and the air was filled with an awful static whine.

The holo's picture became fluid and refused to stabilize. It seemed to be the view out of a tach-ship. Stars spun and blurred, and a blue orb filled the display.

". . . with Xi Virginis . . . bzzt . . . have lost visual contact . . ."

Something blurred the view. The planet pixilated and re-formed, and something clouded the space between the camera and the planet. At first the black specks seemed to be some digital artifact.

Suddenly, a very different voice was speaking. ". . . bzzt . . . coming toward . . . bzzt . . . behold a great . . . bzzt . . ."

It wasn't an artifact. The cloud was real, the specks moving purposefully toward the planet.

". . . seven heads . . . bzzt . . . crowns upon . . . bzzt . . . the third part of the stars . . . cast . . . bzzt . . ."

The transmission died.

"The last part?" Father Mallory asked.

"Behold a great red dragon, having seven heads and ten horns, and seven crowns upon his heads. And his tail drew the third part of the stars of heaven, and did cast them to the earth," quoted Cardinal Anderson, "Revelation, Chapter Twelve." He switched off the holo projection. "We need some-one to investigate."

"What does it mean?"

"We do not know," Cardinal Anderson said. "Analysis of the star field places that planet close to, if not in orbit around, Xi Virginis, on the far side of these colonies."

"Why me?"

"The Church cannot move without attracting attention," he said. "But one man can."

Father Mallory nodded. "How am I to travel there without attracting the Caliphate's attention?"

"Are you familiar with the planet Bakunin?" Cardinal An-derson asked.

CHAPTER THREE

Audience

Power is not the same as knowledge.
> —*The Cynic's Book of Wisdom*

To know all things is not permitted.

> —Horace
> (65–8 bce)

Date: 2525.09.22 (Standard)
Earth–Sol

Cardinal Anderson returned to Vatican City within hours after his transport tached in from Alpha Centauri. Even after the fall of the Confederacy, man's last attempt at an empire spanning all of human space, Earth was still the center of human existence. Certainly that was the case with the Mother Church, which had endured on this spot for over two thousand years, through even the worst years of the Terran Council three hundred years ago.

After those dark days, when the inward-looking Council had been succeeded by the outward-looking Confederacy, St. Peter's had been restored. Today, it was impossible for Cardinal Anderson to tell what parts of the structure had burned down in the twenty-third century, and which had been standing since the sixteenth.

It was very early in the morning in Rome, the sky just purpling with dawn, and there were no crowds as he walked across the square toward the Apostolic Palace. No one challenged him as he entered the palace; most of the Swiss Guard knew him on sight and, more important, the wide-spectrum biometric surveillance that covered St. Peter's Square and the area around the palace would have alerted security if he was anyone other than who he appeared to be.

He made his way through the ancient palace, from the public areas by the Sistine Chapel and the library, into the heavily secured private areas close to the papal apartments.

His Holiness was waiting for him.

Despite the palatial Renaissance décor, and frescoes that appeared as if they could have been contemporary with Michelangelo, the office where the pope received him was one of the more recent additions to the huge complex of the Apostolic Palace. Despite the fifteen-meter-tall windows giving a panoramic view of St. Peter's Square, this room was wrapped in layers of the most sophisticated physical and technological security that had ever been gathered into a single location. Behind the frescoes were walls that were impregnable to fire, explosion, EM radiation, and sound. The grand windows were not even visible from the outside; any observer would see just the blank wall of the palace.

When the ornate gilded doors shut behind him, Cardinal Anderson could hear a slight sucking sound as the portal sealed tight and the office switched to using its own isolated environmental controls. Even the air was screened by several layers of security here.

His Holiness stood in front of the windows, hands clasped behind his back, staring at the dome of the cathedral across the square.

"I trust you had a fruitful journey to Occisis?"

"Yes, Your Holiness. Father Mallory proved to be good choice."

"So was Kennedy, I fear." The pope shook his head. "Does Mallory know?"

"We briefed him with the absolute minimum information," Cardinal Anderson said. "While he saw Kennedy's transmission, he believes it was just another random intercept from the Virginis colonies."

"That is probably for the best." The pope turned around. He was shorter than Cardinal Anderson, and younger. Physically, he reminded Anderson of Father Mallory, though Pope Stephen XII had been born on Earth and was short and stocky through genetics rather than high gravity. "If the Caliphate should uncover Mallory or his mission, better they presume he is the first envoy we've sent to the Virginis colonies."

"Yes," Anderson said. "But the Caliphate will eventually move, regardless of their knowledge of the Church's actions."

The pope nodded. "Eventually. It is certain they know these colonies are out there and as long as they believe those worlds are their own secret, they'll be inclined toward caution."

The exchange couldn't be called an argument, or even a disagreement, except by someone who had access to the decade of subtext behind the words. Cardinal Anderson had never completely approved of the cautious route they took toward these far-flung colonies. He had long debates with the pope about the strategic implications of each move they made.

To Pope Stephen, the longer they went without the Caliphate making any overt move toward these colonies, the better information they had and the better they could react. Even when the Caliphate moved, it would take years to build a substantive connection between the Caliphate and the Virginis colonies. Tach-ships had effective jump ranges of twenty light-years, and while ships could be built that could take the multiple jumps that would be needed to cross the seventy-five light-years between the Caliphate and the nearest of the Virginis colonies, to build a permanent connection, the Caliphate would need to build at least a nominal colony at each jump point to accommodate refueling and repairs if they expected to move trade goods or troops. Building such a corridor took too many resources to remain secret.

To Cardinal Anderson, it didn't matter if the Caliphate had not made such moves as of yet. In his mind, this particular standoff would favor the side that made the first move.

He believed that was true even before they had received Kennedy's transmission. The first envoy they had received any word back from. Kennedy's only words back to them repeated a cryptic message, "Tached into the 89 Leonis system and have lost all visual contact with Xi Virginis," then, overlaid on the transmission, another voice quoting the Book of Revelation.

However, His Holiness still believed they should move clandestinely with low profile assets. So Mallory would be the fourth man sent to the Virginis colonies, and the first one sent to Xi Virginis.

Cardinal Anderson prayed that God would guide him.

Date: 2525.09.29 (Standard)
Bakunin–BD+50°1725

Twenty million people, human and nonhuman, swarmed the sprawling metropolis of Godwin, the largest city on the planet Bakunin. On any other world, it would have been the capital city, but on Bakunin, where any form of State was anathema, the only thing that distinguished Godwin was sheer unwieldy size.

Late in the evening, an elderly gentleman who currently called himself Mr. Antonio walked on the street under the crumbling multilayered walkways of East Godwin. There were no outward signs that distinguished him from the other twenty million residents of the city, or for that matter, any of the five hundred million other inhabitants of Bakunin. Even the most sophisticated medical imaging technology could scan him without registering anything out of place.

Not that he would ever give anyone reason to look for something.

Mr. Antonio walked into the cheap hotel where he had been living for the past six months. The place was a dark, modular hive of windowless rooms that barely fit together. Parts of the composite skin had crumbled with age and had sloughed off, and half the rooms were permanently sealed because of problems with the environmental systems.

Mr. Antonio's room was unremarkable; a single nine-square-meter room that had amenities more appropriate to a tach-ship than a hotel, including the fold-down toilet. The room smelled faintly of mildew.

He sat down on the cot that attached to the wall and checked his watch. At exactly 28:00 local time the comm in his room rang. He picked it up without saying anything.

"It is time," the voice on the comm said. Mr. Antonio did not respond because he knew that this call was one-way. The speaker was light-years away, and had sent a tach-comm to a receiver Mr. Antonio had left in orbit amid all the less distinguished debris that littered Bakunin's sky. That receiver then placed a simpler encrypted transmission to Mr. Antonio that bounced though so many nodes in the patchwork net of Bakunin's communications infrastructure so as to be effectively untraceable.

"The Church is acting on the transmission, and our friend

will perceive this, if he hasn't already. I will need our mole ready when he makes the inevitable move to investigate."

Mr. Antonio switched off the comm and smiled. The groundwork had already been laid. Nickolai would be ready when the time came.

PART ONE

Original Sins

I believe in the incomprehensibility of God.
                              —HONORÉ DE BALZAC
                              (1799–1850)

CHAPTER FOUR

Stigmata

We serve most those beliefs that we first reject.
                    —*The Cynic's Book of Wisdom*

[Animals] do not make me sick discussing their duty to
God.

                    —WALT WHITMAN
                    (1819–1892)

Date: 2525.10.15 (Standard)
Bakunin–BD+50°1725

Nickolai Rajasthan slowly woke from a drugged slumber. For
a few brief, precious moments, he didn't remember the past
year. His subconscious still refused to accept his punishment,
or his exile. For an instant he was ready to find himself in his
own bed in the southern palace, to smell the scent of his siblings, his sisters . . .

Then he remembered.

He wasn't in the southern palace, and he wasn't on Grimalkin. The priests hadn't been able, politically, to have a member
of the royal family put to death, but they had made sure that
he would never set foot on his home planet again.

Nickolai groaned.

"Easy there, big boy." The voice spoke a dialect of the
Fallen. It burned in Nickolai's ears. Even after a year, the
alien, almost squishy, tones of their languages were a constant
reminder of his crime and his exile.

The priests had maimed him and had thrown him to the
chaos of Bakunin to be little more than a beggar in hell. A
lesser person might have spent his time finding an honorable
way to die.

Nickolai always had a contrary nature.

"Are you awake?" the voice repeated.

"Yes," Nickolai slurred.

"Good news. The implants took. I'm going to remove the bandages now. You may want to close your eyes."

Nickolai couldn't bring himself to do so. After a year of blindness, he already could sense a fuzzy light source on the periphery of his vision. Then, suddenly, the bandages came away from his face, and the world was a bright white light that was too intense for his brain to process.

Surprisingly, his new eyes didn't hurt.

He blinked and the world changed, eyes adjusting to the brightness quicker than he had ever remembered. Shapes resolved for him, and he found himself looking at a too-small examination room. He lay in a chair that seemed barely able to hold him.

"Colors seem wrong," Nickolai slurred.

A human face leaned into his field of vision, looking down at him. "Variable spectral sensitivity. Takes a while to get used to." The man reached down and pulled up Nicolai's left eyelid. "Good. No sign of any inflammation."

The man hit a switch, and the chair slowly tilted upright with a pneumatic hiss. The progress was slow, but Nickolai still felt a little dizzy.

"Standard military specs," the human said. Now that he was awake enough to place the voice, Nickolai remembered his name was Dr. Yee.

The doctor took a double handful of bandages from an examination tray and tossed them in a disposal chute. "Once you get used to adjusting the settings, you'll be able to duplicate your natural range of vision. The hard part was scaling up the human design—and the pupil, of course . . ."

Nickolai nodded. It was sinking in. This wasn't just a dream vision, he could actually *see*. If Dr. Yee wasn't here to see the loss of dignity, Nickolai would have been jumping off the wall, and roaring an epic curse on the house of the priests who had burned his eyes.

Compared to that, his right arm was almost an afterthought.

He felt his shoulder itch, and he reached over to scratch it. He felt a new scar and looked down.

He had a new right arm. He touched his bicep, and even the yellow-and-black-striped fur felt real. He flexed his right hand, and his brain told him he could feel bones and tendons flexing even though he knew that the bones were metal and the tendons some sort of mechanical analog.

He extended the claws on his fingers and saw the only obvious sign that this was a prosthetic. The claws on his right hand weren't black, but a gray metallic alloy.

Dr. Yee noticed Nickolai looking and said, "I apologize for that. This was all custom work, and unfortunately the mechanical tolerances on that hand turned out to be too tight for me to apply any sort of finish to the claws."

"You did it all in a single operation?"

"I decided it would be easier to hold your body in stasis until I completed all the work. It shortens the recovery and rehabilitation time not to have multiple surgeries. And your benefactor suggested it would be, uh, *better* if you recovered quickly."

Nickolai shook his head. Could this actually be real? Could he be whole? *No, that is the wrong word . . .*

"Intact" was better. He doubted he could be whole again, not after what happened. And now he was three times removed from his home. Once for his crime, twice for the blasphemous mechanical prosthetics now connected to his flesh, three times for the way he had chosen to pay for that blasphemy. His "benefactor," as Dr. Yee put it.

The priests might have enjoyed the little shame Nickolai felt, until they realized that it was not for his crimes or for Dr. Yee's unclean attentions. Nickolai's shame was only for his own impatience.

He was strong enough. He could have waited another year, another five. To collect enough of his own resources to pay for his reconstruction without accepting the terms dictated by Mr. Antonio.

Perhaps.

As he pushed himself upright, he knew the reality. What value was his pride and the distant possibility of becoming himself again, when measured against the certainty of regaining his eyes, and his arm? If it required a pact with the Fallen, so be it; the priests had declared him damned already.

"Be cautious with that arm until you are used to it," Dr. Yee said. "It is unlikely you can damage it, but it could cause you harm if you miscalculate any aggressive action."

"It is stronger?"

"In some senses. The musculature is calibrated to match your natural limbs, but it has more tensile strength and can move faster—" Dr. Yee touched Nickolai's shoulder. "You do not want to stress where it is attached."

Nickolai touched the scar on his bicep, where the amputation had been.

"Oh, yes, that's the biological skin, but I needed to excavate the remaining bone and much of the muscle that was left so we'd have a clean connection to the joint. Much less likely to have a failure that way."

One more pound of flesh. No matter.

He looked at Dr. Yee, a full meter shorter than him now that he was standing. He wondered if Dr. Yee was short for a human. He was the first one he had actually seen in person.

"Have you been paid?" he asked.

"Oh, yes," Dr. Yee said. "Quite handsomely. If you have any further need—"

Nickolai ducked down and walked out the door of the examination room.

Nickolai stood outside Dr. Yee's offices for a long time, facing the city of Godwin. The chaos of noise and scent was familiar, but he hadn't been prepared to *see* the city for the first time. A clot-red dawn sky scabbed over the nightmares of a mad architect. There was no coherence to the blocks, spires, and twisted forms that made up the buildings of central Godwin. Aircars sped by at every level, dodging pedestrian walkways and tubes that seemed to connect buildings at random. What spaces weren't filled by buildings, and traffic and people were flooded by massive holo displays throbbing with colors too saturated to have originated in this universe.

Godwin was an ugly, overbearing city. It was the most beautiful thing he had ever seen.

New eyes also made him more aware than ever that he was alone among the Fallen. Thousands of people moved around him. All in his sight were human. He had known their scent and had become used to the dull miasma of fear that followed the sons of men around him.

This was the first he had seen their faces. They showed a palette of expression that was alien to him. Most stared at him. Most gave him a wide berth. Most were as short as Dr. Yee.

Nickolai smiled, and that caused the humans nearest to him to turn away and walk faster.

Eventually, he began the long walk back to his apartments. He could have taken a cab, but few were built with the descendants of St. Rajasthan in mind. Most of the world of the Fallen was too small to fit Nickolai. Occasionally, he would stop and close his eyes, because it was easier to remember his way without the visual distractions.

He had reached his neighborhood on the desolate fringes of East Godwin when he heard a familiar voice call his name.

"Yo, Nick, that you?" The words were uglier in this mouth than Dr. Yee's. It was fitting, because the mouth belonged to an uglier person. Nickolai slowly turned to face the speaker. "Has to be, can't be too many tiger-men this side of Tau Ceti, can there?"

The squat man talking to him had just walked out of a bar rank with the smell of alcohol and human musk. The garish pink holo above the entry spelled out "Candyland" in cascades of undulating pink flesh. It was almost a visual expression of one of the scriptures' names for human beings, "Naked Devil."

"Well, fuck me! Eyes, too—went the distance, did you?" The odious little man took off a pair of sunglasses, and before pocketing them, Nickolai could see a streaming display showing several views inside the club, where dozens of naked men and women danced for a packed crowd. He was briefly astonished at the clarity of the image, making him realize that his new eyes were an order of magnitude more sensitive than the ones the priests burned out of his skull. The man rubbed the bridge of his nose. "When you coming back to work?"

Nickolai wondered to himself if he had simply passed this way by oversight, or if on a subconscious level he had planned it.

"Mr. Salvador, I gave you my notice."

Salvador laughed. " 'Notice,' he says." He broke off, coughing. "Really, Nick, I forgive you."

Nickolai noticed movement out of the corner of his eyes.

"And, in fact, I'm feeling real generous. I'm not even going to dock you for the two weeks you missed." Salvador smiled at Nickolai. "A blind one-armed morey was more a novelty than a bouncer—but fully functional? That's useful."

Nickolai could smell the quartet of humans circling behind him. And when he heard Salvador use the ancient slur "morey," Nickolai knew he had come this way on purpose.

He shifted his weight on his digitigrade legs to lower his center of gravity and positioned his arms in preparation for a confrontation. He looked down at Salvador, who was oblivious to Nickolai's shift in posture or what it meant.

"I no longer work for you," Nickolai said.

"Nick, Nick, Nick. I cut you slack because you aren't from round here. You don't know how it works on Bakunin. You *owe* me, tiger-boy. You think a cripple like you'd survive half a day in East Godwin without my protection? You think that ends when you get some flesh hacker to make you nice and pretty? No, you work for me until I give *you* notice."

Nickolai shook his head. "No."

"Nick, I'm disappointed. For a morey, it seemed you had good sense." Salvador shook his head. "Don't mess him up too bad."

The four figures behind him converged. Nickolai didn't need to see them to understand their positions. He could hear the heavy footfalls, and he could smell their sweat. Four males, large ones, and their strides carried a mass beyond their size. Either powered armor or heavy cybernetic implants, and because he heard no servos, Nickolai thought the latter.

He pivoted on one digitigrade leg and crouched to face his attackers. He also did something he had never done while bouncing for Salvador—

He extended his claws.

Four perfectly matched enforcers. Hairless, with muscles so clearly delineated that they might have been taken for dancers inside the club. Time slowed as adrenaline sharpened most of his senses. His vision was already sharper than it ever had been, even in the thick of combat training.

Two grappled him just as he turned, wrapping their arms around his waist, aiming to take him down and make him vulnerable to the others' attacks. Nickolai was already braced against their momentum; they were of secondary importance.

Primary was the man swinging a pipe at his new eyes.

Nickolai grabbed the man's wrist with his left hand and thrust up with his right, at the elbow. Nickolai could feel a jarring sensation in his shoulder as his new arm connected. However, whatever Nickolai might have felt was dwarfed by what his attacker must have felt when his elbow—cyber-enhanced or not—gave way in the wrong direction.

The man's gasping intake of breath had barely begun to turn into something more urgent when the second attacker brought his own club to bear. Nickolai blocked the blow with his new right forearm. The impact shuddered through his whole body, but the new limb withstood it.

That man stopped a moment, as stunned by the lack of re-action as if he had been hit himself. Nickolai did not give him a second chance. His own cybernetic hand struck out, claws first, into the man's neck. It was a blow developed by the warrior-priests of Grimalkin that simultaneously crushed the wind-pipe and opened the jugular. The man instantly dropped his weapon to clutch his throat.

The two men grappling him had just realized something was amiss. They weren't warriors, and they weren't prepared to deal with one.

Nickolai brought his right elbow down on the back of one's neck, dropping him, and as the last one let go, Nicko-lai brought the first attacker's weapon—still clutched in that man's hand—down on the last one's skull.

The fight had lasted five seconds.

Nickolai turned around to face Salvador. The man had backed up to the doorway of his club and was holding a cheap laser handgun pointed at Nickolai.

"You fucked up bad here, Nick."

It was Nickolai's turn to laugh. "Mr. Salvador, I am a scion of the House of Rajasthan. I have been trained to shed blood since before I could speak, and it is the highest sacra-ment of my faith to offer the blood of the Fallen to God. Do you think I cannot kill you before you decide where to aim that toy?" Nickolai struck with his new arm. The laser spun out into the darkness and Salvador gasped, cradling a lacerated hand. Nickolai leaned in toward him, so their faces were only centimeters apart. "Do you forget why we were created?"

"You can't do this, Nick. People will find you."

"My name is Nickolai." Nickolai stood up. "And, despite the pleasure it would give me, I am not going honor you with death at my hands." He glanced back at the four attackers, all quite literally fallen now. "And if you value these men, you should get them medical attention."

Nickolai turned and walked away.

"This is a big mistake, Nick." Salvador shouted after him. "You're going to regret it!"

"I think not," Nickolai growled to himself in his native tongue.

CHAPTER FIVE

Pilgrimage

The risks we see are often those we've already overcome.
—*The Cynic's Book of Wisdom*

One cannot answer for his courage when he has never been
in danger.

—Francois de La Rochefoucauld
(1613–1680)

Date: 2525.11.05 (Standard)
Bakunin–BD+50°1725

He had left the spaceport on Occisis as Father Francis Xavier
Mallory two weeks after meeting with Cardinal Anderson.

Somewhere, in the logs of the Centauri Alliance, Father
Mallory continued on a missionary journey to the Indi Protectorate. And over a year from now, when the transport made
planetfall on Dharma over 160 light-years from Occisis, someone identified properly as Father Mallory would disembark
and begin some good works in the name of Mother Church.

The man who no longer was Father Francis Xavier Mallory had slipped off the long-distance passenger ship before it
tached out of the system, when it made an unscheduled maintenance stop on the fringes of the Occisis planetary system.
By a carefully engineered coincidence, a private freighter was
docked at the same orbital maintenance platform having fixes
made to its life-support system.

The ancient Hegira Aerospace freighter had a manifest
that listed a number of destinations around the core of human
space: Ecdemi, Acheron, Styx, Windsor . . .

Bakunin, typically, was absent from the itinerary. It was a
planet that was rarely logged as an official destination. However,

being one of the core planets, it was much closer than Dharma. A single blink of the tach-drive and nineteen light-years and twenty-seven days vanished.

The longest part of the journey was cruising in from the fringes of the Bakunin planetary system. The captain explained that, since there was no real traffic regulation around the planet, it wasn't safe to tach in too close to the planet. Having one ship tach in or out too close to another while their own drives were still active could cause dangerous power spikes in the engines. Even though all tach-ships had damping systems to both quickly cool down active drive after a jump and control any dangerous spiking, most planets still had strict regulations giving timetables and "safe zones" for all scheduled traffic.

In the case of Bakunin, this captain thought it was just safer to tach in several AU out from the planet, where the chances of interacting with another tach-drive was close to nil.

Forty days after he left, Mallory walked out of the Hegira freighter onto the surface of Bakunin. He walked out into the chill night air, onto a dusty landing zone lit by the glare from dozens of landing lights. The night sky was a black-velvet sheet, the only stars were the engines of spaceport traffic, and the skyline of the city itself was a near subliminal shadow beyond the lights.

The stark-white light was cut briefly by orange as an antique shuttle took off from a pad about half a klick away. Mallory spent a moment watching the ascent. Graceful it wasn't. The shuttle was an insignificant lumpy fuselage on a column of flame. The roar of the ascent made Mallory's molars ache. The orange light faded long before a slight warm breeze carried the burnt chemical smell of the shuttle's engines toward Mallory. Within a few seconds, another, more distant craft headed skyward.

What little glimpses he had of traffic told him that the spaceport extended way beyond the little slice he could see. One bright mote had to be aiming for a landing pad a dozen klicks away.

He lowered his gaze toward the concourse adjacent to his LZ. He could only make out the doors and a few windows beyond the glare of the landing lights. The rest of the building was nothing but a black silhouette against a blacker sky.

Since no one had taken it upon themselves to tell him

where to go, Mallory shouldered his single duffel bag and headed there.

His arrival was nearly surreal in exactly how much he was being ignored. No one asked for his identification, no one was running a security checkpoint, not so much as a customs office. The Proudhon Spaceport Security personnel stood on the fringes of the LZ, clustered next to the lights with a calculated disinterest that was conveyed even at a hundred-meter distance.

It would almost seem that the effort spent manufacturing the identity of John Fitzpatrick, ex-Staff Sergeant in the Occisis Marines—down to removing and reapplying unit tats—had been wasted.

However, the manufactured John Fitzpatrick knew better.

Proudhon Spaceport Security might avoid all the forms of customs and immigration usually tended to by a nation-state, but that didn't mean they didn't know who and what arrived and departed the allegedly stateless rock of Bakunin. Proudhon was the only spaceport on the planet, which gave the Proudhon Spaceport Development Corporation considerable latitude on what they were able to require of ships arriving and leaving. Those ships at least pretended to provide passenger and cargo manifests, and the PSDC at least pretended it wasn't enforcing import, export, or immigration restrictions on allegedly sovereign individuals. But whatever the pretense, the PSDC had a *lot* of antiaircraft—ground based and orbital—backing up whatever it did decide to enforce.

So, while no one *asked* for John Fitzpatrick's carefully constructed passport, that didn't mean that no one knew John Fitzpatrick was here. As he walked across the LZ toward the concourse building, he ran the worst-case scenario through his head—a Caliphate agent in place and knowing of his arrival.

Fortunately, if that hypothetical Caliphate spy took an interest in his arrival, there would be little to John Fitzpatrick that would arouse any suspicion. Ex-Staff Sergeant Fitzpatrick had a checkered career with the Occisis Marines that ended with a court-martial convicting him of assault on an enlisted man. Fitzpatrick had been a career man, no family, who had been about Mallory's age and body type.

He was also conveniently serving a twelve-year sentence, allowing the Church to appropriate his identity. He was exactly the type of man who ended up on Bakunin.

The only part of Fitzpatrick's history that had to be fabricated for Mallory's cover was his pardon and release.

Mallory kept his breath steady and his stride unhurried. His training was coming back, and this time mentally counting the rosary did calm his heart rate and his breathing. It helped that he knew what the threats were. Realities were always easier to deal with than his imagination.

The calm was necessary because there was the off chance someone had some sort of monitor pointed at him. Standard security in any sensitive area—and the LZ certainly was that—not only had video and audio surveillance, but had biometric sensors keyed to stress levels from pulse, skin temperature, kinematics, and facial expression. Civilians were mostly unaware of that level of security until they tried to smuggle a weapon into a bank or a bomb into a government building.

As blasé as these security guards appeared, if Mallory's heart level reached a certain level, or his body language said the wrong thing, they would probably escort him into some private room for a little conversation.

Even if nothing resulted from that, it would raise John Fitzpatrick's profile beyond acceptable levels. Because of that hypothetical Caliphate spy, Staff Sergeant Fitzpatrick needed to be completely unremarkable. Just another bit of human flotsam washed up on the shores of Bakunin—lost in the thousands who came here every day looking for something that only this lawless place could provide.

At the moment, dear Lord, just provide me with anonymity.

He walked right by a pair of the guards and into the concourse. He heard a snippet of dialogue as he passed . . .

"You placed the bet. Fifty grams, pay up."

"You sure it's been a month?"

"Yeah, and Szczytnicki hasn't used deadly force once."

"Damnation and taxes! You putting tranks in his coffee?"

"Give it up, Hōgai—" The doors whooshed shut behind Mallory, cutting off the guard's words.

The concourse was not exactly what he had expected. He was familiar enough with Bakunin's history, and he had done what research he could manage in the two weeks he'd been given. The whole planet was supposedly a maelstrom of lawlessness and piracy, a reputation that led to certain expectations.

Those expectations didn't include the gleaming concourse

that greeted him to the city/spaceport Proudhon. Somehow, Mallory expected the chaos of Bakunin's political climate—an economy constructed around criminal gangs, private armies, and an aggressive social Darwinism that was worthy of the Borgias—to be reflected in its aesthetics. He expected a building choked with street vendors and beggars, a trash-covered update of an ancient novel by Dickens or Gibson.

Instead, he stood on a spotless floor of polished black granite tile edged with stainless steel.

A crystal skylight arced above him, whose individual panes magnified the view above so he could see the ships traveling above Proudhon in excruciating detail. There were hundreds, if not thousands, of vessels visible in the artificially-enhanced sky following so many intricate paths that it seemed a patent impossibility that a single craft could escape a collision somewhere. The fact that traffic flowed at all, without such a disaster, seemed a sign of divine favor.

The concourse was filled with a mass of people in a ground-bound echo of the traffic above. A precise waltz that, however chaotic and patternless, flowed without incident—the people molecules in a turbulent, frictionless fluid.

The floor in the vast space was dotted with tall metallic kiosks, the kind that usually offered directory and comm services. Mallory walked toward one, merging into the fluid crowd.

It could have been a concourse on any of the core planets with a single disconcerting exception. Every person carried a sidearm of some sort. Shoulder holsters predominated, but he saw a fair share of weapons carried on the hip. He saw slug-throwers, lasers, and one plasma rifle slung over a woman's shoulder.

He'd read up a little on the Bakuninite fetish for going around visibly armed, enough that he wore a surplus Marine-issue laser sidearm, but he hadn't really thought what walking among an armed population might feel like. He hoped most of these people knew how to handle all that ordnance.

He was glad for his own sidearm. Not so much out of fear of the gun-toting public, but because the weaponry was so ubiquitous that he began noticing the few people who appeared unarmed. If he'd not walked off the transport with a gun on his hip, someone might have noticed him.

He stepped in front of one of several arched niches in the kiosk and looked at the single-viewpoint holo display it beamed at his arrival. The menu itself was a little overwhelming, much more than the typical listings for currency exchange, vehicle rental, hotel reservations, and the other common traveler's needs. From here he could order up an escort of any given gender and/or species. He could reserve a private surgical unit for procedures lifesaving, cosmetic, experimental, or—anywhere else—highly illegal. He could order a car, or a tank, or a small fighter aircraft. He could have someone deliver a Gilliam Industries manpack plasma cannon in wattages ranging from ludicrous to completely insane. There was a complete directory of mercenaries available for hire . . .

Saints preserve us, enough money and someone could stage a small planetary invasion without leaving the concourse.

Mallory reached in and touched the holo icon for currency exchange.

Immediately he was bombarded with scrolling data, moving graphs and charts, as if he'd been dropped in the middle of the commodities exchange on Windsor.

Bakunin, stateless as it was, had no single currency. And while there was a de facto standard—everything was nominally tied to the price of gold, so much so that currencies were valued in grams—the fact was, unless you had precious metal in hand, everything floated. He was looking at a hundred different currencies, all native to Bakunin, issued from all sorts of agencies—the Proudhon Spaceport Development Corporation; the Insured Bank of the Adam Smith Collective; Lucifer Contracts Incorporated; the Rothbard Investment Group; something called the Bakunin Church of Christ, Avenger . . .

While the money from Lucifer Contracts seemed the most stable, Mallory opted for the notes from Proudhon itself. While the charts told him that he could spend offworld currency as readily as anything else, it was something else that could attract attention—and be more readily traced.

A few icon presses later, the kiosk gave him a chit worth about three kilograms in PSDC currency. He pocketed it and started a hunt for a hotel.

Once he left the concourse, and he was free of the landing lights, he could take in the rest of the nighttime city. Once again, the planet Bakunin sidestepped his expectations, making him wish he had been provided more than the two weeks he'd been given to study his destination.

Everywhere else he could think of, there was an attempt to separate a port from the adjacent urban center. There were dozens of reasons for that, from safety and noise concerns to the fact that a geographical bottleneck made regulations easer to enforce on traffic.

None of these issues seemed to concern the urban planners who designed Proudhon—

What am I thinking? There were no planners . . . except maybe God himself.

Proudhon the spaceport and Proudhon the city not only coexisted, but interpenetrated, two metallic neon-outlined animals in the midst of devouring each other. Landing strips became causeways, high-rises became conn towers, and through it all, weaving between the buildings, the ever-present spaceport traffic dodging not only itself, but also aircraft never meant to leave the atmosphere—everything from aircars to luxury tach-ships vied for its own chunk of the air above Proudhon.

Over everything, a cluster of twelve floodlit white skyscrapers were the only sign of architectural order. Mallory suspected that those were the headquarters of the Proudhon Spaceport Development Corporation.

He had reserved space in a hotel only a few klicks from the concourse. There didn't seem to be a need to go farther afield before he got his bearings here. Bakunin was only a means to an end anyway. It was possible that he could make all the arrangements he needed without leaving his hotel room.

If so, so much the better.

The Hotel Friedman was a retrofitted luxury liner that had grounded and never taken off again. He had only skimmed the description, but it apparently had been outbound from Waldgrave nearly two hundred years ago and suffered mutiny by the ill-treated and underpaid crewmen. During the height of the Confederacy, leaving Bakunin again would invite capture and repatriation of the ship, as well as possible death penalties for the crew members stupid enough to try and fly it away. Instead, the crew sold it to a speculator who then bought the pad it landed on and went into the hotel business.

The reservation chit the kiosk had produced let him into the hotel. His room/cabin wasn't one of the more expensive suites. Like everything else he did, he chose a room based on how likely the selection was to attract attention. He made a point of selecting something in the middle range.

Once in his room, he decided he probably could have saved a few grams of currency and gotten the cheapest room they had.

The Friedman must have dated from a truly decadent episode of Confederacy history, and the current owners had made an extensive effort to preserve the two-hundred-year-old opulence. Walking into the cabin was like walking into a page in a history book; a history book written from the point of view of a post-revolutionary Waldgrave historian who had a point to make about fascistic capitalist excesses.

Every surface in the cabin was detailed in carved hardwoods that age and oxidation had only made richer. All the visible hardware was detailed in engraved brass. And, most lavish—especially when Mallory reflected that this was designed as a cabin in a ship that had to enter and leave a gravity well—was the size. It was really more a suite than a cabin, with three separate rooms. There weren't any windows, but a large holo unit could be programmed to show recorded views of just about any planet in human space, as well as a few that only existed in some artist's imagination.

Mallory set down his duffel bag, found a setting on the holo that actually showed the real-time view of Proudhon outside the skin of the hotel/ship and sank into the leather couch that dominated the living room.

Welcome to Bakunin, he thought.

CHAPTER SIX

Geas

A soul's value tends to appreciate considerably after it is
sold.

> —*The Cynic's Book of Wisdom*

No price is too high to pay for the privilege of owning
yourself.

> —Friedrich Nietzsche
> (1844–1900)

Date: 2525.11.06 (Standard)
Bakunin–BD+50°1725

Nickolai had *met* Mr. Antonio before, of course, but—thanks
to the reconstruction Mr. Antonio had paid for—this was the
first time Nickolai had ever *seen* him.

To Nickolai's new eyes, the man looked weak and pathetic
even for one of the Fallen. He was thin, with twiglike limbs
and a long narrow face. His hairless skin was aged, wrinkled,
and dry. What hair he had was white and as thin as the rest
of him. He smelled of the end of life. However, as close as
this man might have been to death, for Nickolai he just wasn't
close enough.

They sat in a room in a Godwin club that sold privacy
like Nickolai's old employer sold exhibitionism. The room
was sealed to vibration, light, and EM-transmission. Nickolai
knew the screens were active because he had felt a disorienting tingle in his new artificial parts when he had crossed the
threshold.

Beyond that, the room wasn't quite designed for the type
of meeting Mr. Antonio wanted. Leather harnesses dangled
from the ceiling, chains dangled from the walls ending in
velvet-lined cuffs, racks lined another wall holding leather

straps, paddles, and various electrical devices. The dominant piece of furniture was a long padded table with various articulated arms that seemed designed to hold a wide variety of attachments.

Humanity's passion for sin was wide, deep, and more infinitely detailed than any Nickolai had known. Next to the lusts of the Fallen, his own transgressions seemed almost childlike, laughable.

I've been among them too long.

"Are you used to the prosthetics now, Mr. Rajasthan?"

"Yes," Nickolai said, even though he was privately unsure. Just this morning he had torn the handle off the bathroom door in his apartment, and almost daily he had headaches from looking at a world that was too sharp to these new eyes. However, he wasn't going to admit weakness to one such as Mr. Antonio.

"Excellent," Mr. Antonio said, in his uncomfortably fluid language. He smiled, oblivious to the aggression he showed to Nickolai with the flash of his teeth.

Although, Nickolai thought, *perhaps not so oblivious.*

Despite appearances, there were two things Nickolai knew about his human benefactor: the man was not stupid, and he was not weak. It was quite possible that Mr. Antonio knew exactly what was implied with the flash of his own tiny canines.

And the galling thing was that what it implied was correct. In the palace halls on Grimalkin he might have seen fit to scar someone for such an expression—much less one of the Fallen. However, here he was, in service to the naked devil himself.

"Mr. Rajasthan?"

Nickolai realized his attention had wandered, which was disturbingly unlike him. "Forgive me, sir. I was reminded of Grimalkin for a moment."

If Mr. Antonio noticed how forced the honorific sounded, he showed no sign.

"I understand how it is being stranded in an alien land." His smile faded. "Perhaps more than you'd know. But if you would please return to the present moment, however unpleasant the venue?"

He set a case down on the padded tabletop between them.

"The time has come for you to repay my generosity."

"What exactly do you require of me?"

"Your services as a mercenary."

Nickolai said nothing. There was little to say. He had agreed to the devil's bargain. He could almost hear the priests laughing at how far he had fallen, down to prostituting the sacred craft of the warrior.

"I need an agent to attach to a private expedition. You are going to be that agent." He turned the case around and opened it.

"How did you acquire—" Nickolai began, but cut short the outburst.

"A symbol of your service, Mr. Rajasthan. A token from he who gave you succor when you were shunned."

He knows exactly what this means, Nickolai thought.

In the padded case was an antique slugthrower. The design was old, as old in fact as the design of Nickolai's species. However, the handgun was obviously of a post-exodus model. The ancient humans who had designed Nickolai's ancestors for warfare never would have bothered to add gold plating, scrollwork, or mother-of-pearl to something they saw as strictly utilitarian. They certainly never would have engraved quotes from scripture—not that the scripture in question existed at the time the first of these guns had been manufactured.

The 12-millimeter firearm Mr. Antonio had was one that belonged in the ceremonial guard in the temples and palaces on Grimalkin. It had probably been blessed by the temple priests.

Nickolai remembered well when he had passed his first trial as an adult of House Rajasthan. After twelve hours of uninterrupted sparring with priests and acolytes, he had limped, bruised, bleeding, undefeated, up the 367 steps to the cenotaph of St. Rajasthan. At the top, before the statue of the first speaker of his faith, his mother had presented him with a weapon much like the one Mr. Antonio showed him.

The words she spoke were not in the corrupt tongue of the Fallen, but came from the scriptures of his faith:

This is a symbol of your service, my son. A token from He who gives you succor when you are shunned.

Years later, when the priests had come for him, they had taken the gun. They had told him it had been melted down. It had become unclean from his touch.

Now, Mr. Antonio was not only returning his eyes and his arm but, in some sense, his honor as well. In another sense, he was taking all the remnants of honor he had left.

Could he accept the kind of debt this represented?

Nickolai looked into Mr. Antonio's eyes and knew that the deal had already been made, and the debt went deeper than any material accounting. The man he now served was just making the deal explicit in terms he knew Nickolai understood.

Nickolai reached over and picked up the weapon. It was too large for any human to handle comfortably, but it rested perfectly in Nickolai's new hand. The weight felt good, as if it completed the reconstruction of his missing limb.

Mr. Antonio smiled.

"So how do I become this agent you require?"

"You will need to join the Bakunin Mercenaries' Union. That will give you the contacts to apply for the position I need you in."

Nickolai sighted down the barrel of the new weapon, nostrils flaring with the scent of gun oil. "You are certain that I will be hired for this position?"

"Mr. Rajasthan, I have no doubt of it."

Date: 2525.11.07 *(Standard)*
Bakunin–BD+50°1725

It was like he had told Mr. Salvador, *"Do you forget why we were created?"*

Nickolai began to understand why his ancestors were created. Why he existed. Not just the knowledge of what scriptures and history taught, of how mankind—the fallen creation of God—had the arrogance to create thinking creatures to serve man, to praise man, and to give glory unto man.

Nickolai had *known* that he was descended from creatures designed to fight in wars that man didn't have the stomach to fight himself. He had *known* that when all the petty human governments coalesced into the Terran Council that mankind had renounced their creation and cast it out, exiling it to Tau Ceti at a time prior to tach-drives when the only interstellar travel was through a manufactured wormhole, effectively one-way.

He *knew* where he had come from, but on some level he hadn't understood it. He didn't understand until he found himself bound in service to the false god, man. Until he found himself retracing the steps of his ancestors.

This was why he was created—and *this* was why that creation was such a great sin.

But he had pledged himself, so he walked the path that Mr. Antonio had set for him. And that path was very well prepared.

There was already an explanation of why Nickolai was searching for work as a mercenary, and how he had come by prosthetics that cost much more than his income from Mr. Salvador would have allowed. Any investigation would show that the reconstruction was paid for by one of Godwin's many loan sharks—a Mr. Charkov. This debt to Mr. Charkov could not be paid on a bouncer's salary.

To add verisimilitude to the fictitious story, any money Nickolai would receive beyond basic living expenses would disappear directly into an anonymous account that could, with effort, be traced to Mr. Charkov.

So, as dawn crawled over the slums of the city of Godwin, Nickolai walked into an unfamiliar quarter of the city. The Godwin where he had lived in exile had been a city that smelled of smoke, sewage, and crumbling ferrocrete, its sound a mélange of arguments in every possible human language.

Here, west of central Godwin, the streets no longer smelled of garbage and rotting architecture. While the air was still rank with the stink of the Fallen, it didn't stick to his fur. The streets were broader and less crowded, and the cacophony of human voices was less aggressive.

Nickolai walked, because a taxi would be uncomfortable and expensive, but also because actually *seeing* the human hive of Godwin was still a novelty. His vision with his digital eyes was an order of magnitude sharper than his real eyes had ever been and worth the occasional headache. He could read the holo-script crawling up the side of buildings five or ten klicks away. He was able to see the enigmatic human expressions on the drivers of the aircars soaring above him.

And he could *see* as much as hear and smell the difference in the neighborhood around him. The broad avenue of West Lenin wasn't cracked and buckled like the old streets near his apartments. The walls of the buildings around him were still in the colors of steel and stone intended by the builders, not the garish tapestry of graffiti that wrapped the structures where Nickolai lived.

Most different were the human inhabitants. They seemed cleaner, better dressed, and were less prone to obviously avoid his path.

The Godwin branch of the Bakunin Mercenaries' Union was a plain onyx-black cube of a building nestled between a bank and an expensive-looking escort service. The windowless building had a single door and no decoration other than a small bronze plaque with the initials BMU engraved in it. As he approached it, he could faintly smell ozone, a sign of an active broadband Emerson field ionizing stray air molecules.

Nickolai entered the building and faced a long hallway lined with holo screens—the nearest of which showed his approach and the entrance of the building from several points of view and at several different frequencies. One density scan showed a partially exploded skeletal view of his body where the recent reconstruction of his arm was plainly visible, showing bones metallic, dense, and much too smooth and regular to be organic.

He walked along the hallway, past his own image, and past images of a more expected variety—pictures of military hardware, from hand weapons to hovertanks; Paralian-designed assault craft with military-class tach-drives down to manpack contragrav units. Much of the hardware bore trademarks of Bakunin-based industries. The arms industry was the largest sector of the Bakunin economy, supplying not only the bottomless domestic demand, but also equipping probably half the militaries in human space—every government that didn't have the resources to equip its own military and a few that did.

Every *human* government.

Despite historical ties to Bakunin, the nonhuman inhabitants of the Fifteen Worlds—the loose confederation that included Nickolai's homeworld of Grimalkin—avoided any ties to human space; cultural, diplomatic, or economic. Despite being a *de jure* part of the Fifteen Worlds' sphere of influence since the last days of the Confederacy—when it was the *Seven* Worlds—Bakunin's thriving export industry rarely sent anything off in the direction of Tau Ceti.

And, despite the professionalism of the receptionist, it was clear in the man's voice, his posture, and the smell of fear on his skin that the alienation was mutual. The Fallen were still afraid of their creations.

"Can I help you?" asked the receptionist before Nickolai was within six strides of the semicircular desk at the end of the hall.

Nickolai waited until he stood in front of the desk before speaking. "I am here to obtain membership in the Mercenaries' Union."

"Oh," the receptionist nodded, "of course." The man did well hiding his fear. Someone with the half-dead senses of the Fallen might have completely missed the man's discomfort.

Nickolai was tall enough to see over the top of the desk and look down on the receptionist. He watched as the man's hand moved away from a handheld plasma cannon holstered behind the desk. Nickolai frowned slightly. There was little honor in the nasty-looking handgun. It was a single-use desperation weapon—firing it would release all the energy in its fifteen-centimeter–diameter barrel in a cone of plasma at temperatures that would vaporize all organics, most synthetics, and a good many metals in a cone that would fill most of the corridor Nickolai had just walked down.

"We require a one-kilogram deposit as a reserve against your first year's dues," the man told him.

Nickolai nodded and pulled a chit from his belt, placing it on the desk. The man waited for Nickolai's hand to completely withdraw before taking it. "Very good. If you go to one of our interview rooms, you can post an alias and a résumé for our clients, and schedule yourself for a skills assessment. After that we'll archive your DNA signature, and you'll have access to our databases and all our facilities. You'll get an ID badge, but you don't need it for our services as long as you can present a biometric ID. Welcome to the BMU."

CHAPTER SEVEN

Tithes

The most dangerous impulse is to feel safe.
                    —*The Cynic's Book of Wisdom*

In this business you never let your guard down.
                    —SYLVIA HARPER
                    (2008–2081)

Date: 2525.11.10 (Standard)
Bakunin–BD+50°1725

So far, since arriving, Mallory had investigated close to a dozen ships that conceivably could be contracted to go as far as Xi Virginis. Unfortunately, the nature of the trip put severe limits on the kind of vessel that he could hire. The ship had to be able to power several twenty light-year jumps without refueling and needed the capability to skim hydrogen from whatever source happened to be available, since there wouldn't be any processing centers along the way.

It wasn't an impossible criteria. The Indi Protectorate had manufactured thousands of such exploration vessels in its heyday. But those that were still around were old and cranky. The one ship he'd gone to visit today, in his opinion, would require divine intervention to make it as far as Tau Ceti. The only other possibility so far had the ill luck of having a pilot who actually bragged about doing black ops work for the Caliphate.

He was walking back to his hotel from the hangar, when he saw an odd heat-shimmer out of the corner of his eye. He had been retired for forty years, so he didn't react as quickly as he should have. By the time he realized the significance of the visual distortion, the man in the cloak was standing directly in front of him.

The cloak was a military-grade personal camo projector, looking like a cubist heat-shimmer about one and a half times the size of a man in full combat gear. Mallory stopped short when he saw the distortion and realized that there was a near-invisible *something* standing on the walkway in front of him.

He took a step back and felt a metal-clad hand between his shoulder blades. A quick glance back showed more optical distortion, headache-inducing at this range. He was close enough to see the shimmer of the tiny fly-sized optical pickups that orbited the cloaked figure—allowing the occupant to see outside his own photon-twisting cocoon.

The pair had him trapped in a long alley between a featureless gray hangar and a tall office building that showed no ground-level entrances for about twenty meters in either direction.

"Welcome to our fair planet." A voice came from the shimmer in front of him. The voice was amplified, emerged from somewhere around chest level, and was much too cheerful.

From behind him, came a slightly staticky version of the same voice. "We here represent the Proudhon Chamber of Commerce."

"Your donation is greatly appreciated."

Just a few meters away and to the rear, Mallory caught sight of a window—little more than a retail clothing display, but close enough to be an escape. He was ducking down and around the man behind him before he had really started thinking about it; adrenaline and his implants were doing the thinking for him.

Behind him, he heard one of them say, "I really hate new people."

Mallory drew his sidearm and took aim at the window, pointing the barrel between the breasts of the animated mannequin posing in the latest fashion from Banlieue.

Probably should have just given them my money.

The reliable old slugthrower barked in his hand three times, and Bakunin again defied his expectations. Instead of fragmenting, the window simply showed three pancaked slugs embedded in a tight grouping above the mannequin's chest.

What clothing store has bulletproof windows?

Something hard and metal slammed into his back and he

collided face-first into the undamaged window. His sidearm went sailing down the alley. The breath jarred from him, he collapsed on the ground, rolling up to face his shimmering attackers.

"I guess," said the one with static in his voice, "you just don't want to do this nice."

Mallory spat from a bloody lip. "I guess that was a bad idea."

"Bad idea, he says."

"That's funny."

An invisible gauntlet reached down and grabbed the front of Mallory's shirt, and Mallory got the sickeningly surreal vision of most of his torso disappearing as the man lifted him to his feet.

"For your own benefit we're going to have to educate you out of these bad ideas."

Mallory's feet left the ground and his back slammed into the wall. He could hear the servos grinding in his attacker's unseen armor. In his head, Mallory began praying, preparing for the worst.

This close, Mallory could only see the world through the distortion of the camo projection. Through the angular ripples of the projection, he saw a bright flash erupt from the ground behind the man holding him. A ball of smoke rolled upward from the flash, revealing a circle of the walkway melted to black slag. The air was suddenly rank with the smell of hot metal and burned synthetics.

"What the fuck?" The man holding him dropped him and backed away. Mallory staggered against the wall but remained upright. His two attackers were standing right next to him, but Mallory had the sense that he was no longer the focus of their attention.

"Okay, boys, playtime's over." The new voice came from a petite woman standing at the mouth of the alley, back where Mallory had come from. She had brown skin and straight white hair pulled back in a ponytail. She wore a white jumpsuit with a shoulder patch that Mallory couldn't make out at this distance.

Her most distinguishing feature was the razor-thin gamma laser carbine she held pointed down the alley at them.

"This ain't your business, lady."

The woman cocked her head. The barrel of the carbine

didn't move at all. "You know, it might be a good idea for you to think about whether you should be telling me what is and isn't my business."

"Now wait a goddamn minute—"

"Cool it, Reggie."

"Now you going and using my name, what the fuck's wrong with you?"

"She's BMU, Reggie."

"I don't give a shit if she's the fucking pope—"

"Well, I do. Rolling a tourist isn't worth the trouble."

The woman added, "Listen to your brother, Reggie."

"What? No one said anything about who—"

"I told you. BMU. Understand?"

After a long pause, Reggie said, "Okay, cut our losses. Fuck it."

Both shimmers moved away leaving Malloy alone in the alley.

The woman walked down the alley. Without the distortion between him and her, he could now see the shoulder patch on her jumpsuit. It wasn't too surprising to see the initials "BMU" embroidered in gold on a red field. Below the initials were a crossed sword and rifle.

She also had a name embroidered on the left breast of the jumpsuit: "V. Parvi."

She bent over and picked up Mallory's slugthrower.

"Thank you," Mallory said.

"You're welcome," she stepped over to him and handed him his gun. This close, she wasn't just petite, but tiny. She was a full head shorter than his Occisian build—barely 150 centimeters, if that. "But don't go thinking that anything on this planet's free, Staff Sergeant Fitzpatrick."

The woman was named Vijayanagara Parvi. She belonged to an organization with the somewhat generic name of the Bakunin Mercenaries' Union—she was a recruiter. Apparently, Father Mallory's alias, Staff Sergeant Fitzpatrick, had just been recruited by Ms. Parvi. Of course, she told him, he didn't *have* to sign up with the BMU. However, it made economic sense. If he didn't, he would owe the BMU for her services, and he wouldn't have the benefits of being a member of the union.

Of course, the primary benefit would be that he would

cease being a target for bottom-feeders like Reggie and his brother.

"The way it works on this planet," she told him, "you need to be part of something scarier than the shitheads who want a piece of you."

In the end, Staff Sergeant Fitzpatrick went along with her pitch. The whole situation fit so seamlessly into Mallory's cover he chalked it up to divine providence. It didn't even matter that he had the strong suspicion that Reggie and his brother were employed by Ms. Parvi and the BMU to help recruit new blood. Signing up for the BMU was something that Staff Sergeant Fitzpatrick would do even without the extra incentive.

He also felt a level of security when Ms. Parvi confirmed many of the details of Staff Sergeant Fitzpatrick's history. Mallory's cover seemed to have stuck, however rushed it had been.

CHAPTER EIGHT

Mysteries

Knowledge is not the same as intelligence, and having too much of one often leads to having too little of the other.
—*The Cynic's Book of Wisdom*

Sometimes it's smart to know when to be a little ignorant.
—ROBERT CELINE
(1923–1996)

Date: 2525.11.12 (Standard)
Bakunin–BD+50°1725

Tjaele Mosasa sat in a small building in an aircraft graveyard on the outskirts of Proudhon. In the office around him, holo displays crowded the walls. The displays showed unfiltered broadcasts from across all of human space, chattering in every language of the human universe. The data from the signals varied in age from several days to several decades depending on whether Mosasa's receivers were leeching a tach-comm broadcast or a slow light speed signal that wasn't intended to communicate beyond a planetary system. The off-planet broadcasts cycled through signals every few seconds based on some custom filtering algorithms. A dozen other screens showed text data scrolling by quicker than any human would be able to read.

The data flowing through the office, flowing through Mosasa, came from every aspect of human civilization. News broadcasts, soap operas, technical user manuals, tour guides, classified intelligence briefings, personal tach-comms, telemetry data from satellite diagnostic systems, pornography, patent applications, want ads, suicide notes, tax returns, census data—

If someone, somewhere, digitized some scrap of data, it was Mosasa's goal to route it through the hardware in this room. Even when he wasn't present here, he had encrypted transmissions broadcast to receivers implanted in his body.

Mosasa absorbed the data on a preconscious level. The software that formed the highest level of his consciousness, the part of him that thought of himself, was too complicated, slow, and unwieldy to process all the information he gorged on. That duty was reserved for an older part of himself, the part that was designed to process the data, to model it, to give him a view of the universe beyond this office.

The individual holo broadcasts, reports, novels, technical manuals no more impacted his conscious awareness than a single photon. However, like a photon, he didn't need to be aware of any particular data element for it to contribute to his image of the universe.

The core of Mosasa's preconscious mind assembled the unending stream of data into a view of the human cultural and political universe just as his eyes assembled an unending stream of photons into a view of the physical office around him. Both views were completely arbitrary constructions of Mosasa's brain. Both were concrete and unquestionably real.

He saw the twist and political outlines of the Alpha Centauri Alliance as well as the plastic cases holding the holo screens mounted on the walls around him. He could feel the proxy tendrils of the Vatican pushing toward the Caliphate as concretely as he felt the engineered leather of the chair he sat on.

And from a dozen different subtle directions, he felt something pressing into fringes of human space. Information was leaking in from outside . . .

Xi Virginis.

Mosasa knew about the colonies in that direction of space. He knew about them since their founding. He was old enough to have personally known some of the people who had founded them.

He had also known that they didn't interact with the main body of human space. For a decade or so, those colonies' only impact had been the knowledge of their existence in the upper levels of the Caliphate, the Vatican, and their proxies. Mosasa had seen that knowledge channel human actions on the highest levels, a stalemate where those in power did not act for fear of prompting their rivals to act. It was a stable equilibrium that should have endured for decades more.

Something was tipping the equilibrium. Some unseen stream of data was feeding into the equation. Some unknown was moving the Vatican and the Caliphate. Mosasa saw the resources moving, but not the reason.

But like a black hole moving through a galaxy, he might not see the source of the distortion, though seeing the effects was enough for him to give the location of the unknown.

Xi Virginis.

The unknown drew him, even though he knew that if he moved himself, it would further upset the equilibrium. He told himself that, as long as an unknown this large loomed within these far-flung colonies, the stability he saw was illusory.

It wasn't even really a decision. As soon as he knew that the unknown existed, there was a hole in the fabric of his universe. He would *have* to investigate it. The only decision was how he would do so, and what individual threads from the human universe he would pull in behind him to help patch the hole.

Parvi looked at the list of names on the cyberplas sheet in her hand. She read the capsule biographies and shook her head. "Why go to so much trouble? There are plenty of scientists on Bakunin."

"Perspective," Mosasa said. His tone was flat, as always, and it irritated Parvi how it never quite became mechanical. He should speak in a synthetic monotone; sounding like a disinterested human being was just *wrong*.

She knew her irritation was irrational. An artificial voice could sound indistinguishable from human even when not spoken by an illegal self-aware AI. However, most programmers were polite enough to slip in some sort of audible hook, just so you knew there wasn't a real person behind the speech.

Parvi looked up at Mosasa.

That was the other thing. He looked like a real person. A tall, sculpted man with hairless brown skin covered with photoreactive tattoos and body jewelry. He might have been handsome if it wasn't for the dragon's head drawn across the side of his skull and a third of his face. She knew that a long time ago there was a human being named Mosasa, and that man looked pretty much the way Mosasa looked now.

She also knew that man had been dead for at least a couple of centuries.

"What do you mean, 'perspective'?" Her words echoed in the hangar while Mosasa stood with his back to her. He was doing something inscrutable to the drive section of a Scimitar fighter, an old stealth design from the Caliphate that had somehow ended up in the possession of Mosasa Salvage.

"I am investigating something unknown," he said without turning around. "An unknown whose shape implies an impact that could involve all of human space. Having a wide section of social and political background in personnel will be an aid to my analysis."

"I see."

"After you make contact with the science team and arrange for their arrival here, I will need you to assemble the military team."

"I don't see any military personnel here."

"All in time." He waved a hand, dismissing her.

She sighed and turned around, walking out of the hangar.

Parvi hated working for Mosasa. It made her skin crawl whenever she was in his presence. It was with a palpable physical relief that she walked out of the hangar and into the desert air on the outskirts of Proudhon. It wasn't just that he was an AI. That was bad enough. The taboo against Artificial Intelligence devices of any sort were broad and deep in every human culture, dating from the Genocide War with the Race over four hundred years ago. Seeing what the Race-built AIs could do with their social programming was enough to put that tech in a class of evil only shared by self-replicating nano-technology and the genetic engineering of sapient creatures.

No, Mosasa couldn't just be an AI, living on the lawless world Bakunin, the only place where he didn't face summary destruction. No, Mosasa had to be an AI built by the Race itself, a remnant of an old weapon surviving long past the war for which it was built, a weapon that in some sick fashion had learned to mimic a human being.

But Mosasa paid well, and Parvi needed the money.

So she tucked the cyberplas sheet into her pocket, got onto her contragrav bike, and shot back toward Proudhon. She had a bunch of tach-comm calls to make on her boss' behalf.

CHAPTER NINE

Initiations

The shortest freeway will have the highest toll.
                    —*The Cynic's Book of Wisdom*

If you would win a man to your cause, first convince him
that you are his sincere friend.

                    —ABRAHAM LINCOLN
                    (1809–1865)

Date: 2525.11.18 (Standard)
Bakunin–BD+50°1725

The whole process of registering as a member of the BMU
alternately fascinated and appalled Mallory. The academic in
him was fascinated with how the BMU operated and seeing
the detailed workings of a society that operated on completely
different premises than his own. The Marine in him was offended by the military pretense of an organization that, for the
most part, didn't have a chain of command above the squad
level—un-uniformed and mostly unregulated. The Catholic in
him kept seeing the implications of a world whose only military was essentially a group of semiorganized thugs for hire.

To which, the academic in him responded, *How is that different from most of human history?*

The more he saw of the way Bakunin worked, the more he
saw parallels to medieval Europe; the social rationalizations
and beliefs might be different, but the BMU reminded him
of landless knights. All they lacked was dispensation from the
pope to go on a crusade and keep them from ravaging the
countryside.

One major difference, though, was in the area of skill assessment. Apparently, any idiot with a gun and some money

could join the BMU—gun optional. But if you wanted to be a working member, and do more that pay the union protection money, you needed a rating. You could put anything you wanted on your résumé narrative—experience in hand-to-hand combat, fighter pilot, special forces, covert ops—but what mattered was BMU's own assessment.

In the chaotic economy that was Bakunin, it was worth it to pay for a known quantity. Someone hiring a union mercenary was getting a known skill set. It might be more expensive than hiring random thugs off the street, but it was less prone to surprises. Also attractive to a potential employer, a lot of the BMU's few regulations were specifically intended to prevent their members from turning on their employers. Hire someone from BMU, and you were assured that the whole weight of the union would fall on a member who double-crossed you. Of course the converse was also true; union members had the muscle of the BMU to back them if their employer ever double-crossed them.

Membership served the dual purpose of giving Staff Sergeant Fitzpatrick a deeper level to his cover and preventing future incidents with Reggie and his ilk.

He went through their whole system of testing over the course of a week. It was a comprehensive battery of exams; oral, written, and simulated. For Mallory, it was the most rigorous testing he had gone through since he had joined the Marine Special Forces back when he was only twenty standard years old. More so, because he had to keep in the front of his mind that they weren't supposed to be testing a retired member of the most elite combat unit of the Occisis military, but someone who was both more prosaic and more recently employed. Mallory had to work to weight his efforts toward the more basic aspects of infantry skills, and to do more poorly on the more exotic skills like combat demolitions and long-distance marksmanship.

Hardest was the psych evaluation. Mallory decided that he had to give up on Staff Sergeant Fitzpatrick for that. He wasn't trained as a deep-cover agent, and he knew that he didn't know enough to skew that kind of testing in a way that would be seamless. He had to hope that Father Mallory's psych profile wouldn't look too out of place in Fitzpatrick's file.

The psych profile was the last test. Staff Sergeant Fitzpatrick left the testing facility a fully vetted member of the

Bakunin Mercenaries' Union, with certified skills in small-unit ground combat, basic vehicle operation, and logistics. All of which matched the staff sergeant's history with the Occisis Marines. All the other skills rated under 500, the lowest being his sniper rating, at just 150.

The BMU testing facility was on the fringes of Proudhon, sprawling over an area that might have been a series of old landing strips resulting in a low black building that radiated long black rectangular wings at odd angles to itself. On one side the horizon was a humpbacked mountain range, the other was the metallic chaos of Proudhon.

On the Proudhon side was a small private parking area where his rented aircar was waiting. Now that he was done with the BMU for the day, his mind returned to the real reason he was here. Unfortunately, he still had not been having any luck finding potential ships that could take him off in the direction of Xi Virginis.

He was pondering the next place to find someone with an expertise in illicit long-distance travel when he saw Vijayanagara Parvi leaning against his aircar. Instead of a white jumpsuit she wore more civilian clothes. But she still had a BMU logo embroidered on her sky-blue windbreaker and a wicked looking needlegun peeked out from a barely covered shoulder holster.

As he approached he asked, "So, tell me, do Reggie and his brother work for you?"

She smiled. "Tell me if it matters."

"Slamming into that wall hurt."

"You can take it."

Mallory shook his head. "So, are you here to 'save' me from another attack by Bakunin's lowlife?"

"Actually, I'm here to congratulate you. Not many people pass though the exams this quickly."

Mallory's expression didn't change, but he winced inside. He had been making such an effort to have the test scores reflect Fitzpatrick's expertise, he hadn't thought about how much *time* Fitzpatrick would have spent on them. "I wanted to get it over with."

Parvi laughed. "I'd like to see some of your scores if you took some time at it."

"I don't really see the point." Mentally, Mallory scrambled for a new picture of Fitzpatrick that would be consistent with what Parvi had seen of him and the results of his exams. "My money's running out and I need to be working, not being tested by some asshole officer."

"Oh, lord." She was still smiling. "I can see why you never made it past staff sergeant."

Perfect. "You know, maybe I liked where I was."

"Yes. But people are going to hire you based on those scores."

Let's change the subject now. "And how exactly do you go about getting hired?"

"Welcome to ProMex," Parvi said.

It was a cross between an ancient Roman coliseum, a stock exchange, a casino, and hell's own trade show. It was named the Proudhon Military Exchange. In terms of area, it was probably the largest nonaircraft-related structure in the city.

Walking into the massive dome, they passed aisles where hundreds of merchants sold exotic military hardware. Above them, holo screens showed gladiatorial contests being held somewhere else in the complex. Everywhere kiosks gave scrolling displays of symbols that, Parvi explained, gave values of publicly owned paramilitary organizations as well as odds on various conflicts based on current wagering.

It was a little disturbing, but not surprising, that the conflicts were not confined to Bakunin. It was more disturbing exactly how many of them there were. When he commented on it, Parvi said that, "Members of the BMU have seen action on every inhabited planet in human space."

He almost said, *not Occisis,* but he remembered the chaos of the Junta and its aftermath. It was quite possible some off-planet forces were involved at some point.

She led him on a winding path across the floor to a large area clear of the arms dealers. The area was marked by a series of three-meter-high towers, all topped with the chromed spheres of Emerson field generators. Mallory didn't need the red and yellow candy-striping on the towers to know that, while he couldn't see it, the area was protected by an antipersonnel Emerson field.

There was one obvious entry, a round portal mounted between two of the towers. Across the top it said, "BMU Members only." On one side of it, a small open-ended metal cylinder emerged from the skin of the portal. Parvi placed her hand in the cylinder, waited a moment, then walked through.

Well, I'm a member now—several kilograms lighter in the wallet to prove it.

Mallory put his hand inside, waited for a count of three, then walked through after Parvi.

"Genetic sequencer?" he asked.

"Genes, fingerprints, blood pressure, serotonin and adrenaline levels, toxicology—you name it . . ." She led him down a few steps to a large area sunk into the floor enough to hide it from the public area without use of a solid wall. "To answer your question, *this* is how you get hired."

The floor was crowded with men and women, and to Mallory's surprise, a few nonhumans. One of the two standout examples was the Rorschach-faced serpent-necked pseudo-avian form of a Voleran. Its eyeless, hard-beaked head bobbed above everyone, except the other nonhuman. Unlike the Voleran, the other obvious nonhuman wasn't really "alien." At least, its ancestors were of terrestrial origin, victims of morally questionable genetic engineers.

In the twenty-first century, man had not yet established a moral framework around the Heretical Technologies: self-replicating nanotechnology, artificial intelligences, and the genetic engineering of sapient life-forms. The last of these was the most seriously abused before mankind gained control of itself. Thousands of new species, as intelligent as man but—for the most part—less well constructed, were built to fight the wars that ravaged the planet. The weapons outlived the war, and eventually, during the dark days before the rise of the Confederacy, faced exile to the worlds past Tau Ceti.

Understandably, the survivors of that period of human history had very little to do with humanity anymore. Diplomatic communication between human governments and the Fifteen Worlds was practically nil. And even though Bakunin was technically part of the Fifteen Worlds' sphere of influence, this was the first product of that history Mallory had seen here.

The first he had *ever* seen.

The creature was close to three meters tall, and if Mallory had to guess, he'd estimate mass at close to five hundred kilos, all muscle. It had a feline skull and striped fur and moved with a grace that reminded Mallory of a very well-trained martial artist. It wore only a gun belt.

"Never seen a moreau before?" Parvi asked.

Mallory realized he'd been staring and turned away from the giant cat. "No."

"Get used to it. If you stick around Bakunin, you'll see more."

Hearing the tone in Parvi's voice, Mallory turned toward her. "You sound like you don't approve."

Instead of answering him, she led him to one of the kiosks that dotted the floor here, on the opposite corner of the floor from the moreau.

"This ties into the closed BMU database," she told him. "You can see live queries entered by anyone in the system, on-planet or off."

"Off?"

"We have tach-transmit updates on an hourly basis—with a transmission delay, of course."

"Of course." It was disconcerting to think that a completely extra-legal entity like the BMU had outposts on other planets with enough resources to run a tach-transmitter. Mallory faced the kiosk and started running a few searches. The interface was familiar, like searching the want ads anywhere else—except the ads here were "team experienced with infiltration and underwater demolition," "EVA-rated flight crew for Lancer-class drop ship, experience handling pulse cannon/plasma weapon repair/maint a plus," "IW hackers needed, good pay/benefits for low-risk industrial espionage . . ."

For the sake of his cover story, Mallory really looked though the ads searching for positions that resembled anything that might interest Staff Sergeant Fitzpatrick. He'd gather a list of contacts that he could take back to the hotel. He hoped that his search for discreet off-planet transport would bear fruit before he ran into Parvi again and she asked him about his job search. With all the positions available, the longer he went without signing on with someone, the more obvious it would be that he was looking for something more then a source of income.

He went though a series of random sorts when he caught his breath.

Parvi had been staring at the tiger moreau, but she turned to face him. "Is something wrong?"

Mallory shook his head. "No."

He didn't even sound convincing to himself. The deceptions he had trained for with the Marines had involved not being seen by the enemy.

"Just." He stumbled for words as he composed himself. "It just struck me, looking at all these listings . . ." He turned to look at her and the distress on his face was honest, even if his words weren't. "And it hit me that my old life's over. I'm really no longer part of the Marines . . ."

Parvi nodded. "I wish I could say you'd get over that." She turned back to look at the crowd. The tiger moreau was gone now. "Everyone on Bakunin is running from something."

Mallory nodded, turning back to face the kiosk. It was hard not to breathe a sigh of relief that she had bought his little improvised speech.

Please God, he silently prayed, *let me understand what this means.*

On the display, floating near the top of the holo, was a small listing waiting for him to touch it to see greater detail. The current sort was by job location, so various place names glowed brightest, the most common—filling most of the holo—being "undisclosed location."

Of course that made sense. If you were preparing military action, where you were sending the mercenaries was a valuable piece of intel you wouldn't release, even to an allegedly closed database run by the BMU. After all, the members of BMU only owed loyalty to you after they were hired.

However, a few ads did give that sort of information, where it wasn't obviously mission critical to keep it secret. Most of those were prosaic things like jobs as trainers, cargo escorts and security, some of the Information Warfare jobs where geography was irrelevant, jobs as bodyguards or security where the show of force was of more deterrence value, and the one listing that captured Mallory's attention—

"Team needed to protect scientific expedition to vicinity of Xi Virginis."

CHAPTER TEN

Heresies

The one thing more corrosive to a culture than a taboo
without purpose is having no taboos at all.

—*The Cynic's Book of Wisdom*

By identifying the new learning with heresy, you make or-
thodoxy synonymous with ignorance.

—DESIDERIUS ERASMUS
(1465–1536)

Date: 2525.11.21 (Standard)
Bakunin–BD+50°1725

Nickolai, now a fully vetted member of the BMU, walked out
of a cab on the fringes of the city/spaceport of Proudhon. Dusk
was advancing, and the city behind him was already shimmering with light. He had gone through all the union's testing, and
despite the degradation of using his skills for the employ of
the Fallen, there had been something sweet about completely
dropping his constant restraint and allowing himself to fully
exercise his training. He couldn't help but enjoy the fact that
he had demolished the robotic sparring partner they had sent
up against him in the armed hand-to-hand exercise.

All the tests had felt less than serious to Nickolai. He didn't
understand how they could rely on tests that measured people
when nothing was at stake. His coming-of-age trials on Grimalkin had been much more difficult—and conducted by
priests who would maim without hesitation.

If he hadn't been wary about his new arm, he would have
had a perfect score on hand-to-hand combat. With firearms,
his score had been less than appropriate for a scion of House
Rajasthan, but that had been largely due to new eyes—when
he had fixed on a target, he was able to do better than he ever

had with a gun, but if he was off, he was completely off. Still, when the bull's-eyes were averaged with complete misses, his marksmanship greatly exceeded what the BMU considered average.

Judging by the solicitations he had received before his testing was even completed, the Fallen considered him a desirable commodity.

Then that is why we were born, was it not?

The cab flew away behind him, leaving him on a desolate stretch of road that stabbed arrow straight into the desert around Proudhon. The road was stamped with the logo of a company that would have taken a toll from any travelers when this road had a destination in mind. However, the original destination of this highway had been reclaimed by the desert, and the company that built and maintained the way there had similarly vanished.

The road was made of the same grainy ferrocrete that formed most of the landing strips and launchpads in the spaceport/city. Nickolai wasn't used to walking on the material; the streets of Godwin were of cheaper construction and more prone to cracking. Like the temples of Grimalkin, the roads in Proudhon felt as if they were meant to endure an eternity. Solid, flat, and permanent under the pads of his feet . . .

Though, Nickolai saw, like much of the world of the Fallen, that impression was an illusion. The edges of the hundred-meter-wide strip of ferrocrete no longer retained the sharp edges of the streets in the city. The abrasive black sand ground the edges away, advancing a dozen centimeters in a battle it would eventually win. It might take a century or two, Nickolai thought, but the sand had time.

Flanking the ancient highway, ranks of spacecraft of every size and description marched off in all three directions away from the city. Many of the corpses in this aviation necropolis showed bare metal skin, blasted by wind and the volcanic sand. Most had holes in their fuselages showing where some vital component or other had been removed. The skins that still showed markings were graced by a babel of tongues, most of which Nickolai didn't understand.

One of the few he could read graced a small, ornate tach-ship that bore the markings of the Grimalkin royal house. The tach-ship appeared to have been shot down, which Nickolai found alarming. But the seal gracing a half-melted control surface was wrong. It wasn't until he forced his too-new eyes to focus on the tail of the gutted tach-ship, and the illustration shot into headache-inducing relief, that he realized what was different about it. The seal bore the image of a tiger's head holding a blue planet in its jaws, wearing a crown made of seven stars.

Seven stars . . .

The tach-ship was from the age when the chosen people ruled only the *Seven* Worlds, before the fall of the old Terran Confederacy. The ship was at least 175 years old. He spent a few moments wondering how the markings might have survived the blowing sand. He finally decided that it must have been salvaged from orbit.

"Homesick?"

Nickolai spun around, because he hadn't sensed anyone approach. He was immediately tensed and ready to strike out, but there wasn't anyone behind him. Instead, a metallic sphere about the size of his closed fist floated in the air about two meters behind him.

"What is this?" Nickolai growled in his native tongue.

"Security for Mosasa Salvage," the sphere responded in kind. More disturbing than the fact that the machine spoke his language was the fact that it did so without any trace of the soft accent of the Fallen. He could be talking to one of the temple priests.

Of course, that was unlikely.

"I am here to apply for an advertised position," Nickolai said.

The sphere orbited him like a tiny moon. "Yes, Mr. Rajasthan, we've received your data from the BMU. Rather impressive scores, especially for someone who's recently recovered from such traumatic injuries."

Nickolai didn't let his surprise become visible on his face. The surprise was only momentary. How many scions of Rajasthan were in the BMU database, how many were on Bakunin? Anyone with the resources would be able to get almost his entire history on this planet based on his appearance alone, and given the information he had from Mr. Antonio, the owner of Mosasa Salvage had resources to spare.

"You should follow me," the sphere said, finishing its orbit and floating off ahead of Nickolai.

"Where?" Nickolai asked.

"To the hangar," it responded, "with the others."

*   *   *

Nickolai followed the floating sphere through a maze of grounded aircraft and aircraft parts, the pads on his feet warmed by sand that still retained the day's burning heat even as the sun set behind the mountains. The air smelled cold and sterile: metal, oil, and the hint of something long burned.

The ground here felt unnervingly empty of even the soul of the Fallen. The presence of blood and flesh was out of place in the midst of these metallic beasts. For once, on this planet, Nickolai felt out of place not because he was not human, but because he breathed.

The sphere led him to a building that, despite its size, seemed lost in the midst of hundreds of square kilometers of decomposing aviation history. The hangar was a trapezoidal prism of gray, pitted metal. A massive rolling door, close to two hundred meters in width, dominated the side of the building that faced Nickolai. A ferrocrete landing pad sat in front of the hangar, blown clear of sand for about three hundred meters in every direction.

Even with the huge empty space, the wreckage that surrounded this place seemed to loom over Nickolai.

If not for a small red light glowing above a small, human-sized entrance off to the side of the huge rolling hangar door, the cleared surface of the landing pad, and the faint scent of the Fallen drifting on the air, it would have given every appearance of being long abandoned

In this desolate place, the stink of the Fallen was almost reassuring.

"Please wait for the ready light, then enter," the sphere told him, then floated back off into the maze of dead aircraft.

Nickolai walked up to the smaller door with the red light. When he stood a meter away, the red light changed to green. In his mind he briefly pictured himself crossing some irrevocable threshold, that by passing through this door he would no longer be able to turn back.

He wondered at himself. Why would he suddenly think he had choices now?

He ducked through the too-short doorway and walked into the hangar. He felt a tingle in his artificial arm and behind his eyes as he entered, similar but more intense than what he had felt when crossing the EM shielding of the dungeon where he had met Mr. Antonio.

The tap of his claws on the ferrocrete floor echoed in the vast space as he stepped inside. The hangar was windowless and ill lit, but his eyes focused everything into sharp relief almost instantaneously.

Dominating everything was the dark silhouette of a tachship. Little more than a featureless shadow, it loomed over the small gathering of humans by one of its downturned stub wings. The meeting area was defined by a cluster of folding chairs, bordered by the edges of a single spotlight shining down from the scaffolding above.

Nickolai walked slowly, noting the scents and positions of the human mercenaries as he approached. He saw three under the spotlight: two males and one female. That raised his level of caution because he smelled at least two females in the air here, and that meant there were others out of sight, probably inside the ship.

The three he could see had been talking among themselves, but they stopped as soon as they noticed him approaching. They turned toward him, and he could tell by their relaxed posture that they didn't yet see him fully.

These are warriors? he wondered to himself. Unless they had his eyes, they had blinded themselves by sitting in the best-lit place in this hangar. Until they heard him approach, they had been paying more attention to each other than to the vast unprotected space surrounding them. Had he wished to kill them, Nickolai guessed he could finish off two of them before the third realized something was wrong.

"Holy shit," the taller of the men whispered. Nickolai suspected that he wasn't supposed to hear that.

Nickolai walked up to the fringes of the spotlight and stood facing the three humans. He was gratified not to smell the stink of fear around them.

The shorter man walked forward. He was squat and light-skinned, the top of his head barely reaching Nickolai's sternum. The man thrust his hand out. "I'm Staff Sergeant John Fitzpatrick."

The other man laughed and said, "You *were* Staff Sergeant, Fitz. You ain't in the Marines anymore, geehead."

Fitzpatrick's hand hung between them for a few moments. Nickolai knew the human gesture the man was inviting, but Nickolai didn't move his own hand. He could not bring himself to touch the flesh of the Fallen. Unclean he might be, but there were still limits.

When Fitzpatrick realized that he wasn't going to shake hands, he closed his hand and hooked his thumb toward the other man behind him. "And that gentleman is Jusef Wahid—"

"Jusuf," the other man snapped.

"Sorry, *Jusuf* Wahid."

Wahid was tall for a human and had darker coloring and narrower eyes than ex-Staff Sergeant Fitzpatrick.

Fitzpatrick turned and gestured toward the last human in evidence, the female. "And this is Julia Kugara."

The female stepped forward and looked Nickolai up and down. He realized that she was even taller than Wahid. Where Wahid was thin and bony, Kugara was lithe and muscular. She was the first human he had ever seen who didn't appear clumsy.

"So what do we call you?" she asked.

"My name is Nickolai Rajasthan."

Nickolai had been living with the Fallen for over a year, but he had only been *seeing* them for a handful of days. Despite his new eyes, he was still blind to the meanings of facial expressions and body language. Judging by tone of voice and the scent cues that surrounded him, Wahid was the most nervous at his presence.

Fitzpatrick said, "I believe I saw you a few days ago, at the military exchange."

"Perhaps you did."

"Small world," Wahid said. "That's one hell of a coincidence."

Kugara snorted. "God, aren't you a paranoid shit, Jusuf?" She looked Nickolai up and down, her face changing to an inscrutable human expression. "Not like Nickolai here can blend into a crowd at ProMex. Don't mind him," she addressed Nickolai. "Jusuf thinks everyone is a spy."

Wahid snorted. "Everyone can benefit from a little professional paranoia."

Nickolai growled a little in discomfort that he hoped the humans didn't perceive. He glared at Wahid and asked, "Who exactly would I be spying for?"

The odor of fear gratified Nickolai as Wahid backed up a few steps and held up his hands between them. "I wasn't accusing anyone of anything."

Good, he doesn't actually know anything, Nickolai thought.

"I was with the Occisis Marines for ten years before they cut me loose," Fitzpatrick said. "What outfit were you with?"

"I was with no 'outfit.' " Nickolai shook his head. "I served my clan, House Rajasthan."

"What does that mean?" Wahid asked.

"It means he's a member of the royal family on a planet that chooses their leaders based on their prowess at hand-to-hand combat." Kugara turned to look at Wahid. "So don't piss him off."

"How do you know so much about it?" Wahid asked.

"My father came from Dakota," Kugara said, "so don't piss *me* off."

Nickolai caught his breath. With all the information Mr. Antonio provided about the nature of Mosasa, his business, and the type of people he might hire, never was the possibility broached that someone from Dakota might be present.

Dakota.

Dakota was one of the original Seven Worlds, founded when the men of Earth decided that they would no longer live with their damned creations. Having stolen the mantle of God, the naked devil chose to cast his handiwork into exile. It was an exodus of all the sapient products of their genetic engineers.

But more than the chosen were exiled. The Fallen hadn't only raised lesser creatures to become their warriors. They had twisted themselves, re-creating their own flesh into something that was not chosen and was not fallen. And those of once-human ancestry had settled on only one of the old Seven Worlds.

Dakota.

Nickolai could now see the subtle differences that marked Kugara as not quite human. Her scent was different—fainter and less offensive. Her motions were more fluid—quicker, stronger.

He had never met one of the Angels of Dakota. Of all those here, Kugara was closest to God, someone whose flesh bore the mark of God's own creation without being marred by the sin of arrogance that damned the rest of the Fallen.

He might have said something, but someone chose that time to announce, "So has everyone been introduced?"

The new voice came from the shadowed perimeter of the

hangar. A male voice, which was disconcerting since he had not smelled the speaker, still couldn't smell him. Nickolai turned his head, and his eyes shifted spectrum until he saw the newcomer in the darkness. A hairless human form, as tall as Kugara and darker than Wahid. The man wore a gray coverall that covered most of his body. His most distinct feature was a massive tattoo of a fantastic creature drawn with luminescent dye; the neck of the beast emerged from the collar of the coverall, wrapped around the man's neck, and curled around his left ear, leaving the profile of the beast's face drawn across the side of his own.

Mosasa, Nickolai thought, giving the apparition its proper name.

At first the lack of scent made him think he watched a holo projection, but when Mosasa moved, Nickolai heard the scrape of his—*its*—feet across the concrete. Mosasa had been waiting, soundless and motionless, in a corner of the hangar.

Mosasa walked out into the light.

"So this is your job?" Wahid asked Mosasa.

"I am Tjaele Mosasa," it responded.

"Yeah," Wahid said. "Your ad didn't say anything about hiring his kind." He didn't point at Nickolai, but he still felt all the human and near-human attention shift toward him. Nickolai also noticed Kugara fold her arms and take a step toward him while still facing Wahid. She didn't say anything, and Nickolai didn't know quite what to make of the movement.

Mosasa chuckled. "Mr. Wahid, if you find yourself queasy about heretical technologies, you'd perhaps best leave us now."

Wahid started to say something, but Fitzpatrick placed a hand on his shoulder. It was Fitzpatrick who asked, "What do you mean?"

"It means Mosasa is no more human than I am," Nickolai said quietly. Mr. Antonio had told him what Mosasa was, and also told him that Mosasa did little or nothing to conceal his nature. Mosasa would expect his potential employees to research him. That meant that Nickolai didn't have to hide the fact he knew that the thing standing before them was as much a machine as the floating sphere that had led him to the hangar.

Nickolai and his kin, extending to those like Kugara, represented the first of the three Great Sins of the Fallen—what Mosasa had called heretical technologies. Mosasa represented the second, the creation of nonliving machine intelligence. To the followers of the true faith, it was even more unforgivable. With genetic engineering, humanity had only twisted life that had existed beforehand. With artificial intelligence, the Fallen had the arrogance to create thought without life.

To serve Mr. Antonio was a disgrace. Mosasa was an abomination.

And yet, Nickolai still stood here. He wondered if it was because he had completely lost the faith of his mothers, or if he had fallen so far from grace that it no longer mattered what he did.

Nickolai didn't know how the others might feel about Mosasa's true nature, or if they had done enough research to uncover it. In either case, Nickolai couldn't read their reactions to his comment, and Mosasa himself didn't elaborate or explain.

Mosasa only glanced at Nickolai, then back at Wahid. "Mr. Rajasthan is here because the BMU has scored him better than any of you on just about every combat skill outside piloting and Information Warfare."

Fitzpatrick shook his head and asked, "Are you expecting a war?"

"Mr. Fitzpatrick," Mosasa said. "If I knew what to expect, this expedition would not be necessary."

CHAPTER ELEVEN

Acolyte

Everyone worships the God that promises them what they want.

—*The Cynic's Book of Wisdom*

If God did not exist, it would be necessary to invent him.

—Voltaire
(1694–1778)

Date: 2525.11.21 (Standard)
0.98 ly from BD+50°1725

The man Nickolai Rajasthan knew as Mr. Antonio had left the planet shortly after his last meeting with the tiger. Anyone who monitored his departure from Bakunin would have watched the small short-range craft and noted a trajectory that would take the ship toward Banlieue. Even the energy signature of the departure would have matched a small one-man craft taking the sixteen light-year journey. If the observer did the calculations based on energy expenditure and tach-drive capability, they would expect Mr. Antonio to arrive at the 355-year-old Sirius colony within about three months standard.

All of which was a carefully-engineered falsehood.

The craft Mr. Antonio piloted was a rather pedestrian scout ship, a one-hundred-year-old knockoff of a two-hundred-year-old design from the Centauri Trading Company. It had been built in one of the factories orbiting Angkor back when there was a cohesive Indi Protectorate expanding for the sake of expansion. Its construction was functional and ugly, a metallic sheath wrapping the tach-drive that comprised 80 percent of its mass and 98 percent of its volume. The whole ship formed a blocky truncated cone whose outline was defined by the construction of the scout's drives. That outline was only broken by two protrusions; the command blister on top and the single parasitic drop ship attached to a docking ring underneath.

Thanks to the Indi Protectorate's explosive expansion during the years of the Confederacy, and its subsequent decay in the years since, these inexpensive Indi craft were ubiquitous in human space and unlikely to attract any attention even when heavily modified.

And Mr. Antonio's craft was *heavily* modified.

The original tach-drives had been bulky and inefficient and had been replaced by military-grade drives roughly the same size. Those drives were an order of magnitude more efficient than the ones they replaced and would complete the journey to Banlieue in less than twenty-four days standard, if that had been where Mr. Antonio had been headed.

If he had tached to Banlieue under full power, the hypothetical observer monitoring his departure would have seen a power spike five times what would have been expected from the cranky old ship. Instead, the smaller power surge to the military tach-drives took the scout a little over a light-year away from Bakunin. From Mr. Antonio's perspective, the journey was instantaneous. From the perspective of the rest of the universe, the journey had taken a little over thirty-four hours.

Mr. Antonio powered down every system but life support, sat in a dark control cabin, and waited.

There was nothing remarkable about the area where the scout drifted. There was nothing of any substantial mass for light-months in any direction. Even the star Bakunin orbited was little more than a bright reddish star at this distance. The small scout and Mr. Antonio were lost in the big empty, more effectively invisible than if the scout had every ECM and counter-surveillance measure known to man.

He waited, and soon, he was not alone.

About an hour after taching in to this unremarkable volume of space, the reddish dot of Kropotkin, Bakunin's star, vanished. Stars around the missing red dot began winking out in a growing circle. The circular hole in the star field kept growing as something large approached the scout, eclipsing the universe. In a few moments, all of the visible stars vanished.

The scout shook gently from a soft impact. The blackness withdrew from the viewport as if a cloth had been pulled back over the surface of the scout. When the black curtain withdrew, the scout was no longer floating in the void. Mr. Antonio's ship drifted into a large, well-lit ovoid space. The walls swirled with tendrils that ranged in color and texture from matte black to chrome. Several of the chrome tendrils reached out and grabbed the scout, stopping its drift.

Mr. Antonio couldn't see all the tendrils attach themselves, but through the viewport he could see the end of two tendrils deform to mimic mating surfaces to join the surface of his scout. He looked down at the systems monitors for his ship and saw the little fuel and oxy he had used in the one light-year journey was being replaced.

He waited until the green light lit up on the docking controls, showing that the primary air lock had mated and there was pressurization and oxy on the other side. Once it was safe to leave the confines of the scout, he released his harness and pulled himself though the command pod and over to the primary air lock.

He cycled through, and the air lock opened to a long, white, cylindrical corridor, the walls themselves the source of illumination. The shadowless white light combined with the featureless walls to give the impression of an infinite white universe surrounding him. The only visible spatial cues were the door to the scout's air lock and a long cable floating unsupported in the center of the corridor.

Mr. Antonio pulled himself along with the cable, floating through the white. Slowly, weight returned, pulling him down, away from the scout. By the time he reached the end of the cable a slight sense of gravity gave him a definite downward direction.

The cable terminated in the floor of a small hemispherical chamber as white as the corridor that fed into its ceiling. The floor was flat, and slightly textured, which aside from the grayish cable, gave the only visual cues to the geography around him. If it weren't for those two objects, he could have been standing in an endless white void.

The walls did not remain unbroken. A few seconds after his feet touched the floor of the room, an aperture appeared in the wall facing him. The walls withdrew from a circular portal. Beyond was ill lit, nearly black.

Mr. Antonio walked through, and to every appearance found himself standing outside. An unbroken star field wrapped around him in every direction, the view intense enough to be painful. One reddish dot glowed brighter than the others, but the star Kropotkin, even at only a light-year distant, was almost lost in the glare from the Milky Way that wrapped the universe around him. Having just been outside, he knew he was seeing way more stars than were normally visible to the naked eye, even in the emptiness a light-year from Kropotkin.

The aperture closed behind him.

Another man stood nearby, visible as a ghostly silhouette in the starlight. The man faced away from him, staring up at the ruddy star Mr. Antonio had just come from.

Mr. Antonio waited to be addressed.

" 'What a piece of work is a man,' " the other man quoted, without turning around. " 'How noble in reason. How infinite in faculty—' Do you know that, my friend?"

"Shakespeare?"

"Yes, it is. *Hamlet.* 'In form and moving how express and admirable. In action how like an angel. In apprehension how like a god!' " He finally turned and faced Mr. Antonio, a striking figure even in the starlight; tall, hairless, with flesh as sculpted and flawless as an ancient Greek statue. Apollo, was Mr. Antonio's first thought, though Prometheus would probably have been a more apt comparison. "Is our mole in play now?"

"Yes, Adam."

"You have done well. Your acts have helped ensure our success."

"Thank you."

Adam turned away to face the star field surrounding them. As he turned, the red dot of Kropotkin grew in size with vertigo-inducing rapidity. The stars rotated and twisted as their point of view shot around the star.

"I believe you are unsure about this," Adam said as the planet Bakunin swelled in front of him, a white ball with a strip of blue girdling its middle. One green-gray continent cut from ice cap to ice cap dividing the single ocean. The landmass was in the process of rotating from light to dark, the half of it east of the Diderot Mountains shadowed and alive with city lights.

"I have no doubts in you," Mr. Antonio said.

Adam chuckled. "You also know that it's futile to try and hide your feelings from me. I see the pulse of civilizations. The workings of your mind are no mystery."

Mr. Antonio nodded. "I am certain you know the importance of what I do. I'm afraid I do not."

Bakunin grew quickly in front of them, mountains shooting by, and the darkened eastern desert zooming toward them. The lights around the spaceport/city of Proudhon swelled. "You wonder about the importance of Tjaele Mosasa."

Proudhon moved off to the left and the image turned gray as it adjusted for the lack of light. It fell toward a monochrome section of desert filled with ranks of disabled spacecraft.

"If he is a threat, why not—"

"Destroy him?" Adam asked. "He *will* be destroyed."

Their point of view fell toward a single hangar in the midst of the aircraft and stopped a dozen meters from the ground. The image was static, but Mr. Antonio could see a lone figure entering the hangar, the unmistakable form of Nickolai Rajasthan.

"I could have—"

"No," Adam said. "Our actions have been precise for a reason. Mosasa would see an unsubtle attack and not only avoid it, but divine the purpose behind it. No. He has to be drawn from his lair to unfamiliar territory where he will be near blind." The point of view shifted until they seemed to hover just over Nickolai's right shoulder, the tiger's massive foreshortened profile filling the universe in front of them. "Our agent will strike when the quarry is helpless."

"I defer to your wisdom."

"Now, though, with our pieces in place around Mosasa, we should retire our Mr. Antonio."

"How next should I serve?"

"There are things on Earth that should be addressed as soon as my brother begins his tragic expedition."

Mr. Antonio left Adam with a new name, a new appearance, and a new spacecraft.

Replacing the old Indi-built scout was a Paralian-designed luxury transport. Rather than the cramped one-person cabin, the Pegasus V craft had a lush suite with wood paneling, leather seats, carpeting, and solid brass controls. Instead of an ancient serial number, the side of the sleek craft bore a name, *Lillium*.

The person who slipped behind the controls of the *Lillium* bore no resemblance to Mr. Antonio, despite having been him until about fifteen minutes ago. Instead of the old wrinkled

creature with wispy white hair who had hired Nickolai Rajasthan, the pilot who flew the *Lillium* from the bowels of Adam's spacecraft was a middle-aged woman of African descent.
Her hair was black and wrapped her head in tight braids, and
her face was smooth except for the beginning of age lines
around the eyes. She had the long, lithe form of someone who
had grown up in slightly less than Earth gravity, and the musculature of someone who trained in gravity somewhat higher.

Her name was now Ms. Columbia, and she and *Lillium*
were headed to Terra, in the heart of human space.

CHAPTER TWELVE

Portents

The Devil is in the details, and God is right there egging
him on.

—*The Cynic's Book of Wisdom*

Doubt is not a pleasant condition, but certainty is absurd.

—VOLTAIRE
(1694–1778)

Date: 2525.11.21 (Standard)
Bakunin–BD+50°1725

Mallory found Mosasa's response to his question more un-
nerving than a confirmation would have been. He would have
been more comfortable if Mosasa had at least given the impression he knew something of what was happening in the vicinity of Xi Virginis. Mallory looked at his fellow mercenaries
and wondered if any of them, like him, had reasons for being
here other than answering Mosasa's ad.

There was the massive wall of fur and muscle named Nickolai Rajasthan. Mallory didn't know exactly how he felt about
working with someone whose ancestors were created specifically to wage war as a proxy for man. The fact that Nickolai
existed was a testament to how unfit man was to play God,
creating life not out of love, but solely as a tool for destruction. But according to half a millennium of Church doctrine,
Nickolai was spiritually as human as Mallory was, despite his
origins.

Then there was Julia Kugara who, if she wasn't just trying
to bait Wahid, was a descendant of the same genetic engineers who had created Nickolai's kind. Even in the twenty-
first century—when men thought little, if anything, of molding

animals into short-lived faux-humans to kill and die in mankind's stead—even then, men had an inkling of evil when they rebuilt human beings. Even before the secular governments placed the techniques that produced Nickolai's kin on the list of heretical technologies, it was supposedly illegal to genetically modify human beings. Which didn't mean it didn't happen, and happen often enough that descendants of those shadowy experiments still existed.

Mallory knew little of Dakota, the one planet those genetically-engineered humans had made their own after their exile. It was part of the Fifteen Worlds, one of a pair of habitable planets orbiting Tau Ceti—the less inviting one. From what Mallory did know, Dakota was even more xenophobic and insular than the rest of the Fifteen Worlds.

Considering how close it was, Mallory wondered how large a population of Dakota expatriates lived on Bakunin. He also wondered if it was only her father that carried a genetic engineer's legacy and how much of Kugara's genome was artificial.

Finally, there was Jusuf Wahid who came from Davado Poli, a small world that was a remnant of Epsilon Indi's aggressive expansion two hundred years ago; the wrong location and history to be a Caliphate agent. Still, Mallory couldn't help being suspicious of him; even though logic dictated that if the Caliphate was trying to be covert here, it would do its best to use an agent who wasn't an obvious Muslim.

But was there a reason for the Caliphate to be covert? As far as Mallory knew, they had no reason to suspect that the Church knew about the transmissions from Xi Virginis, so they would have no reason to hide their own interest.

Last, there was Mosasa himself. The man was tattooed and jeweled like a pirate from another century. And, according to Nickolai, he was as nonhuman as the tiger. Mallory didn't know exactly what that meant. The cursory research he had been able to do on his potential employer *had* produced the tantalizing fact that Mosasa Salvage had existed on Bakunin almost since the founding of the anarchic colony. The salvage yard actually predated the city of Proudhon. And the images of the salvage yard's owner from nearly three hundred years ago showed a man very similar in appearance to the Tjaele Mosasa who stood before him now.

If Mallory had deigned to risk a more aggressive investigation, tracking down associates and so on, rather than keeping a low profile in his hotel room, he suspected he might have uncovered a few interesting explanations for Mosasa's apparent longevity.

Wahid muttered something about wanting to know who he was working with.

"Well, you know now. If you want to leave, you can be replaced."

Wahid gave Mosasa a wide smile. "Don't mind me. It's all good."

Mallory shook his head. Wahid was the kind of wiseass that annoyed him, especially in a military setting.

"Thank you." Mosasa turned to face all of them. "If you could all take your seats, there are contracts to sign, and then a short briefing."

After Mallory put his alias and genetic signature to a single sheet of cyberplas containing the most pithy legal document he had ever read, Mosasa stood between his seated mercenaries and the shadowed tach-ship and described the mission.

"This is primarily an intelligence gathering mission," Mosasa told them. "There have been a number of political, economic, and scientific anomalies appearing throughout known human space for at least the past five years standard. I have traced the source to an area of space in the vicinity of Xi Virginis—"

"What do you mean 'anomalies'?" Wahid asked.

"Has everyone read the nondisclosure clause?"

That had been one of the pithier parts of the agreement. It simply warned that if the signatory leaked any details of the job, operational or otherwise, Mosasa reserved the right to shoot whomever leaked.

When everyone confirmed they understood that particular detail, Mosasa continued.

"To explain these anomalies, I need to explain some history. I assume you are all a little familiar with the Race and the Genocide War?"

The reference to the Genocide War was a complete non sequitur to Mallory. Of course he was familiar with it. Occisis was founded during that war, a war started covertly by the amoeboid Race decades before humanity reached for the stars. When the Race was discovered manipulating human affairs on Earth, the result was an accelerated spread to the stars and the rise of the twenty-first century United Nations as one of a series of despotic Terran governments.

The founders of Occisis were the survivors, and nominal victors, in mankind's first interstellar war, a war that ended with the near extermination of the first alien species humans had contact with. Since the war, no member of the Race had been allowed off its homeworld. As far as Mallory knew, the old United Nations battle stations still blasted anything that attempted to fly in or out of the Procyon system.

"That's all ancient history," Wahid said.

"A little over four hundred years," Mosasa said, "not quite ancient."

"But there's a point to you going over this?" Wahid asked.

"The point is that there are several details about the Race that aren't mentioned in popular history."

"Like?"

Mosasa grinned. "Perhaps you know why a spacefaring race trying to contain human expansion didn't just drop a large asteroid on Earth?"

Wahid didn't, but Father Mallory, the xenoarchaeology professor, suddenly knew exactly what Mosasa meant. But since that wasn't true of Fitzpatrick, Mallory remained quiet as he mentally fit all the pieces together.

Mallory knew the reason the Race didn't bombard Earth was because the Race had evolved several cultural quirks against direct confrontation. Direct aggression was a strict taboo, so dropping a big rock on another planet was unthinkable, no matter how threatened they felt.

That didn't mean the Race was peaceful. Far from it. The Race was ruthlessly adept at indirect violence, cultural judo where they encouraged enemies to destroy themselves, leaving their own pseudopods free of blood. By the time the Race had a unified government and reached the stars, they had developed sociology, politics, and anthropology into actual sciences, *predictive* sciences. With enough information, they could predict the economic, demographic, and political landscape of a city, nation, or a whole planet decades into the future.

More important, from a warfare standpoint, they knew how to change outcomes. They could see that if this political party received a large funding stream at the same time this corporation in another country was bought out and factories shut down, the end result would be a civil war in country number three.

The Race had covertly used that expertise to severely undermine the situation on Earth for nearly seventy-five years before they were discovered.

"Hold on." Wahid interrupted Mosasa's explanation. "Are you saying that some old Race bogeyman is telling you about 'political, economic, and scientific anomalies'?"

"In a manner of speaking," Mosasa answered.

"You have an AI," Kugara said.

Of course, Mallory thought, even before Mosasa said, "In a sense, I've had several."

The Race's warfare relied on artificial intelligence. Not only was it impossible to run their cultural modeling on anything else—even if humans could duplicate the coding—the only way they could fight against the humans in direct confrontation was to have autonomous weapons that could act without direction. The implication of those weapons, which fought long past the end of the war, was one of many reasons that possession of an AI device was still a capital crime in most of human space.

Except on Bakunin, of course.

But it went deeper than that. Everything slid into unnatural clarity for Mallory. With Nickolai's comment that Mosasa wasn't human, and that even a cursory search for records showed Mosasa Salvage and Mosasa himself being here for over three centuries, there was only one credible explanation.

Mosasa wasn't *using* a Race AI.

He *was* one.

The realization filled Mallory with a moral dread unlike anything he had felt before. He could feel a spiritual eclipse, where the anarchic mass of Bakunin drifted between this small gathering and the light of God, leaving them all in a darkness that was felt rather than seen.

Mallory forced himself to listen to Mosasa explain the details of his expedition. Part of him wanted to leave now, convinced that he sat in the epicenter of something terrifying and godless. Another part, the soldier, the man who was here on a mission for the Church, knew that, if anything, it was God's providence that had taken him here.

And, in the end, Mallory knew that quitting this job was

not something Fitzpatrick would do and would lead to many uncomfortable questions for someone trying to keep a low profile.

That last decision was vindicated when Mosasa introduced the woman who was going to be the military commander for this expedition. When the petite, white-haired woman walked from the shadows of Mosasa's tach-ship, Mallory made little effort to conceal his shock. It was not an emotion that Fitzpatrick would be hiding right now.

"My name is Vijayanagara Parvi," she introduced herself, looking at everyone assembled in front of her in turn. With the exception of Nickolai, Mallory noted. When she looked at Mallory, she said, "Some of you already know me."

This cannot be a coincidence, Mallory thought.

Mallory waited by the exit to the hangar and watched Kugara and the tiger leave together. It only surprised him for a moment, as a moment of reflection told him that the two of them probably shared more in common than any other two members of the small mercenary squad that Mosasa had hired. They weren't his primary concern at the moment. Not his, not Fitzpatrick's.

Wahid left on his own. If things had gone differently during the briefing, he might have chosen to follow him. Either surreptitiously, or in a gesture of false camaraderie akin to what he supposed was happening with Kugara and Nickolai. A drunken conversation might go a long way toward assessing Wahid's potential dual allegiances.

At the moment that wasn't his concern either.

His concern was the short white-haired woman who walked out of the hangar about fifteen minutes later.

When Vijayanagara Parvi stepped alone into the night air, Mallory walked out in front of her. To her credit, she didn't appear too surprised.

"I think we need to talk," Mallory told her.

"Perhaps," Parvi said. "Talk, then."

"Not here," Mallory said.

She cocked her head. "Are you worried about Mosasa hearing this? He's paying me more than he's paying you."

"No," Mallory cocked his head at the hangar. "Back inside."

Parvi shrugged and walked back into the hangar. Mallory already assumed that anything between him and Parvi would make it back to Mosasa. Back inside Mosasa's EM-shielded hangar, he could at least be confident that would be the extent of it.

Mosasa had gone, leaving the vast hangar space empty but for the two of them and the tach-ship. Once they were both inside, with the door shut, Mallory faced Parvi. "I was not expecting you to be part of the first job I have on Bakunin."

Parvi shrugged. "I've recruited a lot of people."

"So you don't find it a little coincidental?"

"The universe is full of coincidences."

"So when you recruited me, were you working for Mosasa?"

"You're acting as if I knew you were going to apply for this particular job."

"Did you?"

"How could I?" she asked. "Did you?"

"No." Mallory was not about to admit that he *had* known the destination, if not the means to get there. But it was clear that if Mosasa had known his goal in advance, he had deftly manipulated Mallory.

"Then I don't know what we're talking about."

"Did Mosasa have you recruit me?"

Parvi laughed. "You're being paranoid."

"Wahid has a good point about professional paranoia."

"You should go get some sleep."

"Did Mosasa have you recruit me?"

"You aren't anything special, Fitzpatrick."

"That isn't an answer."

"You chose to be here."

"That doesn't mean that Mosasa didn't plan for me to be here."

"His AIs aren't magic."

Mallory shook his head. "You aren't going to answer me, are you?"

"What's the point? What if I told you that he had every intention of luring you here, hiring you, and taking you off toward Xi Virginis? Would that make any difference at all? Would you quit and go hire off to fight some corporation's brushfire war?"

Mallory got the strong feeling that Mosasa and Parvi knew quite well why he was here and were exploiting it for some reason. Unfortunately, Parvi's assessment of the situation was accurate. Confirming that knowledge probably wouldn't change what he was doing.

"I still would like to know why."

"Asking that question would presuppose that Mosasa is in the habit of telling me the reasons he does things. I assure you, he doesn't." There was an edge to her voice, and it was hard to tell if the displeasure she felt was directed at him or Mosasa.

"Perhaps I should bring this up with him," he said.

"Perhaps you should." When Mallory turned to go, Parvi added, "For what it's worth, he has me recruit a lot of people."

"What?" He turned around again.

She looked off toward the tach-ship back in the hangar. The displeasure hadn't left her face or her voice, but he began to feel that it wasn't directed at him. "He has me recruit a lot of people."

"What do you mean?"

"I mean that for the past five years I've been paid very well to make sure certain people signed with the BMU. You're one of many, like I said. Nothing special."

"Do you have any idea why?"

She turned and glared at him. "Because the pay is damn good for negligible risk," she snapped at him. "This conversation is over."

The anger was directed at him now, but Mallory got the sense that it was only because he was convenient. He thought back to how she acted around Nickolai and Kugara, and even before that, when he'd pointed out the tiger that almost had to have been Nickolai at ProMex.

"Get used to it. If you stick around Bakunin, you'll see more."

"You sound like you don't approve."

If she *didn't* approve, Mallory wondered how she felt about Mosasa. Working for a Race AI was several steps beyond working with Nickolai. The Church certainly placed machines outside the sphere of God's grace.

She walked to the door, and he asked a last question even though he didn't expect and answer. Not here.

"Why do you work for him?"

She stopped and without turning around she repeated, "Because the pay is damn good for negligible risk."

Mosasa sat in his office lit only by the holos surrounding him. One showed the interior of the hangar and Sergeant Fitzpatrick watching Parvi leave. He barely paid attention; it was just a small drop in the ocean of information that enveloped him, part of a current caused by the mass of the Vatican trailing its massive slow-moving fingers in the human information stream. A necessary data point that would keep him connected to human space after his ship passed into the information desert between here and Xi Virginis.

Do I have to go?

It was a very odd question. It had been literally a century since he had doubted himself. He had built himself so many layers of decisions, so many preplanned branch-points, so many models of so many outcomes, that he never had cause to be uncertain . . .

It is the uncertainty itself I need to eliminate.

The void he faced, the empty in the vast space of light-years between the core of human space and the colonies clustered around Xi Virginis, would be the most isolated he had ever been since his return to Procyon.

Do I have to go?

More than anything else, Mosasa dreaded uncertainty. Ever since he had abandoned his fleshy body to inhabit the remains of one of five salvaged Race AIs, he had inherited the AI's desire to perceive all of its data environment.

There had been five of them, almost a single mind between them.

He was the only one left.

Two had been sacrificed long ago to help fulfill the military directive of the AI's programming. The quintet Mosasa had been part of had managed to bring down the old Confederacy and break the human political hegemony.

The other two Mosasa had lost on the Race homeworld itself when they had finally returned. So long after the war, after the human quarantine of the Procyon system, the Race was dead.

All of them.

What mankind had done, in trapping them on the surface, was to force them to revisit the racial reluctance toward direct physical violence. The taboo that rendered them so weak against mankind.

Unfortunately, they had developed that taboo for a reason. It had been the only thing that had allowed them to survive as long as they had. As soon as enough of them had cast aside such reservations, the results were devastating. Cities in ruins, the entire ecosystem devastated, a planet that was only marginally habitable to begin with had become sterile.

It was a devastating discovery, and possibly due to his imprinted human personality, Mosasa had been the only one mentally strong enough to survive seeing the pointlessness of their victory over the Confederacy.

For some reason, Mosasa had now started to see the void between the stars as the desert on the Race's homeworld—absent of data, absent of people, absent of his creators . . .

Absent of God.

Mosasa dismissed that line of thought and shifted data streams. He had just noticed some local information movement that seemed to flow from the direction of the Caliphate. As expected, placing the destination Xi Virginis on a public database had begun to provoke a reaction.

CHAPTER THIRTEEN

Communion

It is harder to choose your friends than your enemies.
                              —*The Cynic's Book of Wisdom*

Shared hatreds are almost always the basis of friendships.
                              —Alexis de Tocqueville
                              (1805–1859)

Date: 2525.11.21 (Standard)
Bakunin–BD+50°1725

Mosasa's briefing had lasted through the evening, and Nickolai walked outside into a darkened spacecraft graveyard. His new eyes saw every star and every ship with razor clarity. He looked up and allowed himself to feel his own smallness.

I am a scion of House Rajasthan, direct descendant of St. Rajasthan himself. A line bred for five hundred years to fight and to rule.

I am an apostate sinner who held his own will above that of the priests, his masters, and the laws of God.

I am an unclean servant of the Fallen and of things worse than the Fallen.

He stretched his fingers out until his claws emerged, black on one hand, gunmetal gray on the other. In his real hand, he could feel the tendons stretch and the joints crack. In the artificial hand, he only felt the slight feedback as what passed for flesh wrapping it felt a slight increase in tension.

What am I, really?

"So, can I buy you a drink?"

It took a second before he realized the question was

addressed to him. He turned his head away from the stars to look down and see Kugara, the Angel, looking up at him.

"You look like you could use a friend," she told him.

Nickolai turned away. He had fallen out of the habit of looking at people during conversation. "Do I?" he asked. He wasn't quite sure how else to respond. He owed her respect, not only because she wasn't human, but because he would be working with her for the foreseeable future.

He snorted and shook his head, because the irony of that thought wasn't lost on him. Personal feelings were what condemned him in the first place.

"Did I say something funny?" Kugara asked.

"No," Nickolai told her.

When the single word faded, Nickolai realized how quiet it was out here in the desert.

"You aren't going to elaborate on that, are you?"

"What do you mean?"

"Never mind," Kugara said. "How about that drink?"

Kugara had her own transportation, an old contragrav aircar that had the turquoise-and-black markings of a Proudhon Spaceport Security Vehicle, though the skin was now dominated by the matte gray primer color of flexseal patches. It had an open canopy, so it could handle Nickolai's height, though when he got in, the craft briefly suffered a hard tilt to the right before the sensors encouraged the underpowered injection unit to compensate for the mass distribution.

To make room for his legs, Nickolai had to push his seat all the way back, and in response the craft tilted rearward for a moment.

"Gad." Kugara said, watching a few red lights on the dash display in front of her. "Guess no aerobatics with you in the car."

She waited until the craft found its level, then she punched the vector jets, shooting the protesting vehicle across the desert and back toward the city.

Nickolai looked at Kugara. Her hair trailed back in the wind, and her face was dominated by a clenched grin that Nickolai would normally attribute to a huntress just prior to a kill.

"What do you want of me?" he asked.

"We're on the same job," she said against the wind. "Can't I buy a comrade a drink?"

"I notice I'm the only one to whom you offered."

"We both need an ally, scion of House Rajasthan." She turned that predatory grin toward him and said, "Despite what the maps say, you're not in the Fifteen Worlds anymore."

Kugara took him to a bar in a part of Proudhon run-down enough to have been in his old neighborhood in Godwin. It was part of a mall that had taken over an old assembly building. The space was large enough that none of the shops and restaurants inhabiting the space felt the need to build ceilings. The bar was one of the few that felt the need for actual walls.

It took a few moments for Nickolai to realize that Kugara had chosen this place with him in mind. With the ceiling of the original assembly plant a good forty meters above them, he could walk around without ducking. In addition, the bar had circular tables and stools that allowed him to sit without being crammed in a human-sized booth, or wedging his tail into a tall-backed chair.

She let him pick a table. He took one to the rear of the place, putting as much distance between himself and the human crowd as he could. The stares from the patrons were becoming familiar, and he barely noticed the crowd edging away from him. He sat with his back to the wall and wondered what he should think about Kugara's interest in him. He wondered if this was part of Mr. Antonio's plan.

A pitcher of amber liquid slid in front of Nickolai, and Kugara took a seat across the table from him. She had a mug filled with black liquid, with a head the color and texture of foam insulation.

"Allies, you said?" Nickolai asked her.

She raised her glass. "Have a drink," she told him. "To a profitable mission."

Nickolai had worked around humans enough to understand the custom. He took the pitcher in his hand and raised it, echoing the toast. Proportionately, the pitcher fit his hand about the same way her mug fit hers. "A profitable mission," he said. He took a swig with her and set the pitcher down. It wasn't the spiced ale from Grimalkin, but it was more tolerable than most human beverages.

She looked at his pitcher, then at her own mug. Nickolai's pitcher was nearly half-empty, where the head in her mug had only lowered a couple of fingers. "I can see you're an expensive date."

Nickolai pushed his chair back and said, "If you'd rather be alone—"

"Stop it. God, you have no sense of humor."

"What is it you want?"

She shook her head and took another sip from her mug. "I want someone to cover my back. I had the bad sense to go spouting off about Dakota back there . . ." She looked down into her mug. "Sometimes I am an idiot."

"If you don't like working with Wahid, you can find another job."

"You say that as if I have a choice." She lifted her mug and drained about half of what remained. She slammed it down on the table, and after a few moments of silence, she added, "At least you picked up on the fact Wahid seems a bit twitchy. I was beginning to think you were completely oblivious. And you can add that haughty bitch Parvi to the list."

"Parvi?"

"Oh, can't you sense how overjoyed she was to have us in the team?"

"I assume you're trying to be humorous again."

She laughed. "You can say that. So, Nickolai, how do you feel working with a bunch of humans?"

"Mosasa isn't human."

"Yeah, you mentioned that, didn't you? Mind expounding on that little tidbit?"

Nickolai pondered his options for a moment. The fact he carried a rather large secret with him made him reluctant, but Kugara was the only other member of the team he would feel comfortable having as an "ally." He also thought she had a point that they both needed one. This mission was going to take them far outside the grip of the BMU, the only law recognized by their nominal comrades. And would he want to trust his life to humans like Wahid or Parvi, or even Fitzpatrick?

Nickolai finished his pitcher and told Kugara what he could about Mosasa. "Our employer," Nickolai said, "doesn't just *work* with AIs. He doesn't *own* them."

"Meaning?"

"He *is* them."

Kugara lowered her mug. The glass hit the table with a slightly liquid squeak. A similar sound seemed to come from her throat. After a moment she said, "Shit."

"Tjaele Mosasa is a construct controlled by a salvaged

Race AI device. The 'man' who briefed us is no more real than my right arm." He held the arm in front of him; fingers spread so the metallic claws were visible.

She looked at his arm. "That's a prosthetic?"

Nickolai made a fist and lowered it to the table. "Yes. It is."

"It's very well done, I couldn't tell at all." She finished off her dark beverage. She stared at the foam sliding down the edges of her glass. "Why would an AI hire a group of mercenaries?"

"It may be exactly what he said it was."

"Yeah, I'm sure it is." Kugara looked up from the shreds of foam in her glass and asked him, "But if you had a choice, would you be walking into this?"

"No."

"Damn straight." She looked over at the bar. "I think it's time for a second round."

She never asked him why he had no choice in the matter, or why he had a prosthetic arm, or why a scion of House Rajasthan had deigned to prostitute his skills as a mercenary on Bakunin. He returned the favor.

By the end of the third round, and his third pitcher, Nickolai finally felt a comfortable softening of the edges of his perception. Even before coming to Bakunin, he hadn't been much of a social drinker. What little alcohol he consumed was usually ceremonial, toasting saints, fellow warriors, or the person of the sovereign. He was somewhat surprised at how he enjoyed being comfortable with another person, whoever it was.

That might have been why it took him that long to notice their shadow. A trio of men, who had entered some time after he and Kugara had arrived, sat at a corner booth that had a good view of Nickolai's table. They weren't obviously watching them, but they also weren't doing much drinking, or laughing, or talking. The trio might be in civilian clothes, but Nickolai was sensitive to motion and body language, and even out of the corner of his eye he could tell they had body armor restricting their movements under the loose overalls they wore.

Without moving his gaze from Kugara, he cycled though his new spectral sensitivities. When he downshifted the spectrum toward the infrared, he could see square hot spots on their belts that were most likely active Emerson field generators.

The body armor could be innocent, insofar as anything was

innocent in the violent mess that was Bakunin, but an Emerson field sucked enough power that you didn't turn one on unless you imminently expected to be targeted by some energy weapon, otherwise you'd suck the massive power sink dry long before the field would be of any use.

Nickolai did his best not to shift his body language. Raising his pitcher to his lips he said, "Three men behind you." He kept his attention on the three men in his peripheral vision. Either they were very good at covering their reaction, or they didn't have audio surveillance on them.

"What?" Kugara said.

"Body armor, active Emerson fields, LOS on our table."

"Armed?"

"Who isn't?" Nickolai lowered the pitcher and wiped his mouth with the back of his hand as he whispered, "Handguns at most, holstered." He scanned the bar crowd and didn't see anyone else with the telltale of an active field.

Kugara pushed her glass toward the center of the table with both hands, and leaned forward with a smile, as if she was sharing some drunken confidence. "Corner booth, third from the front door?" she whispered.

Nickolai nodded and glanced up at the faraway ceiling. The unusual layout of the mall here made their position unusually exposed. One spotter in the scaffolding above could have a lock on their position almost anywhere they went. The current false-color IR view with which he saw the world showed him two glowing patches up against the ceiling.

He could focus tightly on them, two men in dark clothing. The two of them had taken partial cover near the HVAC duct that pumped cool air into the cavernous space below, and every time they exhaled they released a cloud of warm moist vapor into the cold dry air by the duct.

One spotter, one sniper . . .

"Brace yourself," Nickolai said.

He dropped the pitcher and grappled the edge of the table, throwing the edge upward between him and the watchers in the ceiling. He relied on the fact that his reaction time was quicker than that of the Fallen surrounding him. As he dove for Kugara, the large mass of the moving table had already begun a chain reaction of crashing glass, splintering wood, and human shouts. The air was suddenly filled with the sharp scent of spilled alcohol. He pushed her into a booth against the same wall as the trio of men in the corner booth. They fell on the table between two couples, Kugara landing underneath him with a grunt, spilling the occupants' beverages.

The man to Nickolai's left stood up and yelled, "What the fuck—"

It was the last thing the man ever said. The beam from the sniper's weapon was invisible in normal spectra, but Nickolai was still seeing the world with enhanced IR. He could see the heat of the weapon's trail hanging in the air, tearing through the spot where his head had been a quarter second before, and where this man's chest was now.

Nickolai felt the pulse of combat stretching his sense of time as he rolled on his side, off of Kugara. Adrenaline surged through his muscles, like an electric current, every hair awake, alive, and strung tight as the world slowed down.

Around him, the three others in the booth had just begun sucking in their breaths to scream. His gun was already in his cybernetic hand. He brought it to bear so fast that he could feel the air itself pulling against his artificial flesh.

The sniper's accidental victim had yet to fall as Nickolai pushed himself upright with his free hand. Another blast from the sniper tore through the air, but his reaction time was much slower than Nickolai's, the beam punching into the corner of the table where Nickolai's head had been.

But, to Nickolai's enhanced sight, the heat from the plasma gave a momentarily persistent trail pointing right back to the shooter. The 12mm in his hand spoke, spitting a meter-long tongue of flame that spoke in the voice of a wrathful God. The gunshot echoed thought the massive space, briefly silencing every other sound.

And as in the BMU's training, when Nickolai fixed his new eyes on something, he hit it. There was a brief flare in the infrared as the sniper's weapon vented plasma, then a shadowy human-shaped form fell from the ceiling.

"Shit!" Kugara yelled, throwing herself against his chest. At first he thought it was fear, the smell of it was rank in the bar.

But it wasn't from Kugara.

She wasn't cowering. She was bracing herself against him to give herself cover and steady her aim at the trio of men pushing toward him through the screaming crowd. Her left arm grabbed his side as she held her right out across his chest. In her right hand, braced against the inside of his left elbow, she held a dull gray handgun.

One of the three men pointed his weapon vaguely in their direction. She fired, and he heard a high-pitched buzz as a near-continuous razor-thin stream of silver erupted from the weapon. The smell of molten metal made his nose itch.

Kugara's nasty little weapon was a hyper-velocity needle-gun that fired flechettes at an obscene rate of ten or twenty thousand rounds a second, a speed that essentially vaporized the ammo into a tiny burst of superheated plasma on impact. The thing probably could only sustain fire for two seconds, but a two tenths of a second was enough to decapitate her target.

Around them, the patrons were surging out the exits of the bar in a panic. The two remaining hostiles were caught in the chaos, unable for the moment to close on them or level their weapons.

Nickolai scanned the scaffolding above them and didn't see any sign of other snipers. The engraved 12mm icon Mr. Antonio had provided weighed heavy in his hand. He sucked in deep breaths of air scented with smoke, burned plastic, and human sweat.

He lowered his gun and fired at the hostile on the left. His head snapped back with the force of the 12mm slug and he fell into the mass of the exiting crowd. The deadly silver thread of Kugara's weapon touched the side of the other's face, melting it into a red mist.

"They'll have exits covered, whoever they are," Kugara whispered.

"Good," he told her. "They'll have their hands full, then." He rolled to his feet on the bench seat next to the corpse of the sniper's victim. He held out his left hand about a meter above the table. "Over the wall."

Kugara nodded, pushing herself upright. She stepped up onto his offered hand, pulling herself up on top of the wall with her left hand. She stood on top and crouched, aiming the needlegun alternately left and right. "Clear," she whispered, then dropped down on the other side.

Nickolai spared a glance at the barroom behind him, looking for any other hostiles. The place had cleared out, the last stragglers pushing out the normal exits, leaving the floor a wreck of overturned tables, splintered chairs, and at least three corpses.

He heard Kugara's voice, "Shit!" Followed by the high-frequency whine of her needlegun. He whipped around and leaped up at the top of the wall, cursing his brief division of attention.

He landed on top of the wall, his tail whipping for balance. The sounds of boots on the ferrocrete floor directed his aim down the alley between the bar and the next establishment.

A half dozen men in helmets and body armor had come around from the back of the bar. While they had caught Kugara by surprise, she had likewise surprised them. Two bodies lay sprawled in the alley, helmets trailing wisps of steam. The four others were scrambling for cover around the corner of the buildings as they brought their weapons to bear on Kugara, who was exposed in the middle of the alley.

Prone, she let another burst rip from her gun, emptying quicksilver plasma into the faceplate of the man closest to her. Her latest victim shot wildly, burning a smoldering groove in the wall next to him as he collapsed backward.

Nickolai braced the wrist of his mechanical hand and started pumping the trigger. The first shot hit one in the chest, throwing an electric ripple across his light ballistic armor—the sign of a dying Emerson field cycling down through the visible spectrum. It would have been good against an energy weapon like these men were armed with—and in a fire-team like this, having that protection would prevent friendly fire incidents—but it was useless against a 12mm slug of metal.

His second shot caught another man as he raised his weapon toward him. The slug caught the man in the gut, folding him over and tipping him facedown over a dead or unconscious comrade.

The last man received a bullet in the side of his helmet at the same time a razor-fine stream of flechettes tore across his throat, melting his armor and most of his neck in a cloud of blood and metallic vapor.

Nickolai leaped down from the top of the wall, a deep growl resonating in his chest. As Kugara got up from her crouch, he asked her, "Do you have more ammo for that weapon?"

"Only one clip; I wasn't expecting an ambush."

"Grab a gun from them," Nickolai said. "We need to leave."

She reached down and grabbed a gamma laser from one of the disabled soldiers. She pulled the faceplate off the disarmed man and stared into his face. "Fuck," she said.

Around her, about half the men groaned. The one Nickolai had gut-shot rolled over on his back and fumbled clumsily for his weapon.

"None of you move," Nickolai growled, gun braced. He aimed, but didn't fire. He only had four shots left in the magazine. Fortunately, the man stopped moving.

"Kugara, move!"

Kugara backed away from the man on the ground, shaking her head. "I know these guys," she whispered. Her voice got harder. "I worked with these guys! I was part of this unit!"

"Not anymore," Nickolai told her. He stepped forward, looking at the man who had tried to grab a gun. Nickolai's slug had pancaked against his armor, but that was the extent of his injury. He was probably in the best shape of the men left back here. Nickolai kicked the man's weapon away and dragged him to his feet.

"What are you doing?" she asked.

"Do you know this one?"

She walked over and removed the helmet, revealing a light-skinned man with graying hair and a bushy mustache.

"Wolfe?" she whispered.

"Nothing personal, Julie," he said, keeping his eyes fixed on Nickolai.

"Lead us out of here," Nickolai told her.

"What are you doing with him?" Kugara asked.

"He needs to answer a question or two."

She stared at him a moment, then quietly said, "Yeah." She backed past the fallen men, covering them with the laser. She looked around and pointed with her other hand toward a narrow accessway that ran behind a suddenly empty series of storefronts. "That way."

Nickolai followed, pulling the stumbling Wolfe after him.

CHAPTER FOURTEEN

Limbo

Faith is the first casualty of economics.
                    —*The Cynic's Book of Wisdom*

A bad peace is even worse than war.
                    —CORNELIUS TACITUS
                    (55–130)

Date: 2525.11.22 (Standard)
Bakunin–BD+50°1725

Fortunately for Mallory's spiritual well-being, Staff Sergeant
Fitzpatrick, like 80 percent of the Occisis military, was Roman
Catholic. So it didn't threaten his cover to spend his early
morning hours attending the Church of St. Thomas More, the
only traditional Catholic Church in Proudhon.

Mallory had discovered that, despite Bakunin's origin in
a strain of socialist anarchism that viewed organized religion
with the same zealous hatred as they did the State, the planet's current incarnation was much more tolerant of the former
than the latter. In fact, just searching a directory for a house of
worship he had found nearly a hundred "Catholic" churches.
Almost all of which represented some splinter faith or apostate creed, ranging from Vodoun variants to a conservative
sect that held to Latin service, mortification of the flesh, and
the denial of nonhumans into the Kingdom of God.

But the Church of St. Thomas More recognized the same
pope Mallory did, and fortunately the recognition was mutual.

The church itself was a windowless ferrocrete-and-steel
structure that looked as if it started life as some sort of maintenance structure, perhaps a power substation. The building

made up for the lack of architectural detail by being wrapped in a massive mural showing the Stations of the Cross in sequence around the walls of the building. The artist had used some sort of active paint, so each scene looped through a simple animation; in one scene Jesus repeatedly falls under the weight of the cross; in another, a Roman soldier pounds a nail into Jesus' hand over and over; in another, His body is taken down, repeatedly, never reaching the ground.

Above the entrance, He is placed in his tomb. As Mallory entered, the picture showed Jesus rising and taking a step toward the sealed doorway. Unlike Mallory, the painted Christ never reaches the entrance.

Inside, the layout was more utilitarian; no giant distracting murals, just a large crucifix on the wall above the altar bearing an elongated and strangely antiseptic Christ carved in unpainted black hardwood. Mass had yet to start, and people were still finding their seats on the long pews. Mallory stopped by the basin and crossed himself before finding an unobtrusive seat in the back.

He couldn't help thinking how appalled this diocese's namesake would be at the very nature of Bakunin. Mallory suspected that, despite the protests of Bakunin's socialist founders, Thomas More, the man who wrote *Utopia,* a man who prized harmony and order, would find on this planet its antithesis.

When the priest came to officiate, Mallory did his best to abandon his worldly thoughts. He didn't know what was ahead of him, but he had an uneasy feeling that this could be the last chance he would have to receive communion in the Church.

The unease redoubled when he walked back down the aisle after receiving the Eucharist. Sitting next to the aisle, alone on a pew, was Jusuf Wahid. Mallory wanted to ignore the man. He didn't like the feeling of his spiritual life mixing with the fictitious Fitzpatrick's.

Wahid gave him no choice.

Mallory walked past Wahid's pew without acknowledging the man's presence. However, as soon as he walked by, Wahid stood and slipped into the returning line behind Mallory. "Keep going toward the door," he whispered, breath hot and sour against the side of his neck.

Mallory tried to gauge Wahid's intent, but he couldn't get

a feel from his whisper. It could have been a threat, a request, or a plea.

Mallory kept walking past all the pews and went outside ahead of Wahid. As soon as they got outside, Mallory turned around to face him. "What do you think you're doing?"

"Saving our asses, Fitz." He pushed Mallory's shoulder, turning him toward an aircar that was parked crooked on the pedestrian walkway in front of the church.

"What are you talking about?"

"Apparently, our boss has a good reason for hiring us." He ran over to the aircar, pushed back the canopy, and jumped in. "Come on," Wahid hooked a thumb at the rear seat.

Mallory climbed in and found himself next to a duffel bag. The top was partly unzipped, and inside he could see the barrel of some sort of plasma weapon.

The aircar lifted off before the canopy had closed completely. Looking over the seat in front, Mallory could see a similar duffel bag resting on the seat next to Wahid.

"What's going on?" Mallory asked.

"Someone has taken objection to Mr. Mosasa's little field trip. The lady and the tiger were ambushed last night."

"What? Kugara and Rajasthan? Are they all right?"

Wahid slid the aircar into the frenetic mess that passed for air traffic in Proudhon. The dashboard began a plaintive beeping as proximity alarms began calling for attention that never came. "They're fine," he said as he pulled the aircar up in a climb to pass above a slow-moving taxi. "I think the frank bitch might have cut herself. They took out a hit team of at least ten guys with a pair of effing handguns. And they took prisoners. You believe that?"

For some reason, Mallory thought about what Parvi had said last night about Mosasa.

"He had me recruit a lot of people . . ."

Including Kugara and Rajasthan? Mallory wondered. "Mosasa did say he brought in the best qualified candidates."

Wahid laughed. "The best qualified candidates who applied for a dipshit babysitting mission. You see anything in his ad that would appeal to ninety percent of the mercs on this rock? How many hardcore bastards you think apply for security detail on a scientific expedition?"

"Point taken." Mallory paused as his stomach unexpectedly tried to slam through his diaphragm as the aircar took a sudden dive under a pedestrian bridge. When their flight leveled, he asked Wahid, "So why'd you apply for this dipshit babysitting mission?"

"No offense, Fitz, but that's none of your fucking business."

Wahid took a chaotic route leaving Proudhon, weaving loops around and between buildings, and shadowing random cargo haulers both above and below. He also passed though three parking garages. His path was probably proof against anyone following, short of some tracking device on the vehicle itself.

Wahid explained that the latter wasn't really a problem since he had stolen the aircar less than an hour ago. Mallory decided he had already been on Bakunin too long when he realized that the admission didn't surprise him.

They shot out of the city, parallel to the mountains, and before Wahid dropped the aircar near the surface, Mallory could catch sight of Mosasa Salvage. It wasn't hard to miss, with ranks of aircraft stretching across the desert in all directions. It was even easier to pick out now, with a column of smoke rising from the midst of the aviation graveyard.

"Something's burning." Mallory said as the aircar fell in its asymptotic dive to the desert floor.

"A couple of missiles took out the hangar," Wahid said.

God save us, Mallory thought.

Wahid let that sink in as he flew the speeding aircar over the black desert sand at speeds that would have been suicidal within the congested airspace over Proudhon. They shot away from both Proudhon and Mosasa Salvage at this point. The white central towers of the city were tiny in the distance behind them, the pillar of smoke above Mosasa's business now almost invisible against the morning clouds.

If someone—probably Caliphate agents—had targeted the hangar itself, that meant they had very good inside information.

"What about Mosasa? Is there still a mission?"

"Yeah, there is. Apparently, Mosasa had some information that the Caliphate was interested in what he was doing. He managed to relocate before someone targeted the hangar."

Did he get the ship out?

Mallory had been expecting something from the Caliphate since he had arrived on this planet. Wahid's news was almost a relief, the other shoe finally dropping. But beyond the attacks, something didn't sit right with Mallory. Unlike Staff Sergeant Fitzpatrick, Father Francis Xavier Mallory had retired a full colonel in the Proxima Expeditionary Forces of the Occisis Marines. Colonel Mallory had as much or more command experience than he had on the ground, and because he'd been in the PEF, he had a *lot* of ground experience before they let him near a commission. That meant he knew tactics and planning and how to gauge an enemy.

It also meant he thought Wahid's story made little sense. An enemy with enough intel to target the warehouse had enough intel to keep a watch on the target. It wouldn't require much investment; just a spotter in the mountains or in one of the high buildings in Proudhon could keep unobstructed visual contact. And for all the technology you could use to obscure various mechanical sensors, Mallory knew no way anyone could hide a tach-ship launch from a trained human eyeball. The distortion of any visual camouflage would be detectable by someone who expected to see it, and any spotters would be expecting it.

Mallory didn't believe that their attackers were incompetent, and it didn't seem likely that they had the extraordinarily bad timing to have hit Mosasa after he left with the tach-ship . . .

But Mosasa was an AI.

He knew and planned for it. The ship, the hangar, those had to be decoys . . .

"Where are we going?" Mallory asked.

"The secondary rendezvous point."

"That wasn't mentioned in the briefing."

Wahid shrugged. "Considering what happened to the primary staging area, that was probably for the best. I only knew the place because Parvi gave me the location when she called me. They relocated the staging area to the remains of a bankrupt commune." Wahid continued, "Parvi called it Samhain . . ."

Samhain, Mallory thought. He remembered the meaning from his theology classes back at the university after he retired from the service. The old Celtic month of November, the pagan tradition that became All Souls Day and Halloween.

The idea of going to an abandoned commune named Samhain of all things, made Mallory feel uneasy in a way that had little to do with potential Caliphate hostilities.

Is that the actual staging area? If the hangar was a decoy, what about us?

Could the primary use of the mercenary team be to draw out the Caliphate? If Mallory's assessment of the situation reflected reality, Mosasa's actual site for his Plan B was probably far away from where they were going right now.

Wahid piloted the stolen aircar across the desert barely three meters over the sand, topping three hundred klicks an hour. Samhain was small enough that at the speed they were going, it seemed to appear instantaneously, sprouting from the black dunes. Wahid had to bank severely and turn the aircar in a large loop around the commune before he had decelerated enough to come to a landing.

Mallory knew that outside of the megacorps that dominated the urban centers like Proudhon and Godwin, the main political unit on Bakunin was the commune. On Bakunin, communes were sovereign political entities that he understood, at least on an intellectual level, to be much more diverse than the socialist etymology of the term might suggest. He just didn't know quite how diverse.

This commune was little more than a village. There were some signs that a dome had covered the site at some time in the past; ocher steel fingers pointed up from the ocean of sand in a rough circle around the perimeter. Within, buildings still stood, beaten an even bone gray by wind and weather. Windows were empty black sockets staring blindly from crumbling facades that once mimicked the Tudor style of medieval Terra.

Wahid parked the aircar in an open stretch of sand that had once been a park, now only marked by eroding statues and long dead trees that clawed, barkless and leafless, toward the rust-colored sky.

Mallory opened the duffel bag on the seat next to him and withdrew the plasma weapon that sat on top. He frowned. It wasn't much use at long range and sucked energy like an overloaded tach-drive.

"What's up?" Wahid asked.

"I don't trust this," Mallory said. He pulled out a short-barreled gamma laser, replacing the plasma hand cannon. The laser was a matte-black rectangle with an oblong hole cut in one end for a hand grip. Otherwise it was shaped, and weighed, much like a brick. Almost all of that weight came from the power cells; it was as much a power hog as the plasma cannon. However it had the benefit of accuracy, distance, and the abil-

ity to overload even military-grade Emerson fields with two
or three seconds of continuous fire. He took the laser in hand
and shouldered the duffel bag.

"Trust what?"

"Do you think Mosasa wants to risk leading the Caliphate,
or whoever, to his real staging area? Does a missile attack on
the hangar sound real to you? If they knew what was there,
why'd they wait until after the ship lifted off to attack?"

Wahid shrugged. "They got there late."

"Sure, but they knew where Kugara and Rajasthan were."

"Yeah, I see . . ."

"Professional paranoia, right?"

"Right," Wahid dug out his own gamma laser from the duffel next to him. "Though if there's an ambush waiting, they
should have targeted us by now."

"Maybe they aren't here yet—"

"Or they're waiting for the others." Wahid shot the canopy back, letting in a blast of hot dry air. "Let's get out of the
open."

Mallory stepped out onto the black sand and felt as if he
were stepping into the anteroom of purgatory, if not Hell itself. He kept watch with the laser as he pulled the duffel out
and shouldered it.

Wahid followed, stepping up next to him. "It's like a fucking graveyard."

"Yeah." Mallory said. He looked over at a trio of pitted
statues that dominated the center of the clearing. Most of the
fine detail had been worn away, but he could make out enough
to see a trinity familiar to him from his theology studies. Three
women, one barely adolescent, another obviously heavy with
child, and a third, crooked and stooped.

Maiden, Mother, and Crone . . .

This had been a Wiccan settlement. Mallory wondered
what had happened to it. He realized that on a spiritual level
he was far more disturbed at the emptiness of the place than
he was at the original inhabitants' pagan sensibilities. It felt
very much like he was walking on a grave.

Oddly, his thoughts turned to the Dolbrians, whose known
legacy amounted to a few monumental artifacts and the planets they terraformed. All those planets, including this one;
were they this village writ large?

Was all of humanity living on top of a cosmic grave?

Mallory couldn't help but feel a slight shiver at the thought.

"See something?" Wahid asked him.

Staff Sergeant Fitzpatrick, having gone though only the typical public education on Occisis, wouldn't have any clue about religions other than traditional Roman Catholicism. Wicca and the Triple Goddess would have been lost on the man. So Mallory just said, "No. This place just gives me the creeps."

Mallory looked at the sky, still red with the too-long dawn of Bakunin's thirty-two-hour day. Then he scanned the ruins of the village, looking for likely spots that could hide a waiting enemy. There were a number of buildings with good line of sight on the clearing, but he didn't see signs of anything hostile. One of the blind-windowed Tudors that faced the park and the Goddess trinity sat on a bit of a rise, somewhat removed from its siblings. It would provide the occupants cover and a good view of all the approaches to it.

"Let's take cover," he said as he headed for the building.

He was halfway there when it exploded.

CHAPTER FIFTEEN

Divine Intervention

God favors the side with bigger guns.
—*The Cynic's Book of Wisdom*

There is only one decisive victory: the last.
—KARL VON CLAUSEWITZ
(1780–1831)

Date: 2525.11.22 (Standard)
Bakunin–BD+50°1725

Vijayanagara Parvi flew Mosasa's Scimitar fighter over the desert north of Proudhon. The fighter was a stealth design with an EM profile an order of magnitude smaller than her contragrav bike, despite having thirty times the mass and a thousand times the power plant. The black delta shape slid through the atmosphere like a monocrys scalpel through muscle.

She kept thinking about Fitzpatrick's questioning last night.

"Did Mosasa tell you to recruit me?"

"Yes, you poor bastard," she whispered to the desert whipping by the windscreen. "And he told me to order Wahid to take you to Samhain." The inhuman bastard not only thought moves ahead, Parvi thought, but entire games ahead. It was barely an hour after missiles had taken out his tach-ship and his hangar when Kugara and Rajasthan dragged a bloody mercenary back to him. Mosasa hadn't even bothered to question the man. He had simply ordered the guy to report back to his employers.

One of the things Mosasa had the man report back was the coordinates of the secondary rally site. The one she had sent

Fitzpatrick and Wahid to. She had no idea if Wahid or Fitzpatrick would survive to see her arrive. Though she suspected that Mosasa *would* know.

The navigation unit beeped at her, letting her know that Samhain was just coming over the horizon. The forward LOS sensors started retrieving data, overlaying it on her heads-up display and several secondary monitors. Out the window, a green wire-frame holo mapped onto her view, picking out the spot on the horizon that marked the abandoned commune.

Within two seconds, the green blossomed outward, separating into multiple dots marking the man-made structures in and around the abandoned village. The dots grew into boxy forms outlining walls, roofs, doors, and windows that would have otherwise been invisible at this speed and distance.

Just as the holo display resolved enough detail to pick out individual openings on the buildings still over a dozen klicks away, her heads-up peppered the whole village with red dots.

Samhain wasn't abandoned today.

Parvi flipped a switch to allow the ship to use active sensors. She was two seconds from contact. The hostiles wouldn't have time to react if they detected her spying on them, and after contact, they'd know she was here anyway.

In response, all the secondary screens began scrolling with an extraordinary level of detail, most of which would only be of use in an after-action analysis. The important thing for Parvi were the icons that suddenly overlaid the red dots. These red dots wore powered armor, these red dots had highly charged energy weapons, these red dots were contragrav vehicles, and these red dots, moving across a clearing on the west side of the village, matched biometric data for Fitzpatrick and Wahid.

Half a dozen hostiles in powered armor hid inside the building those last two dots were moving toward. Parvi sent a missile through one of its windows. She had just enough time in the first pass to send another missile into the building housing one of the contragravs. She pulled the fighter up, just ahead of the shock wave from the first explosion.

Mallory was a good fifty meters away from the building when its walls evaporated in a roll of ink-black smoke and bloodred flame. The shock wave knocked him backward and he felt something tear into his leg and his left shoulder.

As he fell into the burning black sand blanketing the courtyard, he mentally chanted the rosary as his implants kicked in. The pain from the shrapnel in his shoulder and his leg faded in his awareness, and he became calmer than anyone in his situation had a right to be. His sense of time telescoped as he rolled around onto his stomach to face the remnants of the building.

Behind the smoke and fire, fifty meters away, another explosion erupted on the other side of the village. Above the new rolling smoke cloud, something flew by at hypersonic speeds, a rocket-fast heat-shimmer slicing the bloody sky in two. It shot past, turning up toward the sky as the shock wave from the second explosion and the sonic blast of the aircraft blowing through the atmosphere slammed into Mallory simultaneously.

In the split second that he took in the presence of the aircraft, the commune of Samhain had ceased being empty. Soldiers were suddenly everywhere. He could see the distortion caused by several active camo projectors by one of the Tudor houses deeper in the village. Closer, by the smoke-shrouded crater that used to be the building in front of him, he saw silhouettes of soldiers in powered armor trying to pull themselves out of the wreckage. They stood out clear as day and moved with halting jerks showing their suits' power was failing or completely fried.

The only cover immediately available was by the Trinity statue, a bowl-like depression that might have once been a fountain. He ran crouched to lower his cross section and dived in. The impact ignited pain in his shoulder and leg that blasted through into his awareness despite the best efforts of his implants.

He braced himself by the lip of the bowl, holding the gamma laser in a shuddering grip. He risked a peek back at the soldiers by the wreckage. By God's grace, and air support, the soldiers weren't paying attention to him.

He saw the fading afterimage of a heavy plasma weapon sending a pulse upward, toward the aircraft, which had looped above the village and was diving down toward them. The pulse was a futile discharge. Even if it unloaded all its power in one burst, forming a microscopic sun that could vaporize a large portion of the attacking craft, it was still akin to throwing a sponge at a bullet.

He looked around, trying to pinpoint where Wahid was. He

couldn't see any sign of him. Around him, the village was lit by flashes of other weapons discharging, and two actual missiles shot up toward the blur diving down toward the village. The missiles hit some sort of countermeasure, blowing up short of the target as the blurred craft broke its dive to shoot over Mallory. Four contrails split off to continue the descent in its wake.

He dove for the lowest part of the bowl as the sonic boom hit. Mallory covered his head as the thunderously low passage of the aircraft blew sand over him.

Then four explosions tore through Samhain, shaking the ground and burning the back of his neck and his hands with their heat. Something that felt like burning gravel pelted him a second later.

The explosions still echoed off the mountains as he shook off the debris that covered his back. Ears ringing, he rolled to the side.

Facing him, less than a meter away, Mallory saw a helmet with a cracked and blackened faceplate. It rested on its side, blown free of whomever it was attached to. The neck was angled away from Mallory, so he couldn't tell if a head was still inside.

"Wahid! What's your status?" he yelled out. His own voice seemed far away and muffled under the ringing.

Wahid's voice was even farther away. *"I'm fine!"*

Mallory turned away from the helmet and pulled himself up to the edge of the bowl so he could look out at the village.

God have mercy . . .

The half of the buildings that still stood, burned. Even the dead trees were on fire. The sky had turned gray-black with smoke, and ash fell like damned snow. On the ground, bits of armor and burned human remains mixed with broken wood and stone. Within the wreckage of the town before him, the only movement he saw came from the licking of flames.

The Maiden statue had been blown into several fragments, and her two sisters had fallen over into a two-meter pile of debris. Despite his leg's protests, he ran for the pile of broken statuary which offered at least the illusion of cover. He fell against the Crone's breast and braced his gamma laser against the Mother's broken left thigh.

He peered over the mound of debris, looking down what had once been the main street of Samhain. The town was fogged by smoke, and a massive fifteen-meter crater, flanked by burning buildings, dominated Main Street. He saw several intact suits of armor scattered on the ground, but none moved.

The heat from the fires burned Mallory's cheeks, and it now seemed that every single structure in the village was completely engulfed.

As long as these buildings had been drying out in the desert air, this whole place was a tinderbox. If there was anyone alive in the town proper, they had other concerns right now. A powered suit might isolate someone from the flames, but the onboard life support could only moderate the temperature for so long.

Mallory slid down to the ground at the base of the rubble.

Back across the courtyard, he saw Wahid in a similar position at the base of a half-blasted statue. Smoldering debris covered the sand between them. He waved, and Wahid waved back, apparently unhurt.

Mallory looked down at his leg. An ugly black length of metal, about as thick as his little finger, stuck out of his thigh about fifteen centimeters or so. Mallory winced as he thought of how his movements must have jammed the shrapnel even deeper.

The implants gave their host an edge, but came with a pretty big downside. Pain might be inconvenient in combat, but it had a purpose. He put a shaking hand on the wound to keep pressure on it. He wasn't going to pull the shrapnel out until he had a medkit handy to deal with any torn blood vessels.

He felt pressure in his left shoulder, and looked down to see blood drenching his sleeve from his shoulder down. Not good.

He set down the laser to move his right hand to put pressure on that injury. Nothing stuck out of it, and the hole was relatively small, but the amount of blood and his light-headedness made him think that the wound might have clipped an artery.

In a strangely detached way he thought, *I'm going into shock.*

The world around him was silent except for the distant crackle of flames he barely heard over the ringing in his ears. Above him, the sky churned, a swirling cauldron of smoke, ash, and embers.

He wondered what had happened to the aircraft.

He blinked and saw Wahid standing over him. After a moment of disorientation Mallory realized he was flat on his back. *I must have blacked out.* Wahid cut away the fabric of his shirt, exposing Mallory's shoulder. He said something, but Mallory couldn't understand him.

Wahid took a canister and sprayed a bandage on Mallory's shoulder. The bandage wrapped his skin in a tight frigid embrace as it compressed the wound and sealed it against blood loss. Mallory felt him inject something in his arm, and he closed his eyes again.

Parvi flew the fighter around the perimeter of the smoldering remains of Samhain, watching her sensors for any potential backup for the hostiles. But no new contacts appeared on any of her screens, and as she orbited the burning commune, the contacts she had already acquired slowly began graying out.

Poor bastards, she thought. The two squads that had died down there were almost certainly fellow mercs. It was possible that she could have recruited them herself.

When she was certain the area was secured, she sent an encrypted burst message to Mosasa and slowed the fighter to come in for a landing near the two remaining live contacts.

The fighter slowed until it was stationary, hovering above the smoke on neutral buoyancy contragrav. She lowered the power to the contragrav, and the ship began slowly sinking through the smoke.

It settled softly on its landing gear about a hundred meters from Wahid and Fitzpatrick. They were together in the one clearing free of burning wreckage, but she could see they hadn't escaped unscathed. Fitzpatrick lay on his back, Wahid bent over him, the contents of an emergency medkit scattered around them.

"Damn," she muttered through clenched teeth. She didn't know if she was more pissed at herself or at Mosasa.

She popped the canopy as the fighter powered itself down. When she jumped down into the sand, Wahid had turned toward her. He leveled a gamma laser at her.

"You?" he sputtered.

"Is Fitzpatrick all right?"

"What the fuck were you and Mosasa doing?" he yelled across at her.

"Is he all right?"

"Yeah, a building exploded in his face. He's fucking wonderful!"

"There was a squad of—"

"You think I'm blind?" Wahid kicked something in the sand at his feet. A half-melted gauntlet arced toward her, landing palm-up between them. A blackened splinter of bone still poked from the wrist. "I saw a whole fucking army waiting for us. I want to know why the fuck they were here, and why the fuck your AI-loving boss decided it was such a fucking great idea to send us here."

Parvi didn't know what to do to defuse the situation. She tried to change the subject. "How's he injured?"

"Just a little shrapnel from some friendly fire." Wahid started walking toward her, the laser aimed squarely at her midsection. "Good old Fitz had you all figured out, too."

"What do you mean?"

"The shits that you blew to hell. They knew the hangar, they took it out, right?"

"Yes."

"Why the fuck weren't we in it when they blew it up?" He shook his head. "Hell, why the fuck didn't a sniper with a missile take out the aircar when I drove all so trusting into Mosasa's little rendezvous?"

"I don't know."

"You think your boss does?"

"I—"

Parvi's answer was cut off by a subsonic rumble. Above them, the smoke swirled into a vortex centered above the open desert beyond Parvi's fighter. The tendrils of smoke twisted and parted, revealing a massive, blocky form that was still slowing to a stop on the strength of massive maneuvering jets. The aircraft's nose was blunt, narrow, and sloped backward to mold into a hundred-meter-long wingless body that managed to look stubby despite its size. The skin of the craft was a patchwork of random paints, patches, and sealant in various shades of gray and brown. It was ugly as hell, and looked nothing like the sleek tach-ship Mosasa had parked in the hangar for the benefit of his new employees.

Wahid stared at the descending cargo ship and seemed to have some trouble deciding where to point the laser.

Inside, Parvi sighed a little in relief. "Why don't you put the laser down and help move Fitzpatrick."

"What is that?"

"That's our ship," Parvi said.

The barrel of the laser pointed down, toward the sand. "But what about—"

Parvi walked past him, toward Fitzpatrick. "Save the questions for Mosasa. I just work here."

CHAPTER SIXTEEN

Exodus

Individuals have free will. Societies do not.
                              —*The Cynic's Book of Wisdom*

Knowledge is more than equivalent to force.
                              —SAMUEL JOHNSON
                              (1709–1784)

Date: 2525.11.22 (Standard)
Bakunin Orbit–BD+50°1725

Mallory woke up from a nightmare. The memory of it faded nearly instantaneously, leaving him with a vague impression of Junta loyalists and a burning church. He opened his eyes and saw a bulkhead curving over him. He felt the vibration of engines running somewhere.

"You awake now, Fitz?"

"Uh," Mallory pushed himself up from the thin mattress he'd been sleeping on. He rose too fast and almost tumbled out of the bunk before he realized he was in low gravity. His stomach did slow rolls as he looked up and saw the small chrome pipes set in the ceiling. *Not gravity . . .*

There were three methods to get some form of "gravity" on a space vessel, none of which were gravity per se. The first, and the most natural feeling, was constant acceleration. Next best was rotating a large container and placing the floor on the outer surface.

Neither worked well when designing a ship to enter an atmosphere.

The last method was perhaps the most nausea-inducing. Contragrav drives had been around a while, relying on a repulsive force inherent in some exotic forms of matter. It wasn't true antigravity, any more than a vectored thrust aircraft, but a kilogram of contramatter would repulse normal matter with a force several orders of magnitude greater than gravity. It had been used as lift for aircraft for centuries. Somewhere along the line, someone realized if they channeled dense plasma from a ship's contragrav drive though manifolds in the ceiling, it could provide a nearly-even downward force through any part of the ship you wanted. And, since the main power requirement of the contragrav drive was creating the exotic matter in the first place, it was actually less expensive than constant acceleration and cost less design-wise than rotating large chunks of the ship.

But it didn't *feel* normal.

Wahid had been bending over him, a small hypo in one hand. Wahid stepped back as far as the small cabin would allow, and Mallory realized that his left bicep was stinging. He rubbed his arm and looked at Wahid. "What did you inject me with?"

Wahid looked a little sheepish. "A little stimulant. You've been out for a few hours."

Mallory nodded. "Thanks for getting me out of there," he looked around the tiny ship's cabin.

"Yeah." Wahid responded to Mallory's curious looks. "Mosasa showed up finally, lucky us."

"The fighter?"

"That was Parvi."

"His own air force?"

"You haven't been on Bakunin long, have you?"

Mallory shook his head.

Wahid laughed, "Well, welcome to Bakunin, where any mother's son can grow up to run as large a tin-pot army as he can afford. And Mosasa can afford quite a bit."

"He can afford more than us," Mallory said.

"Yes, I can."

Mallory turned to see Mosasa standing in the doorway to the cabin. He wore a gray jumpsuit, and the ship's lighting seemed to give the scales on his tattooed dragon an unhealthy green shimmer. He looked at Mallory, then at Wahid. "I can afford to pay well. But I only pay for what is absolutely necessary."

Mallory stood to confront his employer, but he couldn't do much more than crouch on his feet with Wahid already standing in the cabin. "Was it necessary to send us to that ambush?"

"Yes, it was, Staff Sergeant *Fitzpatrick*."

Mallory froze, wondering if he had misheard the emphasis on his alias. He wondered if Wahid heard the same thing that he had . . .

If he had, Wahid didn't show it. "We deserve an explanation."

"Perhaps," Mosasa said. "For now, come forward to the cargo hold, so you can meet the other members of the expedition."

Given recent experience, Mallory had been expecting more mercenaries. Instead, waiting for them in the brightly lit cargo hold along with Nickolai, Kugara, and Parvi, was a five-member scientific team. Four of the five wore the same kind of gray jumpsuit Mosasa wore and were seated with Mallory's three fellow mercenaries in a semicircle facing a small dais.

"Please sit," Mosasa told them, and Mallory and Wahid took the two open seats.

Mosasa stood next to the dais and introduced the new members of the expedition.

Dr. Samson Brody was a hefty black man with a bushy gray beard and a deeply lined face; Mosasa introduced him as a cultural anthropologist. He easily looked the oldest of the group. The youngest-looking of the team was the linguist, Dr. Leon Pak.

More problematic was the xenobiologist, Dr. Sharon Dörner. She was tall, blonde, and came from Acheron. Like Occisis, Acheron was a core planet of the Centauri Alliance. Given the interrelationship between xenobiology and xenoarchaeology, and the focused nature of both fields, the Jesuit xenoarchaeology professor, Father Francis Xavier Mallory, knew of her. Worse, he had *met* her, *twice*.

Dr. Dörner had given guest lectures several times at St. Marbury University, and Mallory had attended all of them. Once he had spent twenty minutes talking about the nature of the Dolbrians with her at a reception afterward, and five years ago he actually had the honor of introducing her.

It took every scrap of will Mallory had not to let the panic show in his face. Fortunately, Dr. Dörner showed no sign of recognizing him. There was little reason she should. Professionally, she would have met hundreds of people like Father

Mallory: teachers, students, fellow scientists. There was no reason one professor should stand out in her memory.

Mosasa continued with introductions, apparently oblivious to Mallory's sudden discomfort.

The last human of the group, the data analyst, didn't have the titular "Doctor" before her name. She was a thin reed of a redhead named Rebecca Tsoravitch.

"Our last team member is a physicist and a mathematician. Since his given name is unpronounceable to a human palate," Mosasa said, "he has adopted the human name Bill."

Mallory had studied for six years at both seminary and the university after his retirement from the Marines. He had studied about the few alien races that human beings had come across in their travels to the stars. Of them all, the Paralians were the most important and influential, especially to anyone residing in the Centauri arm of human space.

The Paralians had been discovered back in the dark ages of the Terran Council. Travel to the stars had been a brutish business, a dangerous one-way affair through manufactured wormholes. When the Paralians had been discovered, the various human colonies had just begun to stabilize and trading among themselves. When the Centauri Trading Company had opened a wormhole above Paralia, they hadn't only found an ocean-covered planet with a tolerable atmosphere, they had found natives.

Natives who, despite being planet-bound and unable to survive at a depth less than ten meters of their oceans' surface, had developed mathematics beyond human comprehension. Within a few short years of first contact, discussions between human scientists and Paralian mathematicians discovered that the Paralians could model the universe in near-miraculous ways; models that led directly to the development of the tach-drive, which led in turn to the disintegration of the Terran Council and the rise of its successor, the Confederacy.

Despite having studied them, Bill was the first Paralian Mallory had ever seen in person. Until now, he'd never known any to have ever left the depths of the oceans on their homeworld.

Bill dominated the team, not just in terms of novelty, but in sheer bulk. Not only was his body itself half again the size and mass of Nickolai's, he also resided within a transparent sphere five meters in diameter containing water under the extreme pressures that existed at Bill's native depth. The sphere was mounted on a mechanical cradle that rested on six robotic limbs that added nearly another meter to the height of the whole apparatus.

Within the sphere, Bill floated. Mallory had heard Paralians described as squid-dolphins, but that was really only a halfhearted approximation of a description. The front of Bill's body resembled a dolphin in the same way and for the same reason that a dolphin resembled a shark, or a submarine.

Like a dolphin, or a submarine, he had a nose; the terminal end of a muscular bullet-shaped body that narrowed to a blunt point at the top—or the front, depending on how Bill was oriented. The muscles on his body defined three lobes that were symmetrical around Bill's long axis, a subtle bump that was emphasized by mottled cobalt blue stripes that followed the length of Bill's body, darkening the farther they traveled from his "nose."

Each bump supported a complex fin that was nearly a meter long and half that wide. Above, or in front of, the fin, each lobe supported a trio of black pits near Bill's nose, each about the size of Mallory's fist.

The "squid" part of the typical description was even further removed from actuality. Bill's body did end in appendages that could be called tentacles, but probably had more in common with an elephant's trunk. Three muscular limbs emerged seamlessly out of the lobes of Bill's body, mottled blue, continuing the striping of his body.

Each limb split into three long fingers about a third of the way down its length. The "fingers" were boneless and flexible, and could deform their shape. If Bill needed to propel himself in the open ocean, he could hold his trio of limbs together and flatten those "fingers" to form a tail fin that would be even more reminiscent of a dolphin.

Mosasa continued introducing the mercenaries for the benefit of the scientific team. Mallory kept his attention on Dörner, wondering if she was the reason that Mosasa placed such an emphasis on Fitzpatrick's alias. If she knew who he was, though, she didn't give any visible sign. She gave Fitzpatrick's introduction no more attention that she'd given the rest of the mercenaries.

As Mosasa went on, Mallory noticed that only Parvi was given the benefit of a title, "Captain," formalizing a chain of command that was already apparent. Also, from Mosasa's introductions, Fitzpatrick and Nickolai were the only members of the military half of the team that didn't have set roles on the ship itself. Parvi was the pilot, Wahid was the copilot and navigator, Kugara was comm, countermeasures, and Information Warfare.

With Nickolai, Mallory shared the somewhat generic role of "security," which meant little in-flight, unless they were boarded or the members of science team were a lot more rowdy than they looked.

"Welcome aboard the *Eclipse*," Mosasa addressed them. He gestured toward the dais where a holo display appeared showing a blunt-nosed brick of a cargo ship, taller than it was wide. Mosasa noticed Mallory's surprise and said, "As Mr. Fitzpatrick pointed out to me earlier, some explanations are in order. As we are en route to our tach-point, it seems a good time to provide some."

"Like why the fuck the secondary rendezvous point became a free-fire zone?" Wahid muttered.

Mosasa pretended not to hear Wahid and gestured to the holo display, which was now replaying footage of a familiar-looking hangar. The light-enhanced view showed a tach-ship of considerably more recent vintage than the *Eclipse* taxiing out to the landing pad outside the doors. "This was the *Vanguard*, a ship that the military among you should remember. It was the latest design, up to date on all surveillance countermeasures, and housed a tach-drive that was easily the most advanced Paralian design available."

Mosasa's use of the past tense was just sinking in when two bright streaks cut across the holo display. One streak entered the open door of the hangar; the second buried itself in the *Vanguard* amidships, directly in front of the drive section. The display whited out for a fraction of a second while the camera adjusted itself to more visible frequencies. When the scene was comprehensible again, the hangar glowed from an internal conflagration, and the *Vanguard* itself was little more than a skeletal framework holding in its own burning remains.

"The *Vanguard* served its purpose."

The cold way Mosasa said it made Mallory more aware than ever that he faced something that was only an approximation of a human being.

Mosasa continued. "Elements within the Caliphate would

have presented an obstacle in assembling this mission. To limit the exposure of the scientific team, and the readying of the *Eclipse,* it was prudent to provide them with somewhat more visible targets."

"You hired us as fucking decoys?" Wahid didn't mutter this time.

"Only one role among several. We are about to depart known territory, and I expect that we will need your skills in a more conventional manner as the mission progresses."

The holo had shifted to an orbital view of Samhain, the village was intact, and Mallory could see Wahid's aircar approaching the site.

Mallory looked back at the others, trying to gauge their reactions. He had no clue as to what Nickolai and Bill might be thinking. Kugara and Parvi weren't showing anything overtly, but he noticed Parvi was not looking directly at the holo where the *Vanguard* burned. He wondered if she had thought of that as her ship, and if Mosasa had clued her in to his misdirection.

The human members of the science team were a little less reserved. Both the linguist, Dr. Pak, and the data analyst Tsoravitch appeared visibly shocked at the display. The older pair, Dörner and Brody, were less visibly upset, but Dörner was slowly shaking her head.

"We have a significant measure of how seriously the Caliphate is taking our expedition." On the holo, buildings began to explode.

"Was this kind of violence necessary?" Dr. Dörner addressed Mosasa.

"Pardon me, Doctor?" Wahid said, whipping around to face the blonde xenobiologist. "You might not notice from this angle, but it's our asses in the sand out there, facing a squad of powered armor."

She gave Wahid a cold, dismissive look. It was a look Mallory knew well. He had seen it often enough back on Occisis, usually from colleagues in the Church or the university, right after they discovered he had once served in the Occisis Marines. He tried to remember if, in her meetings with Professor Mallory, she had discovered his military background. He suspected that, if it had come out, he would have remembered her reaction.

Her words to Wahid were as icy as Mosasa's were detached.

"I was questioning the fact that staging such a confrontation was necessary. I would think, since it was 'your asses in the sand out there,' that you'd wonder that as well."

Mosasa said, "It was quite necessary."

"Why?" Dörner asked sharply.

The cargo hold of the *Eclipse* was quiet, everyone waiting for Mosasa to speak. The only sounds the nearly subliminal hum of the drives, a soft electronic clicking from Bill's massive life-support apparatus, and the quiet jingle of Mosasa's earrings as he paced in front of his display. Behind him, on the holo, the abandoned commune of Samhain silently burned.

"All of you have your own reasons for joining this expedition. And, up to now I've been somewhat reserved about revealing its purpose, though I have told you about 'anomalies' originating from the vicinity of Xi Virginis. I should explain to you all exactly what these 'anomalies' might represent."

The holo changed again, and Mallory saw a star map of a familiar region of human space. He wasn't particularly surprised to see stars highlighted much as they had been in the holo that Cardinal Anderson had shown him.

"The Race developed social, economic, and political models that map flows of information, political power, trade, people—all the factors that comprise what we define as a society or a culture. The best analogy for a layman would be to picture modeling a turbulent flow of a fluid in an N-dimensional space."

Mallory heard Wahid whisper, "That's a layman's description?"

"When a system is closed, such as a planet without space travel or interstellar communication, a Race AI was designed to accurately model social movements, political and technological change, migration and demographics. Over time, I have scaled up that model until I have been able to accurately map the progress and development of all of human space within an acceptable margin of error."

An audible "harrumph" came from the science team.

Mosasa smiled. "Did you have a question, Dr. Brody?"

"No questions," Brody responded. "No questions at all."

"But you think the advancement of the Race's social sciences to have been overstated?"

"I have trouble believing in the miraculous," Brody said.

Mosasa seemed to smile even wider. Mallory wondered

why Dr. Brody had agreed to accompany this mission if he didn't believe Mosasa's claims.

"Leaving miracles aside," Mosasa went on, "these models are very finely tuned. Enough so that I can detect when a system stops being closed. When a new source or sink appears, be it information, people, or trade goods, the drift in actual data versus the model will suggest strongly the nature of the new interaction."

Unlike Dr. Brody, Tsoravitch the data analyst had leaned forward and was hanging on Mosasa's every word. She nervously brushed a strand of red hair off her face and asked, "Is that's what's happening by Xi Virginis?"

"The data points to Xi Virginis as the source—"

"Are there human colonies out there?" Kugara blurted out the question Mallory didn't dare voice.

"Yes." Mosasa said. "Several. All founded during the collapse of the Confederacy. Because of their placement and history, the Caliphate has had an ongoing interest in preventing knowledge of them propagating to the rest of human space."

What? "The Caliphate knew about these worlds?" Mallory said, suddenly less concerned about his cover.

"High levels of the Caliphate have known of them for quite some time, thus their interest in stopping this expedition. As to Dr. Dörner's original question; the necessity of violence was required to draw out and neutralize the Caliphate's somewhat limited resources on Bakunin. By doing so, we've ensured the safety of the expedition."

"I don't follow," Wahid said. "What's to stop the Caliphate from just pouncing on us now?"

"We're no longer their problem. Their public attacks, combined with my public advertisements for mercenaries to travel toward Xi Virginis, has alerted every intelligence agency with an asset on Bakunin that the Caliphate is hiding something in that region of space. There's no secret for them to protect anymore. My small expedition means nothing when they need to rally whole fleets to lay claim to this sector of space before a rival does."

Lord have mercy on us all.

A sick dread slithered into Mallory's belly. Mosasa had just admitted to engineering the conflagration that the Church had been trying to prevent. Samhain was nothing. Mosasa was engineering an interstellar war to provide cover for his expedition.

"Damn it," Wahid snapped. "If everyone already knew there were colonies out there, what the fuck is the anomaly you're talking about?"

"Out here," Mosasa gestured to the holo, "there's also something else. Something alien that defies the Race's modeling capabilities, that radically alters the equations at every point of contact." He faced his audience with a grin that would not be out of place on a portrait of the Devil. "Out there is something completely unknown."

PART TWO

Burnt Offerings

The great act of faith is when man decides that he is not God.

—OLIVER WENDELL HOLMES, JR.
(1841–1935)

CHAPTER SEVENTEEN

Sectarianism

Your friends gain more from your failures than your enemies.

—The Cynic's Book of Wisdom

In every case the guilt of war is confined to a few persons, and the many are friends.

—PLATO
(*ca.* 427 BCE–*ca.* 347 BCE)

Date: 2525.12.12 (Standard)
Earth–Sol

Yousef Al-Hamadi walked slowly as befitted his age. He made his way through the gardens outside the Epsilon Eridani consulate, arms folded behind him. His official title was Minister-at-Large in Charge of External Relations, which meant he was the nominal head of the Eridani Caliphate's intelligence operations and in charge of the Caliphate's covert activity outside its claimed borders.

In large part, it boiled down to cleaning up the messes of other segments of the convoluted rat's nest of agencies and organizations that made up the Caliphate's intelligence community.

Following him at a respectful distance was the tall dark woman he knew as Ms. Columbia.

"Did you have a long journey to Earth?" Al-Hamadi asked as he stopped in front of a large fountain spilling cascades of water across a plain of mosaic tile that formed intricate interlocking patterns with a stylized Arabic script that quoted verses from the Qur'an. Six hundred years ago, in the time of the last Caliphate, the fountain would have been an extravagance. However, to a species that had made Mars habitable, the arid waste of the Rub'al Khali was almost an afterthought.

"My travel caused me little concern."

Al-Hamadi smiled to himself. He couldn't keep, being in the information trade, from trying over and over to pry some scrap of intelligence from the woman herself. However, Ms. Columbia did not reveal a single fact that she wasn't ready to part with. Not that he expected much. As carefully and flawlessly crafted as Ms. Columbia's identity was, the person playing the role would not be prone to sophomoric slips of the tongue.

In the pocket of his jacket, Al-Hamadi had a cyberplas chit with a terabyte or two of detailed information on Ms. Columbia's persona. Data which, he was sure, would bear scrutiny from whatever assets he cared to assign—despite the fact that he was certain it all was a carefully engineered fraud.

However, it was a fraud perpetrated by someone with a historical interest in feeding him very accurate and timely information. This was why he was conversing here, and not having Ms. Columbia taken to one of the airless moonlets whipping around Khamsin where he could ask questions about her and her employer somewhat more aggressively.

"I'm glad your journey was uneventful," Al-Hamadi responded to her non-answer. "I would find it unfortunate if you were delayed. Our meetings always seem so profitable."

"I hope you find this one as profitable," she said as she handed him a cyberplas chit somewhat larger than the one he had in his pocket. This one fit in his hand and had an integrated reader. He touched a finger to one corner and the surface displayed a message in Arabic confirming his identity. He scanned through the contents of the storage device and frowned.

He knew better than to ask where the information had come from.

"My payment?"

"Already done." Al-Hamadi made a dismissive gesture, staring at the device in his hand. Her deliveries were always in person, never trusted to even an encrypted narrow-beam tach-transmission. Even so, the archive in his hand contained background info on events that only just hit his own intelligence feeds two weeks ago, and not in much detail.

The detail here, as usual, required something just short of prescience. It certainly required the efforts of an entire intelligence service with agents on multiple planets and connections with dozens of organizations. A major transplanetary corporation at the least, and more likely one of the Caliphate's rival governments—an entity served as much as the Caliphate by the passing of the information.

Whatever the case, "payment" was almost beside the point for both sides of the transaction.

"Is there something else you wished to discuss?"

Yes. Who employs you? One of the Indi governments? The Centauri Trading Company? Maybe even Sirius?

"Are you aware of the nature of the packages you deliver?"

"On occasion."

"This latest one?"

"Yes."

"Do you have any idea how troublesome this news is?"

"Would it be worth my while to bring you news that was not troublesome?"

"I suppose not."

Al-Hamadi scanned the package and wondered what Caliphate government report detailed the actions of the Waldgrave Militia on Bakunin, and where in the Caliphate bureaucracy it was buried. He knew that the Militia wouldn't engage in an operation without at least the appearance of Caliphate authorization. There would be a report somewhere, approved by someone's cousin on a planetary council just far enough away from the core that the operation would be well underway before Khamsin or Al-Hamadi heard word of it.

If there were two foreign words beloved by the militant factions of the Caliphate, they would be *fait accompli*. This was how the Islamic Revolution on Rubai happened; just take the crumbling central government of Epsilon Indi, and a few dozen rogue militia cells, mix well.

Technically, they aren't rogue when so many politicians support them ...

The problem with the Militia was that they were an incredibly blunt instrument. Their idea of a covert operation was to not take credit for the aftermath. A private expedition toward Xi Virginis was troublesome, but only to persons who knew the significance of that area of space. For a dozen years standard, Al-Hamadi had managed to keep that significance a secret within the highest levels of the Caliphate, presumably far above the level of anyone directly involved with the Militia.

Now that significance had leaked. The expedition from Bakunin was bad enough, but if Al-Hamadi had intercepted that information, it could have been dealt with quietly and without drawing attention.

But the Militia had hired a small army of mercenaries to . . .

Al-Hamadi shook his head. He wasn't even going to try to second-guess their motivation at this point. He had a much bigger problem. The Militia's clumsy actions had done everything but tach-comm every intelligence service in human space with the message, "The Caliphate thinks the space around Xi Virginis is very important. Please allocate all your spare resources toward determining why."

Do they even know? Al-Hamadi wondered.

"Do you believe in God?" he asked Ms. Columbia.

"I doubt the same one as you."

"*There is no God but God,*" Al-Hamadi whispered in Arabic, half reading part of the mosaic underneath the rippling waters. "Sometimes I wonder if that is the case for some of us in the Caliphate. After the fall of the Confederacy, you would think we would be the strongest, most stable transplanetary government in human space. The one government founded not by some accident of history or stellar geography, but a rule based on a common faith, a common law, a common language." He looked at Ms. Columbia, who wore the same distant expression she always did. "It seems that the more common ground we share, the more intractable the differences."

"That seems to be human nature."

"Or God's will." He turned around to start walking back to the consulate. "Please give my regards, and my thanks, to your employer."

Whoever that is, he thought.

He and Ms. Columbia parted ways at the main consulate building. She left the grounds while he went deep into the bowels of the complex, to the secure tach-comm station. He slipped ahead of fifteen diplomats waiting for transmit time because he had the rank to do so, and because the messages he needed to send were probably the most important to ever cross this particular tach-comm array.

The Eridani Caliphate was going to have to send its ships to Xi Virginis years ahead of schedule, and Al-Hamadi needed to get ahead of events before things spun out of control.

Date: 2526.12.17 (Standard)
Khamsin–Epsilon Eridani

It took Al-Hamadi's tach-comm transmission four days to reach Epsilon Eridani and the capital of the Caliphate. The day after Ms. Columbia's revelations propagated through the Caliphate government, Muhammad Hussein al Khamsiti, one of sixteen active-duty admirals in the Caliphate Navy, was enjoying the third week of an extended leave.

He was on a nearly eight-month leave while the Caliphate orchestrated a high-level reorganization of the Caliphate armed forces. Admiral Hussein, along with about a half dozen other admirals, had some time off while their new commands were created.

Until a few months ago, Admiral Hussein had been in command of the defensive fleet around Paschal. It was a position he expected to retire from, until he received the orders to prepare for a reassignment of his command. At first he thought he had offended someone in the bureaucracy, and that he was being ordered back to Khamsin to fill some pointless office role until he could be forced to retire. However, when he had tached into his home system, he had been met by the Minister of the Navy himself, who had assured him otherwise.

"You have been chosen to head one of the Caliphate's newest fleets. Beyond that, all I can tell you is that it's a great honor—until we call you back, enjoy your leave, spend time with your family."

So now he stood in the back garden of his third son's house in the suburbs of Al Meftah, playing catch with his youngest grandson. Little Rahman was barely a toddler and would run after the ball in a lurching gait that seemed always on the verge of toppling over.

Fortunately, the well-irrigated grass in the garden here was forgiving, and when Rahman did fall, which he did frequently, it was followed by a burst of laughter.

When he laughed with his grandson, Admiral Hussein believed that God had specially blessed him. Until two months ago he had not expected to spend any extended time with his family until he retired.

Rahman tossed the ball with a clumsy two-handed overhand throw that landed about a meter short of Admiral Hussein's feet. The boy fell backward, sitting in the grass, and started giggling.

Admiral Hussein took a step forward to retrieve the ball when he heard his daughter-in-law's voice from the back of the house. "Muhammad!"

He stood up, holding the ball in his hand, and saw the Minister of the Navy standing next to his son's wife. He tightened his grip on the ball in his hand.

"Forgive me, Admiral Hussein, but we've been forced to advance the schedule."

"My leave's been cut short?"

The minister nodded. "We need you for a briefing within the hour."

"I understand." He turned toward Rahman, who was still giggling in the grass. "May I have a few minutes to finish playing with my grandson?"

"Of course, Admiral. Your aircar will be waiting out front."

The minister's car took Admiral Hussein to the administrative center of the Caliphate in the center of the city of Al Meftah. The center of the city was formed by massive office buildings—trapezoids of mirrored glass reflecting the turquoise sky and the daytime stars of Khamsin's tiny moons. The aircar didn't land at the Naval Ministry, but at a smaller building at the fringes of the government center. Admiral Hussein didn't notice any obvious markings denoting the building's function, but the roof was dominated by a ground-based tachcomm array and there were very few agencies that would rate their own separate interstellar communications link.

One, of course, was the Ministry of External Relations.

The Naval Minister led him down from the roof, deep into the bowels of the building to a conference room behind several layers of human and automated security. After the third checkpoint, Admiral Hussein looked down at his grass-stained civilian clothes and said, "I probably should have changed."

"It doesn't matter," the minister told him, "Security has a full biometric profile on you."

That wasn't exactly what I meant.

Waiting in the conference room, seated at a long table were three other men, all also in civilian dress. Two he didn't immediately recognize outside a uniform, but one man wore a traditional white cotton thawb. The ankle-length shirt contrasted with the more liberal dress of the other men, but also made the older man more immediately recognizable.

"Admiral Bitar, sir." Admiral Hussein found himself standing at attention before the smiling, gray-bearded man.

He had met Admiral Naji Bitar several times. He was perhaps the most senior officer in the Caliphate Navy. Bitar had been an admiral before Hussein had even commanded his own supply ship, fifteen years ago.

Bitar stood, laughing, and clasped Hussein's shoulder. "Well, I'm glad they chose you for this skullduggery. Considering how impromptu this meeting is, I think we can dispense with the formality." He gestured toward the two other men in the room. "I believe you know Admiral Nijab and Admiral Said?"

"By reputation. We've never met."

Bitar nodded, "I suppose not. Until recently you were serving what, twenty light-years apart?"

The minister cleared his throat. When he had everyone's attention, he said, "I believe we are all here. If you'd all be seated, I think we should begin."

The minister gestured and the lights in the room dimmed. As Hussein took his seat, a holo display lit up showing a schematic of some sort of spacecraft. It didn't seem remarkable at first, until he recognized one of the tiny bumps on the long body as a Scimitar III fighter attached to a docking ring.

That is huge . . .

"You are looking at the newest vessel constructed for the Caliphate Navy. It is an Ibrahim-class carrier. It is the largest tach-capable ship ever constructed. It can move itself along with a battle group of a hundred daughter vessels in a single jump."

A fleet unto itself . . .

"Originally, a year from now, we intended to deploy six of these carriers. However, events have transpired that require us to cut that schedule by more than half. Each of you will be commanding one of the four carriers that will be operational within the next five months."

"What events?" asked Admiral Bitar.

The holo display above the table changed to show a star map.

"These carriers were designed for a specific task, a long-range expedition to a cluster of stars near Xi Virginis."

Date: 2526.1.9 (Standard)
Earth–Sol

The woman named Ms. Columbia, who left the Saudi penin-
sula in a Pegasus V luxury transport named *Lillium,* currently
walked across the ancient grounds of St. Peter's Square in
Rome—in cosmic terms, only a few steps to the left from the
Eridani consulate.

Her relationship with Cardinal Jacob Anderson was similar
to her relationship with Al-Hamadi, for similar reasons. Her
information was too valuable for such men to question her
too closely.

Cardinal Anderson walked next to her as they moved on
the fringes of the crowd filling the square. Unlike Al-Hamadi,
he had not been expecting her arrival. Like all of her actions,
whatever body she wore, that detail was carefully planned by
Adam. Like most of Adam's machinations, the purpose for
surprising Cardinal Anderson was murky to her, but as she
had said, she had faith in him.

"This is alarming, to say the least," the cardinal said, looking at the cyberplas display in his hand. Unlike the data that
greeted Al-Hamadi, the information that greeted Cardinal
Anderson was predominantly engineering data and specifications, telemetry data, and a few video feeds recorded from
orbital construction platforms.

Not much else needed to be added. The details of an
Ibrahim-class carrier betrayed their own significance without
need of much analysis.

"My employer knew it would be of interest to you."

"Your employer is a master of understatement." The cardinal shook his head. "If these specs are accurate, this has just
rendered a decade of strategic planning completely worthless.
No one has ever suspected the Caliphate had this kind of technology. How close to operational is this?"

"At least one will be operational within two months, four
in less than three months, all six should be completed within
eight months."

The cardinal shook his head. "Even if we take into account
training a crew to operate these monsters, they'll effectively
double the size of their fleet in six months."

Ms. Columbia knew that the cardinal's worries extended
beyond the size of the fleet. Numbers mattered much less
at this point than range. One look at the size of the Ibra-

him's tach-drives would be enough to shake even the pope's faith.

The cardinal shook his head. "And given the latest information from Bakunin, they're going to have no incentive to move cautiously." He stopped and faced her. "You'll receive your usual payment. However, if you'll forgive me, I need to act on this information."

The cardinal turned to leave her, walking back toward the Apostolic Palace in a stride just short of a run. She watched him until she lost sight of him in the crowd. Then she smiled.

Adam would be pleased.

CHAPTER EIGHTEEN

Purgatory

Remove the fear of death and you remove the primary constraint on human action.
> —*The Cynic's Book of Wisdom*

History is nothing but the activity of man in pursuit of his ends.

> —KARL MARX
> (1818–1883)

Date: 2526.03.23 (Standard)
39.7 ly from Xi Virginis

Each jump the *Eclipse* made ate up 20 light-years and 684 hours from the universe outside the ship. They were between jumps four and five, now closer to Mosasa's mysterious lost colonies than they were to the rest of human space, and the tiny slice of it Kugara called home. They hung in interstellar space eighty light-years from Bakunin.

"I got something," Kugara said as the display before her showed a multicolor spike that was stark against the universal background radiation.

"Feed it to my station," Tsoravitch told her. "I got a console free."

The redheaded data analyst sat at the secondary comm station at the bridge, and facing her were nearly twenty virtual displays hanging in the air. All showed captured transmissions in various stages of filtering. The two of them spent the downtime between jumps doing what amounted to electromagnetic archaeology. They aimed the ship's sensors at the cluster of stars around Xi Virginis looking for stray EM signals that they might be able to decipher.

Unfortunately, since none of the signals they picked up

were intended to broadcast over interstellar distances, it was not an easy process. Picking up tach-transmissions would be easier for analysis, but actively scanning for them required nearly as much energy as transmitting them, and that kind of power was only really available for a planet-based system.

So they grabbed fragmentary forty-year-old data from a cluster of half a dozen systems—it was close to miraculous that they were able to filter anything intelligible at all—and over two thirds of it consisted of raw digital packets that were meaningless without context. Somehow, though, Tsoravitch was able to occasionally pull snippets of text, audio, and video. She had a knack for correctly guessing what kind of data was encoded in something just by looking at the raw stream.

Kugara was stuck with the much more boring job of looking for artificial signals in the broad spectrum of EM radiation the *Eclipse* could pick up.

One of her displays flashed at her, and Tsoravitch shook her head. "I just sent him the last dozen signals I was able to filter—"

"Mosasa's not very patient."

"I suppose not," Tsoravitch shook her head, "But if he's not even waiting for my analysis, then . . ." She stabbed a few controls, and the various displays in front of her winked out.

Kugara leaned back in her chair and turned to look at her. "Then what?"

"I was expecting something different." Tsoravitch looked down at the control panel.

"From Mosasa?" Kugara asked, trying to keep the incredulous tone out of her voice.

"I think I need a break," Tsoravitch said, standing up. "We'll be making the next jump in an hour anyway."

Kugara watched her go and wondered why she seemed so disappointed. *What did she want out of Mosasa?* She fingered the bio-interface at the base of her skull and wondered. Even though her own ancestors had been the result of someone exploiting heretical technologies, she felt uneasy around Mosasa. Maybe it gave her a level of perspective that Tsoravitch didn't have, but Kugara couldn't help thinking that the woman had *wanted* to work with an AI.

Mosasa sat in his cabin, staring at nothing. Only a fraction of his attention was spared for the data around his immediate physical surroundings. The signals from the maintenance robots scuttling across the skin of the *Eclipse* were higher priority. The small six-legged hemispheres crawled across the skin of the ship, checking seams and the integrity of the hull. Other robots crawled inside the tach-drives, insuring every mechanical system was performing optimally.

The robots, even with the bans on true AI, were largely autonomous within their limited sphere; Mosasa only had to override them occasionally. The task was simple, repetitive, and took only a small fraction of his processing capacity.

At the moment, most of his attention was focused in bathing in the stream of data Tsoravitch had sent him. It was spotty and incomplete, a trickling stream rather than an ocean he could submerge his consciousness in. But he *needed* it. From the *Eclipse*'s reference frame, it had only been out of the immersive data stream he lived in on Bakunin for a hundred and forty hours.

Already his entire being ached with the need. It took a great measure of restraint for him not to forgo all the maintenance checks and order the crew to the bridge so they could make the next jump toward Xi Virginis *now*.

The door to his cabin signaled him unexpectedly.

He shifted his awareness back to the physical world around him; at the same time he grabbed onto the *Eclipse*'s security network to look through the camera in the hall outside his cabin.

Outside his cabin door stood the data analyst from Jokul, Rebecca Tsoravitch. *Oh, yes, I did expect this . . .*

He only wondered briefly at his initial surprise. The same deeply ingrained software that allowed him to perceive the movements of societies allowed him to understand much smaller units. Given enough information, he could see the dynamics of a group of a dozen as easily as a million.

He stood and faced the door as it opened.

"Ms. Tsoravitch?" he asked.

She frowned at him. "Why am I here?"

"I required the services of a data analyst—"

"Bullshit!"

"Pardon me?"

"You're grabbing data from me with only a cursory filtering. I'm barely looking at the data, much less processing it into anything useful. My expertise here seems more than a little redundant."

"I find you useful."

"Why? Why did you ask me on this expedition?"

"Why did you accept?"

She stood in the doorway staring at him. Mosasa watched expressions play across her face, allowing the flood of data about her internal state to wash over him. He could extrapolate her inner thoughts as she asked herself the same question. In some sense he knew her better than she knew herself, even though his observations of her had been remote until this expedition began.

Like all the science team, she was a personality drawn by the exotic but had been forced by circumstances into using her talents for things prosaic and mundane. In Tsoravitch's case, she had a job in the Jokul government managing the software monitors that scrubbed the planetwide data network searching for subversive transmissions. Like many stable authoritarian regimes that managed to keep the populace fed and clothed, the vast majority of their subversives weren't particularly interesting. Not to someone like Tsoravitch.

"I thought I would be working *with* you."

"Even though you know what I am?"

"Because I know what you are."

"Do you?"

"Do I what?"

"Do you know what I am?"

She looked him up and down. "You're a robotic construct camouflaging an AI device, one that was designed by the Race during the Genocide War."

Very deliberately, Mosasa said, "That is, of course, only part of the answer."

Of course, Tsoravitch responded by asking, "Then what's the rest of the answer?"

He explained to Tsoravitch that, three hundred years ago, Tjaele Mosasa had been a human being.

He had lived during the waning years of the Terran Council, before the Centauri Trading Company discovered Bill's homeworld of Paralia, developed the first tach-drive, and upset the already crumbling balance of the human universe.

At that time, before there was such a thing as faster-than-light travel, the use of static wormholes meant there existed a traffic bottleneck, highways between the heavily guarded wormholes defined by gravity and orbital mechanics.

The Mosasa clan had been a large extended family that lived off the traffic moving on those highways in the Sirius system. It was a rich place for pirates, supporting a hundred clans like the Mosasas. Sirius sat in the heart of human space and was a major transit point in humanity's wormhole network, having six outgoing wormholes and eight incoming. Even though the dull rocks orbiting the Sirius system were never meant to support life, the colony world Cynos was one of the richest planets aside from Earth itself.

Tjaele Mosasa was the youngest unmarried adult of the pirate clan, a third-generation inhabitant of the lawless void between the wormhole and Cynos. While his brothers and sisters would attack and board a prize, he made sure their patchwork vessel the *Nomad* didn't fall apart. He spent the first six years of his adult life in a vacsuit patching holes, rerouting power around fried connections, and repairing the Frankenstein's monster of a ship's computer.

When the *Nomad* found a pair of derelicts off the main route to Cynos, that was where he was, in a narrow unpressurized maintenance tunnel, in a vacsuit making sure that the power system didn't overheat. He was annoyed that he wasn't able to watch the approach with the rest of his crew, his family. However, the *Nomad* was a cranky old ship, older than Cynos itself, and someone had to make sure they didn't blow the thing up.

He was looking forward to the prize, though. Most of their livelihood came from raiding cargo tugs that rarely gave them anything with which to upgrade the *Nomad*. Food, fuel, and trade goods were well and good, but a new ship's computer was high on his own priority list.

A derelict vessel would be a godsend for maintaining this boat. He allowed himself to daydream about finding a vessel in good enough condition that they could retire the *Nomad*.

He smiled at his own unjustified optimism, and tapped the finger of his gauntlet on an ancient meter. When he jostled the mechanism, the numbers slid back from the impossible down to the merely improbable.

Just an intact computer core—

His thoughts broke off as the tunnel whipped around, slamming his faceplate into the meter he had been reading. He floated away from the impact as fragments of wires and electronics drifted in front of him. In his brief contacts with the walls, his suit filled with the hideous noise of something tearing the *Nomad* apart.

The lights in the tunnel went out.

For several seconds after the impact, he couldn't move. His vision was confined to a narrow cone of the work lights in his helmet. The emergency lights didn't come on.

He knew something bad had happened. He could see that in the debris drifting through the light-cone in front of his face. He could see it in a cloud of vapor that drifted in front of his faceplate, a mist of tiny white crystals.

Something was venting into the corridor, under pressure. None of the possibilities were good; fuel, hydraulic fluid, or—worst of all—atmosphere from the pressurized part of the ship.

He grabbed a wall and turned himself to point up the corridor, back toward the main body of the *Nomad*. Now that the shock of the impact faded, he was preoccupied with one thought: *were the crew compartments intact?* That thought overrode even the basic question of what the hell happened.

He pulled himself through the debris-filled corridor, the work light on his helmet cutting silver cones out of the clouds of ice crystals that now filled the corridor. The ice stuck to the outside of his faceplate, gradually blurring his view until he had to wipe it off with one of his gauntlets, leaving long streaks across his field of vision.

If the emergency doors came down, they'll be fine. If they were all still on the bridge, there would at least fifteen minutes of air even if the CO_2 recyclers were off-line, time enough to get the emergency vacsuits to them. That'd keep everyone alive as long as he could keep the suits powered. Enough time to patch the hull and get life support together.

That's what Mosasa told himself. That's what gave him the strength to keep pulling down the corridor, through the near-opaque fog of venting atmosphere. He held on to the hope even when he reached the end of the corridor, where the air lock should have been.

He pulled himself though the wreckage of the air lock, still believing that there was a chance that his family survived.

Then he was through the confined space of the air lock and

free of most of the crystalline fog, and realized there was no hope at all.

Mosasa floated above the floor of the *Nomad*'s cargo hold. The bridge and the pressurized crew area should have been above him.

They weren't.

The ceiling of the cargo hold was a mass of twisted metal, torn cable, and hoses. Nothing remained of form or function in the midst of the wreckage. Through the rat's nest of twisted girders, he could see the stars. No sealed compartments where he might find his brothers and sisters, aunts, uncles, or cousins. The inhabited portion of the *Nomad* no longer existed.

Mosasa, barely breathing, lowered his gaze to the rest of the cargo hold to see something that had survived the devastation; something that was not part of the *Nomad*.

The lights from his helmet fell across something smooth and metallic embedded in the twisted metal wreckage. At first it made no sense. He could only see it in brief glimpses as his light shone on it through the twisted steel that filled half the cargo hold.

The surface was silvered and might have once had a mirror sheen, but it had been scarred and pitted and heavily gouged by the wreckage surrounding it, allowing glimpses of duller metal to show through the skin. Unlike the *Nomad* around it, the mirrored spacecraft—that was the only thing Mosasa could assume it was—showed little visible structural damage beyond the superficial tears in its skin.

He carefully pulled himself through a maze of wreckage toward the thing, telling himself he was pulling himself toward the bridge and any potential survivors even as he knew he was lying to himself.

The mirrored craft was thin and broad, like an arrowhead. And it had pierced the *Nomad* in the same manner. Mosasa saw no markings on the skin of the craft, just oblong apertures that could have been maneuvering jets, sensors, or weapon ports. The damn thing was also too small for an interplanetary vehicle. Even a solo craft that barely gave the pilot room to piss would carry more mass and volume just for life support. The alien design, without markings, almost looked like an unmanned torpedo.

When Mosasa cleared the top of the wreckage, where the bridge should have been, he floated in open space. Stunned as he was, survival training took over; he connected one of his suit's tethers to a firmly wedged girder. Even a few cm/s velocity in the wrong direction could doom someone in open space without them even being aware of it until it was too late and they had drifted beyond reach of the ship. His suit had small vector jets, but those took power, and he knew, as soon as the unobscured stars revealed themselves above him and the *Nomad,* he was going to need every joule.

The space that had been the *Nomad*'s bridge was now dominated by the drive section of the mirrored ship. Its engines had slagged, and the metal/ceramic rear thrusters glowed in the darkness like a dying star.

Around Mosasa, shadows drifted in the blackness, eclipsing the stars. His light picked out fragments of the *Nomad* floating out into space; a computer console; a chair; a twisted nest of wires . . .

And bodies. He saw bodies tumbling into the void. His family. Most were already too far away for him to make out features, but his younger sister Naja was only fifteen meters away, facing him as she drifted away from the *Nomad,* the only home she had ever known.

She was close enough for him to see blood frozen, crusted on the gold rings in her lips, nose, and ears. Close enough that his work light reflected dully in her eyes. Her expression wasn't of shock, or horror, but of somewhat muted surprise. Mosasa lowered his head so that the light left her face.

He thought briefly of trying to retrieve the bodies. But there was no point. The Mosasa clan buried their dead in space anyway. At least his family had a living relative to speak for their souls as they returned to the dark.

He spent a long time floating by the cooling drive section of the assassin spacecraft, and said prayers for twenty-four men, women, and children. When he finished, he looked up and noticed something else in the darkness beyond the *Nomad*. It eclipsed stars but was far enough away that his helmet light didn't illuminate it.

He had a stronger lamp on his belt, and he had passed beyond caring about power conservation. He was dead, and had been for an hour. Everything else was delaying the inevitable.

He pulled the lamp from his belt; it had a beam as wide as his fully spread hand, and could pump out lumens an order of magnitude beyond his helmet work lights. He shone it out in the direction of the shadow, and it seemed a universe of floating debris flicked into existence. A spreading galaxy of wreckage of objects ranging in size from tiny bolts and metal shavings to a sphere encased in torn tubing about twenty meters across that must have been wrenched from the drive section.

The distant shadow was much bigger. He was able to pick it out with the lamp. Light splashed its side, dappled with shadows from the *Nomad*'s wreckage. Distance was hard to judge, but it seemed it could be as far as a klick away. And if that was the case, it was twice the size of the *Nomad*.

To Mosasa's eye, the derelict craft was untouched.

The side was painted and Mosasa could see the blue and white of the old United Nations flag on the side. Beyond that, in three-meter-tall letters in a half dozen languages, Mosasa saw the name of the ship.

Luxembourg.

And, after staring a long time, Mosasa realized that the *Nomad* was still drifting toward it.

The *Luxembourg* had been a ghost ship from the Genocide War. When the *Nomad* drifted close enough, Mosasa jumped the gap with an umbilical to anchor the two wrecks together. Even before he attached the cables, he could see that the *Luxembourg* was largely intact. The mirrored arrowhead that had buried itself into the *Nomad* and had killed his family had been an old Race-built weapon, AI driven, autonomous so none of the Race would actually be involved in a direct confrontation.

For some reason, it had been guarding the derelict.

When he entered the *Luxembourg*, he discovered that the attack that had killed the old United Nations ship had been very careful to do very little damage to the machine itself. Each hole in the skin managed to avoid holing vital equipment and ended in a vacuum-desiccated crew member. The *Luxembourg* had been neutralized in a matter of moments. He even found one corpse strapped to the ship's toilet.

The backup battery systems still had a charge, and the secondary life support still had an oxy reserve in the tanks. None of the emergency systems had come on-line. About all that was missing was a decent ship's computer.

It took weeks, but Mosasa revived the late twenty-first-century ship. In that time he discovered two things. The first was that the *Luxembourg* wasn't strictly military. It had been run by the United Nations Intelligence Service. The second thing he discovered was deep in the belly of the ship, in the only armored compartment, flanked by incendiary devices that the crew never got the chance to fire.

Four cylindrical crystals; four Race-built artificial intelligence devices. The machines were tied into the ship's systems, and had gone cold and dormant.

It was the first time that Mosasa had realized that human beings had co-opted the same heretical technologies the Race had used. Understanding that probably made the next thing he did easier.

After days of trying to revive them, he thought of the mirrored arrowhead that had impaled the *Nomad*. The Race used AI-piloted drones, so the device onboard the weapon had been operational enough to pilot the drone.

It was insane, and went against every taboo against these devices, but Mosasa was a pirate, alone, and close to the limit of his resources. If he was to survive, he needed the *Luxembourg* fully functional. He removed the brain from that weapon and wired it into the *Luxembourg*.

"I was able to jumpstart those old AIs." Mosasa looked at Tsoravitch and said, "But three centuries is a long time, and there's only the one left. Me."

Tsoravitch shook her head, and Mosasa could tell the tale of his human origins had left an impression. She seemed to stare past him as she asked, "But you're not him, you're one of the AIs."

"I'm both. Mosasa lived long enough to emigrate to Bakunin, shortly after we recorded his identity. We needed a human consciousness to properly interact with the human world. Those memories are as much mine as they were the human Mosasa's."

"What happened to the other AIs?"

"Two were destroyed in the days before the Confederacy's collapse."

"The other two?"

"They were lost when I tried to go home."

"Home?"

Mosasa nodded. "But we need to go back up to the bridge. We're due for the next jump."

CHAPTER NINETEEN

Faith of Our Fathers

Truth is not monopolized by seniority.
                    —*The Cynic's Book of Wisdom*

The memories of men are too frail a thread to hang history
from.

                    —JOHN STILL
                    (1543–1608)

Date: 2526.3.27 (Standard)
Salmagundi–HD 101534

Flynn Nathaniel Jorgenson hated funerals almost as much as
he disliked crowds. He would have much rather been on wilderness patrol, cataloging new species, away from the small
metropolis of Ashley, away from the Hall of Minds, away from
the stares and the whispers.

However, since it was his father being archived for posterity, he couldn't avoid the ceremony. Not in good conscience,
anyway.

His dad rested on an old contragrav sled, floating a meter
above the marble avenue. The sled was a relic of the founding of Salmagundi 150 years ago. The chassis had been rebuilt
long ago, in line with its ceremonial repurposing. The bed was
boxed in by ornate wood carvings, painted in lavish primary
colors.

Flynn walked next to his mother, behind his father, at the
head of the brightly colored procession. The pride of place
held by immediate family. He had to fight the urge to look
behind him, to see who might be staring at him.

"Good lord, Flynn. Who cares what they think?"

"Shut up, Grandma."

The procession ended at the entrance to the Hall of Minds. It hadn't changed since Flynn had last been here, on his first equinox. That was close to seventeen standard years ago. Four solstices come and gone, and four equinoxes as well, and before the next solstice he planned to be as far away from here as he could get.

"Am I that bad?"

"Give it a rest—please."

The Triad awaited his father's body at the entrance; the three oldest people on Salmagundi, shaved bald so their forehead tattoos were more visible. Where most people had four or five glyphs marking each pilgrimage to the Hall of Minds, these three had dozens. Flynn only had one, and he could not imagine what now lived behind these Elders' eyes. Their faces were expressionless, and they gazed out at the procession in a way that didn't seem quite human.

His father bore six glyphs on his brow. Six ancestors. Six residents of the Hall of Minds.

The Triad led his father's body and the procession into the central rotunda. The space was vast and echoing, occupying half the aboveground volume of the building. It easily held the thousand-plus people of the procession.

The Triad led Flynn's father to the center of the rotunda, where a circular dais supported a pair of square obelisks about twice the height of a man. One member of the Triad stood in front of each pillar, while the sled floated to rest between them. The last member, a woman by her voice, stood at the head of the contragrav sled and spoke.

"We are here to commit Augustus David Jorgenson to posterity. We are ready to cast his shell aside and commit him to the archive, where this unique individual will enrich our lives in perpetuity."

"God, how I hate the way they say 'unique' . . ."

"They do end up looking alike, don't they?"

"Yeah, Gram. They do."

The reception after Augustus Jorgenson's funeral was held at the Jorgenson estate, another place that Flynn had avoided for over a decade. It was probably the largest house in Ashley, and one of the oldest. Fitting, perhaps, for one of the chief founding families of Salmagundi.

Also a sign of the importance of Flynn's father, there were

at least twelve people there to eulogize him before the wake proper. Of course, each eulogy had little to do with Augustus David Jorgenson himself. Flynn had to listen to all of them, out of respect for his father, or who his father had once been.

The series of speakers talked about the people Augustus David Jorgenson had chosen to make part of his own mind, the people he had ritually downloaded. They spoke briefly of them, and of the people they had downloaded, and those they had downloaded . . .

Long passages became little more than a mélange of names and dates without any context. A muddy narrative that became as bland and meaningless as most of the people around him.

It was never supposed to be like this. Gram had explained to him the founding of Salmagundi. How once they were a hundred light-years from the crumbling Confederacy, and free of the laws against the heretical technologies, the founders had decided to record their minds not to build a culture, but to preserve a knowledge base in a population that was just on the edge of sustainability. With a human mind archived, they would never again want for a sanitary engineer, an astrophysicist, a neurosurgeon, a hydroponics expert—

Over the course of 150 years, it had become something other than necessity. It had become a combination of ancestor worship and a promise of immortality. Flynn wondered if many people knew how much a fraud it all was.

He wondered how many cared.

After the endless eulogy ending with the—to Flynn, ironic—toast to the Founders, he drifted through the wake like a ghost. The crowd and the conversations obligingly parted around him. No one seemed to be eager to engage Augustus' only son in conversation. The lone tattoo on his brow was a beacon of his oddball status even to those who didn't know him personally.

That was fine by Flynn. He walked up to the buffet, removed a small meat-filled roll, and retreated to the empty solarium. He sat on a wrought-iron chair and looked up through the tinted glass at the small golden ball of Salmagundi's sun.

There were no plants here anymore, not like when he was a child, when his father was his own age. Then, this room was filled with flowers. Teased and tended by his father, when Augustus was still his dad. He had a love of the natural world, and the endless abundance of the planet Salmagundi with its two-year-long seasons. A love that Flynn had inherited.

A love that died with Augustus' fourth trip to the Hall of Minds.

Flynn had been barely old enough to understand the change that accompanied his father's fourth glyph. When he had come back from his turn at the solstice festival, he was colder. More like the ancient automatons of the Triad. His voice lost passion, and inflection, and affection.

And he had let his flowers die.

The seasons turned again and the following equinox came with the associated festivals. Like the solstices, the equinoxes marked the time when pilgrims came from all corners of Salmagundi to visit the Hall of Minds. During the festival, the population of Ashley doubled, crowding with a press of people coming to select a new tattoo for their brow, and a new ancestor to merge into their own mind.

It also marked the time when those who had reached their fifteenth year since the prior festival were expected to select their first ancestor and become an adult. By then Flynn had been almost seventeen, the oldest child there to come of age, and the first selected to walk into the Hall of Minds. He hadn't the authority—or the courage—to refuse. All he had been able to do was choose which ancestor he would come to host.

"Here you are."

Flynn turned and saw his mother standing in the doorway, facing him. He wished he had taken a glass of scotch. "Hello, Mother."

"You're ignoring our guests. That isn't polite."

"God forbid we're rude, chicky."

"Gram, that's my mother."

"Yeah, yeah."

"I needed some time to myself—"

"Flynn, you're by yourself all the time. You live out in the wilderness. Can you please be social?"

"They don't want to talk to me. You know that. I make them uncomfortable."

"Uh-huh, sonny, the feeling's mutual, and you know it."

"You can change that—"

"Don't start—"

"Come back, be a part of society. Isn't there someone—"

"Stop it!"

"You're rejecting the lives of everyone who came before us, their knowledge, their expertise, your father—"

Flynn stood up. "My father died eighteen years ago!"

His mother took a step back. Flynn could hear a few gasps back in the reception area. He didn't care any longer.

"Son—"

"Where was the memorial when the Triad jacked him into the Hall and diluted his soul to the point of nonexistence? What about you? Did you mourn him the morning when he couldn't remember what was him and what was a decade-old recording?"

"Please lower your voice."

"Why? Everybody here knows what I think. Hell, everyone here is the same fucking person. The same tepid average of everyone the consensus made important." Flynn pushed past his mother and faced the crowd, who was now all staring at him. "Here's a little game, folks. That same shocked expression you're all wearing, is that you, or someone you downloaded?"

He slammed the door on the way out.

Flynn had walked the winding path into the overgrown estate gardens for about fifteen minutes before the female voice in his head spoke up. *"You sure know how to make an exit."*

"Do you enjoy dwelling on the obvious, Gram?"

"Well, you made me feel a little unwelcome back there."

Flynn turned a corner and faced a secluded patio hidden by yellow-green foliage. A stone bench was nestled, almost buried, in a nest of vines, facing a long-silent fountain. On the bench sat a young woman about 150 centimeters tall, with almond-shaped green eyes and straight black hair cut in an asymmetrical diagonal. She wore the same black leather jacket, pants, and boots she always wore. She looked up at him and said, "And you know I don't like it when you call me Gram. It makes me feel old."

Flynn shook his head distractedly. "Yeah, sure."

She looked down at herself. "Do you mind? I waited until we were alone again."

"No, Tetsami, you're fine." He sat down next to the apparition.

His experience in the Hall of Minds, as far as he could tell, was unique. It was supposed to be a melding, a merging of an elder's knowledge and experience with your own. In most cases, it also meant the merging of those that elder had himself merged with, and so on, and so on . . . Achieving some sort of higher unified consciousness.

With Flynn, a combination of his own panicked resistance and his choice of Kari Tetsami manifested itself differently. Most people—most recordings of people, that is—downloaded from the Hall of Minds knew what was happening, expected it, understood it. Tetsami's mind, the oldest one in the archive, had been stored before Salmagundi had established itself, and before the biannual rite at the Hall of Minds existed.

If anything, the event panicked Tetsami as much as Flynn, and she escaped into some distant part of his brain. They remained two separate individuals. Flynn, and his twenty-five-year-old great-great-great-great-grandmother.

"Look," Flynn said, "I'm sorry if it sounded like I included you in that outburst."

"I know." Tetsami patted his hand, sort of. Her visual manifestation couldn't actually touch him, though he felt it inside. "I'm in there with you."

"Ever think it would have been better if the download went the way it was supposed to?"

"Hell, no. You know that creeps me out as much as it does you. I'm me, you're you, and let's keep it that way."

Flynn shook his head. "I just don't know how long I can keep this up."

"Standing up to their stupid ancestor worship isn't a crime."

"Yeah, but it might cost me my job."

Tetsami sighed. "I was kind of hoping that you didn't notice Robert was there."

"We were staring right at him, you know. Only one set of eyes between us." Robert Sheldon was manager of the wilderness corps, Flynn's employer, and about as conservative an example of Ashley high society as you could find. He was a lifelong colleague of Flynn's father—he would hesitate to use the term friend—and probably only allowed Flynn to work there as a favor. Between his father's death and his outburst, Flynn thought that Robert would have little reason to keep him employed.

"Come on, your father just died. Don't you think that's enough reason to cut you some slack?"

Flynn chuckled. "I know you're old-fashioned, but you've seen enough of things to realize my people don't see death quite the same way you do."

"Yeah," she sighed. "I've seen plenty of religions that promise resurrection. Yours is the only one I've ever seen that delivers." She leaned back and stared at the sky, even though Flynn knew the only thing she saw was what his own eyes were looking at. "You'd think my particular situation would make me a little more sympathetic to them."

"So, any suggestion how to deal with this?"

She turned and looked at him. "Ignore it. Either Mr. Sheldon will hold it against you, or not. Worst thing that can happen, you find another job."

"I guess so."

"I'm sure, if you worked at it, you could find something more important to worry about."

Flynn looked up at the sky. The sun had set and the stars were just coming out. "I suppose I could," he whispered.

CHAPTER TWENTY

Service

Freedom is often simple ignorance of whom you serve.
 —*The Cynic's Book of Wisdom*

It is easier to meet expectations than to question them.
 —SYLVIA HARPER
 (2008–2081)

Date: 2526.04.22 (Standard)
19.8 ly from Xi Virginis

Nickolai moved through the corridors of the *Eclipse* alone. The modified cargo ship was deep into its slog toward Xi Virginis. The star was nearly seventy-five light years past Helminth, whose scientific outpost marked what was supposed to be the fringes of human expansion in this direction.

Despite having the most advanced drives Mosasa could buy, the *Eclipse* was still limited to making tach-jumps twenty light-years at a time. However, Mosasa had retrofitted the *Eclipse* so that most of its volume was power plant. It could make the round trip without needing to refuel, with two jumps to spare.

Each jump took close to a month, despite being instantaneous as far as the ship and those aboard were concerned. It was the downtime between jumps that ate up time for the crew. For forty-eight hours the *Eclipse* drifted between jumps.

The *Eclipse*'s engines were so large that, even with their massive damping systems, it still took four or five times as long as a normal ship for the drives to cool down from being fully active. While having drives active for four hours after a jump was technically dangerous, in those four hours it was far more likely that they'd be struck by a random asteroid than it would be for a tach-ship to suddenly appear close enough to cause so much as an oscillation in the drives' power levels.

After the cool-down period, when the drives were no longer active, the rest of the time was spent with maintenance checks. This trip was riding on the very edge of the performance specs for those engines. For the crew, they had been traveling for a little over a week, but the rest of the universe had aged 150 days.

The next jump would take them to Xi Virginis.

Mr. Antonio had explained the necessity of the downtime in the dead space between stars, about the maintenance and the observations Mosasa would wish to make. Mr. Antonio had also told him what he needed to do at this particular down period, once they had tached within twenty light-years of their target.

Nickolai pulled himself down one of the rear corridors of the ship, a maintenance area that didn't bother with the pseudo-gravity maintained in the crew areas, the bridge, and the one open cargo bay where the Paralian stayed.

Nickolai floated between cargo holds that held extra power plants for the *Eclipse*'s long journey. He was going aft, toward the tach-drives and, more important to him right now, the tach-transmitter.

The ship was on a nighttime cycle, so most of the others who had no job to do were sleeping. He saw no one else before he slipped into the rearmost chamber of the *Eclipse*. The access corridor to the tach-drives was short, less than ten meters long, and ended at an observation room, little more than a widening of the corridor in front of a massive port set into the rear bulkhead. The effect made it seem that the corridor abruptly ended in empty space.

Several hatches lined the corridor, walls, floor, and ceiling. Several had active displays showing details of what was happening behind them, almost all the graphs and numbers low into the green.

Few meant anything to Nickolai. He wasn't an engineer. He glanced from panel to panel, until he found a display that was completely quiescent. Along the top, he saw the words Mr. Antonio had told him to look for: "Coherent Tachyon Emitter."

On the wall above him was the access panel for the business end of the ship's tach-comm. Without it, the *Eclipse* was limited to light speed communications, effectively mute to the rest of the universe.

Before he moved, he checked back toward the door. Above the door was a holo pickup that should be providing a view down this corridor. "Should be" were the operative words. Two jumps ago, Nickolai had engineered his first sabotage on Mr. Antonio's behalf. He had taken a cartridge from his slugthrower, punctured the soft metal tip of the bullet, and allowed three drops of the clear liquid inside to spill into a junction box that served the optical cabling for the surveillance system. The chemicals in the liquid accelerated the oxidation of several key components, causing a hardware failure that was both hard to diagnose and hard to repair, and would appear perfectly natural in a ship this old.

The camera down here was still blind as of three hours ago. Nickolai confirmed that by standing on the bridge where several monitors scanned through all the security feeds. It was unlikely that anyone had gotten around to fixing it in the past three hours.

He just wished there was some visual indication that the camera was nonoperational.

Nickolai reached up and tapped his artificial claw on the button to open the panel. It slid aside, revealing the coils on the meter-diameter cylinder that directed the FTL particles that would compose any transmission. The coils were cold, idle, hanging about ten centimeters above the open hatch.

From his belt, Nickolai removed one of the devices that Mr. Antonio had given him. Like everything else, it resembled something other than what it actually was. To even a thorough examination, the small palm-sized device was nothing more than a personal Emerson field generator, designed to detect and absorb the effects of energy weapons within a specific range of frequencies, and provide the wearer a measure of protection from everything short of a plasma cannon, at least until the batteries overloaded.

It would be completely unremarkable until someone opened up the computer and examined the source code in the small device. Then they might see some oddities, such as the frequency sensitivity, which was set to wavelengths that didn't make sense in terms of energy weapons, or even in terms of normal massy particles. The settings only made sense when interpreted to involve the complex numbers associated with a stream of tachyons.

Nickolai slid the field generator under the emitter tube, back as close to the rear bulkhead as he could manage. According to Mr. Antonio, the generator would be completely passive and undetectable to any diagnostics. It would only switch on during a full-bore tach-transmission, and then cause a failure that would be nearly impossible to trace.

The important part wasn't how it worked, the important part was this act would be another step in clearing his debt to Mr. Antonio. Honorless as this sabotage was, Nickolai told himself that he owed Mosasa and his hirelings no loyalty. A demonic machine and a crew of the Fallen—honor did not apply.

He slid the panel shut and flexed his mechanical hand.

He wondered if he would feel the same about serving Mr. Antonio if Mosasa was simply another damned human. He wondered if Mr. Antonio had only told him Mosasa's nature because he anticipated the bad taste of doubt that would fill Nickolai's mouth about now.

He stayed there, lost in thought, until he caught a faint near-human scent. He was aware of her only a few moments before he heard her voice. "Nickolai?"

Nickolai turned at Kugara's voice. Somehow he retained enough composure to avoid looking startled or spinning his whole body in an awkward tumble. It helped that he was in a cramped human-sized space that prevented someone his size from moving quickly.

"Yes?" he said. She floated in the doorway of the maintenance corridor, staring at him. He couldn't read her expression enough to see if she noticed his proximity to the tach-comm. She was in charge of the comm and the integrity of the data systems. Could she have somehow detected what he was doing?

He almost hoped she had.

"What are you doing back here?" she asked him. Nickolai was better at human tones of voice than he was at expression, but the way she addressed him was puzzling. It wasn't aggressive or accusatory—if anything, her voice was borderline submissive. Worried? Maybe even embarrassed?

Maybe she didn't realize what I was doing. "I came back here to look out the observation port." He provided the explanation he had prepared. "I feel cramped in here."

She smiled, and Nickolai wondered if she made a point of not showing her teeth to him. "That, I understand." She massaged the neural interface on the back of her neck and shook her head. "Even the ship's internal network feels closed in. Which makes no sense, but there you are."

"Why are you down here?" Nickolai asked.

"Same reason." She shook her head. "But you were here first. I can go back and jack into an observatory program. Get a better view that way."

"Then why come down here?"

"Oh, just something about seeing it with my own eyes. Doesn't make a lot of sense."

"I understand."

She turned to go, and Nickolai said, "Wait."

She looked over her shoulder at him. "What?"

"There's room by the portal, if you want . . ." Nickolai didn't know why he was saying the words, and he trailed off in the middle of the sentence.

"To join you?"

"I understand if you want to be alone," Nickolai said. He turned to face the empty stars. In reality, staring out the observation portal was the last thing he wanted to do, but it was the only explanation he had for being here, and now that Kugara had seen him, he didn't have much choice but to face the void.

"Nickolai," she said, "we've been alone since we boarded this ship."

"Longer than that," Nickolai whispered, pulling himself into the small circular room in front of the observation port. He pressed himself against the wall so he squatted on his haunches. If the *Eclipse* was pointed at their destination right now, then he was probably facing all of human space. The home of his own people, the Fifteen Worlds, he could probably cover with his hand.

To his surprise, Kugara joined him. She floated up behind him, and placed a hand on his shoulder. "You know, it's not as roomy as you think it is."

Nickolai edged to the side, and Kugara squeezed through the top of the doorway. She pressed against his arm, grunting. Once past him, she twisted to hold herself against the wall on the other side of the door, facing out the portal toward the stars.

"Damn," she whispered.

"What?"

"Nothing." She looked down at the wall behind her. "The view would be better if I killed the lights. Here . . ."

She touched a control on the wall behind her, and the lights in the corridor dimmed until the only illumination came from the control readouts and the stars. Beyond the window, the star field erupted into painful clarity. Nickolai's artificial eyes shifted frequencies and sensitivities, showing more and more stars, a view of the universe he had never experienced before. A vastness that was beautiful, stark, and completely disinterested in him.

"Damn," Kugara repeated.

Why are we here? Nickolai thought. Staring out at the stars, the question took on an unintended depth beyond the simple self-doubt of inviting Kugara to share this view.

After a long silence, Kugara asked, "Do you trust Mosasa?"

"No."

"But you agreed to work for him."

"You say that as if I had a choice," Nickolai quoted her words back at her.

"Touché." She pulled her legs up until her knees were drawn up in front of her. She folded her arms across her knees, and rested her chin on her arms. "He's so cold."

"He's a machine."

"You told me that. But the idea he knew, about the ambush—*ambushes*—and that he might have triggered an interplanetary invasion. Don't you feel you're working for the Devil?"

Nickolai laughed for the first time in a long while. He only stopped when he realized that Kugara was staring at him.

"My apologies," Nickolai said. "That was amusing."

"What was amusing?"

Nickolai looked out at the stars. "Of course we're working for the Devil. Mosasa is lifeless thought, the personification of the sins of the Fallen."

"The Fallen?"

"Humanity. Our creators."

"Our creators?" She sucked in a breath. "Oh."

There was a long period of silence before she asked, "If Mosasa is the Devil, what does that make us?"

"Souls untainted by the arrogance of the Fallen who have

the possibility of redemption in the eyes of God. You more than I, because you are closer to His creation before the Fall."

"You believe this?"

"I was raised in the faith of St. Rajasthan."

"Is that an answer?"

"What I believe is not important. I'm as damned as Mosasa."

"Why?"

"You never asked me about my arm."

He couldn't read her expression, but he could almost feel what she was thinking. She could ask him about his past, but that would open up the opportunity for him to question her about her own.

Kugara didn't speak for a long time. Then she said, "You truly think I'm closer to God than you are?"

"In my faith, you are considered an Angel."

He heard her make some soft rhythmic sounds, like she was gasping for breath.

Crying? Why?

She extended her legs, pushing against the portal to shoot out the door above him, out into the corridor. Nickolai turned, body slowly tumbling in the observation room. "Kugara?"

"Shut up, you stupid morey bastard."

Nickolai drew back, the unexpected slur stinging him more than he thought possible.

"You know nothing about me," she shouted at him without turning her head. "Nothing! How dare you!" She disappeared out the doorway before Nickolai could pull himself out of the observation room.

He floated alone, in the dark, with the stars.

There was a small area forward of the crew quarters of the *Eclipse* that served as a common area. Mallory made a point to take meals there when there was a quorum of the scientific team in attendance. On some level he wanted to avoid Dr. Dörner, but that was not really possible on a ship this size, and going to the effort of trying to avoid her would have attracted way more attention to himself.

In the end, his cover was only a means to an end, the end being intelligence on what was happening out toward Xi Virginis. And after Mosasa's revelations about the Caliphate,

Mallory suspected that information was more important than ever.

He hoped the scientific team Mosasa had assembled would be the closest to knowing the answer. That was the theory, anyway.

So, at each meal, he took a seat and eavesdropped, and if they didn't actively engage him in their conversations, they didn't shun him either—though Dr. Dörner's icy stares came close.

Fine, Mallory thought, *the more you see me as a mercenary thug, the less likely you'll see a Jesuit colleague.*

Over the past week, just by listening to their small talk, he discovered that none of them had been recruited from Bakunin itself. They came from several far-flung corners of human space. Bill—who was only ever present as a synthetic voice on a comm unit, his massive life-support system never leaving his cargo bay—was from Paralia, of course. Dr. Dörner, Mallory knew, came from Acheron, and that caused Dr. Pak to make an unsubtle comment about the planet contributing to her icy personality. Dr. Pak actually came from Terra, which usually granted him some deference beyond his relative youth but didn't keep Dr. Dörner from making a sharp comment about people who peaked young looking forward to a "slow, sad decline."

Of the last two, Brody came from Bulawayo in the Trianguli Union, and Tsoravitch came from Jokul in the Sirius Economic Community. Two planets fifty light-years apart; both close to forty light-years from Acheron. Mosasa had cast an extremely wide net, one that made the concentrated effort on Bakunin seem designed to catch the Caliphate's attention.

Which was probably the point . . .

Mallory didn't like to think of what would happen when the Caliphate moved toward these outlying colonies. The Vatican had no fleet, as such, but should the Bishop of Rome speak to some secular rulers, Mallory suspected that the Caliphate's move wouldn't be uncontested.

The only thing preventing him from seizing the tach-comm and sending a desperate message back home was the fact he knew that the Caliphate was closely observed. Their moves would be known by other assets soon after they made a decision. It wasn't worth blowing his cover before he had gathered information at the source.

The source of what, that was the question. And the science team was as unenlightening on the point of this expedition as Mosasa had been.

Tsoravitch had just made a point about Mosasa's less than edifying briefings. She leaned back in a corner of the common room, sipping a container of what passed for coffee on the *Eclipse,* and shook her head at Brody. "If he didn't give you any more information, why'd you agree to come along on this bizarre little field trip?"

Brody sat facing away from Mallory, so he couldn't see the doctor's expression from his spot on the couch in the opposite corner of the common room, though the tone of voice Brody used was almost wistful. "I really could care less about Mosasa's 'anomaly.' But I've been in a teaching chair at Sokoto University for nearly twenty years standard. I study culture, and I haven't stepped foot outside the Trianguli Union since I finished my graduate work. Now I get the chance to see colonies that have been isolated from the rest of human space for at least a century? I jumped at the chance."

"Amen to that." Pak raised his glass in a toast to the others.

"Same reason?" Tsoravitch asked.

Pak nodded. "A hundred years isn't a huge time for linguistic drift, even if they are isolated. But if these colonies were founded during the collapse of the Confederacy, with a substantial mix of languages, there could be a whole class of new Creole to study. The first person to write a paper on these outliers could make a career." He looked over at Tsoravitch. "What about you?"

"You know any other chance I'd get to work with an AI?"

There was a long pause at the table. Brody broke the silence with a nervous chuckle. "She's got you there, Leon."

"You still there, Bill?" Pak called out.

"I am listening," Bill's voice came from a comm unit in the middle of the table. The synthetic voice was male, deep, and had a slight Windsor accent. Though the voice was completely naturalistic, it was so lacking in affect that Mallory would have preferred something that sounded like a computer.

He wondered if Bill picked it out himself, though Paralians perceived sound so differently Mallory doubted that Bill would be able to easily interpret the characteristics that made human voices unique.

"Well, what about you?" Pak said. "Are you anticipating some new branch of physics or mathematics?"

"No, I am not."

"Why'd you agree to join Mosasa's little expedition?" Pak asked.

"I wish to go where I have not."

"You're a tourist?" Pak asked.

"Mr. Mosasa provided me the means to leave the Ocean."

Pak looked at Brody, smiling. "He *is* a tourist. Bill, we'll have to get some holos of you that you can tach to the folks back home."

"I do not understand what you mean."

"Don't mind him," Brody said. "He's just—"

Brody was interrupted by a klaxon over the PA system. After a single *whoop*, Mosasa's voice came over the address system.

"Attention. We have our course programmed and we have engines primed for our final jump. We will be taching to the Xi Virginis system in fifteen minutes. Everyone who can, please report to the bridge."

"This is it," Brody said, pushing himself from the table. "Sorry you can't come up with us, Bill."

"Can you clarify? Are you apologizing or expressing sympathy?"

Mallory slipped out of the common room first, not staying to hear them explain things to Bill. Before the door slid shut behind him, he heard Bill explain in great detail how he had a full holographic feed from the bridge and didn't need to be present for the critical jump.

Fifteen minutes, Mallory thought. *Fifteen minutes and we'll be in the Xi Virginis system.*

The thought was unsettling.

Nickolai was one of the last people to step onto the bridge of the *Eclipse*. He waited for the last minute so he would avoid the possibility of running into Kugara, who had turned from possible ally to a complete enigma. Besides, it simplified things if his only allegiance was to Mr. Antonio.

The *Eclipse* had a huge bridge, with a ceiling high enough to provide Nickolai the headroom to stand fully upright. It easily accommodated all of Mosasa's crew, and could have held the Paralian and his elaborate life support, if there was a way for the huge apparatus to make it up here. The layout of the room was a sphere with the bottom flattened out. Stations ringed a large holo display intended for more redundant positions than were supplied by Mosasa's crew.

Parvi and Wahid sat at elaborate consoles on either side of the holo display, which showed an image of the space outside. Staring into the display was like looking out the observation port in back, out at the emptiness light-years from everything. However, with his cybernetic eyes, Nickolai could tell that the holo only honored a narrowly-defined visible spectrum. With little effort, he could make out the ghost of Mosasa on the opposite side of the display from him. Kugara sat at a fourth console, opposite Mosasa, her back to Nickolai and most of the other spectators on the bridge.

"Drive is hot," Parvi said. "All systems check okay to go."

Wahid answered, "We have a fix on target. Current course window opens in ninety seconds."

"Mass sensors clear," Kugara said. "Nothing significant within two AU."

"Are we okay to fire the tach-drives?" Parvi addressed Mosasa.

"Go ahead, Captain."

"Sixty seconds to window."

"Course approved," Parvi said. "Switching the tach-drives to auto."

The bridge was silent for a few long seconds. Nickolai idly wondered if being present here would somehow make the act of taching somewhere more impressive. It didn't seem appropriate that leaving a gravity well—barely moving a few hundred kilometers—always *felt* more dramatic than the sensation of moving twenty light-years. No matter how much time supposedly passed in the interim, on the ship it never felt like anything at all. No sensation, no passing of time, not even a slight unease to let you know that something significant had happened. If you stayed locked in a cabin, you could tach halfway across the galaxy and never know you had moved.

"Twenty seconds to window." Wahid said. "Fifteen seconds to last-chance abort."

"All systems nominal," Parvi said.

"Mass sensors still clear."

"Ten seconds. Five to commit." No one answered, and Wahid said. "Five seconds to window, drives are committed. Three . . . two . . . one . . ."

There wasn't even a sound to mark the jump to Xi Virginis.

CHAPTER TWENTY-ONE

Fallen Angel

An event is dangerous in direct proportion to how unexpected it is.

—*The Cynic's Book of Wisdom*

A civilization that cannot envision its own demise has already begun to die.

—JEAN HONORÉ CHEVIOT
(2065–2128)

Date: 2526.4.30 (Standard)
Salmagundi–HD 101534

A month after his outburst at his father's wake, Flynn shot his flier out over the forests of Salmagundi. Despite his worries, Robert Sheldon hadn't seen fit to fire him, or even mention the incident. Things had since settled back into a routine, with him spending long days surveying the dense forests east of Ashley, cataloging stands of trees mature enough to be harvested. If people were slightly less likely to engage him in conversation, that was fine with him; most people didn't have much to talk about anyway.

He flew on manual—which, technically, was a breach of regulations. Allowing a human being to pilot an aircraft was supposedly only an emergency procedure. However, not only did he feel better with the craft under his direct control, it also meant the computer couldn't override him and turn it around if someone back at Ashley decided he should come back. It never happened, but he still didn't like the idea that someone could make that kind of remote control decision.

As long as he did his job, no one should have reason to complain how he did it. He shot over the trees at three hundred meters, the sensor batteries underneath the craft picking up moisture and chlorophyll levels in the foliage, filling in the topographic map on his display with bands of reds, yellows, and blues, showing which areas of the forest had matured the fastest from the last dry season—

"Flynn! Look up."

"Huh, what?"

"North, about thirty degrees above the horizon."

Tetsami's voice in his head drew his attention to something that was just visible out of the canopy, on the fringes of his peripheral vision. He turned his head to look at it.

Something moved, high and fast, leaving a glowing contrail. Oddly, the object itself didn't reflect any light. It was a black smudge at the head of the turbulent atmosphere.

Flynn whispered, "A meteor?"

The object closed on the horizon in front of him, following a downward path. "The way that thing's moving, it's going to make one hell of a—"

The object hit the forest in front of the flier. The world outside the windscreen went white with the impact, then immediately black as the light levels caused the windows to tint themselves. Less than a second later, turbulence hit the small flier, tumbling the nose up and to the left. All the control surfaces stopped responding, and Flynn's stomach lurched as the vector jets started throwing the craft in an uncontrolled spin.

He cut the vectors a little over three seconds after the computer would have done, allowing the flier to coast on neutral buoyancy contragravs. In a few moments air resistance and inertia brought the craft to a standstill.

The windscreen became transparent again. Outside, he saw an inverted horizon tilted at a fifteen-degree angle. The flier was about a hundred meters closer to the forest canopy and pointed about two hundred degrees off course—in addition to floating upside down.

"That's why the regulations want the computer to fly this thing."

"We're fine, Gram," Flynn muttered. "No damage."

He gingerly opened the vectors to right the flier, waiting until it was upright before spinning the nose around to look at the impact.

"Look at that."

They were about fifty kilometers out from Ashley, but Flynn wouldn't be surprised if the rolling pillar of smoke might be visible from town. The edges of the burn zone formed a ragged ellipse about two or three klicks long and about half a klick wide. The trees inside the burn zone were shattered and charred black, and the ones still standing at the edges were smoldering.

Fortunately, despite the clear sky at the moment, they were in the wet season. The trees were already too saturated to burn very well. If it had been the dry season, Flynn would have already been looking at thousands of hectares of smoldering forest.

He flew down close to the site, looping it twice, recording all the data he could with the craft sensors. Then he approached for a landing in the thickest part of the burn zone.

"Shouldn't you call this in?"

"Yeah, I should." The little craft slowed until it was lifted only by the contragrav, and slowly began to drift down. "I should also clear any landings with base before descent."

"As long as we're clear on the rules here."

Flynn tweaked the descent until the craft was over a relatively flat patch of bare ground. With the contragrav at 85 percent, the little flier drifted gently to the ground, rocking slightly on its landing skids. Once settled, he cut the contragrav, and the whole ship shifted as the ground took the ship's full five-thousand-kilo weight.

"We're here." Flynn threw off the harness, turned around in the pilot's chair, and grabbed the survey kit from its slot behind the cockpit.

"Hey, I understand—I want to see this, too. But call this in before you step out there. I'm just as fucked as you if you get pinned under a burning tree and no one knows where we are."

Flynn sighed. He turned around and flipped a switch. A light flashed on the console showing an active beacon. He turned on the communicator and said, "This is Flynn Jorgenson, in survey craft 103. Disembarking at 0°15'5.25" North, 78°42'14.38" West. Assessing probable meteor impact site." He hit the "Transmit Repeat" button without waiting for base to acknowledge him.

"Happy, Grandma?" He grabbed the survey kit again, and hit the release for the hatch.

The hatch slid aside along the fuselage, letting in air thick with the smell of smoke and steam. It was bad enough that Flynn's eyes burned. He grabbed a respirator mask and fitted it over his face. The gasket sealed flush with his overalls, which were made of fireproof ballistic fiber and had their own environmental controls.

He stepped outside and his feet sank into about twenty centimeters of mud and ash. At ground level, the scar of the impact was even more apparent, if that was possible. A trench of bare earth cut down the center of the blast zone, razor-straight. On either side, the splintered remnants of charred trees leaned aside, pointing away from the scar in the ground.

Flynn pulled the camera out of the survey kit and began recording images, topography, infrared, and spectroscopic data.

"You're quiet," Flynn said as he slogged through the mud and ash toward the hot spot at the end of this gradually deepening trench.

"I have a bad feeling about this."

"Why?"

"Does this look like a normal meteor impact?"

Tetsami had a point. Something with enough mass to survive reentry and still be visible during descent should have left a bigger scar. And the oblique angle? Atmospheric breaking and gravity should bring the path near vertical—but this almost looked like a controlled impact . . .

"Holy Jesus Tap-dancing Christ!"

"What?" Flynn snapped his head up from the camera and looked around, suddenly afraid that Tetsami's burning tree was about to fall on him.

"No, damn it, look at it, look at the fucking egg!"

"Egg? What egg?"

He suddenly saw Tetsami's effigy appear in his field of vision, face twisted in fear and frustration. She pointed. *"THERE! Look THERE!"*

Flynn turned around and found himself standing about three hundred meters from the terminus of the impact site. The object was still steaming, and half buried under the mound of mud and clay it had pushed up in front of itself. It was obviously an artifact, not a meteor. The surface was way too smooth. It was also small, much smaller than it had appeared when Flynn saw its descent.

It was egg-shaped, and from what he could see of it, he'd guess that its long axis would be two or three meters long, four at the most. Small enough that Flynn had initially lost sight of it in the devastation caused by the impact.

He raised the camera to it and zoomed in . . .

"What the . . . ?"

At first he thought the calibration was blown on his equipment, but several spectrum and configuration changes gave him the same picture. The mud and ash around the egg was boiling hot, averaging over a hundred degrees, and hot spots all around five or six times that.

The egg itself was cold. It radiated no heat at all.

Radiated nothing.

Flynn's equipment picked nothing radiating *or* reflecting from the matte-black surface. No infrared, ultraviolet, or visible light. The laser and radar range finders couldn't fix on the thing; when he swept the beam past it, he saw the numbers go from 268.25 meters to infinity.

Flynn shook his head, "It's a black hole."

"No," Tetsami said, still standing next to him, "It's something a lot more complicated."

Flynn looked at her. "You *know* what this is?"

Tetsami nodded. "Yes." Her voice was little more than a whisper. It quavered a bit, and for a moment Flynn saw his several-greats grandmother as a little girl. "Eigne called it a seed."

Eigne called it a seed.

In the seventeen years Tetsami had been part of him, Flynn had learned a lot about her history. History that, not too surprisingly, was not part of the normal educational curriculum on Salmagundi—not that there was much of a curriculum to begin with. The schooling Flynn had gotten was pretty much limited to the basics of literacy, linguistic and otherwise. Their ancestors had done all the heavy lifting on those points, so what was the point of *teaching* history?

So over the years, he had heard a lot from Tetsami that no one else had ever bothered to tell him. The details of the founding of Salmagundi weren't the only things she had told him about. Eigne and the Proteans were another part of that secret history.

Tetsami, as had most of the Founders, had come from the planet Bakunin as the Terran Confederacy was collapsing. Bakunin was a lawless world that respected no human State, and because of that attracted every form of deviant belief, every persecuted form of worship, every refugee from anywhere.

Every one.

The Founders of Salmagundi, free of the Confederacy's constraints on heretical technologies, built the infrastructure that would become the Hall of Minds, something that would be anathema to the men who declared the operation of an AI a capital crime. Compared to the Proteans, the sins committed by the Founders of Salmagundi were insignificant. There were other heresies, graver sins.

Before the stars were in easy reach, man had tried to terraform the worlds in his home system using molecule-sized self-replicating intelligent machines. However, something had gone wrong on a distant moon, Titan. The machines took over, and the war that followed sterilized all of man's outposts in the outer part of humanity's home system. A billion people died in that war, five million in the immediate aftermath, others in subsequent efforts to sterilize the sites of banned nanotech experiments, including one long-dead planet where the Confederacy killed nearly fifty million people by dropping a hundred-kilometer asteroid through the planet's crust.

But those who dealt with such things had never been completely wiped out. A small sect of human beings—at least a sect of people who had once been human—equated spiritual transcendence with the physical and mental transformations granted by the machines. The cult of Proteus found refuge, if not a home, on Bakunin. And the entity that had spoken for the Proteans on Bakunin had called herself Eigne.

Before the Confederacy, in its death throes, used an orbital linear accelerator to vaporize the Protean outpost on Bakunin, that outpost had manufactured and launched thousands of seeds. Seeds that contained millions of minds archived from eras back as far as the catastrophe on Titan, as well as the entire collected sum of human knowledge up to that point in human history.

In large part, the reason for the existence of the Proteans was to propagate their existence as far as possible in space and time.

One of those seeds had just crashed here, on Salmagundi.

For several hours, Flynn radioed information back to Base. Despite the "seed's" enigmatic nature, he was able to produce some information. The thing was a matte-black egg exactly 3.127 meters along its long axis. The mass readings, if they were accurate, showed it much denser than normal matter, about a kilogram per square centimeter, which meant that the thing, small as it was, massed more than most of the aircraft in Ashley combined. The thing had found its place on the planet's surface, and Flynn doubted it was going to move.

However, he had a lot more information than the sensor data on the seed itself. For once, he had relevant ancestral information, and it was exhilarating. Flynn, the habitual singleton, actually had useful knowledge from his sole extra mind. For most of his life, he had felt as if he wasn't quite in on the joke, that the people around him with two or three glyphs on their brow had access to a subtext he wasn't quite aware of.

Finally he had something over everybody. It felt good. So good, in fact, that he completely missed the warning signs; the shift to encrypted protocols, the change in radio operators to people he wasn't familiar with, the occasional and emphatic order for him not to leave the site of the impact, the repeated questions about who else might know this information, who he had discussed the Proteans with.

He couldn't really blame Tetsami either. Normally, she was a little more paranoid than he was, but if he was caught up in the novelty of having something new to report on and having the expertise to analyze it, Tetsami was overtaken by her awe at seeing a remnant of Proteus showing up on Salmagundi. Enough so that, like Flynn, she hadn't given herself the opportunity to think through exactly how the powers-that-be back at Ashley might react to their visitor or its history.

Ten hours after the impact, after the sun had set, the first security contragrav arrived. Flynn ran up to the craft as soon as it landed, waving his arms, still oblivious as the doors opened and two men stepped out. The name tags on their jumpsuits read Frank and Tony.

"Hey, it's about five hundred meters that way—" Flynn pointed.

"Uh, they seem more interested in us."

Frank stepped up to Flynn while Tony walked past him toward the flier. Flynn turned, finally realizing that something was wrong. "What are you doing—"

Frank grabbed him and, before Flynn could object, had him in handcuffs and a restraint collar.

"What the fuck?"

Frank hustled him into the back of the security contragrav

and pushed him down into a seat. As the door closed, Flynn saw Tony pulling the comm unit and all the data recordings from his flier.

"Okay, that's not good—"

"No, Gram, it isn't."

CHAPTER TWENTY-TWO

Jihad

Right and wrong are defined by what you do, not what you serve.

—*The Cynic's Book of Wisdom*

A conqueror is always a lover of peace.

—KARL VON CLAUSEWITZ
(1780–1831)

Date: 2526.5.6 (Standard)
10.3 ly from Beta Comae Berenices

It had all been leading to this. Almost six months ago, Admiral Muhammad Hussein al Khamsiti had taken command of a battle group that barely existed. Now, after half a year of accelerated construction and the crash training of nearly ten thousand men, the *Prophet's Voice* floated in the interstellar void ten light-years from Beta Comae Berenices and the planet Falcion, preparing for its maiden voyage.

Attached to the kilometer-long vessel, over a hundred individual spacecraft docked, ranging from troop transports to fighters to heavy drop-ships—an entire fleet unto itself.

On the bridge, Admiral Hussein stood and waited for their last tach-jump. There was no technical reason for any of the command staff to be here during the jump, much less Admiral Hussein himself. However, it had been impressed upon the entire command staff of the Caliphate that this mission was as much about diplomacy as it was about military force. To that end, forms of ceremony were meticulously adhered to.

Admiral Hussein stood along with a senior officer from each of the larger vessels in the *Voice*'s battle group. Each officer wore the emerald dress uniform of the Caliphate Navy, boots polished to a mirror shine. Golden braids of command outnumbered the enlisted men and noncommissioned officers doing the work maneuvering the *Voice* and syncing the tach-jump.

The admiral thought that his command staff would cut quite the impressive figure when they made their first broadcast down to the surface of the "lost" colony orbiting the star HD 101534, the *Voice*'s destination.

Of course, the hundred warships accompanying the *Voice* would probably be a fair bit more impressive.

He expected that the Caliphate's politicians were right, and they would have a victory without firing a shot. All the admiral would require of the colony would be a formal treaty of alliance, no large matter for a planet so far removed from the rest of human space.

Just enough to keep the Caliphate's rivals at bay.

The admiral steepled his fingers as he waited for the klaxons to announce their last tach-jump. He wondered idly if any of the command staff at attention in front of and below the command dais were as happy as he about the prospect of a largely peaceful mission. The admiral was a veteran of conflicts on Rubai and Waldgrave, and he was not a timid commander, but the *Prophet's Voice* was a brand new flagship. Many of its hallways still smelled faintly of new paint.

Not only a new ship, but a new ship *design*. The Caliphate had spent an unprecedented amount of time and treasure in the creation of the Ibrahim-class of carriers, each with its own fleet of warships, fifty tach-capable vessels and another fifty short-range fighters, all attached to the great ship like parasitic young.

In addition, the Ibrahim-class of carrier had the largest and most sophisticated tach-drive in existence. Until the Caliphate's engineers built the antimatter-fueled monstrosities filling the guts of these new carriers, the limits of existing tach-drives peaked out at twenty light-years and $256c$—and that only effectively reachable by ships a third of the *Voice*'s mass, without the attached warships.

The *Voice*'s tach-drives showed a fourfold increase in speed, mass, and distance. It could clear eighty light-years in a jump that took only slightly over twenty-eight days standard. Even if the drives sucked the energy equivalent of a small sun, it placed every world in human space in tactical reach of the

Caliphate. Including the far-flung colonies seventy light-years past Helminth.

The potential of the new warships was limitless.

However, the admiral was very much aware that the potential was untested. It was distressing how quickly the *Voice* and her sisters were promoted from an abbreviated shake-down into active duty. When the orders came for this mission nearly six months ago, the *Voice* was still being constructed. It had been barely three weeks since the last of the construction crew had left the ship.

The admiral was keenly aware of the rush to space-worthiness. They had not even been able to test the power-hungry tach-drives at their full capacity.

Not until this moment.

The *Voice* was the last of the four to dive out toward the worlds clustered around Xi Virginis. Their target was a small world eight light-years away from that star, and right at the theoretical outer limit of the *Voice*'s massive drives from their current position.

The crew functioned admirably under the gaze of so many command officers. He was proud of having his people perform so well after the bare-bones training they were forced through to fully man the *Voice* in such a short time frame. Checklists were completed, final broadcasts made through the ship, the last engineering details were triple-checked and the navigation team ran the final models on the massive computer cores that pondered the longest tach-jump in human history.

The complicated electronic ballet concluded with a chorus of "Ready" cascading across the bridge, starting at navigation, through communications, environmental and weapon systems, and finally ending with Captain Gamal Rasheed, the commander of the *Voice* and therefore the highest ranking member of the battle group under Admiral Hussein. The captain turned to him and said, "All stations report we are prepared to jump."

The admiral nodded. "Give the order, Captain."

"Engage the tach-drive."

Date: 2526.5.10 (Standard)
Earth–Sol

Sydney was probably about as far as one could get from Rome and still remain on the same planet—not only geographically, but in spirit. Where the Vatican, and most of Europe, seemed to embody the roots of mankind, its ties to Earth, the Australian city seemed the reverse, aggressively tying itself to the star-flung traces of humanity. It still wore its history as the capital of the old Confederacy.

Once the nominal seat of the last attempt at a universal human government, and more than 250 years old, the Confederacy Tower stabbed a kilometer-long finger into the Australian sky. It dominated this city the way it had once dominated all of known space.

To Cardinal Anderson, the building seemed to reach beyond the bounds of Earth, a modern Tower of Babel that was still, in a sense, caught in a slow motion collapse that began 175 years ago. The power still held by the building was represented by the extensive diplomatic compounds that clustered near it. The embassy and consulates here had remained in continual operation even through the collapse of the old Confederacy. No place else would anyone find representatives from more human colonized planets. Across all of human space, there were probably only a dozen planets that didn't have a diplomat here. And that was including the cluster of colonies around the star Xi Virginis.

Cardinal Anderson stood on a balcony of one of those diplomatic compounds. The Vatican had had a token embassy here from the days of the Confederacy; it was a small structure on the fringes of the diplomatic hive surrounding the spire reflecting its unique status. Even before man had left the bounds of Earth, the Vatican had the strange distinction of having all the functions of a state without most of the secular trappings of that authority. It had been near a millennium since the Bishop of Rome had commanded a nonspiritual army.

However, in some ways, the Church was more powerful now than it had been then. He certainly doubted a request from any other entity would have sufficed to gather together the people meeting here tonight.

He stood and watched as the sun set behind the massive spire, backlighting it so that its silhouette parted the sky as if the clouds were a pair of theater curtains just beginning to open, revealing something dark behind them.

"Your Grace?" came a voice transmitted into the office behind him.

"Yes?" he responded without turning around.

"Mr. Xaing from the Indi Protectorate has just arrived."

"Thank you. Let the representatives know I'm on my way down."

He turned away from the shadowed spire caught between a sense of satisfaction at bringing this meeting to fruition and a sense of foreboding over what he had to impart.

Twelve people waited for him downstairs. He had called on representatives not just from the large states of the Indi Protectorate, the Centauri Alliance, and the Sirius Economic Community, but he also invited diplomats from the Union of Independent Worlds, and had even appealed to the non-humans of the Fifteen Worlds.

When he walked into the conference room in the basement of the Vatican consulate, he faced representatives from every transplanetary government outside of the Caliphate itself. As he walked up to the head of the table, a holo of the Caliphate's newest Ibrahim-class carrier was projected above the long axis of the table. It was sobering to think this ship was as massive as the Confederacy spire itself.

"Thank you all for coming. I know the logistics of this meeting were complex, but the willingness of your governments to meet here should illustrate the gravity of this situation."

A dozen pairs of eyes focused on him with emotions that ranged from support from the Vatican's nominal allies, Centauri and Sirius, to enigmatic disinterest coming from the in-human eyes belonging to the canid from the Fifteen Worlds, to outright hostility coming from the camp of Indi and the Independent Worlds.

But all were here to hear him speak.

"It is the desire of His Holiness to share what we know about the Caliphate's capabilities and intentions, because their implications affect every government represented in this room."

With that, Cardinal Anderson made the same arguments that he had been making to the pope for the last decade. By the grace of God, these people would not take as long to convince.

CHAPTER TWENTY-THREE

Revelation

The more prepared the attack, the less expected the outcome.

—*The Cynic's Book of Wisdom*

No battle plan survives contact with the enemy.

—HELMUTH VON MOLTKE
(1800–1891)

Date: 2526.05.22 (Standard)
Xi Virginis

There wasn't even a sound to mark the *Eclipse*'s jump, just an abrupt shift in the star field shown in the holo.

Another twenty light-years, Nickolai thought. *Here we are.*

For the drama, and the plotting, and the hushed admonitions of Mr. Antonio, the *Eclipse*'s arrival at the point of Mr. Mosasa's anomaly was anticlimactic.

"We're still nominal on all systems," Parvi said. "Drives are cold."

"Mass sensors negative for two AU."

Wahid didn't say anything. After a long pause, Mosasa said, "Navigation?"

"Hold on a minute." Wahid shook his head, and for all the trouble Nickolai had in interpreting human expressions, even he could tell something was seriously wrong.

"What's the problem?" Parvi asked. "Are we off course?"

Nickolai knew that the *Eclipse* was fueled for multiple jumps at this distance, but even so, the thought of taching twenty light-years in the wrong direction tightened something in his gut.

Could what I did have affected the engines? Nickolai began to realize that there was no particular motive for Mr. Antonio to keep him alive. Mr. Antonio wasn't like Nickolai; he was a man and had no honor to keep, even to himself.

"No, we're right where we're supposed to be," Wahid said slowly. It almost sounded as if he didn't believe it himself. "All the landmarks check out . . ."

"What's wrong, then?" Parvi asked.

"Look at the damn holo!" Wahid said, thrusting a hand at the display as if he wanted to bat it out of his face.

"What?" Parvi looked at the holo of stars between them, and her eyes widened, and she shook her head. "No . . ."

"Kugara?" Mosasa snapped.

"I'm ahead of you. Mass scans out to the full range of the sensors. No sign of anything bigger than an asteroid for a hundred AU. We got background radiation consistent with interstellar media—"

One of the scientists, the female with yellow hair, spoke up. "What happened? Is there some sort of problem?"

"Bet your ass there's a problem." Wahid spun around on his chair and faced the spectators, pointing a finger at the holo display. "We're missing a whole star."

"What?"

"Xi Virginis is gone, Dr. Dörner."

Behold a great red dragon, having seven heads and ten horns, and seven crowns upon his heads. And his tail drew the third part of the stars of heaven, and did cast them to the earth. The words echoed in Mallory's head, the transmission Cardinal Anderson had played for him, the voice quoting Revelation burning in his memory.

Mallory stood back and watched everyone react to the news that an A-spectrum main sequence dwarf star had ceased to exist. More than one member of the science team said, "A star can't just disappear."

Apparently that was wrong.

Bill's synthetic Windsor monotone asked for sensor data, and told them to look for stellar remnants. Even without any affect, Mallory could sense a slight desperation just in the nature of the request. Kugara had already done a mass scan of the region and found nothing significant for one hundred AU; no dark stellar remnants, no remains of a planetary system. Just dust and some widely-spaced asteroids.

Perhaps most disturbing was Mosasa's reaction. He seemed as shocked as everyone else, running duplicate scans at his own station, shouting orders at his trio of bridge officers.

You were looking for some sort of anomaly, Mallory thought. *Here it is.*

Wahid made several attempts to disprove their location. But all the other stars were right where they should be. The background showed that they couldn't be more than a third of a light-year off in any direction; right on top of Xi Virginis in interstellar terms.

"What the hell happened?" Wahid muttered. "Did it blow up? Did it fall into a black hole?"

"No remnants of any such event are observable," Bill's synthetic voice answered Wahid.

"There was a colony here?" Dr. Dörner had joined the bridge crew around the holo, where data now scrolled by the star field.

Mosasa ignored her and kept shaking his head. "This can't—"

Dörner grabbed Mosasa's shoulder and pulled him around to face her. "You said there was a colony here?"

The emotion drained from Mosasa's face, and he suddenly looked as flat as Bill's voice. He reached up and removed Dörner's hand from his shoulder. The dragon tattoo glinted in reflected light from the holo next to them. "Yes," Mosasa said, "there was a colony here. Kugara and Tsoravitch isolated one hundred forty-seven distinct EM signals from it during our approach. The colony, or its capital city, was named Xanadu."

Dörner stepped back, as if the enormity of the situation was just beginning to sink in. "How many people—"

"My population estimate was five hundred thousand to one point five million."

Dörner blinked, staring at Mosasa.

Wahid and Bill were still carrying on a conversation. "We had a damn star here twenty years ago, right?"

"The light sphere from the unknown event had not reached our last position when our course was laid in. That places the unknown event no more than 19.875 standard years ago."

Mosasa stepped back. "This is completely outside every scenario—"

"One and a half million people?" Dörner shook her head. "One and a half million people?"

Mallory stepped forward; and slowed as he realized that Fitzpatrick, his alter ego, would not have the immediate impulse to comfort someone. When Dörner turned toward him, he had an uneasy feeling reminding him that she was a potential disaster for his cover story if she remembered seeing him before as Father Mallory.

His hesitation allowed Brody to be the one to step forward. The anthropologist took Dörner away from the bridge crew, quietly talking. "We don't know what happened, Sharon. We don't know there was anyone here when whatever happened, happened."

He walked her back to the other two members of the scientific team, who were watching everything in stunned fascination. Mallory looked over at Nickolai to see how the tiger was reacting. He couldn't tell from the feline expression if Nickolai was frightened, amused, or smelled something odd.

"Kugara," Mosasa said, his voice still oddly flat. "Power up the tach-comm unit."

Did Nickolai's eyes just widen? Mallory could swear something just changed.

"Yes? Transmit where?"

"Earth. We're going to hit every diplomatic consulate in turn, broad, unencrypted."

Kugara hesitated, "Okay? Even the Caliph—"

Mosasa turned around and snapped, "Yes! *Everyone!* If anything trumps your narcissistic human political divisions, it's this. This changes *everything*. I can't account for this kind—" He abruptly stopped and stood up straighter. He allowed the emotion to leak out of his voice again. "You need to burst transmit all our telemetry and recon data. Now."

"I'm packaging the data now."

Nickolai closed his eyes and looked almost as if he was bracing for something.

"Transmitting," Kugara said.

Something like a large rifle shot shook the bridge.

"What was that?" Dr. Dörner asked.

"—the hell?" Wahid said, and he began tapping madly at the display. "You see that, Parvi?"

"I have depressurization in the main maintenance tunnel. Damn. Major power drains on the main tach-drive."

"I lost all data readings on the tach-comm," Kugara said.

"Shit," Wahid said, "that's because we don't have one anymore."

The main holo display switched to one of the external cameras, pointing down at the stern of the *Eclipse*. A long contrail of ice crystals and debris emerged from a small hole in the skin of the ship, as if the ship was being followed by a small comet.

Did the tach-comm just blow up?

Mallory looked around and realized that Dr. Dörner was staring at him. *Did I say something? Did I give myself away?*

"What happened to the tach-comm unit?" Mosasa snapped.

"The diagnostic logs show an intense power spike at the time of transmission," Kugara replied quietly.

"It spiked across the whole system," Parvi said. "The drives are intact, but the tach-comm is interlinked with the damping system. It drained two thirds of the power reserves before vaporizing. We only have one damping conduit left at about fifty percent capacity."

"No!" Mosasa snapped, slamming his hands down on the console in front of him. "We cannot have the tach-comm down. That communications link is *essential*."

"Sir? Did you hear what I said?" Parvi's voice was on the verge of cracking. "We're down two thirds of our power reserves. That's our return trip *and* our margin."

"We have to repair the tach-comm. Communication is our number one priority!"

Everyone, bridge crew and scientists, stared at Mosasa as their nominal leader stared into the holo before him, watching the ice cloud of venting gases fade as the ship sealed off the damaged section. "We *need* the communication link back up."

If anything, the look of shock on Mosasa's face was worse now than when he heard an entire star was missing.

"I'm sorry," Wahid said. "From all the engineering data, there's nothing left to repair. The surge completely vaporized the main transmission coils, as well as the primary power damping coils. We only got half of one secondary coil to keep the drives from overheating. We're damn lucky we didn't suffer a main drive failure. We don't even have the power to spare for a transmission, even if I could pull a new coherent emitter out of my ass."

Mosasa shook his head, hands clutching the console in front of him. At the moment he looked way too human.

Only one third power, Mallory thought. *That's less than two fully-powered jumps. That can't even get us halfway back.*

He could see that understanding sinking into the faces of the rest of the crew, except for Nickolai's, who appeared as enigmatic as ever. Mosasa stared at the console in front of him, whispering, "Was this planned?"

"Sir?" Parvi asked.

Mosasa pushed himself upright. "We need to conserve power and get to a colony where we might be able to repower the ship and repair the damage. Everyone on maintenance duty, I want the drives checked out. Make sure they suffered no other damage."

"What colony?" Wahid asked.

"The closest one is HD 101534. It is eight light-years away and leaves us with an acceptable margin in our remaining power reserves."

If it is still there, Mallory thought.

Most of the crew had things to do, checking out the integrity of the tach-drive, doing what they could to fix the damping system, repairing the breach made by the failing tach-comm, plotting a course to the next nearest "lost" colony. Even the scientists finally had some work, trying to decipher exactly what happened to Xi Virginis.

That left Mallory alone in the common room, wondering exactly what the meaning of all of this was. Even if the tach-drives themselves were undamaged, they were effectively stranded, as isolated from the rest of humanity as these far-flung colonies themselves.

And, deep in his soul, he felt an approaching doom. It wasn't a fear of death. The doom he felt coming was far from that personal.

Xi Virginis is missing . . .

And his tail drew the third part of the stars of heaven, and did cast them to the earth . . .

He was Catholic, and a Jesuit, so he had always had a pragmatic view of his own faith in the face of the observable universe. He was comfortable with a God that spoke to him in allegory and metaphor, the beauty of the natural world was enough to shore his faith in God, and the wickedness of his fellow man was enough for him to believe in Satan. He believed in the spiritual world, the presence of Christ at the

Mass, and in the holiness of the saints. He believed in good
and evil.

And, deep in his soul, he felt that the *Eclipse* had crossed
into something whose evil was nearly beyond human comprehension. He could not objectify the feeling, give himself
a rational basis for it. A missing star was strange, but across
creation there were certainly things stranger. It would be the
height of arrogance to presume that man had plumbed the
depths of what was possible.

But, to Mallory, the absence of Xi Virginis was worse than
unexplained, it was malignant. It represented something ab-
horrent in the universe: the snake in Eden, Satan tempting
Christ in the desert, the Dragon from Revelation.

The more he thought of the magnitude of evil, the more he
thought he was a poor instrument to face it. He could draw on
his military experience to face the worldly issues posed by the
Caliphate. But this? He was a professor. He didn't even have a
parish. When it came to spiritual matters, he was as weak and
insignificant a priest as anyone could hope to find.

"God give me the strength to do your will," he prayed.
"And grant me the wisdom to know what that is . . ."

"Amen, brother," came Wahid's voice from the doorway.

Mallory turned, startled, to look at his fellow mercenary. "I
didn't hear you come in."

Wahid shrugged. "Who's expecting an enemy to jump them
on their own ship?" He walked over and sat down on the couch
across from Mallory. "Professional paranoia or not, it's natural
to let your guard down when you're on your own ship."

Mallory didn't like where this was going, so he changed the
subject. "So, you have the course to the next colony plotted
in?"

"Yes, if the bastard's still there."

"Yeah . . ."

Wahid leaned forward. "You ever hear of a tach-comm failing like that?"

"No."

"Neither has anyone else, you know. It's one of those things
that just doesn't happen. Hell, it took Bill to come up with a
model of exactly what happened."

"What happened?"

"You want to take a guess?"

"Huh?"

"Go on Fitz, take a guess."

"I have no idea what—"

"An Emerson field."

"What?"

"Apparently, if you do the right math, you can tune an Emerson field to imaginary wavelengths that interact rather interestingly with a coherent beam of tachyons. According to Bill, exactly the massive power sink and overload that took out our comm array and half the drive sensors."

Mallory looked at Wahid and the silence stretched for nearly a full minute before Mallory said, "That means someone sabotaged us."

"Someone with access to disable the security cams in the maint tunnel."

Such as someone whose nominal shipboard duty was security. Mallory started to stand up. "I think you might have the wrong—"

Wahid put a hand on Mallory's chest and eased him back down into a sitting position. "That news got everyone on the bridge a little upset. The idea one of our colleagues shafted us, stranding us in the ass-end of nowhere without even the ability to call for help. Now figuring out who, that's an issue. I mean we got four or five people who had access. Mosasa and Parvi can go anywhere, of course. The technical folks. Security, of course." Wahid stared into Mallory's eyes. Mallory didn't say anything for fear of betraying himself. "You're Catholic. Right, Fitz?"

"Yes."

"I figured, since I had to fetch you out of a church of all places."

"What are you—"

"You know, Dr. Dörner of all people, she remembered you when I mentioned that. Funny thing is, the guy she remembered wasn't named Fitzpatrick." Wahid leaned back and said, "Why the fuck did you screw us over like this, *Mallory?*"

"I didn't. I don't know what you're talking about."

"Hand me your gun, slowly."

"You're making a mistake."

Wahid drew his own weapon and pointed it at Mallory. "You know, Mosasa doesn't think so. Last I checked, he's in charge. Hand it over. Now."

Mallory didn't have much choice, he pulled his sidearm out of its holster and held it out butt first. Wahid took it.

"I think we need to talk—" Mallory started to say. His words were cut short when Wahid struck the side of his face with his own gun, hitting him hard enough to knock him sideways out of his seat. Mallory landed on hands and knees, spitting up blood.

"Believe me," Wahid told him, "we're going to have a nice *long* talk. But right now, you're going back to your cabin, locked up and out of the way."

CHAPTER TWENTY-FOUR

Confession

> We are defined by the secrets we choose to keep.
> —*The Cynic's Book of Wisdom*

> Every man must get to heaven in his own way.
> —FREDERICK II "THE GREAT"
> (1712–1786)

Date: 2526.05.24 (Standard)
Xi Virginis

Mallory had been confined to his cabin for nearly twenty hours, isolated from the rest of the ship, having no idea if they had tached to a new colony yet or not. During that time, his mind was divided between the enormity of what was happening in the universe around them and the enormity of what was happening aboard the *Eclipse*.

Someone had sabotaged the tach-comm and had done so in a very sophisticated manner. Mallory immediately suspected a Caliphate agent, but he couldn't force that scenario to make sense. Why would the Caliphate want to destroy the tach-comm? Did they know what happened to the star that used to be here?

Why then destroy the tach-comm and not the whole ship? Mallory knew enough to realize that the same sabotage that neutralized their FTL communications could have easily wiped out their engines, stranding them or destroying the ship long before they reached Xi Virginis.

As unstable as he had appeared on the bridge, Mallory wondered if it was possible that Mosasa had done it.

He wasn't prepared when the door to his cabin finally slid open.

He was expecting Wahid, or perhaps Mosasa himself. He wasn't expecting Nickolai. *It makes sense, doesn't it? He's the other half of the security detail.*

The three-meter-tall tiger filled the doorway, a wall of muscle and fur. Mallory wondered what kind of interrogation techniques the tiger had been trained in.

"Your real name is Francis Xavier Mallory?" Nickolai asked.

Mallory decided that he had long passed the point where Sergeant Fitzpatrick served any use, and Mallory allowed his alias to die alone and unmourned. "Yes," he said quietly.

"You are a priest."

"Yes." *The next thing you'll ask is why I blew up the tach-comm and stranded us here.* The problem was, his alias made it hard to produce a credible denial. He wondered how deep the interrogation would have to go before his denials *were* credible— or he gave in and told them what they wanted to hear.

"May I speak with you?" Nickolai asked.

"I'm not in a position to refuse."

Nickolai stepped into Mallory's cabin and allowed the door to slide shut behind him. Nickolai loomed over Mallory, seeming to take up half the volume of the cabin. Mallory could feel the tiger's breath on his face, and it took an effort of will to keep his body from reacting.

For several moments they stood on opposite sides of the cabin, Mallory staring at Nickolai, waiting for the questioning to begin. The questions, however, were not what Mallory had anticipated.

"Are you a servant of God, Father Mallory?" Nickolai asked.

The question was not rhetorical, and Nickolai used an earnest tone that was out of place in a voice that was a half-register away from a growl. Mallory nodded, "That is my calling, however weak an instrument I am. I've devoted my life to the service of God and the Church."

"The Roman Catholic Church?"

"The Society of Jesus, to be precise."

Nickolai looked away from him, as if he was considering something. After a moment he spoke. "Do you know of my faith, Father Mallory? The faith of St. Rajasthan?"

Mallory shook his head. "I studied many religions in my seminary training. But that isn't familiar."

"It is just as well. Rajasthan didn't speak to the Fallen. I shouldn't have come here." He began an awkward turn to leave.

Something in his manner, something that came across as very human despite his origins, made Mallory reach out and touch the tiger's shoulder. "What is troubling you?"

Nickolai pulled away and snarled at his touch. Mallory almost recoiled, but managed to restrain himself. Something serious was bothering Nickolai, and it was visible even through his predatory feline expression.

He faced Mallory, his cheeks wrinkled in apparent disgust. "Why should that concern you?"

"It's part of my vocation."

"I'm not human, nor part of your church."

"My God preaches compassion," Mallory said. "If you don't wish to share your troubles, stay and tell me of St. Rajasthan."

Nickolai's expression softened slightly, and he lowered his gaze. "Do you wish to hear of your own damnation, Father Mallory? My God teaches that humanity has long ago left His grace."

"My own faith tells me that I am a sinner in the eyes of the Lord. That we are all fallen, since the first man walked the Earth. And it is God's mercy alone that allows us a chance at redemption."

"God is not merciful, Father Mallory. He is cruel."

"Is this what St. Rajasthan teaches?"

"No. This is what life teaches."

Mallory listened to Nickolai as he began talking of his religion, and his life. He started slow, halting, obviously uncertain about speaking to a human. Something inside the tiger had broken down, and each sentence seemed to break down his restraint a little more. He needed to open up to someone, and obviously had needed to for a long, long time.

Apparently, it was Mallory's identification as a priest that allowed Nickolai to permit himself to talk. He said, more than once, "Even the Fallen can be servants of God."

Nickolai had been born to the House of Rajasthan on the planet Grimalkin. House Rajasthan, in addition to tracing its

descent from the founder of the primary religion on Grimalkin, was the ruling clan in the theocratic monarchy that reigned
over the planet. Nickolai had been a prince, which amounted
to nearly unlimited wealth and power. Since childhood, he had
been trained as a warrior as a form of devotion.

When Nickolai spoke of God and his religion, Mallory was
fascinated. The nonhumans that founded Grimalkin originally
had no religion of their own, though many identified as Catholic as it was one of the few human faiths that allowed for the
fact that even nonhumans could have an immortal soul.

The faith of St. Rajasthan had taken the Abrahamic religions, Christianity in particular, as a starting point, just as
Christianity had built upon Judaism, or Islam had built upon
both. The religion of St. Rajasthan grew out of the beliefs of
his contemporaries. And those beliefs were predominantly
Roman Catholic.

What divided Nickolai's faith from Mallory's was the ines-
capable fact that his ancestors *knew* their creator, humanity; a
creator that was less than divine, a creator that in some senses
was less capable than its creation, and a creator that rejected
them and subsequently declared the processes that created
them a great heresy on the level of self-replicating nanoma-
chines or artificial intelligence.

And, while Mallory was surprised to discover that many
of the books of his Bible were part of the scriptures Nickolai
knew, the interpretation was very different. In the scriptures
of St. Rajasthan, the Christian Bible was a tale of mankind
repeatedly being granted favor then falling from God's grace,
starting with Eden, the first fall and banishment from the garden, through the destruction of Sodom and Gomorrah, the
Flood, and the Israelites and the golden calf. . . .

To St. Rajasthan, the story of Christ was not one of redemption, it was another temporary reprieve until humankind made
its final wicked mistake, its attempt to take God's mantle for
itself. The scriptures of St. Rajasthan told of God finally turning away from mankind for the sin of arrogance and pride,
and as He did with Lucifer, casting the whole of man from His
kingdom.

In this new faith, mankind became the Fallen, a new Satan.
It was little wonder why the Fifteen Worlds had little contact
with human space.

It also made Nickolai's presence in the midst of the Fallen

all the more remarkable. He obviously held to these scriptures, so merely being in the presence of men would be threatening to his soul.

The only ones with any hope of God's grace were those poor instruments mankind had imperfectly molded from the clay. Untainted by man's sin, they still had some chance to attain the Kingdom of Heaven. But mixing with the Fallen threatened to taint Nickolai as well.

Nickolai explained to Mallory that he had been damned before he had ever set foot on Bakunin. He had been young and foolish, and had thought that his family was more powerful than the priests. He had thought that he could do what he wanted without fear of retribution.

He had been wrong, and in payment for his sins the priests had burned out his eyes and severed his right arm and left him to live as a beggar on Bakunin.

"Your eyes and arm?" Mallory asked.

"Yes. This," he said as he held out his right arm and extended his claws. Mallory could see a metallic glint from them. It was the only sign that the arm was artificial. "And my eyes are reconstructions, made for me on Bakunin. I am present here in order to repay the debt I incurred for them."

"But why did they punish you so harshly?"

"Harsh?" Nickolai whispered. "They allowed me to live."

Nickolai's sin was grave in the eyes of St. Rajasthan.

Man had created many species before abandoning that kind of genetic engineering. Originally, there had been thousands. The simple act of reproduction was of grave concern. One of the first commandments of the nonhuman faith was "Mate only with your own kind."

The world Grimalkin was in many ways similar to the world Mallory knew. The more secular power someone had, the more they could bend the rules of the Church. Humanity might have fallen, but they had no monopoly on corruption and hypocrisy. As long as the transgressions of the royal family were kept private, the priests ignored them.

So at first, when Nickolai was involved in a dalliance with a servant, a panther-black feline who was not only a different social class but a different species, no one overtly cared as long as the affair was discreet. Young royals often bedded servants

before the family chose a mate for them. Such liberties never
lasted long and were of little consequence.

Both truisms proved false in Nickolai's case. The affair
lasted months, when weeks were more typical. It became obvious to everyone in House Rajasthan that things had passed
beyond the venting of adolescent lust. Nickolai had entangled
himself in an impossible romance, and his family had to intervene, taking his lover and sending her to an estate on the
opposite end of the planet while they rushed him into a hastily
arranged marriage.

Nickolai's family had acted too late. Cross-species fertility was very low, but hybrids were possible, and by the time
his family relocated his panther lover, she was already heavy
with his cubs. When his children were born, the public evidence of Nickolai's sin was too great for the priests to ignore.
In the Church's eyes, the sterile crossbreed infants were
abominations.

Nickolai's children were drowned before he knew they existed while their mother was flayed alive.

"But you, they let live?"

"I am a scion of House Rajasthan. Executing me would
have been problematic, preferable as that might have been."

*That, and allowing him to live with this on his memory. That
was as much punishment as taking a limb.* Mallory couldn't
help but think that St. Rajasthan was correct in the near-Gnostic interpretation of his species' creation. Man had aped
God and made creatures in Man's image, and in so doing bequeathed the creatures the worst of human nature.

*God save Nickolai, and God forgive the men responsible for
his existence.*

"I'll pray for you, Nickolai."

Nickolai shook his head slowly. "Save your breath, priest. I
am as damned as you are."

"You hold no hope for forgiveness?"

"I have done worse. I've taken the instruments of the Devil
into my own flesh. I have prostituted myself to the Fallen."

"What comfort can I give you, then?"

"In my faith, it is a matter of honor to bear witness for your
sins before a servant of God. We do this in anticipation of our
final judgment. I wish to face that moment with dignity, and
not as a frightened cub mewling for its mother."

"My faith has a similar ritual. Do you wish me to consider this your confession?"

"If that is what you call it."

"Yes, I will do so, my son. And I will still pray for your soul."

Nickolai paused, but eventually he said, "Thank you."

"Is there anything more that you wish to confess?"

Nickolai nodded. "Yes. And I need your forgiveness more than God's."

Nickolai knew that he was going to die, and it would be sooner rather than later. He knew it as soon as the *Eclipse* shuddered in response to the aborted tach-comm signal. Even if the ship was still functional, they were cast into the void, alone in every possible sense of the word.

All that was left was to make his testimony to the closest representative of God he had available, the falsely-accused priest. The fact that he was human might have been better than talking to his own kind. Testifying his sins to the Fallen was humbling, and damned as he was, God was still scourging him for his arrogance.

St. Rajasthan had preached that pride was first among sins, the cause of Lucifer's fall and likewise cause of Mankind's fall. Nickolai had been guilty of more than his share.

When he finished talking, he watched the man that until recently he had known as Staff Sergeant Fitzpatrick. He still was unable to read subtle human expressions, but Nickolai could tell from the long time that it took Father Mallory to respond that he had made an impression.

"You sabotaged the tach-comm." It wasn't a question, or an accusation, just a flat statement.

"Yes."

"Do you know why?"

"I was paying a debt. Perhaps I owe too much."

"But you don't know why this Mr. Antonio wanted you to do this?"

"No. He told me many things, but never his own reasons."

"What *did* he tell you?"

Nickolai told the priest what Mr. Antonio had told him, of how he knew that Nickolai would be selected for this mission, and what he knew of Mosasa's nature and history. He told Mallory Mosasa's story from the old pirate's first life on the *Nomad* and his discovery of the AI cluster on the derelict *Luxembourg* to Mosasa's final co-option by the AIs he kept. He told how Mosasa and the four other AIs were involved in the founding of Bakunin, and how their social engineering kept the anarchic planet stable in the face of the Confederacy, and how that same social engineering used Bakunin as a fulcrum to destabilize and ultimately destroy the old Terran Confederacy—the long deferred goal of the Race that had built the AIs, the last pyrrhic victory of the Genocide War.

He also told the priest how the single Race AI forming Mosasa's brain was the only one of the five to survive to the present. Two had been lost during the Confederacy's collapse, two more when Mosasa returned to the home planet of the Race.

Mallory shook his head. "This man who hired you knew all this?"

"This is what he told me."

"Do you know if any of this is true?"

"I cannot say—" Nickolai was interrupted by static over the PA system.

Mosasa's voice came from above. *"I can."*

Mallory looked up at the ceiling even though the speakers were invisible. "Mosasa? How *dare* you!" Nickolai was sensitive to the scent of human emotion, and the room was suddenly ripe with the smell of rage. Mallory's fists clenched so hard that his forearms vibrated.

"Father Mallory—"

"This was a *confession,* you mechanical atrocity. Do you have no respect—"

"Stop testing me, priest."

"Mosasa!" Mallory yelled to the ceiling. Mosasa didn't respond. "Mosasa!"

"Father Mallory?"

"Please forgive me, I didn't realize—"

"I did," Nickolai told him.

"You knew he would be watching?"

"He is a creature of Satan. He lives in wires, not in flesh. He sees though every camera on this ship, hears through every microphone. I knew he would hear this."

"Why?"

"We will die soon, and I needed to make my final testimony."

CHAPTER TWENTY-FIVE

Apocrypha

When you ask if you want to know, you don't.
> —*The Cynic's Book of Wisdom*

The trick to leadership is keep moving forward, even if you're wrong.

> —BORIS KALECSKY
> (2103–2200)

Date: 2526.05.24 (Standard)
Xi Virginis

For the first time in a century, Mosasa felt as if he was floundering. The holes in the fabric of his world were growing with each passing moment, opening into unknowns vast, deep, and larger than the sparse data that surrounded them. For the first time in 175 years, he moved without any idea of what the consequences of his actions might be. The data flowing to him now was practically nonexistent, and he was fumbling blindly.

Worse than the missing star, which was completely unexpected, was the sabotage. There was no way he had to make the act comprehensible. He had imprisoned the Vatican agent, Father Mallory, because he couldn't propose any other logical alternative.

But Mallory hadn't destroyed the tach-comm. He couldn't have. The purpose of having him here was as a data conduit back to the Vatican, and through them, to the non-Caliphate powers. Having a communication channel was primary to Mallory's mission, and their situation now, with the loss of the comm and the power drain, was as dire for him as it was for Mosasa.

But once the crew had discovered Fitzpatrick's was an alias, Mosasa had to confine him. The dynamics of the crew allowed no other action if he desired to keep a stable equilibrium.

But the very fact that the comm had been sabotaged meant that the equilibrium Mosasa perceived was illusory. And if he couldn't truly understand the dynamics within the confines of the microscopic universe of the *Eclipse,* how could he trust what he saw of the universe outside it?

Even if Kugara and Tsoravitch found EM signals leaking from the colony at HD 101534, those were eight years old. How could he be certain that, when they tached into the system, the world, the star, would still be there?

His isolation from the data streams that fueled the awareness of his machine half allowed uncertainty to grow within him like a cancer. Before leaving Bakunin, he could see the turbulent flow of society, economics, politics as easily as ripples in a pond. . . .

Now he was so blind that it was becoming hard to credit that he had ever seen at all. The longer he was isolated from the flow of information, the larger his blind spots became—infecting scenarios he had already plotted. He could no longer even be sure of decisions he had made before this point.

Mosasa stood, locked inside his own cabin, funneling every data channel on the ship through his internal sensors. He obsessively watched every millimeter of the *Eclipse* trying to fill the void of not-knowing. The flow of data traveled through his mind like windblown leaves through an abandoned city.

Included with the pathetic trickle of data were feeds from every security camera and microphone on the ship. A universe of information so small that even the shell of his human consciousness was aware of the content. He saw the crew working on making the *Eclipse* ready for the next jump. He saw the scientists at computers trying to make sense of the impossible absence of Xi Virginis. He saw Nickolai enter Mallory's cabin.

Nickolai?

At first Mosasa was confused at the interaction. The nonhuman now formed the security detail with Kugara, so he was one of four people who could open the seal on Mallory's cabin. But he didn't have any reason to interact with the traitor priest. . . .

Then he heard the talk and realized the ritual nature of the discussion. Nickolai had a legitimate fear that they wouldn't survive the journey and had sought Mallory out because of his status as a priest. It all made sense.

Except, in Mosasa's analysis, Nickolai wouldn't be driven toward such a ritual exercise unless he believed he carried some weight of guilt. Guilt beyond the circumstances of his exile, which was largely neutralized by a sense of pride and determination.

Mosasa realized what that guilt had to be before Nickolai actually confirmed it.

How did I not see it was him? Why did I not see?

Mosasa realized why. Trying to see the tiger's own personality next to the overwhelming force of belief, tradition, and ritual was like trying to see an asteroid whipping across the surface of a star. His own motives were practically invisible, and if Nickolai's employer had the sense to use the forms of his culture to direct his action, manipulate him . . .

The very things that made him a perfect candidate for Mosasa—the nonhuman perspective, the predictability of his indoctrination, his ingrained prejudices—those same things made Nickolai the perfect spy.

Can someone have targeted me so well?

When Nickolai told Mallory of Mosasa's origin, Mosasa began to truly feel fear. He revealed the story he had told Tsoravitch, but he didn't stop. He told of how the five AIs had helped stabilize Bakunin in the face of the Confederacy, and how they had helped lead to the Confederacy's downfall, leaving three AIs surviving.

Until then, the data was all what Mosasa would have considered discoverable by some human agency. But the tiger didn't stop there.

Nickolai's employer, Mr. Antonio, had revealed things that no human should have known. Mr. Antonio had told Nickolai what had happened at Procyon, when Mosasa had returned to his homeworld.

Long before there had been a Tjaele Mosasa, Race AIs had been used in the covert war the Race waged on Earth. When the intelligence agencies on Earth had discovered the Race's social manipulation, they had managed to capture the Race's own devices and had begun understanding how to use them.

By the time the Genocide War with the Race had erupted

in full force, the United Nations had intelligence ships like the *Luxembourg* equipped with ranks of alien AIs. Near the end of the war, the *Luxembourg* had been neutralized by a Race drone weapon that then guarded the captured ship for a Race salvage team that never came.

The pirate Tjaele Mosasa had revived five of those AI units, including the brain from the drone weapon. Mosasa had used the devices to gain an insurmountable business advantage and amass a considerable fortune. Eventually, the living Mosasa had traded his fleshy body for a cybernetic one, gifting his thoughts and memories to one of those AIs.

The AIs, however, never forgot their purpose. Autonomy alone was not enough to undo the directives the Race had programmed into their being. Free of human constraint, they had worked for their ultimate goal; the fall of the human political hegemony and freedom for the Race who had been confined to their planet by automated battle stations since the end of the Genocide War.

The quintet of AIs had helped stabilize Bakunin, preventing a founding of a state, causing a weak point in the Terran Confederacy. The five of them could mimic humanity enough to interact, infiltrate, and directly implement the kind of social engineering the Race had designed them for. In the end, after centuries of work, they had achieved their goal. The Confederacy had collapsed.

Of the original five, only three had survived to depart for Procyon and the Race homeworld; Mosasa of course; Random Walk, who had once been formed of two AIs and was now half himself and somewhat unstable; and Ambrose, a hybrid of flesh and cybernetics who had smuggled one of the five brains into the heart of the Confederacy.

Only Mosasa survived to depart the Race homeworld and return to Bakunin, the only one to see the truth and remain willing to survive.

The Race was dead.

All of them.

What mankind had done, in trapping them on the surface, was force them to revisit the racial reluctance toward direct physical violence. The taboo that had rendered them so weak against mankind.

But that taboo had existed for a reason: it had been the only thing that had allowed the Race to survive as long as it had. As soon as enough of them had cast aside such reservations, the results had been catastrophic. Cities lay in ruins, entire eco-systems had been devastated, and a planet that had been only marginally habitable to begin with had become sterile.

The surviving half of Random Walk had simply shut himself off. Either the sacrifice had been too much or he couldn't accept the loss of what had been their reason for existence, their reason for acting at all. Without their creators, there was no purpose left to serve.

Ambrose, on the other hand, went insane. He attacked Mosasa, accusing him of allowing this to happen. His attempt to strangle Mosasa proved fruitless—Mosasa's neck was completely cybernetic, while Ambrose's half-human body was still in large part flesh and bone. Failing the attempt to kill Mosasa, he ran off, screaming that he would find someone, some member of the Race still alive.

But their creators no longer existed, and Mosasa returned alone.

Mosasa was speaking though the PA system to Mallory, shouting, before he was quite aware of what he was doing. *No, this is bad, I don't act impulsively, I don't act on fear . . .*

He sealed the door to Mallory's cabin and cut his transmission even as Mallory responded to his interruption.

Mosasa reined in his desperate emotions and contacted Kugara, the only security team he had left. She looked up from a console on the bridge, surprised at Mosasa's disembodied voice. "Kugara, take Wahid and go to Fitzpatrick's cabin. Take Nickolai into custody."

She looked around, as if searching for him. "Nickolai, why?"

"He confessed to sabotaging the tach-comm—"

"What?"

"He is in the employ of unknown forces and is unpredictable. I want him restrained in a cabin, and I want you guarding him during the jump. Tsoravitch will handle your station."

"But—"

"*Now!* I'm not going to allow this to delay our jump!"

Less than a minute after Mosasa had said, *"Stop testing me, priest,"* The door to Mallory's cabin slid open. Nickolai turned and saw Wahid and Kugara standing on the other side.

"Yeah, I was fucking paranoid." Wahid shook his head and

gave the two of them a thin little smile. He pointed the brick of a gamma laser at Nickolai's midsection. "Do me a favor," he said. "Unholster that slug thrower and toss it over here."

Kugara pointed her needlegun at him and looked at him with a hard expression that told him nothing.

Nickolai knew that he could easily take out the two threats in front of him, disarm them before they fired, if he cared to. But what point was there to it? He could take over this ship, and then what? Drift until the abyss claimed him?

Better to accept his fate with what little dignity he had left.

He took Mr. Antonio's gun from its holster and gently tossed the weapon to Wahid. It felt blasphemous, watching one of the Fallen catch the icon.

"We're going back to your cabin, tiger-boy." Wahid told him.

Nickolai nodded.

Wahid grimaced and gestured with the gamma laser. "Move it."

The two of them allowed him to take the lead, and as he passed them he noted his last chance to overpower both of them before getting shot.

"What the hell were you trying to do?" Wahid said from behind him. "Why didn't you just strap a bomb to your chest, you morey fuck? It'd be quicker."

Nickolai didn't answer. For himself, he knew the answer. If Mr. Antonio had told him the consequences of his sabotage, he never would have agreed. Suicide was the ultimate cowardice, and while Nickolai might have been damned for many things, cowardice would never be one of them.

But why did Mr. Antonio wish Mosasa dead in this particular fashion? Nickolai was a warrior and had access to the whole mission. Had he been given simple instructions to eliminate the AI—or even the whole crew here—he could have done so. Even if there was some doubt about the location of Mosasa's AI brain while they were planetside, once they were on the *Eclipse* the nature of interstellar communication meant that the thing had to be on board.

Nickolai went quietly to his cabin. Kugara stepped in behind him. "Arms behind you."

"What?"

"Do what she says," Wahid told him.

Nickolai complied. He felt her grab his wrists and start wrapping something around them. He glanced back, and saw her pulling a roll of emergency sealant tape around his limbs, the same material that you'd use to seal tears and punctures in an environment suit or a ship's hull in a pinch. It bonded to itself and other synthetic materials instantly.

"My arm . . ." Nickolai began to say. But it was pointless. Did it matter that the tape binding him permanently fused to the pseudoflesh of his arm?

His real arm felt the warmth as the tape bonded to his artificial limb.

"Legs," she told him.

Nickolai complied, bringing his two digitigrade feet together. She started taping below the ankle, and stopped a little below the knee. Nickolai now stood, immobile.

Kugara grabbed his shoulder, spun him so he faced the door, and pushed. His back hit the wall next to his cot.

With his back to the wall, Kugara pulled one last strip of the sealant tape across his neck, attaching him to the wall.

Wahid shook his head. "You think you got him tied up enough?"

"If he wanted to, he could have disemboweled you five times while we came up here. One thing I learned in the DPS, if you arrest a morey, you *restrain* them. They were engineered to tear you apart hand-to-hand."

DPS?

Nickolai stared at her, wondering. The DPS was Dakota Planetary Security, the secret police, and the main enforcers of the planetary government. Kugara wasn't a typical refugee from Dakota, of which there were plenty on Bakunin. She was what the refugees were running *from*.

He suddenly wished he had asked her more about her past.

"Well you certainly have restrained him. Though you might want to strap his legs to the wall, too, unless you *want* his neck to snap if something goes funny with the jump."

She turned around and ran several strips of tape across his torso, waist, and legs. "There," she said. "Happy?"

Wahid shrugged. "Hell, I'd shoot the furball right now if it wasn't for the fact our boss will want to talk to him after we tach into civilization."

Kugara subvocalized so Wahid wouldn't hear, but Nickolai could make out her saying, "*If* we tach into civilization."

"Speaking of which, we got thirty minutes if Mosasa didn't push back the jump." He looked Nickolai up and down. "You're okay sitting on this particular package until after the jump?"

"Yeah, the bridge is short-staffed as it is. Get back up there."

Wahid shut the door and Kugara leaned against the wall opposite Nickolai. "This is going to be long half hour," she said.

Nickolai was inclined to agree.

Parvi sat at the pilot's station fifteen minutes before jump and ran though all the scenarios she could think of. Having power reserves so low made her uncomfortably aware of the differences between a fighter pilot and a tach-ship pilot. If something went wrong with the *Eclipse,* there was no bailing out. They didn't have the resources to compensate for any navigational errors.

Worse, they were taching completely blind, with half the sensors gone from the drive systems. Those were the last line of defense for the engines if they had the bad luck to tach into the wake from another ship. They allowed the engines to modulate and keep things from overheating or blowing up like the tach-comm.

Of course, that was unlikely to happen. While another tach-ship could cause a disturbance that could affect their engines, such wakes were short-lived and propagated only a few AU. They would have to tach right on top of another ship in astronomical terms for it to be a worry, sensors or no sensors.

Much worse was the more likely prospect of more sabotage.

We've gone over the ship with every diagnostic we have; everything's in working order . . .

At eleven minutes to go, Wahid came in, holstering a gamma laser and sat himself at the nav station. He started going through the checks without a word to anyone else.

Tsoravitch sat at the comm station, not that the *Eclipse* had much communication left. She had slipped into the seat when Mosasa had ordered Kugara and Wahid to restrain the tiger. For all the distaste Parvi had for Nickolai, she still had yet to

wrap her head around that one. *How the hell did Mosasa's pis-
sant little adventure rate* two *spies?*

Were there people back home who *knew* what they'd find
here?

Eight minutes. The bridge was disturbingly silent. As a precaution, Mosasa had ordered all the nonbridge crew to the
cabins which doubled as escape pods, just in case.

Of course, if it came to that, the people on the bridge were
screwed, along with Bill, trapped in the cargo hold by his massive environment suit.

Mosasa came in, completing the bridge crew. Just the four
of them, Parvi, Tsoravitch, Wahid, Mosasa. Rotating in the
central holo glowed a schematic description of their route.
Eight light-years to the closest colony and a habitable planet.

If it is still there.

Six minutes and the door to the bridge slid shut with a
pneumatic hiss. Parvi watched the display as her readout on
the ship's systems showed each compartment isolating itself.
In a few moments each segment of the ship with people inside
was on an isolated life-support system.

Just in case.

"Bill's given the computer models the all clear," Wahid
said.

Three minutes, and Mosasa looked at Tsoravitch. "Give the
bridge feed to the rest of the ship."

Tsoravitch nodded, tapping a few controls, releasing a small
snap of static across the PA system. Parvi did the final checks
on the power plants to the tach-drive and heard her voice
echo around her when she said, "Drive is hot. The systems are
on-line and within acceptable ranges."

Wahid tapped a few controls and the schematic on the main
holo stopped its subtle rotation and began to glow slightly
more solid. "Target fixed. Course window opens in one hundred seconds."

Tsoravitch nodded and stared at her own readouts. "No
problematic mass concentrations within five AU." Sweat
beaded on her forehead. Parvi wished Kugara was at her
station.

Parvi asked the rote question, "Okay to fire the tach-drive?"
This time, the question didn't seem so rote.

"Yes," Mosasa said mechanically.

Wahid announced, "Sixty seconds to window."

"Our tach-drive is on auto," Parvi announced.

Wahid's voice sounded distressingly calm. "Twenty seconds to window. Fifteen seconds to last-chance abort."

There was little calm in Tsoravitch's voice. There was a little vibrato in her voice when she said, "Mass sensors still clear."

"Ten seconds. Five to commit," Wahid said. "The drive is committed. Three . . . Two . . . One . . ."

For the first time in her life, Parvi physically felt when a ship fired its tach-drive.

CHAPTER TWENTY-SIX

Relic

Nothing moves a State quicker than fear, and nothing a State fears so much as change.
—*The Cynic's Book of Wisdom*

What governs men is the fear of truth.
—HENRI FRÉDÉRIC AMIEL
(1821–1881)

Date: 2526.5.29 (Standard)
Salmagundi–HD 101534

In the month since the egg landed, a small village of temporary buildings had sprung up around the egg. Most of the buildings had been moved from one of Robert Sheldon's mobile logging camps.

It wasn't long after Frank and Tony landed and took Flynn into custody before the first of the portable outbuildings arrived. They shoved him into one of the barracks buildings shortly after it landed. The building was little more than a large modular container that could mate with the bottom of a large cargo aircraft. The skin was heavy and well-insulated enough to survive a wildfire in the dry season. The people inside would survive, too, if they didn't run out of air.

The structure could house twenty or thirty people. But it also made a fairly good impromptu prison. Even without cuffs or a restraint collar, Flynn would have had an impossible time trying to get out of it without someone opening the armored, fireproof doors for him.

Fortunately, they removed the cuffs within the first forty-eight hours, and provided relatively decent food and clean clothing. But they wouldn't remove the restraint collar, and the comm units were completely isolated inside the new camp's network. He could call security, and that was about it.

At least it had something of an entertainment library, since it was designed to support a working camp, though about half was porn and 90 percent of the rest was thinly disguised work-safety tutorials. Flynn and Tetsami spent most of their time playing chess against each other, and replaying variants of the same conversation.

"I don't believe that thing is here." Tetsami rubbed her neck, mirroring the placement of the restraint collar. "I don't even remember how far we are from Bakunin here—"

"One hundred and fourteen light-years," Flynn said. "You've told me often enough." He moved a rook on the small comm screen.

"Those things don't have tach-drives. It's been traveling for a couple of centuries at least."

Flynn shook his head. "I find it hard to believe that such an advanced society would settle for sub-light speeds. Your move."

"The Proteans were a little weird," Tetsami agreed, castling. "Very much kept to themselves. But I think the word 'seed' covers what they're doing, propagating themselves."

"That slow?"

"Think of the energy a tach-drive requires for each jump. That thing is what, three meters long? They get it to speed and coast and it requires the same energy to get here as it does to get to the next galaxy. All it takes is time."

"A *lot* of time."

Tetsami shrugged. "I can see a little of their perspective. I mean, back when I first heard of them, I never expected to be in lockup with my great-to-the-seventh-power grandson one hundred and seventy-five years later, waiting for him to move something."

"Yeah." Flynn moved a knight behind his rook and smiled. "Check."

"Christ on a unicycle," she muttered at the screen.

"One hundred and seventy-five is one thing, millions is another—"

"Millions of what?" Robert Sheldon asked from the doorway to the barracks.

Flynn blinked Tetsami's image away and looked at his boss. The man had sandy hair gone half gray. He had four glyphs on his forehead, and like most of the people with four or more, he had a somewhat flat voice and an expression that Flynn thought of as mechanical.

"Years," Flynn said without any explanatory comment. "Are you going to explain why Ashley security has locked me up for nearly a month?"

Sheldon walked up, shaking his head. "You're an impulsive young man." He sat down on the bunk opposite him and next to the comm still showing the game in progress, almost precisely where Tetsami had been sitting. "And naive as well, even for knowing one of the Founders."

Flynn squirmed a little inside at Sheldon's language. He never liked the way people used the word "knowing" someone to refer to what Flynn had come to see as ritualized psychic cannibalism. Having Tetsami with him as a separate person made the way it was *supposed* to happen, the merging of personalities, seem so *wrong*. Who was the hell was anyone to deny her her own identity, or that of any of the millions of people archived in the Hall of Minds? Everyone looked at Flynn the singleton as having no respect for the ancestors of Salmagundi, but was it more respectful to see their ancestors as little more than an undifferentiated data source? No more individuals than they were themselves?

Flynn did something he usually avoided in conversation; he looked Sheldon in the eye. "Why did you have me locked up here?"

God, his eyes look dead.

Please, Gram, let me talk to him.

"Mr. Jorgenson, you did not have authorization—"

"That's bullshit." Flynn stood up, and the move was fast enough for the restraint collar in his neck to send a warning pulse that fired a nasty wave of numbness down his legs and arms. "There was an impact in my survey zone, and it turns out that I had some particular knowledge—"

"Any investigation needed to be cleared before—"

"So I broke a regulation; you don't *imprison* someone for that. Sure, fire me. *But what the fuck is this?*"

Sheldon reached up and clasped Flynn's hands, lowering them. Sheldon's hands were cold and hard, like being touched by a headstone.

"Lower your voice, son. I am here as a favor to your father."

"My father's dead."

"Sit."

"Are you going to explain—"

"Sit!" Sheldon's voice changed, making Flynn realize that, up to this point, Sheldon's voice had still retained a trace of human warmth and character to it; characteristics that evaporated in the single command.

Flynn sat.

"Mr. Jorgenson," Flynn noticed this time that Sheldon seemed uncomfortable using the address. "Do you realize what would happen to you if I did not intervene on your behalf?"

"My behalf?"

"Quiet!"

Flynn shut up.

"You may know one of the Founders, but you seem to have forgotten why they came here."

No, Bobby, Flynn remembers just fine. It's you assholes who decided to misinterpret and take things out of context—

Gram, not now.

Sorry.

"Contact with the decadent cultures beyond this planet is a grave assault on our purpose here. A violation of the commandments of our Founders."

"But—"

"Please listen." Sheldon placed his hand on Flynn's shoulder and almost sounded human. "The thing that makes us what we are, our communion with the past, *that* would be the first thing they take away from us."

Inside Flynn's head, a quiet voice whispered to itself, *Christ on a crutch, I'm going to be sick.*

"I told you what this is. You *know* it isn't some Confederacy artifact."

Sheldon shook his head. "You are young and haven't known enough of our history to understand. We cannot allow this kind of disruption to our way of life. It matters little where this thing is from."

"Disruption?" Flynn shook his head. "This thing is from a culture that's so far beyond the Confederacy the Founders escaped that it's nearly inconceivable. Just understanding the smallest bit of it could—"

"It could destroy everything we've built here."

"What?"

"This arrival is too dangerous to be made public knowledge. By association, the Triad has decided that you are too dangerous as well. I intervened, out of respect for your father, to spare your life."

Flynn opened his mouth, and nothing came out.

"You see the gravity of this now? The Triad was prepared to erase you, completely, without archival—"

Flynn could care less about the Hall of Minds. But the thought that the Triad considered killing him—the current, flesh-and-blood person—just to avoid some sort of "disruption," that was worse than appalling. But, thanks to his boss, Flynn had stayed alive, under house arrest in the barracks by the fallen seed.

"Why are you here?" Flynn asked.

"I wanted you to know that this will be over soon." He looked into Flynn's face. "When things return to normal, I want your promise not to make any waves. Don't make me regret helping you."

"I—"

"Please, Flynn. Your father was my friend."

Do you even have friends? Flynn thought.

He didn't trust himself to speak, so he just nodded.

Sheldon let go of Flynn's shoulder and said, "Thank you." As he got up to leave he glanced at the comm screen and said, "White has mate in three moves."

Flynn heard Tetsami whisper inside his skull, *What are they going to do?*

Date: 2526.5.30 (Standard)
Salmagundi–HD 101534

The next day, they had an answer.

Flynn and Tetsami watched as three tracked vehicles rolled across the clearing in the direction of the seed. The vehicles were ocher metal, squat, and carried large cylindrical power plants on their backs.

"What the hell are those?" Flynn muttered.

"Mining equipment," Tetsami said, an invisible presence next to him. *"We had dozens of the things when we founded this misbegotten planet."*

"Mining equipment? What for?"

"Those things have the highest energy gamma lasers on this rock, unless someone's gone and started building hovertanks I don't know about."

"Oh." Flynn paused. He finally said, "Fuck."

The closed-minded bastards of the Triad were going to destroy the seed. Forget that it was the space-borne equivalent of their sacred Hall of Minds, it was *disruptive*.

Worse, Flynn knew that the debate that probably had raged in the Triad and the upper echelons of the Salmagundi leadership in the last month—and, good lord, how those old farts loved a debate—wouldn't even have touched on the moral question of incinerating a million minds or the progeny of an unimaginably advanced civilization. What would have taken a month of debate would have been the logistics of how to incinerate the damn thing.

"We should do something," Flynn said.

"Do you mean that?"

"What are you asking, Gram?"

"Do you really want to get into more trouble then you're already in?"

Flynn stopped speaking out loud. *"If you got some other option in mind, let me know."*

"I might be able to hack us out of this box—"

"Damn it, Gram! We've been locked up here for weeks. Why didn't you say something earlier?"

"I need you to give me our body."

" . . ."

"And stop calling me Gram."

On some level Tetsami didn't blame Flynn for being pissed. When she had been young and stupid, she had the same problems with people trying to do what was best for her. She knew, on some level, the kid never really understood it when she told him how lucky he was. When Tetsami was his age, she could only wish for the kind of stability Flynn had. Back in the bad old days when she was a software hacker on Bakunin, she had barely scraped by from job to job, the last one nearly killing her.

No one ever shot at Flynn Nathaniel Jorgenson. His job didn't carry a risk of frying his brain on the wrong side of a black security program. He was able to take things like food, clothing, and shelter for granted. Until the damn Protean egg-thing showed up, all the kid ever had to worry about were the occasional stare and harsh language. Even those were low key compared to what Tetsami had gotten because of her ancestry from Dakota.

For all his angst about being the oddball, he didn't understand that just the fact she was here meant that his society accepted him. He might not be a model citizen by the bizarre rules that had evolved on Salmagundi, but he wasn't really an outcast.

Not yet.

She was still regretting opening her big mouth when she felt Flynn withdraw. She blinked, and it was her body that was blinking. She reached up and touched the restraint collar with Flynn's hands.

"What are you going to do?"

"Get you more trouble than you deserve," she said, her voice now sounding like the one in her head. "Now shut up, we don't have a lot of time."

Fortunately, she and Flynn had traded off enough that wearing his body wasn't nearly as disorienting as it could have been. In her own mind it had been seventeen years since she had a female body, or had been shorter than Flynn's 200 centimeters, her 150-year-old mental image notwithstanding.

She felt around the edge of the restraint collar and found the hatch on the control panel.

"What're you doing? You force that thing, it'll zap us—"

"Sonny, zip it."

She kept her finger on the panel as she walked over to the bathroom. She would have liked to run, but the collar *would* zap them if she moved quicker than it wanted her to. She wasn't planning to give the thing the excuse.

In the bathroom she faced the mirror. She had seen Flynn's lean face, tattooed brow, and sandy hair often enough—but it still was startling to her when she was actually in control. When she was just along for the ride, somehow the reflection wasn't her.

The restraint collar was a thin toroid wrapping their neck, just loose enough to slip a finger underneath. Buried inside were some sophisticated electronics, position sensors, and a little Emerson field generator; the kind that, when it activated, interfered with human neural impulses enough to knock the victim out.

Fortunately, since bio-interfaces were universal on Salmagundi, she didn't have to worry about the damn thing being lethal. Back in her days in the Confederacy, some people didn't bother to calibrate these things to accommodate folks with wired skulls—a badly adjusted one could've cooked their brain. Techs here knew better.

That didn't mean they didn't have blind spots.

Flynn's face smiled back from the mirror as his stubby fingers and blunted nails managed to pry open the hinged cover on the restraint collar's control panel. There was little to see underneath, just a little socket to receive an optical cable—

"What are you . . ." Flynn's mental voice trailed off as she turned and pulled a panel off the ceiling.

The fact was, for all the security people Sheldon had camped here, no one on Salmagundi really understood security. Because of the culture they developed, one that bred a conformist personality into nearly every citizen, they had all but forgotten that people like Tetsami had ever existed. Crime, such as it was, tended to be petty and personal. When these people went to the Hall of Minds, they didn't choose singletons like Tetsami to receive. They picked people who had status in living memory, or those who held the memories of a dozen others whose skills spelled their own advancement.

Tetsami, however, had a skill set that was largely forgotten about, and as such, inadequately protected against.

Behind the ceiling panel were several cables, one leading to the hidden camera that watched the interior of the barracks itself. Once she made sure that the bathroom door was locked, she reached up and grabbed the data cable. She pulled one end out of the camera socket, disconnecting it.

Flynn didn't vocalize anything, but she felt his apprehension. *"Don't worry,"* she thought at him, *"Your Gram knows what she's doing."*

She reached into the recess and pulled the cable free from another camera, pulling two three-meter lengths of optical cable into the bathroom. She knew Flynn's worry. Both cameras go dead, and he had the amateur worry that security would fall on them at that very moment.

Tetsami knew well, however, human nature being what it was, the drone manning the camera feed would make the easy assumption that it was a technical fault, which it sort of was.

The security spud would waste a few minutes on technical diagnostics trying to troubleshoot the problem before calling the live guards to check things out. If they were in luck, there wasn't any alarm on the feed—this wasn't a prison after all— and the spud on duty was involved in something less boring— like a game of solitaire or watching the mining lasers—and wouldn't even clue into the missing feed for awhile.

Even though she had kept her skills on ice for years, she was sure she wouldn't need more than a minute or two. Especially since, unlike at her old stomping ground, the connections for wide-band optical data feeds on this planet were somewhat standard.

One cable she jacked into the port on the restraint collar. The other one she set into the small concave bio-interface set in Flynn's neck. The connection found the magnetic socket just under the skin and set itself with a click that resonated in Flynn's jaw. She could sense his growing panic as she connected. Bad memories, she thought. But she couldn't spare the time for reassurances now; he was going to have to hang on for the ride.

The data line she connected to wasn't designed for a bio-interface, so it took several interminable seconds to sift through the sensory garbage that flooded her brain, random flashes of color, icy pins and needles racing across skin, white noise, a floral chemical smell that combined with the taste of rotten bananas. All sense of her body was gone, except for the vague feeling of Flynn's body beginning to hyperventilate. The panicked gasps for air were far away and slow, her time sense had begun to telescope seconds into minutes.

Most people on Salmagundi, even those trained to use a biojack for something other than ancestor worship, would have probably drowned in the chaos of sensation, lost without a prefab software shell to guide them.

Not her.

Tetsami programmed a custom shell on the fly. Not as quickly as she could have in her prime, but Flynn's brain still had some of the Tetsami genes, and that gave her something of the edge she used to have. In moments she had wrapped her senses in a simple blue shell that gave everything but her eyes and the kinesthetic/tactile impulses from her hands back to the nonvirtual world.

She heard and felt Flynn's body breathing real time, and felt the sweat on his skin. Fortunately, he seemed to be calming now that the world had ordered itself around her.

There was security on the data line, but only on the human-interface level. The pipe for the video was wide open and un-encrypted, and let her in without even asking for a handshake. In seconds, she was in the heart of the security network, pulling up every I/O signal she could identify.

Instantly, she pulled up visuals on every camera linked up to the security system, surrounding her point of view with visual feedback from every camera tied to the security net.

In the small arena of Sheldon's temporary camp, she was briefly omniscient, surrounded by views of every building, every vehicle, down to the security guard sitting in a shack watching his holo monitors. It was either Frank or Tony—she had never bothered to keep those guys straight. Frank/Tony was just now noticing the loss of two video feeds from Flynn's barracks.

She paused and addressed a question to Flynn's consciousness. *"You still want to do this?"*

"Yesss . . ." Flynn's mental voice seemed slow and echoey, as if he wasn't quite caught up to the speed Tetsami was processing. *"Look what they're doing . . ."*

Tetsami could see one of the monitors showing the mine equipment taking position. They fired bursts in turn, low power, but nearly overloading the optics of the cameras watching them; probably calibrating things before they went all out.

Unfortunately, the machines weren't on the security net like the cameras; otherwise, Tetsami might have been able to stop them from where she was.

Frank/Tony was raising an alarm, but only four guards' worth. The cameras outside Flynn's barracks showed no disturbance and gave a full 360 of the area. The doors were sealed and unmolested. As she expected, they were assuming a technical glitch and just sending the guards to make sure.

She sent her attention down the cable that connected to the restraint collar on Flynn's neck. That connection had some rudimentary security on it, but not enough to even slow her down. In a fraction of a second she was in a much smoother shell program provided by the collar itself; with a few choice menu selections, she had drilled down to the collar's built-in development environment; left over from whoever designed and built this thing.

She didn't know the physics of an Emerson field, but the

collar had software that allowed her to design the equations for a new field geometry as well as ditch some of the safety protocols as far as power consumption went.

While she jury-rigged the collar, she kept a point of her awareness back watching the cameras. Slowly, to her anyway, four guards walked up to the door of Flynn's barracks. They opened the door just as she finished rigging her collar.

The quartet showed their lack of understanding of basic security principles by all walking inside at once.

Outside the virtual world, she heard someone shout, *"Jorgenson!"*

She shouted back, "I'm in the fucking bathroom."

She waited until she heard pounding on the door to the bathroom. *"Get out here, now!"*

The door to the barracks hung open, and the guards weren't visible anymore. "Here I come," she shouted back with Flynn's voice, then she fired the restraint collar.

CHAPTER TWENTY-SEVEN

Resurrection

The universe does not go out of its way to conform to our expectations.

—The Cynic's Book of Wisdom

Mind moves matter.

—Virgil
(70 bce–19 bce)

Date: 2526.5.30 (Standard)
Salmagundi–HD 101534

The mind was damaged.

It remembered the egg's short journey. It remembered launch +228.326 years, when it had called upon the inhabitants of the egg to decide on a course of action. It remembered launch +229.528 years when it changed course to bring it close to Xi Virginis. It remembered closing on the disintegrating star and understanding that it was no natural phenomenon.

It remembered the cloud.

It remembered fighting wave after wave of hostile sentience as the cloud tried to envelop the egg. It remembered the panic as the living minds within itself understood that something was trying to destroy the egg. It remembered the horror its passengers felt when they realized that the same thing in the cloud that tried to digest the egg had already done so to a whole solar system, one that had once been inhabited.

The mind remembered its charges ordering the egg to change course for the nearest inhabited system. Spreading a warning of what they faced was more important than any individual's survival.

It remembered using all the energy reserves of the egg to fight free of the cloud and change course.

It remembered, but only in terms of the raw data. The sense of experience was missing. It knew what had happened, could replay the recorded data, but it wasn't connected to it anymore, as if it were another mind entirely.

That was frightening, and that fear was the first emotion the mind remembered ever feeling. More frightening was the lack of data regarding planetfall, and the horrible absence of other minds in the egg. Sometime between the escape from the cloud and now, the egg had used up almost all of its energy reserves. It had gone dormant and had struck its new target without even the mind's awareness to guide it.

Since then, the egg had absorbed enough energy from its environment to revive the mind. But the mind was deaf and blind and alone. The sense array it remembered from its disconnected memories was gone. The hyperawareness was gone, leaving only a dim sense of arrival as its sole connection to the world outside the surface of the egg.

The mind examined itself, and found something as dismaying as the absence of senses and the confusion of emotion that overwhelmed it. The mind was no longer whole. The damage, first caused by the cloud, then caused by the near-exhaustion of the energy reserves in its escape, had left the mind with a tiny fraction of processing capability. The mind was blind because it no longer was capable of interpreting the wide array of senses the egg provided.

Unlike the host of other minds the egg had carried, the mind itself had survived only because of its nature. It had been distributed across the whole of the egg; no one piece of it could be identified as the mind's brain. So even as crippled as the egg was, there was still enough of the mind left to become aware.

But not enough to be whole.

Not enough, the mind realized, to even be the same entity that had efficiently protected the egg from danger for over two hundred years; the entity that could have selflessly piloted the egg for a million more. The mind inside the egg realized that it was no longer that mind. Too much was gone, and, in a wave of despair, it knew that too much was *added*.

Tiny fragments of the egg's passengers had merged with the mind's psyche. Their presence manifested in waves of emotion that the mind had never been designed to feel. Every decision the mind tried to make found itself blocked by unfamiliar feelings of fear, grief, loss . . .

And *anger*.

The field the restraint collar generated was typically programmed to point inward at low power, screwing up human neural impulses and usually leading to pain, temporary paralysis, and unconsciousness. But those characteristics were all software. With the right program the same device could, for instance, become the equivalent of the Emerson field generators that were used to protect the body from energy weapons.

So, with the right programming, the restraint collar didn't need to direct its field inward, or at low power.

When Tetsami fired the thing, instead of blasting her and Flynn unconscious, it pulsed its effect outward, at max power, draining its charge in about a fifth of a second and, if the software was correct, in a radius that covered a good 75 percent of the barracks trailer.

Before she disconnected, Tetsami left a virus on the network that would kill every camera connected to it within a few seconds, starting with the one pointed at the barracks door.

She pulled the cables and stood in the bathroom again.

"See," she whispered, "I know what I'm doing."

"That was impressive."

"No." She yanked open the now unlocked, dead, and uncomfortably hot restraint collar and let it fall to the bathroom floor. "That was Salmagundi security being less than impressive."

She took a step back and opened the bathroom door. One of the guards flopped down across the doorway, drooling on the floor. The other three were crumpled, one by the door, one on a bunk, one nearly on top of the guy blocking the bathroom door. Two had nosebleeds, but all seemed to be breathing.

The guys weren't heavily armed, basically just shotguns and rifles. She stepped over the guys in the bathroom doorway and bent over to pick up a shotgun off the floor.

"What are you doing?"

"Jumping Jesus on a pogo stick! Why do you think I kept asking if you were sure about this? We're criminals now, kid. Wrap your head around it." She checked the load on the shotgun. It had a full load, ten shots worth of caseless ammo.

"Who are you planning on shooting?"

"Anyone who tries shooting us, for starters." She ran to the open doorway and looked around for more guards. She didn't see any in evidence, and with the cameras dead, she was probably unobserved. The air smelled rank with smoke and ozone from the mining lasers.

Yeah, we wanted to do something about that, didn't we? she thought privately. If the things were automated, she could pinpoint the control center and get in to hack—

Over to her right, where the Protean egg/seed was, there was a violent flash of purple light and a blast of hot air. Hot embers and gravel shot by the doorway and Tetsami had to duck inside to avoid being pelted. When the light faded, a nasty mechanical whine filled the air.

"What the hell?"

"We're too late. They blew it up."

Tetsami wasn't so sure about that. She ducked outside to look in that direction.

They hadn't blown it up.

The matte-black ellipsoid hadn't moved, but the ground around it had. It now floated at the center of a ten-meter-diameter crater that was nearly hemispherical. The perimeter of the crater encompassed the area where the heavy mining equipment had been. Of the mining lasers, or the tons of earth that had been underneath the Protean seed, there was no sign. As Tetsami watched, the near-mirror surface of the hemispherical crater crumbled as the soil began collapsing back into the hole.

"Somehow," Tetsami whispered, "I think it didn't need our help."

The mind focused on the anger, a stable rock in the swirling maelstrom of emotion that filled its empty world. Whatever was responsible for the destruction of Xi Virginis—whatever intelligence was behind the cloud that had damaged the egg—that entity had to pay. The mind didn't know how, but it clutched to that single desire.

The mind would see that entity cease to exist. It would erase it from the face of the universe. It would destroy the thing on an altar of the mind's righteous fury.

With the anger, came focus and a dim awareness of the universe outside the egg.

The mind could not use all the egg's senses at once, but it realized that if it focused on a narrow array of the sensory capability, it could see, after a fashion. Despite the subjective eternity in which the new mind had floated in the dark womb of the egg, it had in fact only been 2.38 seconds since the mind had revived.

As slow as the new mind moved in comparison to the old, it still had time to assess the presence of the mining lasers pumping terawatts into the egg. That energy had been absorbed and used by the lowest autonomic functions of the egg to repair the physical damage. The lasers themselves, as pure energy weapons, posed no threat to the egg itself.

However, the mind knew their purpose. The beams were an attack.

Like the cloud.

The mind reacted before it even understood the ramifications of the act. It extended one of the quantum fields enveloping the egg out to a diameter past the extent of the mining lasers. Space rippled, tore, and reformed in a shell around the egg, letting out a flash of light as a sphere of matter ten meters in diameter was twisted *elsewhere*. The energy required to destroy the lasers was barely balanced by the release of energy caused by the vanishing matter.

What have I done?

The mind did not understand its own actions. It had acted without thinking and had done something violent, aggressive, and probably counterproductive. Reviewing the record of the incident, it could see that human beings had piloted the lasers.

It had been under no risk, but it had killed nine people.

The anger leeched out of it as it wondered what it had become.

Tetsami heard Flynn's panicked thought, *"What the hell IS that thing?"*

Tetsami started taking slow steps backward. She knew what it was, conceptually, but seeing the thing there, a matte-black hole in reality hovering over the crater, ignited a visceral fear. One nasty thought in her direction, and both she and Flynn could cease to exist.

"Freeze!" someone yelled at her. "Drop the shotgun!"

Tetsami glanced behind her and saw a trio of Sheldon's security goons leveling more shotguns at her. She spread her arms, holding the gun by the barrel to keep them from freaking out and shooting her.

"I'm not your biggest problem," she said.

One of the other guards had already come to that realization. He was looking past her, where the egg/seed was. "Fathers save us," he whispered.

Klaxons sounded throughout the compound. Someone in the stellar security staff must have just realized that they were down three mining lasers and one prisoner.

The first guard decided to stay on task, though. "Drop the gun, Flynn, and get on the ground. I *will* shoot you."

"Do what he says, Gram."

"Don't rush things, kiddo."

She did her best to remain calm and move slowly. No need to add to the chaos. She slowly knelt down, arms out, still holding the shotgun by the barrel.

"I said, drop the fucking gun!"

She carefully laid the gun next to her as she lay facedown on the ground.

One of his friends yelled, "Holy shit!" and started pumping shells toward the crater.

A distraction was a distraction, and Tetsami used it to roll away into a drainage ditch next to one of the prefab buildings. More shots exploded above and behind her, but none came near her. She scrambled out of the mud and crawled up to the lip of the ditch to look over back toward the crater.

The floating black seed was leaking. Black poured out of it, spilling into the crater below it, oily tendrils that seemed almost tears in the fabric of space.

"Why the hell are they shooting at it?" Tetsami whispered.

"Do you see the same thing I do? It ATE those mining lasers."

"Yeah, and a shotgun shell is going to do what, exactly?"

The three guards must have come to the same conclusion, as the firing ceased. They stood, facing the crater, as the egg dissolved into a viscous pool in the crater.

"Did they shoot a hole in it?" Flynn sounded confused.

Tetsami shook her head. Whatever was happening, it was not that simple. The black pool in the crater was no longer the black nonstuff that had made the egg. She could see reflective highlights and ripples. There was *something* there.

No. Tell me you aren't going to do that, she thought as one of the guards knelt down and poked the substance with the barrel of his shotgun.

Black tendrils shot up the barrel, crawling across the man's arm before he could react. His two companions stumbled back as a net of shiny black threads wrapped every surface of his body. He didn't move, aside from a tense vibration. His eyes bulged as the net seemed to tighten, the threads forming it thinning.

For a moment it gave every appearance that the net was going to crush the man alive. Then the threads constricted and pulled *into* his flesh. His head snapped back and he released a strangled gurgling sound. His body shook as the tendrils withdrew along his arm and down the shotgun.

He collapsed backward as the last black filament let go of the gun barrel. He fell into a fetal position on the ground, hyperventilating. The parts of his skin that Tetsami could see bore a fine webbing of welts that corresponded to where the fluid web had penetrated.

"What the hell was that?"

"I don't know," Tetsami answered Flynn. She inched along the ditch on her stomach, away from both the crater and the guards. The guards, at least, were paying her no attention. Their focus was divided between dragging away their fallen comrade, and keeping an eye on the black-filled crater.

The black began rolling out of the crater. The liquid spread out, over the lip, in a strangely geometric webwork.

The guards ran, pulling the welt-covered guy to his feet so he could stumble along after them. Tetsami pushed herself to her feet, but she felt a thundering panic in her gut that wasn't wholly her own.

"We got to get out of here!"

"Damn it, Flynn, that's what I'm doing. Let me drive!"

However, Tetsami hadn't done quite enough to accommodate Flynn's emotions. She felt him desperately grasping for control as she tried to run up out of the ditch. Their nervous system spasmed from two sets of conflicting motor instructions, and both of them took a running face-first tumble into the ground. Gravel dug into Flynn's face and tore the meat of his left arm though his shirt.

He barely realized that Tetsami had completely withdrawn as he tried to get on his feet. When he did, pain shot through his ankle all the way up his leg, intense enough that his leg collapsed when he put weight on it.

He fell on the ground again and looked behind him at the advancing black spiderweb. It was as if the personification of the Abyss was reaching for him. The strange order of the tendrils reached the first of the prefab buildings, and it crawled up the walls of the building as if it was some non-Euclidian vine.

Flynn flipped on his back and started pushing away from the advancing web with his good foot. The advancing web held to some strange geometry and, as it closed, he saw that within the holes formed by the black tendrils, the regular web pattern was repeated by thinner tendrils. Even closer, and he saw that inside the smaller webs, there was even a thinner pattern repeating.

The ground changed under the fractal net. Irregularities smoothed out, and the muddy surface turned uniform and smooth. Flynn only managed to keep ahead of the web because its advance slowed. The web enveloped two large prefab buildings. Flynn glanced and saw a dozen people running for the perimeter fence.

It seemed like a good idea, if he could get to his feet.

Now that the web's advance seemed complete, he tried to push himself upright. But his ankle collapsed under him with a blinding flare of pain.

Shit! I'm sorry, Gram.

Just shut up and crawl.

Flynn crawled, putting distance between himself and the web as fast as he could manage. It didn't feel nearly fast enough.

He glanced back over his shoulder and saw the enveloped buildings moving, folding in on themselves. He stopped and stared, because they weren't collapsing. Instead the walls fragmented and each piece slowly turned on an impossible axis, as if each building was a puzzle box being manipulated by an unseen giant. Also, like the web itself, the motion seemed to replicate itself on smaller scales, each rotating fragment itself formed by dozens of smaller rotating fragments. The material of the buildings changed character from dull utilitarian metal into something lighter and more reflective.

Like a cloud, or a snowstorm—

Damn it, Flynn, move your ass!

Someone had decided that two outbuildings turning into

rolling cloudbanks constituted a threat. Shots came from the direction of the perimeter fence, some striking too close for comfort.

"Don't those idiots realize how well that worked the first time?"

"As you point out, they're all too much the same person. They keep making the same mistakes."

Flynn pushed himself to try and put at least one building between him and the shooters. As he did, he saw something streak through the air toward the closest alien building/cloudbank.

A missile? Flynn thought.

The missile sailed through it, and buried itself in the surrounding woods before exploding. Flynn felt a hot wind as the roar of the explosion rolled past him.

The hole in the cloud healed itself.

Then the air was alive with missile tracks. Flynn curled into a ball and covered his head as explosions began echoing across the compound. "Shit! Shit! Shit!"

Heat burned his back and he could smell his own hair smoldering. His ears rang with the almost continuous roar of the missile strikes. They rang until he could hear nothing else but the ringing.

He stayed like that until he realized the ground was no longer shaking, and his back wasn't on fire. The ringing persisted, and he whispered, "Hello?"

He could hear his own voice. He wasn't deaf.

Flynn rolled over and faced what should have been the sky. It took several moments to make sense of what he did see. Above him, he saw the underside of a semitransparent hemisphere two or three hundred meters in diameter covering most of the central portion of the temporary camp, a dome centered on the point the egg had landed.

The skin of the hemisphere shimmered various shades of blue as missiles from the outside collided with the semitransparent shell. The weapons broke soundlessly against the perfectly curved skin in cascades of blue-and-violet-tinted flames and smoke.

"Gram?" Flynn whispered.

"Yeah, I see it, too."

"What is—" Flynn's question was interrupted by a low voice that didn't sound human.

"It is coming."

Flynn lowered his gaze and faced a man, or something in the shape of a man. The speaker stood under the shimmering blue dome, in the midst of what had become a landscape of fractal crystalline geometry.

The man was naked, hairless, and his skin was shiny midnight black, showing no fine detail. He stared at Flynn with featureless black eyes and, when he spoke, he flashed teeth that were perfect black mirrors.

"It is coming here," he said.

CHAPTER TWENTY-EIGHT

Harbinger

Fear the new, but fear more the obsessive grasp on the old.
—*The Cynic's Book of Wisdom*

There comes a point where the debate ends and you must pick up a gun.

—DATIA RAJASTHAN
(?–2042)

Date: 2526.5.30 (Standard)
Salmagundi–HD 101534

The Great Triad had been in continuous session for thirty days. Representatives from each Triad from each region across Salmagundi were here; over a hundred men and women, carrying the memories and experience of tens of thousands, representing the whole of the planet.

Alexander Shane, the oldest human being here, bore fifteen tattoos across his brow; more than anyone else living. Seven of those marks represented people who had borne at least as many when they had lived. The combined wisdom of a thousand of Salmagundi's past citizens informed every word he spoke, every move he made. As the senior among them, he was the one to preside.

He sat, with the others at a great circular table in one of the many great rooms in the Ashley Hall of Minds. There were other halls where they could have met, in other cities, but the authority of the Great Triad came from their persons, and not their location. Ashley happened to be closest to the reason they met.

Alexander watched the debate, contributing little of his own wisdom. He felt the pervasive panic as much as anyone else here. The presence of the offworld object threatened everything that their ancestors had built here.

"We are relying on the words of this singleton Flynn Jorgenson as to the nature of this invader," one of the younger women spoke. She only had ten tattoos across her brow and her hair still had hints of brown in the midst of the silver. "It could be prelude to an invasion."

"We've seen no evidence of this," someone countered.

"No," she replied. "But Mr. Jorgenson's statement is at odds with the facts. The trajectory of this object does not lead back to the old systems."

"It had been traveling for centuries," another woman said, "and could have maneuvered any number of times before entering our space."

"Where it came from is irrelevant," a man agreed from across the room.

"It is only irrelevant if it is not a harbinger of a greater threat," she told them all. "Need I remind you where its trail points back to?"

"Coincidence," someone muttered.

"No evidence at all—"

"You are looking for problems where there are none—"

"Once it is destroyed—"

Alexander let the dialogue shoot back and forth without enforcing any rules of order. A limited amount of chaos was necessary so that when the final consensus was reached, every member could feel their voice as having been part of coming to it.

Usually, though, consensus was quicker in arriving. Rarely did the members' opinions diverge on anything of substance. However, this session was as anomalous as the event they debated.

What concerned the woman, and a substantive minority of the Grand Triad membership, was the fact that the review of what records existed showing the object's entry into the system revealed a path that led from the direction not of the of Confederacy, but of a star that had vanished from Salmagundi's sky a decade ago.

Alexander remembered the event from three different points of view: his own and two more that had been bequeathed to him from the Hall of Minds since then. It had been a subject of interest and debate in Salmagundi's scientific community a decade ago when Xi Virginis winked out of the sky. Then, the debate in the Grand Triad had been whether to expend the resources to investigate. There had even been a half-dozen advocates for building a tach-ship to send to the Xi Virginis system.

Alexander remembered the debates. They had lasted for nearly an entire season, and in the end Salmagundi's essentially insular nature won out. The star had not exploded, and the scientists accepted the idea that something had simply caused it to burn itself out.

The thought that the object Flynn Jorgenson described was somehow a remnant of that event was disturbing. Enough that members of the Triad who, like Alexander, had been present during that first event were dusting off the rhetoric from the earlier session as if the decade-old incident were still being debated.

The Great Triad had a memory broad and deep. No member forgot any slight, any error, any insult—to the point that every word spoken had such a ponderous history associated with it that it was wondrous that anyone spoke at all.

The debate launched into a tangent about Xi Virginis, and Alexander was about to use his authority as the chair to rein in the arguments when the comm on the table in front of him began flashing. He picked up the device and hit the receive button. The device was muted, so the caller's voice was translated to text that silently scrolled across the screen in front of an image of the woods southeast of Ashley.

The text jerked, stuttered, and mistyped some words, and Alexander could almost hear the panicked excitement of the caller embedded in the fragmented text.

"WE LOST THE MINGLASERS. OBJECT EMITTED SOME SORT WEAPON. DESTROY TWO OUTBUILD-INGS MULTIPLE MISSLE HITS."

The text kept scrolling past an image of a ruddy translucent dome shedding the effects of multiple missiles.

"Order!" Alexander snapped at the room before him. The arguments broke off instantly, and a sea of elderly tattooed faces turned toward him.

"There has been a development," Alexander said. He then piped the feed from his comm to the room's main display screen and unmuted it. The flat, shaky images came from someone's handheld comm. As the view of Mr. Sheldon's camp filled the giant curving screen above the meeting table, another missile trail sliced the right side of the image in half, ending in the skin of the hemisphere. The hemisphere beyond the rolling explosion turned a deeper red, almost black, as smoke and flame lapped across the surface.

The voice accompanying the image was shaky. "The thing has taken hits from every missile we have. I have no idea how, but it has a mass-capable Emerson field."

Alexander spoke to the comm in his hand, "Can you please repeat the damage?"

The speaker took a deep breath and said, "We lost the mining lasers and crew. It . . . ate . . . two of our outbuildings closest to the impact site. The shield you see there is two hundred seventy-five meters in diameter."

"Has it grown? Moved?"

"No."

"Then conserve your weapons. Let us consider it."

"Did you hear me? The mining crew is gone. We don't even have bodies."

"Conserve your weapons."

"Yes, sir."

Alexander remuted the comm and looked out at the Grand Triad. "It seems," he said, "we face a larger threat than we anticipated."

The debate erupted again. This time Alexander waited only until the first obvious lines of argument played themselves out. When he spoke, he was the first one to mention nukes.

It was admittedly drastic, but he was protecting their whole way of life.

PART THREE

Prodigal Son

More individuals are born than can possibly survive.
—CHARLES DARWIN
(1809–1882)

CHAPTER TWENTY-NINE

Test of Faith

Sometimes you get a miracle. Don't expect another one.
> —*The Cynic's Book of Wisdom*

It is not necessary to hope in order to undertake, nor to succeed in order to persevere.

> —CHARLES THE BOLD
> (1433–1477)

Date: 2526.6.3 (Standard)
750,000 km from Salmagundi–HD 101534

For the first time in her life, Parvi physically felt when a ship fired its tach-drive. A very slight physical jerk as all the indicators on the console in front of her soared toward the red. None showed dangerous levels, but the drive came out of the jump hotter than it should have. The one damping coil that they'd gotten back up to 75 percent capacity was much too narrow an aperture to cool off the drives. The indicators were still edging upward.

Parvi held her breath until, one by one, very slowly, the readouts started going back down.

"Isn't that a beautiful sight?" Wahid said, and Parvi silently agreed.

Then she realized that he wasn't talking about the fact that the *Eclipse*'s engines weren't going to melt. She looked up and saw a blue-green planet filling most of the holo above the bridge console.

"I have radio traffic all over the place," Tsoravitch announced. "Video, audio, data traffic. Our sensors are completely saturated. I have commsats, and at least half a dozen major population centers on the coast of the main continent."

Parvi saw Mosasa smiling out of the corner of her eye.

"We made it," Wahid said over the PA system. "We fucking made it!"

Parvi looked at the planet hanging in the holo as she asked, "How close are we?"

Wahid was grinning, "A fucking bull's-eye. Point-seven-five million klicks out."

"Shit," Parvi stared at the meters on the console in front of her.

"What's the matter?" Wahid said.

"We're too close," Mosasa said, the smile leaving his face. He turned toward Parvi. "How long before the drives cool to safe levels?"

Parvi shook her head. "I don't know. At the current rate, twelve hours, but we only have one damaged coil working. Venting continuously that long, it may start to degrade or fail entirely."

"How much of a problem are we talking about?"

Parvi leaned back. "Worst case, if the coil fails completely, the drives will still go cold in about forty-eight hours all by themselves. Being hot that long increases the chance of an eventual failure. We're also vulnerable if someone operates a tach-drive too close to us. That will cause the drives to heat up again."

"Damn."

Mosasa turned to Tsoravitch. "Our first priority, make contact with the surface. We can at least warn away outgoing tach-ships and request them to send someone up for repairs. Bill? Are you on-line here?"

"Yes."

"Can you do anything to help cool the drives?" Parvi asked Bill.

"We unfortunately lack the equipment. We did everything possible before the jump."

"What kind of danger are we in?" she asked. "What if someone does tach in on top of us?"

"A high-efficiency twenty light-year jump arriving within a two-million-kilometer radius will severely damage the drives. The effect drops off exponentially as the jump distance and drive efficiency decreases."

"I just wish there was an AU or two between us and the planet," Parvi said. "How the hell did we get that kind of navigational error?"

"Most probably a significant concentration of dark matter directly between here and the former location of Xi Virginis which caused an unexpected space-time curvature. I will be able to give a more thorough analysis once I've been able to review the telemetry data from the jump."

"At this point," Mosasa said, "Our main concern is contact. And once the drives are cold, I want preparations for landing."

Date: 2526.6.3 (Standard)
Salmagundi–HD 101534

Alexander had never seen the Grand Triad gripped by such chaos. Only yesterday they had come to grips with the alien invader southeast of Ashley. Despite the objections of the Ashley Triad and the area lumber interests, Alexander had finally gotten consensus around the idea of using their limited nuclear arsenal to eliminate the threat from the invader. The site was far enough away from Ashley that they should be able to avoid dangerous levels of contamination.

Even in a worst case scenario, moving the city's population was preferable than allowing this alien infection to take root here.

But even as they had begun discussing the logistics of the strike in their ponderous manner, they faced another invasion.

On the massive holo screen facing the conference room an image showed a blunt-nosed tach-ship, a hundred meters long, hanging in space less than a million kilometers from Salmagundi. It was close enough that the satellite observatory feeding the image could pick out the rough patchwork of gray-and-brown repairs forming most of the ship's skin.

Inset over the image was a transmission showing a redhaired young woman with an unmarked brow. The sound was muted, but Alexander could read the captions on the looped transmission, "This is the Bakunin-registered tach-ship *Eclipse*. Our drives are hot and we request a safe zone around our position for the next twelve hours at least. We need assistance in repairing our damping coils, and would also like clearance to land within the next forty-eight hours."

Next to the young woman's transmission was telemetry data gathered by the satellites when the *Eclipse* tached in, as well as transponder information from the ship itself that, predictably, corresponded with the woman's assertion that the ship was registered on Bakunin and was named the *Eclipse*.

Most problematic was the telemetry data, which showed a point of origin corresponding to Xi Virginis.

Just like Flynn's Protean artifact, Alexander thought.

"We cannot let this craft land," someone contended for the dozenth time.

"And how do we prevent that?" someone else countered.

"They may have information about the alien craft," a third person said. "We need to direct them to a site that can be contained, and sterilized if necessary."

Alexander looked at the *Eclipse* on the monitor. Was this the prelude to an invasion? It was clearly not a military vessel, and the sensors they'd been able to train on it showed that the ship's drives *were* hot. They were not trying to hide their presence, and they weren't being subtle about their transmissions. It was only a matter of time before some civilian received the *Eclipse*'s transmissions.

And, worse, it wouldn't be long before someone started a dialogue.

It would be bad enough to have unfiltered alien information leaking into the carefully balanced society of Salmagundi, but Alexander had faith in the ability of their culture to absorb such shocks. It might actually be a good thing if the Great Triad had to deal with some public discontent. It might improve their flexibility.

What concerned Alexander, and what made this a grave event, was the possibility that information from Salmagundi might leak out to the Confederacy. Salmagundi's culture was based on technologies that the rest of humanity believed heretical, and history made it seem unlikely that the Confederacy, or its successor, would suffer the Hall of Minds to exist.

Of even more concern was the presence of the Protean artifact. That technology was even more antithetical to the Confederacy Alexander's ancestors had fled. The Confederacy had rendered entire planets uninhabitable to destroy the kind of self-replicating nanotech that the Proteans represented. An attack might only focus on the alien artifact, but Alexander couldn't count on that.

For all they knew, the *Eclipse* might only be the vanguard following the Protean artifact, determining how thoroughly they had been contaminated by its contents. In which case, simply destroying them might, in fact, provoke exactly the kind of devastating attack he wanted to avoid.

"We need to let them land," Alexander said when one of the debating factions asked for his opinion. "If they put down in an isolated area, we can better control their contact with the population. More important, we can control the information they gather about us."

Date: 2526.6.3 (Standard)
2,250,000 km from Salmagundi–HD 101534

"Engage the tach-drive."

A chorus of "Yes, sir!" came from the bridge. The *Voice*'s sisters may have preceded her by taking these huge leaps into the void, but the edge of excitement in the crew's acknowledgment showed that, for the men here, they may as well have been the first.

For all the excitement in the air, the actual jump was anticlimactic. A short series of warning klaxons, a brief flicker as all the holo displays on the bridge reflected the instantaneous changes rendered in the universe outside and in the systems of the *Voice*. Even so, a subdued cheer went up on the bridge that was even shared by the command staff. The *Prophet's Voice* had made it. It had tached a distance quadruple that of any prior drive design. Admiral Hussein didn't join in the cheering, but he did smile. For a people whose history was tainted with humiliation and oppression, this vessel represented a high point. It was *here* when the Caliphate surpassed the rest of humanity.

The bridge crew moved quickly from congratulations back into routine. Things had gone smoothly. They were in orbit around the star HD 101534. During the nonevent of firing the tach-drive, the universe had moved on for a little over twenty-eight days standard.

A blue planet hung in the holo display, their destination.

Is that right? Admiral Hussein thought to himself, reviewing the ranging readout next to the planet's display. It was the first sign that this mission was diverging seriously from the plan.

"We are confirmed two-point-two-five million kilometers from target," called an ensign from the nav station repeating what the numbers on the main display told them. That was a serious navigational error; the *Voice* was supposed to tach in at least two AU from their target. The *Voice*'s tach-drives were so powerful that they could be dangerously disruptive to any native tach-drives that might be active close to the planet. They had come in way too close.

It was almost certain, at this range, that the residents of this planet had already detected their presence. If not simply by a visual contact, the *Voice* was close in enough for the energy spike of their arrival to be detectable on the surface of the planet.

It took thirty seconds for the other shoe to drop. An NCO at the comm station announced, "We have a distress beacon at oh-point-seven-five million kilometers from target."

Admiral Hussein rubbed his temple. This was a worst case scenario, their arrival damaging some native vessel. At best, it was a horrifying diplomatic misstep; at worst, it could be interpreted as an act of war.

Captain Rasheed ordered the communications officers to attempt contact with the distressed ship and assess its situation.

The main holo changed from the planet to show a blocky cargo ship tumbling through space with ragged holes where much of the drive section should have been. Clouds of debris and venting atmosphere followed the craft. The ranging read-out showed the craft at a little over a million kilometers from the *Voice*, almost directly between them and the planet.

God help us all.

"Sirs, I have a transponder signal. It's standard encoding, and identifies the ship as the *Eclipse,* owned by the Mosasa Salvage Corporation, registered on Bakunin."

"Bakunin?" Hussein repeated along with Captain Rasheed.

"Yes, sir."

The crippled vessel was over ninety light-years away from anywhere it had a right to be. Everything had suddenly become a lot more complicated.

CHAPTER THIRTY

Seraphim

Sometimes your allies are chosen for you.
          —*The Cynic's Book of Wisdom*

Survive first, all else comes after.

                                        —MARBURY SHANE
                                          (2044–*2074)

Date: 2526.6.3 (Standard)
750,000 km from Salmagundi–HD 101534

A little over thirty minutes after Kugara taped Nickolai to the wall, Wahid's voice came over the PA system. "We made it! We fucking made it!"

I guess that means the colony, not to mention the star, is still here. She allowed herself a small measure of relief and looked across at her prisoner.

She hadn't wanted to be the one to guard Nickolai, but her years as an enforcer for the DPS had given her the training to handle someone like him. She was probably the only one in seventy light-years who could. Mosasa was certainly aware of that.

Mosasa's voice followed Wahid. "We are currently approaching a planetary orbit, and we will commence landing procedures as soon as our drives are cold. That will be approximately twelve hours."

Twelve hours? The engines must have suffered a bigger hit than I thought.

"As a precaution," he continued, "anyone who is not bridge crew, please remain in your cabins unless absolutely necessary."

She was stuck here for twelve *hours*?

Kugara shook her head. She stood in the corner of the room opposite the wall where she had secured Nickolai. If their situation hadn't been so dire, it might have been comical. Kugara's restraints on Nickolai looked almost like a DPS academy hazing.

But not really.

Nickolai hadn't been beaten, dragged through the slush, or taped to a freezing metal pole. She briefly remembered participating, dousing vodka on the skin of shivering plebes and igniting it, watching the blue flames ripple across naked skin before burning themselves out. The alcohol content was never quite enough to do permanent physical damage, but the poor bastards training to be part of the DPS didn't know that, and with their heads taped to the pole, they couldn't see the vodka burning, allowing them to imagine the worst.

Kugara remembered laughing at the screams when the victims lost the ability to tell cold from heat, and felt the sting of ice on their arms as if it was a branding iron.

She stared at Nickolai and thought, *And you called me an Angel?*

Kugara didn't like the universe's sense of humor.

The room was silent for a long time before Nickolai finally spoke. "Why haven't you asked me?"

Why didn't I gag you? "Ask you what?"

"Why?"

Kugara shook her head. "I don't care. I'm a hired gun, and I'm not paid to care about your motives. Not unless Mosasa orders me to do an interrogation. I don't think you want that."

There was another long silence, and then Nickolai said, "I apologize for what happened on the observation deck."

"What?" For a moment Kugara was confused. Things had happened too quickly for her to fit Nickolai's confession—the little Mosasa had passed along—into her memory of events on the *Eclipse*.

It struck her much harder than it should have when she realized what his apology meant. "That's when you rigged the tach-comm!"

It was all crap, from their first meeting onward, a way to distract the one member of the crew that had any training to deal with him. He probably knew enough about her history with the DPS to know exactly how she was going to react when he brought up his damn furry theology.

"I—" Nickolai started to say.

"Shut up. Don't say another word, or I ignore the fact Mosasa wants you in shape for questioning." She could easily picture herself slowly tearing bits of flesh away from him, not even for the sake of gaining information, just to teach the tiger a lesson. She was no stranger to that kind of procedure; she had broken people with little more than a pocketknife.

And she hated him for making her remember that.

Over the next couple of hours, the PA broadcast updates; no communication from the planet; drive continuing to cool down; other ship's systems nominal. About three hours into the silent ordeal, Tsoravitch, who'd taken over the role of bridge communications officer, announced, "We have a transmission from the planet. They're giving us communications and landing protocols."

"About time," Kugara whispered. "We've been calling them for three hours."

"Maybe they don't want us here." Nickolai said.

"What?"

"They came out here for a reason. Maybe they don't welcome visitors from their past."

Kugara opened her mouth to say something, but she stopped herself. It was a possibility that should have been patently obvious to any native of the Fifteen Worlds. Dakota certainly wouldn't welcome an unannounced visitor from anywhere, Grimalkin wasn't much better.

We may be lucky no one is shooting at us.

Twenty minutes later the whole cabin shook.

"What the hell?" Kugara said, trying to keep her feet as the ship violently vibrated. Emergency klaxons sounded, and the cabin lights began flashing red. *That's the signal for a hull breach!*

Parvi's voice came over the PA, "Everyone to the nearest lifeboat/cabin now! We've had a critical overlo—"

Her voice was cut short by the sound of a massive explosion that threw Kugara toward the ceiling. As she fell back down, she could feel the weight of her body sucking away, telling her that the gravity manifolds were failing. When she hit the floor again, she bounced lightly off.

The lights in the cabin died, plunging both of them into

complete darkness. The PA no longer spoke, and for a few moments the only sound in the cabin came from the two of them breathing.

"Were we attacked?" Nickolai whispered.

"I don't know," Kugara answered. She fumbled for a handhold in the dark and found one next to the door. She pulled herself against the wall. Through the wall she could feel vibrations that made her stomach churn. *Something overloaded the power plant,* she thought. *Emergency power should be returning shortly . . .*

As if in response to her thought, a dull red light came on above the doorway. Then it began flashing rhythmically.

"Oh, shit," she whispered through clenched teeth. She opened the console next to the door and confirmed her fears.

"What is it?" Nickolai asked.

"Shut up!" she yelled at him, as if there was anything she could have done at this point. The emergency systems had fully taken over. The cabin was sealed. She tried to get the comm to the rest of the *Eclipse* responsive, but the cabin's connection to the rest of the ship was dead.

The display, unresponsive to her touches as it was, helpfully showed a schematic of the cabin's systems. Power and life support were now on a fully closed loop, helpfully illustrated by two animated arrows pointing at themselves. Six colored blocks connected the square cabin schematic to the rest of the schematic of *Eclipse.*

One of the blocks turned from green to yellow to red. The small block on the screen broke in half. At the same time a pop like a rifle shot resonated through the walls of the cabin.

"Kugara?" Nickolai asked.

The first block faded from red to black as the next block broke in half. Another rifle shot shook the walls of the cabin. She shook her head.

"Kugara?"

"It's the escape sequence," she whispered. Another shot resonated through the skin of the cabin. This time the vibration didn't fade away completely. Holding on to the wall next to the display, Kugara had the morbid sense of being trapped inside a loose tooth. "This cabin's about to be blown free from the rest of the ship." Another rifle shot and the vibrations were noticeably larger in amplitude. "If there's even still a ship on the other side of this door."

She pushed off the wall and grabbed the edge of the cot, the only piece of furniture in the room. She braced her feet on the floor and lifted, folding it into the wall, slamming it shut.

Another rifle shot; this time the sound of twisting and grinding metal accompanied the amped-up vibrations.

She pushed off and grabbed the handle of a yellow-and-red outlined panel in the wall. She pulled it open, and a padded bench with crash webbing unfolded. She pulled herself into it and spared a glance at Nickolai, bound to the wall. She muttered, "Shit!" as the last rifle shot echoed through the cabin.

The shot was followed by a thundering roar, and suddenly they were no longer weightless. Kugara felt herself sinking deep into the padding beneath her as the whole cabin shook. The floor of the cabin was now the wall behind her, and Nickolai was secured sideways on the wall to her left.

She stared at Nickolai and could see the strain on the sealant tape as his body pulled against it. His head bent toward her and slightly away from the wall, and his lips curled back in a snarl revealing his massive teeth. His head shook with the vibrating cabin. The cabin jerked, and Kugara winced in sympathy as his head slammed back against the wall.

"Nickolai!" she called out to him, the shaking cabin giving her voice a manic vibrato.

He grunted something and shook his head. She didn't know if he was telling her he was okay or that he wasn't. A shiny thread of saliva and blood trailed from his lips to the wall/floor where Kugara had strapped herself in. The vibration stopped, but the acceleration continued.

"The engine's going to burn until the computer thinks we're clear," she yelled above the sound of the engine. The acceleration wasn't painful, two, maybe two and a half gees. But it kept going. And going.

God, how much delta-V does this lifeboat need?

She didn't know the full specs on the *Eclipse*'s lifeboats, but it was very unlikely that they packed more than a few minutes' worth of fuel. The job of the disposable engines on these things was to get the lifeboat clear of dangerous debris, and if possible maneuver the boat toward rescue . . .

Or a habitable planet.

The acceleration cut out, leaving them both in free fall again. Over the PA system a computer-generated voice said flatly, "Three hours until atmospheric insertion."

"Atmospheric insertion?" Nickolai said. His voice was a little bubbly, blood massing at the corner of his mouth.

"The lifeboat's going to try and land us," Kugara said, undoing the straps holding her to the acceleration couch. "So much for Tsoravitch's communications and landing protocols."

She pulled herself over to the console by the door, hoping to get some feedback on the state of the *Eclipse,* how fast they were going, and the integrity of the lifeboat. The little display wasn't that accommodating, giving her little more than the fact that inside was oxygen, outside was hard vacuum.

Not that she could have done anything if the lifeboat was damaged. The lifeboat was going to burn off its velocity hitting atmosphere until the boat was slowed enough for the drag chutes to deploy. If either the shielding or the chutes had been damaged, their reentry would be painful and short.

She looked up at Nickolai and realized that even if the lifeboat worked perfectly, his ride would still be painful and short. He'd been severely beaten by the two-G escape from the *Eclipse.* If this thing hit atmosphere, it was going to go in ass-first and pull a lot more than two Gs deceleration, and it was going to be a hell of a lot rougher.

"I'm going to have to get you into one of the crash couches."

Nickolai laughed. "You should leave me here. I'm not going to fit in a human cradle."

"Maybe if you were bound to the right wall."

"Leave me here." Nickolai spat, and an oblong glob of blood and saliva went on a tumbling slow-motion odyssey toward the nominal ceiling.

Kugara pulled herself down to one of the emergency panels under the folded-up cot and ejected the medkit. *Probably going to need this when we land, if we survive.* "Do that, and we reenter the atmosphere, if your skull isn't turned to jelly slamming into the bulkhead, your internal organs are probably going to be perforated on the splinters that used to be the right side of your rib cage."

"So? I betrayed you all. Why should you care what happens to me?"

"Your damned Angel has too much blood on her hands already to just let someone die out of spite." She pulled out a cutter from the emergency medkit. It was designed to liberate victims from damaged environment suits or, in a pinch, more substantial wreckage. The shiny fifteen-centimeter crystalline blade was designed to vibrate through most inorganic materials and leave flesh intact.

She pulled herself up in front of the tiger and said, "Don't make me regret this."

She started with his legs, slicing through the sealant tape. The knife hummed in her hands as she traced the outlines of his thigh and his calf. The tape came free in small segments, which she plucked from the air and pressed to the wall. Fortunately for Nickolai, the sealant tape only bonded to synthetic material, so she didn't pull free patches of fur with the tape. She worked her way up to his waist and for the first time found herself disconcerted by the fact that Nickolai didn't wear any clothing.

His balls are as furry as the rest of him. She had to snort to keep herself from an uncharacteristic giggle.

"Are you all right?" Nickolai asked. His voice was still slurred from the blood pooling in his mouth.

You're asking me? "I'm fine."

She wondered if she should check the oxy levels in the lifeboat. Not that it mattered; either there was enough and the recycler was working or they were screwed. *More things are getting to me than lack of air.*

She kept cutting, freeing his torso, pulling long strips off his chest and abdomen, finally his neck. He floated free of the wall, arms bound behind him. She grabbed his shoulder and maneuvered so she was behind him. When she did, he said, "My arm's a construct."

Oh, shit. She had completely forgotten about Nickolai's arm. She placed her hand against the tape wrapping his right arm. The tape was a rigid shell in the shape of his arm. It had also changed color. The normal tape was a matte gray color, but it shifted toward green as it bonded to something. Even in the ruddy emergency lighting, she could tell the tape on Nickolai's right arm had shifted all the way to the fluorescent green of a fully bonded seal.

The damn stuff was tougher than most steel alloys. Even if she freed that arm, there was no way he could move it.

She stared at it and said, "I'm sorry. I wasn't thinking."

Nickolai shook his head and spat some more blood. "It doesn't matter. Just don't use that tool against it."

"Yes." The cutting knife would leave flesh intact, but could probably slice Nickolai's cybernetic arm in half. At least it could do a lot more damage than the sealant tape already had. She carefully cut along his left arm, avoiding coming near his right and the hardened tape.

It took a few minutes, but she freed his left arm. He swung both arms in front of him, the right arm immobile in its impromptu cast. She pushed a little away, giving him some room. She had some fear that he might turn on her. He was the reason they were in this situation, by his own admission a traitor.

Though she wondered if that was the right word. Traitor? They both were mercenaries. In the end, their loyalty was to whoever hired them. Nickolai may have broken a BMU contract, but did that carry the weight of that word?

And why the hell am I thinking like this?

Nickolai pushed against the wall with his left hand and rotated to face her. He extended that hand toward her and asked, "May I have that tool?"

Kugara wondered a moment about the knife's usefulness as a weapon, then berated herself. Nickolai was deadlier unarmed than she would be with most hand-to-hand weapons. If he wanted to attack her, he would have done so already.

She handed him the knife.

Nickolai wrapped his hand around the handle and held up the blade, staring at it. In his grip, the blade seemed tiny, almost a surgical instrument. She watched as his jaw clenched, and his blood-smeared lips pulled back in a silent snarl revealing his huge canines.

He lifted his right arm up, and inserting the blade at a shallow angle, he started to cut. The blade sank deeper under the sealant tape than it should have, and Nickolai winced.

He didn't stop cutting.

He worked the blade down the length of the bindings, from the shoulder, along the bulge of his bicep, across the elbow, down the forearm. Liquid beaded along the cut, spheres of clear fluid more viscous than water floating free of the wound.

Even though it was artificial, the way Nickolai worked was too much like someone skinning themselves alive. She whispered, "Stop," but he either didn't hear her or he ignored her.

Under the pseudoflesh of Nickolai's right arm were muscles and bones and nerves; the bones metallic, the muscles some synthetic polymer, and the nerves filaments of gold or some other nonreactive metal. They weren't alive, but they mimicked life too well. The polymer muscles glistened wetly under the emergency light, sliding and swelling as he moved his arm.

When he was done, his right arm was flayed like a holographic medical display. Kugara couldn't stop staring at it.

"Why?" she asked him.

"It was necessary," Nickolai said.

"Does it hurt?"

Nickolai flexed the fingers on his right hand, and she could see the tendons sliding along his wrist. "The neural feedback shut down about halfway in."

She opened the medkit and pulled out some heavy-duty bandaging spray.

"You don't need to—"

"Hell I don't. Even if you don't feel that, I know that wasn't designed to be exposed to the air." She grabbed his right wrist, near the hand where it was still wrapped in fur and something that felt like skin. He allowed her to pull it forward. She sprayed the can onto the faux wound that was Nickolai's arm. The spray dried white and flexible, giving his arm the character of a well-defined corpse.

She let his arm go, and he bent it, flexing his hand again. "Thank you."

"Yeah, right." She took handfuls of hardened sealant tape still attached to ragged clumps of almost-flesh, and shoved them into a cabinet so the debris wouldn't bounce around the cabin and kill them during reentry.

The computer voice spoke. "Two hours until atmospheric insertion."

"Now that you're free," Kugara told him, "Help me rig an acceleration couch that will fit your oversized body."

CHAPTER THIRTY-ONE

Good Samaritans

Surviving the worst will always complicate the matter.
—*The Cynic's Book of Wisdom*

Truth will sooner come out of error than from confusion.
—Francis Bacon
(1561–1626)

Date: 2526.6.3 (Standard)
750,000 km from Salmagundi–HD 101534

Everything had been going as smoothly as could be expected, the bridge crew making periodic announcements over the PA system while Parvi sat at her station obsessively nursing as much efficiency as she could out of the damaged damping coil. Things were going better than she had a right to expect, the engines were already down to 50 percent ahead of her projection.

Then every meter on the console before her redlined. The power spike was sudden, and she lost all readout from the damping coil at the same time the emergency klaxons announced a hull breach.

She slammed her hand on the PA broadcast and shouted, "Everyone to the nearest lifeboat/cabin now! We've had a critical overload."

Before she finished her sentence, the drives blew. She could see the displays go critical in the split second before the explosions. Everything lurched out from underneath her as every display went dead, plunging the bridge into darkness.

More explosions, and Parvi could feel her ass drifting out of the seat in the darkness.

Gravity's gone.

She grabbed the dead console blindly, trying to keep from drifting away. *Hull breach, lost gravity, how long before we're breathing vacuum?*

After a moment, emergency lights flickered on around the bridge, bathing them in a red glow. "What the fuck just happened?" Wahid called from the far side of the bridge. Now that there was some light, he kicked off the wall, back toward the console.

"The drives overloaded," Parvi said, not quite believing it herself.

"Did the damping coil cause it?" Mosasa asked.

Parvi shook her head. "The spike happened before it failed."

"Someone tached in," Tsoravitch whispered.

"That's bullshit," Wahid said, pulling back into his seat. "They'd have to be right on top of us. You heard Bill."

Parvi looked down at the pilot's station, and even under emergency power, all the displays were dead. She tried calling up details on the drives, the maneuvering jets, life support, and structural integrity. She couldn't get anything except the internal diagnostics of the bridge itself. "I can't communicate with the ship's systems. Everything in the pilot's station is cut off . . ."

"Wahid?" Mosasa snapped.

"I can't raise the bridge's nav console."

"Tsoravitch?"

"It's dead. *Everything's dead!*" She slammed her fists against the console in front of her. *"Nothing."*

Parvi stared at Tsoravitch and felt the same edge of panic herself.

"Snap out of it," Mosasa said. Parvi heard desperation in his voice that went deeper than Tsoravitch's panic. His voice grew brittle as he yelled at her. "We need the external sensors online, and that's not going to happen with you breaking down!"

Before Parvi could intervene, Wahid said, "Listen."

The bridge fell silent. After a few seconds, a sound resonated through the skin of the *Eclipse*, a distant hammer blow echoing though the whole vessel. Another few seconds and the sound repeated.

It took a moment for Parvi to realize what was happening.

"The lifeboats," Parvi said to Wahid.

"What?"

"The drive failure caused enough damage to trigger the emergency systems to abandon ship." Another distant hammer blow. "The *Eclipse* is launching the lifeboats. Everyone locked in the cabins is being evacuated."

That meant everyone except Bill and the people on the bridge.

Tsoravitch sucked in a ragged breath and asked. "What could make that happen?"

"A catastrophic failure," Mosasa said quietly. "Complete loss of shipwide life support, imminent structural failure, fire, explosion—"

Another hammer blow, and a slight lurch felt through the floor.

Mosasa pushed away from the bridge console and pulled himself toward the wall. Once there, he began pulling open access panels.

"What are you doing?" Tsoravitch asked.

"A failure in the data lines to the main console," Mosasa said, "We shouldn't have lost the feed from the rest of the *Eclipse*."

He's assuming there's still something out there to get a feed from.

"Tsoravitch," he shouted, "get over here. I'm going to need your help."

Another hammer blow, and another lurch.

Parvi could picture the lifeboats bursting from the skin of the *Eclipse*, like parasitic larvae burrowing out of the flesh of their host.

Tsoravitch pulled herself over to Mosasa, and the two of them began digging into the guts of the bridge's data network.

Wahid turned to look at Parvi. "Think our boss saw this one coming in his AI crystal ball?"

Parvi shook her head as another hammer blow echoed through the bridge. This one seemed farther away, and the lurch that followed weaker. "No," she told him. "I don't think he had any idea."

Parvi saw strands of optical cable and electronic components floating between Mosasa and Tsoravitch. She wondered if they did get the bridge reconnected to any external sensors whether she would want to know what it showed.

The central holo fuzzed a moment, then came to life. She looked up and found herself staring down a surreal view of one of the *Eclipse*'s central corridors. For a moment it felt as if she were suddenly floating down somewhere else in the ship.

"They got the security cameras on-line," Wahid said. He slid over to the comm station and started trying to control the display. The view panned as Wahid manipulated the controls.

The corridor appeared undamaged at first, just dully lit by the emergency lights. Then Parvi noticed the debris floating in the air, shiny flecks of silver. "Ice," she whispered. Faint clouds of ice crystals floated in the corridor. Something bad had happened to the life-support systems.

The camera panned past one of the emergency lamps and Parvi saw that some dull particulate matter floated alongside the ice crystals—soot, or ash. Then the camera panned to one of the cabin doors.

"Holy fuck," Wahid whispered.

The cabins were all behind two doors sandwiched together. The outer door was supposed to remain sealed when the lifeboats ejected, but this one had failed, completely. Either the outer door had never closed at all, or the force of the lifeboat ejecting opened it again. The cabin door looked out on empty space.

Wahid cycled through other security cameras, showing more empty corridors. He found the open cargo bay, and Parvi saw the Paralian in his massive life-support equipment, his manipulator arms buried deep in an open control panel.

"Probably trying to do the same thing we are," Wahid said.

"Can you contact him?" Parvi asked.

He shook his head. "All I got here are the cameras. I don't even have the PA system yet."

He cycled though some more cameras until he found a view of the engines. Of what *used* to be the engines. It took several moments for Parvi to recognize what she saw, only partly because the camera itself was damaged and giving everything blurry rainbow halos and fuzzy unstable outlines.

The tach-drive had torn itself apart. Parvi could only see the anchorages where the massive coils used to be. Nothing recognizable remained of the drive itself. Metal twisted in on itself and melted into odd, puttylike forms. The skin of the *Eclipse* had peeled back from the engine compartment, exposing everything to the stars.

Parvi stared at the wreckage openmouthed. The tach-drive had completely consumed itself; it was miraculous that they were still alive.

Date: 2526.6.3 (Standard)
2,250,000 km from Salmagundi–HD 101534

The bridge of the *Voice* had become less crowded in the past fifteen minutes. Shortly after seeing the *Eclipse,* Admiral Hussein had given the order, "Every command officer must return to his ship, and I want each vessel in the fleet crewed, powered, and ready to disengage within the next hour."

His staff had nodded, a few with widened eyes. Those were the younger men who had not held command long enough to take to heart the old truism, "Battle plans never survive contact with the enemy."

The more experienced staff had seen immediately what Admiral Hussein had seen. The presence of the *Eclipse* in the space around HD 101534 changed the entire tenor of their mission here. There was a good chance that they were not making first contact, and that they might face forces from Indi, or Centauri, or even Sirius. Only God Himself knew what might be waiting for them on this planet.

They needed to be ready for it, whatever it was.

The main display on the *Prophet's Voice* was dominated by tactical holos. On the main holo, two million kilometers from the green triangle representing the *Voice,* glowed a dotted yellow line representing the orbital path of the inhabited planet that the *Voice* was supposed to bring into the Caliphate's fold. On that yellow line was a small blue sphere representing the planet's current location.

A little past and above the midpoint between the green triangle and the blue sphere flashed a bright red triangle. Fortunately, there was no sign of any other craft in orbit.

"Any contact with the *Eclipse* yet?" Captain Rasheed asked the NCO at the communications station.

"No, just the transponder and six distress beacons leaving the ship."

"Lifeboats?" Hussein asked the captain. "Can we intercept them?"

Captain Rasheed ordered the lifeboats highlighted on the main screen. Six red dotted trails sprang up between the *Eclipse* and the planet. He stared at the display a moment, as velocity and bearings started to appear next to the six contacts. "No, we can't ready an intercept craft and get it there before they reach the planet."

Admiral Hussein rubbed his temple. "The ship itself, can we intercept it?"

The captain nodded, "If we launch a salvage team within the next thirty minutes, we might reach them in two hours."

"Do it."

The captain ordered a pair of ships, the *Jeddah* and the *Jizan,* to launch on an intercept course. The *Jizan* was an engineering vessel, capable of repairs and salvage. The *Jeddah* was a fully-armed drop-ship capable of planetside engagements.

Within half an hour, the tactical display showed a pair of green triangles departing from the *Voice* and speeding toward the new ship.

Date: 2526.6.3 (Standard)
750,000 km from Salmagundi–HD 101534

In the hours since the engines failed, the bridge slowly filled with floating debris as Mosasa and Tsoravitch pulled out burned-out components from the panels around the bridge. Parvi wasn't remotely technical, and until they resurrected something she could fly, she was relegated to watching the other three work on the electronics of the bridge in relative silence, retrieving any segments of cable, broken fragments of plastic insulation, or discolored circuits as they floated by. She stashed the debris in a mesh bag so they didn't float into something important and cause them worse problems.

As if things could get worse.

Despite the best efforts from Mosasa and Tsoravitch to contain the stuff, every few minutes, Parvi had to grab some migrating fragment of flayed electronics. She was in the midst of bagging a fragment of optical cable that had gotten caught in her ponytail when Wahid shouted "I got contact with Bill!"

Parvi pulled herself upright. "Is he okay?"

Over the PA system, Bill's synthetic human voice spoke. *"I find myself and my support systems unharmed."*

Mosasa turned around. His dragon tattoo seemed particularly sinister in the dim emergency lighting. "What the hell happened to my ship?"

"An unprecedented surge in the engines," Bill said. *"It is*

unique in my experience, but the energy surge was exponentially higher than expected for normal tach-drive interference."

"Did you *see* what the fuck happened to that drive?" Wahid said.

"*I salvaged the data. And I have detected something I believe is important.*"

Mosasa floated up and grabbed the console next to the navigator's station, bringing himself to a stop. "What?" he asked.

"*I have connected to an external camera array. I will patch the images up to you. Can you see the data?*"

"I've got it, Bill." Wahid said.

As Wahid connected Bill's data to the main holo display, Tsoravitch floated up next to Parvi.

The holo shimmered and stabilized into a view of a star field that, at first, looked unremarkable.

"Well, what the hell? Look at that." Wahid broke out in a grin. "Look at that!"

In a moment, Parvi could tell why Wahid was grinning. Centered in the image, barely visible, was a pair of spacecraft. As she watched, they got noticeably larger.

Tsoravitch grabbed Parvi's arm and shouted, "Yes! Yes!"

"Can we magnify this at all?" Mosasa asked.

"Sure," Wahid said, and the image zoomed in on the two vessels. One was clearly a drop-ship with a smooth skin and the profile of a lifting body that could provide some sort of maneuvering capability in an atmosphere. The other had the spidery appearance of a vessel never meant to descend into a gravity well.

Parvi could also now see the green-and-white crescent markings of the Caliphate.

"Apparently," Wahid said, "we didn't beat them here."

"Do we have any of our communications array up?" Parvi asked.

"Not yet," Tsoravitch whispered. Parvi could tell that she was remembering the holo of the attack on Mosasa's salvage yard.

Parvi hugged her shoulder. "Don't worry. If they had evil intent, we'd know by now. We're well within range of that ship's missile battery."

Mosasa shook his head. "It's wrong . . ."

"What's wrong?" Wahid asked. "You said yourself that they were going—"

Mosasa slammed his hand against the console. "They didn't have the *time*."

"Uh, should I point out the obvious," Wahid said. "They *are* here. You know, maybe your crystal ball's a little cloudy."

Mosasa looked at Wahid, and all the expression drained from his face. "Perhaps it is over," he whispered.

The flat way he said it chilled Parvi. It was as if he had given up.

"Are you still there, Bill?"

"Yes, Mr. Mosasa."

"They will probably come through the cargo bay. Prepare to greet our visitors."

CHAPTER THIRTY-TWO

Descent

Know when to hang on, when to let go, and when not to get on the ride.

—*The Cynic's Book of Wisdom*

On the road to hell, seat belts are optional.

—ROBERT CELINE
(1923–1996)

Date: 2526.6.3 (Standard)
750,000 km from Salmagundi–HD 101534

Hours after they took Nickolai away, Mallory prayed for the wisdom to know what his purpose in this debacle was. Even as they approached a planet and relative safety, Nickolai's words still burned in his ears, his accusations about Mosasa and his fatalistic belief that the *Eclipse* was doomed.

Half of him wasn't even surprised when the cabin started shaking.

The klaxons and emergency lights announced a hull breach and Parvi's panicked voice burst though the PA, "Everyone to the nearest lifeboat/cabin now! We've had a critical overlo—"

A massive explosion threw Mallory out of his cot. When he pushed himself off the floor, he found himself floating upward. Something jerked, and the lights went out.

After several moments, a dull red light came on above the doorway and began flashing rhythmically.

The lifeboat's going to launch.

Mallory pulled himself to the wall so he could fold the cot shut, locking it against the wall. Then he pushed himself to the opposite wall as his cabin vibrated with the first shock of the bolts blowing free between the lifeboat and the rest of the ship. He unfolded the acceleration couch as the second shock hit. *How many?* he wondered as he wrapped himself into the safety harness. He counted the third shock, and the cabin felt as if it was half floating. Four. Five. Six.

A giant invisible fist slammed into his gut as the lifeboat's engine kicked in, blowing him away from the *Eclipse*. It only took a second or two for him to realize that the lifeboat was doing more than clearing the vicinity of the *Eclipse*. Even through the blast of two or three Gs of forward acceleration, he could feel the pitch and yaw of the boat maneuvering beyond the impulse to escape.

The too-long acceleration must have nearly played out the small disposable drive attached to the boat. Once it cut out and Mallory was able to free himself from the acceleration couch, the nav computer spoke over the PA. "Three hours until atmospheric insertion."

Date: 2526.6.3 (Standard)
300,000 km from Salmagundi–HD 101534

All the lifeboats would have jettisoned, and the nav computers would attempt to put them down in a cluster close to population, if there were any obvious population centers. The computers would try to put the boats someplace survivable—no mountain ranges, deep oceans, desert, or tundra.

The operative word there was *try*.

If they were lucky, the beacons would be working and the survivors would be able to reach each other on foot. Mallory pulled out the emergency kit and found the comm beacon for his lifeboat. He pulled out the little handheld unit and scanned for the other lifeboats. The display showed six active beacons out there, but no sign which of them had survivors—no transmissions other than the standard emergency broadcasts.

Someone has to be first, Mallory thought. He switched the unit to transmit.

"This is Fitz— This is Mallory, from the *Eclipse*. Is anyone receiving this transmission?"

He repeated himself a half dozen times before he heard a voice return, "Hello, hello, hello?"

It was coming from beacon number five.

"Yes, I can hear you."

"—bzzt—ron Dörner. I'm with Dr. Pak and Dr. Brody. Dr. Brody's injured."

"What happened?"

"—bzzt—during acceleration. His wrist is broken—bzzt—unconscious."

"Do you have the medkit out?"

"Yes."

Mallory talked her through treating Brody. The doctor had a compound fracture and a head wound. Fortunately he was breathing okay and his pupils were responsive. Mallory spent a half hour talking Dr. Dörner through stabilizing the fracture and getting Brody strapped into one of the acceleration couches. If they were lucky, that would be enough to get him to ground safely.

"Stow everything you can for reentry." Mallory told her. "It isn't going to be pleasant."

"Yes—"

"When you land, don't leave the vicinity of the lifeboat unless you're in immediate danger. These things will try to cluster their landings, and if you stay by the beacon, I can probably reach you before anyone else."

He could hear the hesitation in her voice before she said, "Yes."

She is the one who ID'd me to Wahid and Mosasa . . .

The air went dead for a moment, then he heard another voice. "Mallory?"

He thought he recognized the voice. "Kugara?"

"Yes. Had some issues to clean up here before I hunted down the radio."

"Everything all right with you?"

"We're alive here."

"Did you hear Dörner?"

"The tail end. Rendezvous at boat five?"

"Yes."

"I'm shutting down to conserve power. See you on the ground."

"See you on the ground." He shut down his own transmission.

Date: 2526.6.4 (Standard)
Salmagundi Orbit–HD 101534

When the PA gave him the ten-minute warning, he had already stowed everything in the cabin and strapped himself into an acceleration couch. Mallory felt the rotation of the cabin as it turned the bulkhead he was strapped to toward the direction of motion.

The planet's atmosphere announced itself with a vibration and the beginnings of pressure in his gut as the lifeboat began to decelerate. The vibration continued, intensifying. The fist in Mallory's gut kept pressing, joined by invisible thumbs pressing into his eyes and a choking pressure in his throat. His pulse throbbed in his ears, vying with the sound of his cabin shaking apart.

Another sound joined the vibration, a demonic wind. The sound of superheated atmosphere shredding past the shielding of the lifeboat. Mallory's vision grayed, and the cabin plunged into darkness. He didn't know if his eyesight failed or if the emergency lighting died.

The vibration, the roaring of the atmosphere, and the pressure all increased until it felt as if the lifeboat was about to collapse into a crumpled ball and burn up.

It didn't, and after a short eternity the shaking stopped and the pressure eased. The boat had made it into the atmosphere, and the braking hadn't incinerated it. He felt weightless again, but this time it was because he was in free fall.

The lights flickered back on and he felt the drag of gravity as the lifeboat hit its terminal velocity.

Mallory swallowed and waited for the jerk of the drag chute. For several long moments he imagined the chutes failing, and the lifeboat slamming into the ground at full speed. The wait was long enough for him to pray that the shock of the initial impact would kill him instantaneously, before the bulkhead above him slammed down like a boot crushing a cockroach.

He tensed, fists clenched, eyes closed, expecting the fatal impact at any moment. His implants drove adrenaline through his system enhancing his perception and reaction times to absolutely no effect except to distort his time sense to the point he had no idea how long he had been falling.

When he felt the sudden deceleration pressing into his gut, it took him a few seconds past the panicked shock to realize that he hadn't slammed into the ground. The chute had deployed.

Thank you, Lord, Mallory thought. He stared up at the bulkhead above him with watering eyes and whispered, "If it isn't too much to ask, after all this, please grant me a soft landing."

Date: 2526.6.4 (Standard)
Salmagundi–HD 101534

The boat slammed into something, rolling forward until something snapped, resonating through the cabin. The whole lifeboat slid forward, shaking and tumbling. The cabin flipped over completely four times before coming to a rocking, unsteady rest.

It took five seconds after the boat stopped moving for Mallory to get his bearings. The lifeboat had rolled so that the original floor was at a forty-five-degree angle sloping down from his feet toward the ground. He dangled from his acceleration couch, facing down.

He undid the straps, one by one, feeling the whole descent in every joint. That combined with the crashing fatigue that was the aftereffect of his implants hyping his metabolism. Climbing out of the couch was a complicated maneuver, disengaging himself from the acceleration couch without falling the three meters into the bulkhead below him. He had to hold onto the crash webbing while he undid the buckles. Even though he was prepared for the drop, he released the last buckle too fast and almost dislocated his shoulder rolling out.

He hung on, half standing on the sloped floor, half dangling from the harness. Standing there, it struck him full force.

I'm still alive.

If he had made it, the others had a good chance, too. And Brody was going to need some help. He let himself go, falling to lean against the bulkhead where the cot was still stowed. He pulled out all the emergency gear.

He took out the comm unit and tried raising the *Eclipse,* but got no response. But he didn't expect one.

He tried to call the two occupied lifeboats, but didn't get a response there either. While he could see the beacons for the lifeboats with Brody and Kugara, both stationary, he couldn't raise them.

He clipped the unit to his belt. He could try periodically

once he got moving. Until they were in contact again, the plan was to rendezvous at lifeboat number five.

Thankfully the range given by the beacon put all the lifeboats within a fifty-klick radius. Lifeboat five, fortunately, landed close to the center of the cluster. So while Mallory was about thirty kilometers from Kugara's lifeboat, he was about fifteen kilometers from lifeboat five. Nickolai and Kugara had ten more klicks than he did to get to the rendezvous, but that was still closer to them than Mallory's lifeboat.

Though it still remained to be seen where it was they had landed. All kilometers were not created equal. Despite the lifeboat's best efforts, it was still quite possible that they had made landfall someplace impassable.

Mallory edged up to the door to the lifeboat. Like the floor, it was canted at a forty-five-degree angle. Next to the controls, a line of lights flashed green. So according to the lifeboat, not only did the mechanism work, but the environment on the other side of the door was in the acceptable range of temperature, pressure, and oxygen content.

If he believed the sensors, it was safe to open the door.

It occurred to him that this was the last time he would have to rely on the lifeboat for his survival. Outside the door, it would just be him and God.

He hit the control to open the door. It slid aside with a horrid scraping noise and stuck about halfway. Hot air blew in, carrying the scent of burned synthetics and woodsmoke. Though the open doorway he could see a slice of night sky, the purple tint and shimmering of the stars giving the reassuring feel of an atmosphere above him. The stars flickered in heat shimmers coming from the skin of the lifeboat.

He didn't want to wait for the shielding to cool off, so he found an insulating blanket in the emergency stores and draped it over the bottom corner of the open doorway. With that, he was able to pull himself up enough to look at the landing site without burning himself.

The lifeboat had landed in a hardwood temperate forest. The tumbling Mallory had felt early was the boat crashing through the forest canopy and tumbling to the ground. The force had been enough to tear a hole in the canopy for him to see the stars. The chute from the lifeboat's descent was tangled

in the treetops, little more than a ragged shadow from where
Mallory stood.

The lifeboat hadn't put down in absolutely optimal condi-
tions, but it was closer than Mallory had any right to expect.
The terrain was relatively level, and the forest was old growth
with wide-spaced trees and underbrush that wasn't terribly
dense. If lifeboat five was in a similar site, he could reach them
on foot in a matter of hours.

He shouldered the medkit and the emergency pack from
his lifeboat and set off in the direction of lifeboat five.

CHAPTER THIRTY-THREE

Hubris

Great power does not foster great flexibility.
—*The Cynic's Book of Wisdom*

The love of power is the love of ourselves.
—WILLIAM HAZLITT
(1778–1830)

Date: 2526.6.4 (Standard)
1,800,000 km from Salmagundi–HD 101534

After an hour of chaos, the bridge on the *Voice* had settled down into a more normal operation. The battle group had disengaged and spread out into a close formation around the *Voice*. The *Jeddah* and the *Jizan* had established radio contact with the *Eclipse*, and the *Jizan* was in the process of docking. And Admiral Hussein had recorded a revised diplomatic message for the planet, one that the *Voice*'s communications officers were repeatedly beaming down to the surface. They still waited for a response.

And all the shipboard clocks turned over to mark a new day. As the timer on the main holo changed to read 00:00:00, one of the ensigns from navigation walked up to Captain Rasheed.

Admiral Hussein distinctly heard Captain Rasheed say, "That can't be right."

"What's the problem, Captain?"

Captain Rasheed straightened up and said, "Give your report to Admiral Hussein, Ensign."

"Yes, sir!" The ensign came to attention facing the admiral. "The observatory data we're receiving is not syncing with our mapped projections, sir."

Admiral Hussein frowned. "You're not saying we're not on course, Ensign?"

"No, sir. The map projection is only wrong for one star."

Captain Rasheed called over to the nav station and said, "Put the anomaly up on the main holo."

In response, the main display for the bridge changed to show a segment of a star field overlaid with the vector map generated by the navigational system. The actual stars fit in the overlay, none off by a fraction of a degree. However, in the center of the display, a single red circle was disconcertingly empty. There was no sign of the star that should have been contained within the marker, it wasn't off by a degree here or there, it was just *gone*.

The text next to the empty circle read "Xi Virginis."

Admiral Hussein's first thought was of their sister ship, the *Prophet's Sword*, which had tached to Xi Virginis barely a week before their own departure. Things had already gone far beyond the operational parameters of this mission; this did not feel good.

"Is some outer planet eclipsing the star?" he asked.

"We've been checking for something occluding our observations, sir. If anything is, it's showing no detectable radiation of its own, inherent or reflected, and it is far enough away not to interfere with any other visible landmark."

Coincidence? Something just happened to be eclipsing the destination of our sister ship so precisely?

Admiral Hussein leaned forward and said to Captain Rasheed, "I want every scrap of data you can get on Xi Virginis, and scan for any tach-transmissions from the *Sword*."

"Yes, sir."

Communications identified a signal almost instantaneously. They had a lock on a data transmission, a tach-burst specifically coded for the *Voice,* and the encryption wrapping it identified the *Sword* better than a fingerprint.

When the signal was decrypted, the main holo on the *Voice's* bridge filled with the face of Admiral Naji Bitar, the commander of the *Sword's* fleet. Hussein wondered if his discomfort over Bitar's grinning expression was simply a matter of decorum.

"Greetings, Admiral Hussein," said Bitar's smiling face. "My communications officers have timed this to reach you upon your arrival. I wish to provide you with some good news.

Our contact with the colony at Xi Virginis has been quite positive. Not only are they enthusiastic to ally with the Caliphate, but they have been willing to share technological advances that are ... extraordinary."

The star. What happened to the star?

"Your observations will have detected that the star Xi Virginis has ceased radiating. This shouldn't alarm you. The colonists here have discovered a means to harness all the energy produced by the star. This technology is part of what they wish to share."

A Dyson Sphere? Is that what he's talking about?

"Needless to say, you must communicate home as discreetly as possible. The Caliphate has many enemies, and we cannot risk communicating this news back in any way that might alert them."

Admiral Hussein heard Captain Rasheed pass some orders on to the communications officers, restricting physical access to the tach-comm.

"You will receive a more personal contact within eighteen hours standard after your arrival. You will have a more in-depth briefing on what we have discovered here. We are about to embark on a new age, Muhammad, my friend. God is great."

The feed swapped Bitar's face for the green-and-white crescent of the Caliphate, then ended. Admiral Hussein didn't know what to make of the transmission. It felt inauthentic from the address all the way to his closing. There was an aggressive cheer pervading the message that was more than unprofessional. . . .

Creepy, Hussein thought. *The word is "creepy."*

Captain Rasheed turned toward Hussein. A gulf of silence filled the bridge. All waiting for him.

Hussein had known the operation had changed as soon as he had seen the *Eclipse*. Now, after hearing Bitar's message, he wondered if there would be anything of the original operation left. At the very least, Bitar's short speech, bolstered by the missing Xi Virginis, completely revised Hussein's risk assessment.

He looked up to the bridge at large. "No mention of Admiral Bitar's speech or Xi Virginis is to occur beyond the people present here. You are not to discuss it among yourselves unless a superior officer is present and has given permission. Understood?"

"Yes, sir," from the bridge crew.

"If anyone mentions the disappearance of Xi Virginis to any of you, you will only confirm that command is aware of the situation. That is the only statement permitted. Understood?"

"Yes, sir."

He looked down at Captain Rasheed. "I want you to detail a science officer and someone from the medical staff to analyze that tach-broadcast. Now."

Date: 2526.6.4 (Standard)
750,000 km from Salmagundi–HD 101534

Mosasa stared at the holo, where the security cameras showed the spidery form of the *Jizan* drawing the wreckage of the *Eclipse* into itself. A dozen robots, and a half dozen men in hardshell EVA suits, crawled through the wreckage by the drive section like fat white aphids invading a rotten log. The invaders connected cables, secured debris, and attached umbilicals from the Caliphate ship to what remained of the *Eclipse*'s power and life support . . .

And data . . .

He barely listened to Parvi as she talked to the crew of the *Jizan,* guiding them through the heavily modified and severely damaged systems. For all the activity, movement, the babble around him, he felt as alone as he had ever been at any point in his ersatz life. His world had shrunk from the universe to the claustrophobic prison of the *Eclipse*. For the first time in hundreds of years, he felt trapped inside his own skin.

He had built his identity on being aware. Unknowns were solidly delineated areas to explore, not this vast all-encompassing darkness.

The Caliphate should not be here. Not yet. Not with this kind of force. They had no political or economic impetus to launch their reclamation of the colonies out here so soon. Travel time and the limits of tach-drives made it impractical for them to take physical possession. Of course they'd come out here eventually, but only after the forces impelling the various states out here had reached a political equilibrium *and* they put in place the infrastructure to support the journey out here.

It should have taken *years*.

But the Caliphate was here, with a whole fleet of ships.

Mosasa knew his view of the future was imperfect, and the

smaller the scale of the projection, the less accurate it was. But this wasn't a simple error or a slight divergence. This was a wholesale failure to see a major shift in resources on a planetary scale.

It was enough of a failure to completely shatter his faith in his understanding of the universe. Seeing the patterns of political, social, and economic energy had been as basic to his worldview as the ability to perceive color.

He looked at his hands and had difficulty being fully convinced that they were actually there.

I am Mosasa, he thought, *but I am also a machine. Can I be sure that I ever left the* Luxembourg? *Can I know that I've not just suffered a prolonged hallucinatory systems failure?*

"Mosasa!"

He looked away from the holo and saw Parvi looking at him. He should be able to understand the emotion in her face, but right now he found himself unable to interpret it. "Yes?"

"Did you hear what I said?" Parvi snapped.

"What?"

"They're ordering us onto the *Jizan,*" Parvi said. "That means losing contact with all our comm gear— God only knows what they're intending to do to the planet. Our people are down there."

"What do you want me to do?" Mosasa asked.

Parvi stared at him, and he thought he could understand her expression now. She was afraid.

Date: 2526.6.4 (Standard)
1,200,000 km from Salmagundi–HD 101534

An hour later, Admiral Hussein sat in a briefing room with a group of engineers, scientists, and medical officers. On the table between them was a frozen image of Admiral Naji Bitar.

"We've done a comprehensive analysis of the transmission itself," said Lieutenant Abdem, one of the *Voice's* senior communications engineers. "It is unquestionably from the *Sword's* tach-transmitter. The encryption protocol is embedded in the hardware, and every transmitter is imperfect enough to give a unique temporal distortion to any broadcast. No way to duplicate it precisely."

Admiral Hussein nodded and looked toward the medical officers.

"We've checked every biometric marker we can given the

data transmitted. Voice-print, facial structure, iris variegation, kinematics. All are consistent with Admiral Bitar's medical profile."

"What about his emotional and psychological state?"

"It seems unusual," said Lieutenant Deshem, the psychologist. "The admiral is displaying no abnormal stress levels at all."

"That is unusual?"

"Consider what he's reporting to us. This represents a radical change—even if it's a positive one, change always engenders a stress response."

"Could he be lying?"

"There's no indication of that from what we can analyze. It seems that he believes everything he's saying in this transmission."

"Any sign of external influences, drugs, hallucination . . ."

Deshem shook his head. "He is lucid to all appearances—"

"But?"

"His body language, at the end of the transmission, it seems to suggest that he is withholding something. As if he's not telling the whole truth."

Hussein shook his head. Aside from all the technical resources they had, he could tell the same thing just from the deliberate vagueness of how Bitar phrased things. *"You will receive a more personal contact within eighteen hours standard after your arrival. You will have a more in-depth briefing on what we have discovered here."*

Before he could ask another question, his personal comm buzzed for his attention. The *Jizan* was returning with what was left of the *Eclipse* and her crew. He excused himself and listened to the briefing from the captain of the *Jizan* on what they had found, and what the *Eclipse* had been doing so far from human space.

What he heard was not reassuring.

CHAPTER THIRTY-FOUR

My Brother's Keeper

Never discount the possibility you might live through it.
— *The Cynic's Book of Wisdom*

Those who are prepared to die are unprepared to live.
— SYLVIA HARPER
(2008–2081)

Date: 2526.6.4 (Standard)
Salmagundi–HD 101534

Nickolai had mentally and spiritually prepared to die. Because of that, he found it disconcerting to open his eyes in the dark confines of the lifeboat and realize he still drew breath. He lay there, strapped to the jury-rigged acceleration couch, staring up into complete darkness, wondering if he was being rewarded or punished.

His last memory had been the slam into atmosphere. He had thought the shielding had failed the way the boat had shuddered.

He smelled blood.

Blinking, he adjusted the photoreceptors in his new eyes and the interior of the cabin came into focus. He saw the monochrome cabin in sharper relief than he'd ever be able to with his natural eyes, despite his species' excellent night vision. His sight edged into the infrared, and he could see the form of Kugara radiating heat next to him. He heard her breathe and found himself grateful.

The lifeboat had taken a beating. The lack of lights showed a general power failure, and the bulkhead above him had been bowed inward by the impact of landing. The cot had been blown out of its stowed position to dangle like a half-severed limb. The emergency stores had also broken free, scattering medkit, food packets, and survival tools all through the cabin.

He now appreciated the effort Kugara had put into extending the acceleration couch. It had taken both of them an hour to unbolt parts of the third and fourth couches and attach them above and below a standard-sized couch. The effort had probably saved his life, given the violent landing.

As it was, it was an agonizingly slow process, untangling himself from the harness, except for his right arm, which gave him no pain at all. It no longer even felt a part of him. Fortunately, given how unsteady he was, the lifeboat had come to rest with the acceleration couches on the bottom. He was able to peel himself out of the couch without falling over.

"Kugara?" He spoke to her, but she was unconscious. Bending over her, Nickolai could see a sheet of blood trailing over the side of her face from a wound in her temple. Something had struck her during the descent, probably when the storage compartments burst open. She groaned, and he searched through the wreckage for the remains of the medkit.

He grabbed the kit, half of which was missing, and did what he could to treat the wound. He was gratified to see that it wasn't as bad as it first appeared. It had bled profusely, but it was just a superficial tear in the skin. The blow causing it hadn't been enough to knock her out. She'd probably blacked out from the deceleration as Nickolai had.

She groaned a few times, but didn't wake up until after he had flushed the wound and had sprayed the last of the bandage on her scalp.

"Shit, that's hot."

"You have a bad laceration."

"Am I bleeding to death? Save that stuff."

The can hissed and died. "It's empty now. You used most of it on my arm."

She blinked and fumbled with her restraints. She raised her head and bumped it on his wrist. He barely felt it, but she flopped back, pressing her hands to her forehead muttering, "Shit."

"Are you all right?"

"Where're the damn lights?"

He had forgotten that she would be unable to see. He stood up and looked at the scattered emergency supplies until he saw a flashlight.

"What are you doing?"

"Getting you some light." He picked up the flashlight and turned it on, still amazed at how quickly his new eyes adjusted from the monochrome dark to the starkly colored cabin interior.

"Shit, warn someone, would you?" Kugara held her hand up between her and Nickolai, shading her eyes. He noticed he was pointing the light right at her. He moved the beam away and pointed it at the door to the lifeboat.

"Thanks," Kugara whispered as she undid the harness holding her down.

Nickolai stared at the door. It was now oriented horizontally. The floor he stood on, with the acceleration couches, had been the right wall when this cabin had been part of the *Eclipse*. It was hard for him to tell, but it looked as if the frame had warped outward with the same impact that had dented in the bulkhead above.

Kugara stood up next to him, shaking her head. She looked at the debris on the floor, and the unpleasantly curving bulkhead above them, and said, "That was one rough mother of a landing."

"Seems like it."

"Don't you remember the descent?"

"No. I blacked out."

She nodded. "Me, too. Right after the chute gave up."

"What?"

"Sometime between reentry and the ground, the chute cut out and we hit free fall again." She rubbed the bandage bonded to her temple.

Examining the door more closely, Nickolai could see that the frame was warped, bowed outward nearly five centimeters. The door itself had buckled a little, becoming very slightly concave. There was no way it was going to slide back home, even if there was power left.

"How do we open this?"

"Well, first we should get some heads-up on what it's like outside." Kugara walked to the door and pulled open the emergency control panel for the door, the same one that had shown the schematics of the lifeboat's launch. It was one of the few panels that hadn't popped open during landing, and for a few moments it looked as if it never would. She strained against it, and the warping bulkhead seemed to have jammed it as badly as the main door.

Just before Nickolai stepped up to help her with it, the panel opened with a nasty screech that hurt his ears. It also released the smell of burned electronics.

"Damn," she said. "It's dead."

He wasn't surprised. However, he smelled something beyond superheated metal and roasted ceramics.

"Okay," she said, "Maybe one of the other boats can give us an idea." She hunted around on the floor and found the handheld comm unit. When she picked it up, half the unit stayed on the floor. *"Damn it!"*

Nickolai took another deep breath. Under the smell of the dead lifeboat, he could smell cool air, the woody, earthy smell of some sort of plant life.

Kugara stared at the fragments of the comm unit and repeated, "Damn it!"

"I think it is safe to open the door."

"What?"

"The skin's already been breached. Can't you smell the air?"

She wrinkled her nose. "All I can smell is my own blood gumming my nostrils."

"By the panel you opened."

She stepped back over to the door and bent down. "No, I can't smell—" She froze a moment. "Well, what do you know? I can feel a draft." She stood up. "We must have hit hard enough to crack the shielding. The leftover heat from reentry must have been enough to fry the circuits in this thing."

"So? How do we open the door?"

"There's a manual emergency release that should blow out the whole door mechanism," Kugara said. She knelt and opened a red-and-yellow-striped panel to the left of the dead control panel. In a recess behind it was a T-shaped handle. She grabbed it and pulled it out to the right—which would have been up had the lifeboat been docked on the *Eclipse* and the floor had been the floor. The handle pulled out a lever that extended about fifteen centimeters. She looked back at Nickolai. "You might want to back up a bit."

He took a step back and found his back against a bulkhead.

"Okay," she said. She turned away from the door and pushed the lever to the left, toward the original floor.

The whole lifeboat resonated with a rapid series of bangs that rocked the cabin briefly back toward Nickolai. In a moment, he could smell freshly vaporized metal drifting in from outside.

The door still hung in place.

Kugara stared at it, shaking her head. "I don't believe it. There shouldn't be anything left holding that door in place."

Nickolai stepped up to the door and pushed.

The metal creaked, then a massive shudder gripped the bulkhead in front of them. The door leaned outward and the whole outer skin of the bulkhead seemed to slough off in a cloud of ceramic dust and an odor of heated metal. In its wake, the falling door revealed the bark of a massive tree trunk.

A cool wind blew into the lifeboat, carrying the odor of a living forest.

The lifeboat had come to rest on the edge of a hardwood forest. From the divots in the ground and broken trees, it appeared that it had actually made landfall on a small rocky mountain about two thousand meters above the tree line. It had then bounced, slid, and rolled down a 40 percent grade and a couple of cliffs until it slammed to a stop against a massive tree with a fifteen-meter-diameter trunk.

The impact hadn't killed the tree, but it now tilted at a perceptible angle away from the lifeboat, which had recoiled and rolled to its final stop about ten meters away in the direction from which it had come. Judging by the scar burned in the tree's trunk, and the orientation of the lifeboat, Nickolai suspected that slamming into the tree was what had dented the bulkhead.

Another twenty meters downslope, and the other side of the lifeboat would have slammed into it; the bulkhead where they'd been strapped in. That might have been the most heavily-shielded portion of the lifeboat, but if it had been that bulkhead taking the brunt of the impact, the two of them might not have survived.

At least not in shape to crawl out of the lifeboat.

"The beacon's still active," Kugara said, "but that'd survive anything. Comm's for shit though."

Nickolai stood between the tree and the wreck of the lifeboat staring up at the bluest sky he had ever seen. A tiny yellow flare of a sun heated his face, especially the leather of his nose, way out of proportion to its size.

He wondered why he was still alive.

"Nickolai?"

He turned around to face her. She was crouched down, the broken comm unit spread out on sheet before her. It was in a half dozen pieces. "Are you listening to me?"

"Can you fix it?"

She laughed. "The main circuit snapped in half. Even if I had an electronic repair kit and knew exactly what I was doing, we'd still have to replace the thing. This is pretty much a disposable unit."

"We set up a rendezvous at lifeboat five."

"Yeah, but no telling where they landed without this." She tossed the part she was holding into the pile. "They could be two klicks away and we'd never find them."

"So what do we do?"

Kugara stood. "We got two choices." She looked at the wreckage. "We stand pat and wait for our dubious comrade Mallory, or someone else, to catch up with the emergency beacon." She looked back at him. "Or we strike out independently to find civilization or another lifeboat with a working comm."

Nickolai nodded. "There's a third choice."

She arched an eyebrow, an expression that Nickolai still didn't quite know how to interpret. "Oh, really?"

"One of us can stay by the lifeboat, the other go out and—"

"Oh, *hell* no!" She folded her arms. "You think I'm letting you out of my sight, tiger-man? Have you forgotten why we're in this mess in the first place?"

"You think I—"

"I'm not stupid, Nickolai. I know you don't want to kill me, otherwise I'd be several flavors of dead right now. That does not mean I trust you."

"Then what do you want *us* to do?"

She sighed, and thought a moment. "If we're lucky, another lifeboat put down in line of sight." She glanced up at the trees. "Think you can get to the high ground with that arm?"

As large as the trees were, they were easy enough to climb. The bark was rock-hard and scaled in a semiregular pattern of hexagons that spiraled up the trunk. The six-sided plates were the size of Nickolai's fist, and the gaps between them were more than wide and deep enough for him to insert his claws. Almost a ladder.

He pulled himself up the side, climbing up over a hundred meters until he got a good, mostly unobstructed, view of their surroundings. It helped that they landed on the side of a small mountain. He might not have climbed the highest tree, but the tree's placement on the slope meant that he was hanging on above the tree line for most of the forest.

From his perch he had a good view to about 120 degrees' worth of horizon before the mountain range behind him started interfering with his view.

Below him, Kugara shouted up, "What do you see?"

"Forest goes south all the way to the horizon. There's a large body of water to the southeast, about sixty kilometers away at its closest, I'd guess. Down the shoreline I see some sort of settlement. It's too far away to see details, but there are a few very large buildings."

"How far?"

"Possibly a hundred and fifty klicks—it's just at the horizon." Of course, the estimate could be way off, considering he had no idea how big the planet was, and barely had a feel for how high above the forest he actually was.

"Anything closer?"

He shouted down an inventory for her. He could see a couple of spots of color which could be drag chutes caught in the forest canopy at fifty and sixty klicks. He saw a couple of large cleared areas that might have been signs of logging activity. Those were farther away, close to the settlement.

Southwest of them, Nickolai saw a closer scar in the woods. It almost seemed to be a scar from some oblique impact. But he could see some sort of structures dotting the clearing.

"How far is that?"

"Fifteen kilometers, twenty at most."

"Okay, get a good bearing on that site. That's where we're going."

CHAPTER THIRTY-FIVE

Mixed Blessings

Sometimes victory is simply deciding to act.
—*The Cynic's Book of Wisdom*

One person with a belief is equal to a force of ninety-nine who have only interests.

—JOHN STUART MILL
(1806–1873)

Date: 2526.6.4 (Standard)
Salmagundi–HD 101534

Mallory had already made four kilometers toward lifeboat number five by the time dawn broke. He kept trying to radio the others, and the yellow point of the sun had begun poking through the canopy at him before he finally got a response.

"Father Mallory?" came Dr. Dörner's voice.

"Yes, what's your situation?"

"Dr. Brody is still unconscious, but Dr. Pak and I are both all right."

Mallory thanked God that they had made it through reentry in one piece. "Good, that's good. Have you heard anything from the *Eclipse* or Kugara?"

"No. But it took a while to get to the comm unit. We have a little problem."

Mallory's breath caught. "What?"

"We seem to be stuck in a tree."

Mallory picked up his pace through the woods as he got the details from Dr. Dörner. Their lifeboat had made a softer landing than anyone had a right to expect. The unfortunate side of this was that, unlike Mallory's lifeboat, lifeboat number five didn't hit with quite enough force to break the trees it landed on. Dr. Dörner had managed to open the door and discovered that they were at least fifty meters up. There was rope in the emergency kit somewhere, but their perch was precarious enough that Dr. Dörner didn't want to risk the movement that would be required to find it in the jumble of debris that filled the lifeboat. Even if they had the rope at hand, they had no way to safely get Brody to the ground.

"Can you see how the lifeboat is supported?"

"N–no." Her voice was thick with fear.

"We need to get all of you out of that lifeboat," Mallory said.

"I don't know how we can."

Mallory heard creaking wood over the open link. They had to get out of there before the support gave way. "Look, don't worry about getting down. The immediate problem is getting Brody to a stable location. Look out the door. You must see other branches big enough to support you."

He heard her suck in a breath, then the comm followed with rustling movement and more creaking. "I'm here." Now her voice was cut with the sound of wind. More creaking, followed by a snap, and she gasped.

"Are you all right?"

"The lifeboat shifted," she whispered.

"Do you see anything within reach?"

"I'm looking . . . There's a branch below the door. It's about a meter in diameter."

"Perfect, can one of you get to it?"

"I don't know if I—" Her voice was cut off by more rustling and creaking, and Mallory heard muffled voices he couldn't make out.

"Dr. Dörner?"

"Leon said he can try."

"Okay," Mallory sucked in a breath. "What kind of shape is Dr. Brody in? Is he conscious?"

"No. We've tried waking him."

Mallory sucked in a breath. None of the options were particularly good, but they couldn't stay in the lifeboat. "Can you move him yourself?"

"I–I don't think so."

"Then you and Dr. Pak need to move him to the doorway. Then Dr. Pak can go outside and help you pass Dr. Brody through the doorway."

"You make it sound simple."

"I know it isn't," Mallory said. "Slow and careful. You can't stay in that lifeboat."

"Father Mallory?"

"Yes?"

"Why did you pretend to be someone else? Isn't that a sin?"

Mallory paused and then said, "I've only done what the Church asked of me. We're all sinners looking for God's forgiveness. Now, please, get yourself and Dr. Brody out of there."

"I'll need two hands," she said. He heard her set down the comm unit. He started walking again, hearing only the protesting tree, grunts, and soft, inarticulate speech. Every passing minute, the groaning wood seemed to get louder, and occasionally something would pop.

He felt his chest tighten when he heard static blare over the comm followed by a horribly loud crashing sound.

"Dr. Dörner!" he shouted into the unit, breaking into a run even though he was still at least nine kilometers away from them. "Dr. Dörner!"

After nearly thirty seconds of panic, the comm came alive again. "We're fine. The comm fell from my belt while we were moving Dr. Brody."

Mallory stopped running, the relief almost a physical blow. "Is everyone out?"

"Not me, not yet."

"Can you make it?"

"Yes. But can I ask you something, Father Mallory?"

"What?"

"Do you know what happened to Xi Virginis?"

"No, Dr. Dörner. But I think God led me here to find out."

"God or Mosasa?"

"God is free to choose any instrument to work His will."

She hesitated before asking, "Did you sabotage our communications?"

"No, I didn't."

"I'm going out the door now." She added, almost in a whisper, "Pray for me."

Mallory did as she asked.

Alexander had never seen the Grand Triad gripped by such chaos. Progress of the Salmagundi government was always slow and deliberative, filled as it was by minds self-selected for their caution and traditional nature. It was always annoying, but now it had verged on the dangerous.

Alexander had, through debate, reason, cajoling, and very subtle threats, brought the Triad around to his position both on eliminating the Protean threat and allowing the *Eclipse* to land. For a few hours, things had gone smoothly, the *Eclipse* making no objections to their traffic control directions, maneuvering to approach and limiting their radio traffic as requested.

And, despite the objections of the Ashley Triad and the area lumber interests, Alexander had gotten consensus around the idea of using their limited nuclear arsenal to eliminate the threat from the invader. Once the *Eclipse* was on the surface and under guard, a single attack would wipe the alien object from the face of the planet. The crew of the *Eclipse,* whoever they were, would have no need to know that the Proteans ever existed.

Then the *Eclipse* had exploded.

Alexander had watched the observatory footage as the engines of the ship had blown themselves into space, carrying a good part of the ship with them. Then the lifeboats burst from the skin of the craft, and suddenly their contact with the rest of the universe was less direct and controlled.

Worse, the *Eclipse* was not alone.

The display above the meeting room showed a schematic view of the space in orbit around Salmagundi. The location of the *Eclipse* highlighted in red, two other ships showing up blue, one of the two attached parasitically to the wreckage of the *Eclipse*. An inset showed a map of the area to the west of Ashley covering about a hundred thousand square kilometers. The inset was from a weather satellite, and if Alexander stared at it hard enough, he could see the scar from the alien's impact about two hundred kilometers into the woods southwest of Ashley. The site was highlighted by a red circle.

Six other circles now dotted the woods southwest of Ashley. One of the *Eclipse*'s lifeboats had made landfall within a dozen klicks of the city, and would have been in full view of the population if it had landed in daylight.

"We need to secure these landing sites *now;* it's been nearly six hours."

"Calling up a larger security detail will make it impossible to contain this news. There are already unacceptable rumors surrounding the existing incident—"

"And when we detonate a nuclear weapon? Are you going to contain those rumors?"

"We have a limited supply of militarily capable units. We should not risk them—"

"If not on this, what? We're being invaded. We need to focus on the craft approaching us. Did they see the damage to the *Eclipse* as an attack?"

Alexander glanced up at the schematic. At the edge of the view, maybe a million kilometers from the planet, a spreading line of blue contacts were edging into view. He counted twelve. Fifteen minutes ago, there had been six.

The Grand Triad had been debating for hours, and for once Alexander could see no hint of consensus coming. *We will collapse under the weight of our own arguments. . . .*

With the eyes of his ancestors, he watched the room and saw the shape of the coming disaster. If the civilization they'd built on Salmagundi had a weakness, it was this hesitation in the face of the unknown. He knew that it was only going to worsen as the stakes increased. He had seen it growing as they debated the nuclear option, but even then it hadn't reached the crisis point. Then, the Grand Triad had reached a conclusion.

This was different.

There was no way they could defend themselves if they vested power in the disparate parts of the Triad. As much as they wanted to, there was no way they could emulate the merger of minds and souls exemplified by the Hall of Minds outside of a single skull.

Even knowing all this, the internal debate Alexander Shane underwent in coming to his own personal consensus was almost as long in coming as the nonexistent decision of the Triad. But when his own decision came, he welcomed it and started it into motion.

He checked the chronometer on his comm and it showed 10:00, a third of the way into Salmagundi's thirty-hour day. He stood up and formally excused himself. The debate around him barely rippled, acknowledging his departure. Harrison took over the chair and did less to rein in the chaos than Alexander had.

Like Alexander, he had the experience of enough lives to

know how pointless it was to attempt to force the Triad toward action at a time like this. Unlike Alexander, he was satisfied with the traditional inaction.

Alexander stepped outside the meeting room and was met by a dozen men in full militia gear. Each of the men had been handpicked by Alexander. Every single one had two or three glyphs matching some of the fifteen across Alexander's brow. So each one shared several lifetimes with him. Each one thought enough like Alexander that they could be trusted with what was about to happen.

They all saluted him.

Alexander saluted back.

"It is time," he told them. "Secure the building."

Several ran to seal the various entrances to the Hall of Minds. Others ran to take over the security control center.

He picked up his handheld comm and transmitted a prerecorded message to the security chiefs of every city on Salmagundi.

"This is Alexander Shane, Chairman of the Great Triad. Acting on behalf of the Triad, all security and militia members, active and reserve, are now under my command. All available personnel are to report for duty immediately and await further instructions."

Alexander suspected that it might be another hour or two before the rest of the Grand Triad realized that the doors to the meeting room were sealed and all external communication was cut.

He met up with his own personal guard in the security office of the Ashley Hall of Minds. It wasn't much space to run a whole government from but—outside the meeting room where the Grand Triad was imprisoned—it had the most bandwidth to handle the kind of multitiered communications he needed right now.

The normal security detail had been ushered out, and Alexander had to remove a half-eaten sandwich from the console as he sat down. Two other men, the highest-ranking militia members in Ashley, joined him by taking the other two available seats.

Alexander turned to one. "We're going to need intel from everyone who's got an eye on orbit. I'll need to know anything coming into our space, and what it is. Coordinate that and get views up there." He pointed to the ranks of security monitors. "And get the satellite imagery from around Ashley up on the main screen there."

He turned in the chair to face the other man, "I want six militia units ready to go to secure the lifeboat landing sites within the next fifteen minutes. If anyone gives you any problems, route them to me."

Both men began making calls. Alexander didn't expect any problems. Authority was accepted on Salmagundi, and a challenge to his assumption of command would require as extraordinary a deviation from the norm as he had just committed. He was rather secure in the fact that kind of initiative was rare.

The small sun rose higher above the forest canopy as Mallory closed on the location of lifeboat five. The trees closed in, but not closer than a few meters. It didn't slow his progress too much.

He was within two kilometers of them when he got a frantic voice on his comm unit.

"We have aircraft!"

"Dr. Dörner?"

"Two aircraft just flew over. Can you hear?"

"I—" Before he finished the statement, he heard them overhead. He looked up and saw two shadows shooting low over the forest canopy. The fans roared as they passed almost directly over him. The two craft were large cargo or personnel transports. Though their blocky forms and slow progress showed their lift to be from contragrav engines, their maneuvering fans were oversized, and still vectored enough thrust that the downdraft shredded foliage. Fragments of spiky green leaves rained down on Mallory as the blocky vehicles passed over him.

"Here! We're over here!" He heard Dr. Dörner's voice as the engine noise retreated with the aircraft. There was a pleading note in her voice.

"They've seen you," Mallory said. "If they didn't see the drag chute, they picked up on the beacon. They're probably looking for a landing site."

"We're over here!" the comm continued.

Mallory wondered if she heard him at all. He could hear Dr. Pak shouting something in the background.

Mallory tried to raise them, but in their excitement over seeing the rescue craft, she must have set down their comm unit. He couldn't really blame them. His own spirits had been raised just seeing it.

It felt miraculous. Enough so that Mallory wondered if it was literally miraculous. It felt as if the hand of God had helped them safely to ground. The only thing that tempered that thought was his inability to contact the *Eclipse* or Kugara. He knew better than to try to interpret his survival as divine favor and others' fate as divine punishment. That kind of simplistic thinking was spiritually wrongheaded, shown by Job onward.

However, it was very human to wonder *why* God had spared them.

Mallory broke into a jog toward the lifeboat, trying to get there in time for the rescue party. As he ran through the woods, he heard the aircraft returning.

What? They need an LZ, don't they?

They returned, moving much more slowly. They passed above him again, vector fans roaring, and came to a stop about five hundred meters away from him. Right above where the lifeboat had to be. He broke into a run, and he was able to resolve details on the craft. Mallory recognized the design.

It was two centuries out of date, but the design had been a popular version of an airborne troop carrier. It was the kind of ubiquitous vehicle that you'd find in the vehicle pool of every riot police force and planetary militia in the days of the Confederacy.

As Mallory closed on the lifeboat, he saw the side doors slide open to reveal ranks of soldiers in full armor, one of whom was bent over a large plasma cannon aiming out the door on a pintle mount.

Is this a rescue?

Mallory came to a stop as soldiers started dropping out of the aircraft on zip lines. He backed up and crouched for some cover as two dozen men dropped to the ground.

He knew enough tactics to realize that he was pinned. The aircraft would have the imaging gear to see if he ran. His only hope to avoid detection was to hug the base of this tree and hope they hadn't bothered to sweep this area of the woods yet.

He waited, hearing nothing but the massive roar of the hovering aircraft. If they hadn't picked up his transmissions, if they hadn't seen his IR signature running through the woods, if they hadn't caught sight of him any of the times he was in LOS.

Those were too many ifs.

It only took the soldiers five minutes to have a trio of armed men surround him. Mallory took some comfort in the fact they didn't shoot him out of hand.

On some level then, it still counted as a rescue.

CHAPTER THIRTY-SIX

Hallowed Ground

Sometimes the crazy person is right.
—*The Cynic's Book of Wisdom*

Never make the mistake of assuming the universe is sane.
—AUGUST BENITO GALIANI
(2019–*2105)

Date: 2526.6.4 (Standard)
Salmagundi–HD 101534

Nickolai followed Kugara through the woods. It was mostly clear and downhill, meaning they made good time, probably doing better than eight kilometers in the first hour. That made it all the more annoying when a pair of aircraft passed within a klick of them, heading to their northeast, back to where their lifeboat landed.

Kugara stated at the shadows visible through the canopy and said, "I don't believe it."

"Should we go back?"

Kugara stared after the aircraft and sighed. "No, we're closer to the outpost you spotted." She turned around. "Hand me the flare gun."

Nickolai reached into the emergency pack and retrieved the flare gun. It was the last in a long list of signaling devices stowed on the lifeboat and, being the one object not reliant on electronics, it was the one that had survived their lifeboat's impact. Unfortunately most of their high-tech equipment had either taken too much of a beating or was burned by the same shielding breach that had fried the internal electronics of the lifeboat itself. Only the ship's distress beacon survived all of it, and they couldn't take that without taking the whole lifeboat. So they only had a single flare gun that was included in the sparse survival kit almost as an afterthought.

He handed it, butt first, to Kugara.

"Let's hope they see this," she said. "We have only, what, three more flares for this thing?"

Nickolai nodded.

She backed up, looking upward, as the sound of aircrafts' maneuvering fans receded. She held the gun two-handed, pointing up and away from both of them while looking for a hole in the forest canopy. She smiled as she looked up to a ragged blue opening in the green above them.

She aimed the gun upward and fired.

Nickolai heard a click followed by a sharp snap. Nothing happened. Then the gun started hissing.

Kugara screamed, "Shit!" and tossed the flare gun away from her, running toward Nickolai. Before the gun hit the ground, a horribly bright red flame shot out the barrel in a continuous stream. Even with his eyes auto-adjusting, the forest was briefly turned into a two-tone image in blazing red-white and ink black. The air filled with the smell of molten metal, burning leaves, and the toxic smell of melting synthetics. The hiss grew into an insistent low-level roaring, not quite as loud as the aircraft engines in the distance.

Kugara, running blind, tripped on a dead branch. Nickolai stepped forward and caught her before she fell face-first into the dirt.

"Damn Mosasa," she shouted into his chest. "You're supposed to check those things periodically!"

The air choked with acrid smoke as the light died, finally sputtering out. "Are you hurt?" he asked.

She pushed away from him. "I'm fine." She turned around and stepped over to the smoldering crater where the flare gun had landed. She stared at the remains of the gun. The barrel was still recognizable, but the mouth was black, fading to a series of rainbows back toward where the handgrip and the trigger used to be. Those parts had been synthetic, and were melted where they hadn't burned away completely.

The smell of it made his nose itch. His eyes watered, but while he expected his eyes to itch, he realized he didn't feel anything at all. *Like my arm . . .*

"Well, that's a lost cause," she said. She looked up at the wisps of smoke trailing up through the trees. "And if they see that, they're better spotters than I've seen. Back to Plan A."

Kugara picked up the pack she dropped, looked at her compass, and resumed the walk to the outpost. He followed. If luck and the terrain was with them, they'd reach it within the hour.

Forty-five minutes after leaving the smoldering remnants of the flare gun, they found the first sign of civilization. About five hundred meters from their destination, they faced a ten-meter-high fence. The fence was shiny new and dotted with signs saying, "Restricted/Warning/No Admittance."

Kugara looked at the signs and said, "I guess they speak English here. Dr. Pak will be disappointed."

Nickolai looked up at the top of the fence. Small black spheres topped fence posts, sign of either a stun field or surveillance devices. Probably both.

Kugara stepped back from the fence and looked around. "Left or right?"

"Most of the buildings were clustered on the eastern end." He pointed.

"Right it is, then."

After walking a minute or so, Nickolai said, "This is recent."

"I noticed. Those trees are still bleeding whatever they use for sap where they cut the overhangs."

"What are they protecting?"

"You know, I don't really give a shit. We obey the signage and get the guards to call in the cavalry."

Nickolai looked through the fence as they walked, but the woods were still too dense for him to see much of anything on the other side. "Then what?"

"What?"

"What do we do then?"

She spun around. "You know what I want? I want you to shut up." She turned and marched off along the fence. Nickolai followed without asking any more questions.

Not vocally, anyway.

The fact was they were stranded nearly a hundred light-years away from Bakunin. The *Eclipse* was most likely destroyed, along with their nominal employer. Nickolai doubted that a far-flung colony like this would be willing to expend the time and resources to return them—if the Fallen here were even willing to deal with a nonhuman like him. . . .

Dying would have been simpler.

There was a gate only a few hundred meters farther along the fence. It opened to a rough road that was little more than a muddy track. There were signs of a couple of heavy tracked vehicles traveling this way not too long ago. The weight of them had left trenches six to ten centimeters deep in the earth. He saw some sign of foot traffic around the gate, but none that went more than ten meters away from the fence. All of the tracks were the club-shaped boots of the Fallen.

A guard shack sat about five meters inside the fence, to their right. The gate itself was designed to slide aside for the large traffic on the road. Inside the sliding gate was a smaller human-sized doorway, hanging open.

"Hello?" Kugara called out.

Nothing stirred. The guard shack was apparently empty.

She looked around. "I don't get it."

Nickolai took a deep breath and shook his head. "No humans here, not for hours. But . . ."

"But, what?"

"I smell old fires, explosives. Human blood."

"Jesus. And they just leave the door open?"

"Maybe there's nothing left to protect."

Kugara pulled her small flechette gun and pointed it at the ground. "If you would do me the favor?" She nodded to the open gate.

Nickolai supposed that he should be grateful that she did him the favor of at least making the pretense of asking. He walked over to the door. There was some logic to being the experimental subject here; any traps were going to be scaled for a human intruder and might not affect him as badly. Even so, he suspected that tactics was only a secondary consideration in having him take the lead.

He pushed the gate with his artificial hand, and it swung inward. He had to crouch and step through sidewise to avoid touching the frame of the door, which could still be charged.

No traps were sprung on him, no sudden stun fields, and no guards emerging from the trees. Nothing happened other than leaves rustling in the breeze and the door slowly creaking shut. He walked over to the guard shack. It was a small temporary structure with one-way windows, barely twice as wide as he was; just tall and deep enough for a human to stand comfortably inside.

Around back was the entrance, which hung open like the gate. He opened it, and no one was inside.

"Nickolai?" Kugara shouted, still on the other side of the fence.

"No one's here!" Nickolai shouted back from behind the guard shack.

There wasn't room for him inside the building, but its shallow depth put the control panel within easy reach. He touched the panel and called up a series of small views of the perimeter fence. A few more taps, and he was looking at a series of views, presumably from inside the fence. He saw a number of temporary structures, and what looked like a landing area, but no people and no vehicles.

Also, many of the buildings showed signs of withstanding some sort of firefight. The area between the structures showed debris and shrapnel.

He heard Kugara approach him, but he was still startled when her voice came from near his right elbow.

"What the *HELL* is that?"

It only took a moment for him to realize what she was talking about. A camera had just panned to bring into view something that didn't belong here. Something that didn't belong anywhere, as far as Nickolai was concerned.

The camera panned from a series of temporary prefab buildings to something that Nickolai couldn't classify as a building or a plant or a geological feature. It was a twisting crystalline structure that seemed to grow out of the ground and repeatedly fold into itself as it reached up into the sky. The camera kept panning over more geometric forms that seemed to have been born out of the hallucinations of a Paralian mathematician.

Nickolai stared at the images in the small holo and couldn't turn them into anything more than pure abstractions. If the shiny forms held a function, he couldn't discern it.

"What is it?" Kugara repeated.

"It must be what they were fencing in."

"Is it some sort of natural formation?"

He shook his head. "There's no sign of anyone here. If

these are the comm channels," he tapped on a quiet part of the console removed from the security cam display, "there's no talking going on around here."

"So we have some sort of firefight, and an evacuation."

"That's what it looks like."

"And *that*." She gestured toward the holo that was panning back across the crystal enigma.

Nickolai nodded. "And that."

"It would be just our luck to make landfall in the middle of a war." She stepped back and gestured down the road with her gun. "Well we should check out exactly what kind of mess we're facing. I'm almost glad our flare gun failed."

The small outpost nestled in an oblong clearing in the woods, one that *had* been some sort of impact site. When they walked from the woods to the clearing itself, Nickolai could see the signs in the trees. Many were blackened, and the massive hexagonal plates that passed for bark had sloughed off the trees that still stood at the perimeter, revealing a dull-red interior that seemed to be a sign the tree was dying. In front of the wounded sentinels, their broken comrades had been piled into deadfalls on the edges of the clearing.

The clearing itself was populated by two ranks of temporary buildings that marched down toward the opposite end of the clearing, where the site turned alien and crystalline. Seeing it with his own eyes, and not through a holo camera, Nickolai could see something he hadn't noticed through the security cameras; the buildings showed more combat damage the closer they got to the crystal. The buildings directly adjacent showed severe burning, shrapnel and blast damage. The abstract geometry of the crystals appeared untouched.

Nickolai could smell the remnants of explosives and old fire stronger than ever. He could also smell the scent of a human being.

"In front of us," he whispered, "in the crystals, our one o'clock."

Kugara turned to face that direction, and he heard a gunshot from some sort of slugthrower. The source was impossible to pin down precisely. The crystal structures vibrated in sympathy with the sound and contributed distorted echoes.

"Drop the weapon!" The accent was odd and distorted by the same crystal echoes, but it was understandable.

Kugara looked at him and lowered the flechette gun. That wasn't enough for the sniper. "I said drop it!"

Kugara tossed the gun on the ground in front of them. "We aren't part of what's happening here. Our lifeboat crashed—"

"Who are you? What is that . . . creature?"

"I'm Julie Kugara, my companion is Nickolai Rajasthan. We are crew members from the tach-ship *Eclipse*. Our lifeboat landed in the woods southwest of—"

"Are you from Xi Virginis?"

"What?"

"Are you from Xi Virginis?!"

"No," Nickolai answered, interrupting Kugara. "The *Eclipse* was based out of Bakunin."

"Bakunin?" The voice's tone changed, becoming less confrontational. "There's still a Bakunin out there?"

"As far as we know." Kugara said. "We've been in tach-space for over six months."

Nickolai saw a shadow move in the crystalline landscape. It resolved into a relatively young human male holding a shotgun. The man was shorter than Kugara and wore a pair of tan overalls. He walked with a bit of a limp.

"You two are really from Bakunin?" He brushed some hair from in front of his face, revealing a tattoo in the middle of his forehead. He was staring at Nickolai. "You talk?"

"Yes." If it wasn't for Kugara's presence, he would have leaped and disabled this man already. He could tell this youth had no military training just by the way he held his shotgun and ignored Kugara's discarded weapon as he walked toward them. Considering how much attention he was paying to Nickolai, Kugara could probably clear the distance between them and disarm him before he realized she had moved.

For a moment, the man didn't seem to be paying attention to either of them, then he said, "Moreau, right? From the Seven Worlds?"

"It hasn't been the Seven Worlds for a hundred and seventy-five years," Nickolai said. "It's the Fifteen Worlds now."

"Of course it is. We've been out of touch." He walked around them, keeping what he must have assumed was a safe distance. "A lot of you on Bakunin now? Since it became 'officially' part of the Sev—Fifteen Worlds?"

Nickolai wondered what was going on. When this man first saw them, it seemed clear he had no idea who or what Nickolai was. Now he seemed to be aware of the history of Nickolai's people, at least up until one hundred seventy-five years ago. He wondered if he was in radio contact with someone else. He didn't see signs of the man wearing a radio, but that didn't mean anything. He could have anything implanted, could be in contact with anyone on the planet as far as they knew.

"There aren't very many; most are exiles, like me."

"Bakunin's still a great place to run away from something?" He turned and looked up at Kugara, who was a good head taller than he was. "That your story? You running away from something?"

"I retired."

"From?"

"Dakota Planetary Security."

The man paused and took a step back, looking at her. He whispered to himself. Nickolai heard his nearly-subvocalized words, "Oh, boy, Gram." Then, after a pause, "Go right ahead."

There was a strange and abrupt shift in the man's body language. His grip on the shotgun changed, so he was now a lot more able to bring it to bear quickly. The cock of his head, and even his facial expression seemed different.

Most different was the voice. It suddenly seemed older, more confident. "Forgive me if I'm a little incredulous that my long-lost sister from Dakota just walked into our little no-man's land. You got some convincing to do, chicky, starting with what in the name of Jesus Christ on a unicycle you're doing a hundred light-years from what's left of the ass-end of the Confederacy."

CHAPTER THIRTY-SEVEN

Zealots

War does not exist when all parties have perfect knowledge.

—*The Cynic's Book of Wisdom*

The greater the ignorance the greater the dogmatism.

—Sir William Osler
(1849–1919)

Date: 2526.6.4 (Standard)
Salmagundi–HD 101534

Alexander sat in his impromptu command center within the Ashley Hall of Minds, trying to improve the glacial response time of the Salmagundi government. Even in the face of his coup, and his direct control of every police department, security agency, and militia on the planet, events conspired to move faster than Salmagundi could react.

On the screens before him, he could see the recon team securing the last lifeboat site. Three of the six lifeboats had been unoccupied, and they had secured the occupants of two others. The teams had sterilized the sites, using plasma grenades to reduce the lifeboats themselves to slag.

It was the kind of direct action the Triad spent days debating, worrying over its effect on the general population. As if the presence of offworlders and offworld artifacts would be somehow *less* disruptive.

At least that concern was moderated by the fact that they had already evacuated the civilian population from the forest east of Ashley in preparation for using their nuclear stores on Flynn Jorgenson's alien invader. The evacuation was fortunate on many levels. It helped ensure that no civilian agency came

across the lifeboats before the militia got there—even with
the intolerable delay caused by the Grand Triad's debate.

Alexander idly wondered if they were *still* debating.

The preliminary abbreviated debriefing conducted by the
on-site commander with the four *Eclipse* crew members they
had retrieved indicated that there were two lifeboat occupants
who still remained at large. They were his immediate concern.
He needed them in his control or confirmed deceased. His
militia scouts had identified the lifeboat the missing two had
landed in, and after slagging the wreck, they now engaged in
a search pattern, spiraling out from the landing site. It concerned Alexander, because it placed a militia team in uncomfortable proximity to Flynn Jorgenson's Protean anomaly. He
had the nuclear strike on hold, but the other militia teams had
already retreated out of the red zone. Alexander did not want
one of the militia teams in harm's way if he had to launch the
attack. They weren't an expendable resource.

One of the militia officers with him solved the problem.

"Sir, we have something on holo five."

Alexander looked up, and saw a security feed from the
camp around the Protean artifact. The camp was abandoned
in anticipation of the coming strike, but he saw three figures
standing in the middle of a muddy track. One was Flynn
Jorgenson, the unfortunate who had discovered the Protean
artifact's impact site. The other two were unquestionably
the two missing invaders from the lifeboat. One wasn't even
human. It had striped fur, a tail, and looked as if it stood
three meters tall.

They were too close to the Protean site for the militia to
retrieve them, even if he wanted to risk contact with something so obviously nonhuman. He would have to be satisfied
with the strike.

He ordered the last militia aircraft out of the red zone and
resumed the countdown for the nuclear strike.

Date: 2526.6.4 (Standard)
650,000 km from Salmagundi–HD 101534

While the *Jizan* approached with the troublesome remains of
the *Eclipse* and its crew, Admiral Hussein had the data from
the crew interviews piped into the same meeting room where
he had been reviewing the transmission from Admiral Bitar.

He watched the debriefing of the *Eclipse*'s owner, Mosasa,

as it was transmitted back to the *Voice*. He wanted to believe that it was some sort of elaborate misinformation ploy. Even while the human-shaped AI was still talking, he pulled half of the intelligence analysts on the *Voice* to do what fact-checking they could using the resources on the *Voice* against what data the *Jizan* could recover from the dead ship.

By the grace of God, how did all this fall into my lap?

The medical officers who had been doing the analysis of Bitar's transmission were still with him, observing the android's statement for much the same reason.

"What do you make of it?" he asked them, still watching the hairless Mosasa's passion play. The medical officers sat at a square table in the observation room while Hussein paced around the perimeter. In the center of the table was a holo projecting an image of the seated Mosasa and his interrogator on board the *Jizan*.

Lieutenant Deshem folded his hands, watching the confession, and shaking his head. "I don't know what value I can provide. The medical team has done everything possible with a noninvasive scan to confirm that this—*thing*—is exactly what it says it is."

"And everything else it's saying?"

"Admiral, sir, this thing is a machine. All I can tell you is how well or poorly it is mimicking human responses. Unlike a human being, we have to assume that every response—voice, body language, pupil dilation—may be engineered for our benefit."

"I understand your caution," Admiral Hussein said. "We're facing something that admits its own design was for the purpose of manipulating human responses. That said, if we take all those cues—voice, body language, pupil dilation—at face value, what is Mosasa telling us?"

"As if this was the interview of a human being?"

"Yes."

Deshem nodded. "Mosasa shows signs of being dangerously psychopathic and potentially suicidal."

"What?"

"I see no exhibition of empathy, and he—it—displays a narcissism bordering on megalomania. It is the center of its own universe, and it has rewritten its own personal narrative so that it is not just the hero, but it is God. A human being with those traits would be, at the very least, sociopathic. Combine this with a series of failures aboard the *Eclipse* and we have a situation where reality contradicts its personal worldview. Its self-image is incompatible with powerlessness, and that conflict is manifesting as signs of depression."

Hussein stared into the holo and asked, "And you think Mosasa would want us to see that? Make that interpretation of his story?"

"No, I do not—which is precisely why I distrust the conclusion."

Hussein stared into the holographic Mosasa's eyes and felt a deep unease.

The *Jizan* had a fully operational medical unit that had shown him the scans of the creature sitting in this holographic interrogation room. Never mind how human Mosasa looked, or how human he behaved, there wasn't a single biological component to the thing being interrogated on the *Jizan*. It didn't matter if Hussein could recognize the pain and fear in Mosasa's expression. It didn't matter if he could see the loss in Mosasa's holographic eyes. There was nothing behind them, no soul, only an imitation of life. A facade constructed solely for the purpose of deceit and manipulation.

If the Father of Lies was to attempt to create a man, Hussein suspected the result would resemble Mosasa.

The more Hussein stared at Mosasa's expression, the more he thought Deshem had described a psych profile that perfectly fit an AI, and *this* AI in particular.

This is why we do not suffer such things to exist.

As the *Voice* caught up with the *Jizan,* Admiral Hussein watched the other surviving crew members being debriefed. Between the statements, and the data from the dead ship, he confirmed the *Eclipse* had been Mosasa's scientific expedition toward Xi Virginis.

The *Eclipse* had accumulated a large amount of scientific data observing the site where Xi Virginis had been. If it was to be trusted, the star didn't exist anymore.

Admiral Hussein thought of Admiral Bitar and the *Sword*'s fleet. He supposed that the pilot of the *Eclipse* could have tached out before the *Sword*'s arrival, but where were the technologically advanced natives of Xi Virginis that Admiral Bitar had told them about?

It would take a significant effort to completely map the

Eclipse's transit history, but a cursory review of the logs supported the crew's story. The *Eclipse* had been in transit for months. Even with the fastest standard tach-drive available, it took the *Eclipse* as long to make its twenty light-year hops as the *Voice* took to make its eighty light-year leap.

Hussein found it incredible that a civilian had been able to secure such an advanced drive system. What was more incredible was the fact when the crew of the *Voice* was receiving its crash training on a virgin ship Mosasa's expedition was well underway.

It seemed unlikely that such an undertaking would have gone completely unnoticed. Hussein suspected that Caliphate intelligence discovered Mosasa's expedition and moved up the timetable for launching the new fleets. Of course, he would have liked it if his own intelligence officers had known about that beforehand.

A cursory examination of the *Eclipse*'s logs recovered names, biometric identification, and some history on all the crew members. Mosasa had split his people between a science team and a group of mercenaries from Bakunin. It seemed a lot of military talent for a scientific expedition, but that was probably par for the course on Bakunin.

The science team seemed fairly straightforward, including a linguist, a data analyst, an anthropologist, and a xenobiologist. Add to that a Paralian, who was an expert on theoretical physics and went by the alias Bill. The nature of the team pretty much demonstrated that Mosasa expected to encounter a human colony out here.

The mercenary team was *interesting*.

Not only had the *Eclipse* been sabotaged, it had harbored a Vatican spy. The presence of a Vatican agent gave weight to the idea that the *Eclipse* was actually the impetus that set the *Voice* and her sisters in motion early.

When the *Eclipse*'s crew was brought on board the *Voice*, Admiral Hussein made it a point to meet the most diplomatically sensitive crew member first, the Paralian.

Having one of the creatures on board the *Voice* was troublesome, and he intended to show the creature the respect he would any diplomatic envoy. It was also a logistic issue, since the creature's life support resided in a machine that was nearly six meters tall and five wide. There was no way it would fit in any of the human spaces in the *Voice*, so at the moment their alien guest resided in an unpressurized loading bay that served one of the hundred spacecraft that formed the *Voice*'s battle group.

A set of engineers was scrambling to figure out what to do with Bill once the fleet had to reattach to the carrier.

It also meant that a face-to-face required an environment suit, and the only record was the low-res holo camera embedded in the chest of that suit. Out here, open to space, blocked only by a safety grille across the thirty-meter docking portal, there was none of the sophisticated monitoring equipment they had in the interrogation rooms. Not that all the physical monitoring in the world would make sense looking at Bill.

To his surprise, Bill, or, more accurately, the communications software Bill used, was as fluent in Arabic as it was in English.

Admiral Hussein questioned the creature over the comm link, watching the tentacled bullet-bodied thing for some clue to its emotional state. It was as hopeless as trying to read the mood of a jellyfish.

Even so, the history Bill provided him was congruent with the stories from the others and the *Eclipse*'s logs. All had been hired by Mosasa to uncover some sort of ill-defined anomaly originating from the direction of Xi Virginis.

It also confirmed the details of what they found there, or failed to find there. It provided a wealth of technical details especially on how the *Eclipse* ended up damaged and inbound to this system. Most of those details were completely opaque to Admiral Hussein, but they would help the engineers in going over the wreck of the *Eclipse*.

It was that technical discussion, opaque as it was, where Bill complicated the diplomatic issue.

"I am impressed with your ship," Bill radioed from his electronic voice box. Even in Arabic, the words carried a Windsor accent.

"What do you mean?"

"I never would have thought human engineers would be able to build a tach-drive that worked beyond the asymptotic barrier."

Admiral Hussein just stared at the creature in its glass globe.

"I apologize, was I unclear?"

"No, go on, please."

"Even the highest acolytes of our universities within Paralia have failed in designing a stable generator that could manipulate a field complex enough to move the asymptotic barrier. In theory it was always possible, but the dimensions involved increase with the cube of the distance, so solving the equations for a three-dimensional reference frame—"

"Bill?"

"Yes, Admiral? Do I need to explain something?"

"Just tell me how you know the capabilities of this ship?"

"Simple observation; the data provided when the *Eclipse*'s own drive failed provided enough data to describe a boundary model of your drive capability. The mass/drive ratios visible on this ship speak to an unorthodox sixfold redundancy or a new drive design. Mosasa implied that his expedition would be the impetus driving the Caliphate outward, meaning you left after us, yet arrived before us, despite the necessity of supplying and outfitting a vessel this large for a hundred-light-year journey."

"I see." Admiral Hussein turned away from the Paralian and looked out the grate and toward the stars. The planet they were here for was a small blue-white disk, brighter than the stars behind it.

He had known that these capabilities would be known as soon as they were used, but it was discomforting to realize that even the Paralian considered them extraordinary. He was not in the habit of questioning his government, but for several moments he wondered where the expertise had come from.

"What is it you see?" asked the Paralian. It took a moment for Admiral Hussein to realize that it was in response to the last thing he had said. He turned to face his massive guest and was about to explain the figure of speech when his suit's comm called for his attention on the command channel. He switched the comm from the closed channel he shared with the Paralian and immediately heard Captain Rasheed's voice.

"Admiral Hussein?"

"Yes, Captain?"

"We just detected an energy spike on the other side of the planet. We don't have visual contact yet, but it's consistent with the *Sword*'s tach-drive signature."

"Are you sure?"

"It has to be an Ibrahim-class carrier. No other drives leave as large a footprint."

Instead of an envoy, Bitar comes in person?

"I'm coming to the bridge."

Admiral Hussein turned the comm back to the Paralian's channel. "I have to go now," he told it.

"Is there a problem?"

"No," he lied.

Date: 2526.6.4 (Standard)
Salmagundi–HD 101534

In less than an hour, Alexander had confirmation that the last of the militia aircraft was safely out of the red zone. He ordered the drone aircraft bearing the nuke to head for the target. In ten minutes, the low altitude airburst would vaporize everything at the impact site. On the security footage, the two offworlders still stood with Flynn.

"Mr. Shane," one of the militia officers said shortly after he ordered the nuke into position.

"What?"

"We have developments in orbit. I'm putting the feed on holo one."

The main display in front of Alexander shifted to show the schematic of the space around Salmagundi. It had changed since he had left the rest of the Grand Triad to their debate. When he'd left the meeting room, there had been a dozen unidentified spacecraft, one identified as the source of the lifeboats and of the offworlders standing in the security footage showing on holo five.

The red-highlighted spacecraft was no longer shown on the schematic. Now on the fringes of the image, Alexander saw thirty or forty blue icons pushing in from the edge. As he watched, three more appeared in range.

Closer in, in orbit above them, there were suddenly dozens of vessels.

"What the hell?"

"Our observatories are picking up dozens of spacecraft just now taking up positions in orbit."

"How many?"

"At least sixty."

Alexander settled back into his seat, staring at the screen. He had moved, but not quickly enough. He watched the icons maneuver in discreet jumps as observations were made and fed again into the model he was watching.

The militia officer spoke again, "We have sixty-three confirmed contacts. Sixty-five. Sixty-eight."

"Stop counting," Alexander whispered. Salmagundi had, maybe, a dozen craft capable of orbit. All dated from the original colonization. The Confederacy was about to descend upon them, and there was nothing they could do about it.

"Mr. Shane? We need confirmation to detonate the nuke."

Alexander looked at the security monitor. Flynn and the offworlders were looking up.

"Mr. Shane, sir?"

Tetsami faced the newcomers and said, "Forgive me if I'm a little incredulous that my long-lost sister from Dakota just walked into our little no-man's land. You got some convincing to do, chicky, starting with what in the name of Jesus Christ on a unicycle you're doing a hundred light-years from what's left of the ass-end of the Confederacy."

She looked from the tall woman to the taller moreau. Her own genes, at least the genes for the last body that had been exclusively her own, had come from Dakota. However, unlike the three-meter-tall furry tiger-man, just by looking, there was usually no way to tell someone from Dakota from a human whose genetic history didn't include a couple of genetic engineers trying to "improve" something a few centuries ago. A century or two of mixing bloodlines and the more-or-less "normal" human morphology dominated.

One thing was clear, the presence of tiger-boy proved that this couple was as definitively from off-planet as their nameless Protean.

But from *Dakota?* What the hell was going on here?

It didn't get better.

The woman, Kugara, did most of the talking. She told Tetsami and Flynn about their ship, the *Eclipse,* and the ill-fated expedition it made to Xi Virginis. The story uncomfortably synced with the Protean's warnings, and Tetsami tightened the grip on her shotgun. Even more than when the nonhuman pair walked into the deserted outpost, she stared at them looking for some sign of infection, some wrongness, some symptom that these two had been touched by the same darkness that had consumed the Xi Virginis system.

Then Kugara mentioned his name.

Tetsami jumped backward, leveling the shotgun at the space between Kugara's gut and Nickolai's groin. "What was that name?" she yelled at them, finger aching against the cold metal of the shotgun's trigger.

What the hell? Gram?

Shut up!

The tall woman backed up, stopping only when she bumped into the tiger. "Mosasa, Tjaele Mosasa." Nickolai put his arm around her in a gesture that was almost protective.

"What the hell does that bastard have to do with this?" Tetsami screamed at them. The barrel of the shotgun shook, and she concentrated on steadying her aim.

What, you know this person?

Shut up!

It could just be someone with the same name . . .

"SHUT UP!" Kugara looked at her as if Tetsami had just lost her mind. *I just said that out loud, fuck.* "Mosasa," Tetsami said. "Tjaele Mosasa."

"Yes."

"Bald, lots of earrings, dragon tattoo, looks like a pirate?"

"Yes."

"Christ on the cross with his tap-dancing apostles!" Tetsami leveled the shotgun at Kugara's head and yelled, "You *work* for that robotic bastard?"

Nickolai stepped in front of Kugara and it spooked Tetsami so much she almost shot him in the chest. "Yes," Nickolai said. "We are members of the Bakunin Mercenaries' Union, and we were hired by Mosasa. But Kugara wasn't aware of what he was until I told her."

"You know what that amoral Machiavellian machine actually is?"

"I did," Nickolai said. "She didn't."

Tetsami raised the shotgun so it was centered on Nickolai's face. The tiger didn't even flinch.

Gram, what are you doing? She felt Flynn pushing to take control back, but she wouldn't let go. "Then why shouldn't I blow your head off for working for that thing?"

The tiger stared down the barrel of the shotgun and said, "If you wish to kill me, kill me."

"Damn it," Kugara's voice came from behind the tiger as

she tried to push past his arm. "Thanks to Nickolai here, that amoral Machiavellian machine is probably dead."

The barrel lowered a fraction. "What?"

Kugara managed to step around the tiger's bandaged arm. "This furry prick sabotaged the *Eclipse*. He's the reason we were on a lifeboat landing on this godforsaken world."

Tetsami lowered the shotgun and shook her head. She still couldn't get her brain around the idea that Mosasa, of all things, had followed her nearly two hundred years and a hundred light-years from Bakunin. She had come out here, so far, just to get away from that thrice-damned planet.

But this was Mosasa they were talking about. It's quite possible that she was trapped, again, in some long-term plot created by the AI to manipulate the universe into some form that was more to its liking. The pair here might be just as trapped in the AI's web.

"Anomalies around Xi Virginis?" Tetsami whispered. "But damn vague about them, I bet."

"You know Mosasa?" Kugara asked her. "Good lord, how?"

Yeah, Gram, how?

Tetsami laughed. "Mosasa's why I'm here, why this colony's here. Hell, I wouldn't be surprised if he was why Xi Virginis disappeared."

"What?" both said in unison.

"Short version," Tetsami told them. "I came from that pit Bakunin. I escaped the shitstorm that pretty much collapsed the Terran Confederacy. A shitstorm your friend Mosasa largely took credit for."

"He's not our friend," the tiger said. "He was our employer."

"Mosasa took credit for the collapse of the Confederacy?" Kugara asked.

"Oh, come on," Tetsami said. "You just said you knew what he was. Don't you know what those Race AIs were designed for? The kind of social engineering they're responsible for? It's how the Race waged war." She lowered the shotgun and gestured with her free hand, taking in the whole horizon. "This planet was on a Dolbrian star map buried under the Diderot Mountains on Bakunin. A star map that one of Mosasa's AIs just happened to find while the old Confederacy was trying a military takeover of the planet. A star map that got handed over to the Seven Worlds and caused enough chaos in the

Confederacy's congress that the whole shebang started collapsing under its own weight."

The two of them stared at her as if she wasn't speaking the same language.

"It's the Fifteen Worlds now," Tetsami said. "Go thank Mosasa for that. And the Dolbrians."

"How do you know all this," Kugara asked. "This planet's been out of contact since it was founded—"

"I'm older than I look," Tetsami said. "About a hundred and seventy-five years older."

CHAPTER THIRTY-EIGHT

Destiny

Nothing is so destructive as what we believe to be true.
—The Cynic's Book of Wisdom

No passion so effectually robs the mind of all its powers of
acting and reasoning as fear.

—EDMUND BURKE
(1729–1797)

Date: 2526.6.4 (Standard)
Salmagundi–HD 101534

Nickolai stared at the man with the shotgun and tried to understand what was happening. Something—Mosasa, fate, or
divine will—was conspiring to draw these threads around
them. If what this man said was true, Mosasa knew of these
colonies long ago. He would have known when they had been
founded.

All of this, everything that was happening, could be the result of a centuries-old AI attempting to manipulate events.

He admitted as much, Nickolai thought, remembering the
dialogue between Mosasa and Wahid when the *Eclipse* had
just gotten underway.

*"High levels of the Caliphate have known of them for quite
some time, thus their interest in stopping this expedition. As to
Dr. Dörner's original question; the necessity of violence was
required to draw out and neutralize the Caliphate's somewhat
limited resources on Bakunin. By doing so, we've ensured the
safety of the expedition."*

"What's to stop the Caliphate from just pouncing on us now?"

*"We're no longer their problem. Their public attacks, combined
with my public advertisements for mercenaries to travel toward*

Xi Virginis, has alerted every intelligence agency with an asset on Bakunin that the Caliphate is hiding something in that region of space. There's no secret for them to protect anymore. My small expedition means nothing when they need to rally whole fleets to lay claim to this sector of space before a rival does."

At the time, Nickolai had been too preoccupied with his own ill-fated duty to Mr. Antonio to think deeply on the human politics involved. In retrospect, Mosasa had offhandedly taken credit for possibly starting a war.

It also raised the question of exactly what Mr. Antonio was trying to accomplish. At first, it was simply an internecine battle between the Fallen. Even when Mr. Antonio told him of Mosasa's artificial nature, Nickolai never thought of the implications.

Mosasa was designed to anticipate, to see the forces of society arrayed around him. See them and manipulate them. He maneuvered the Caliphate into moving entire fleets ...

How did he not anticipate what Nickolai did? How did he not know until Nickolai made his testament to the human priest? How did he not know about Mr. Antonio or his employers?

Who was Mr. Antonio?

Nicolai forced himself to pay attention to more immediate concerns, like the man with the gun. Fortunately, he had lowered the weapon. The way the man talked, Nickolai wondered if it was because he finally trusted they weren't a threat, or because he was overcome with some sort of contagious fatalism.

The man talked of the founding of this colony, named Salmagundi, by refugees from a war on Bakunin 175 years ago. The colonists came from destroyed communes and bankrupt corporations and planets in upheaval during the Confederacy's long, slow collapse. Apparently, they were talking to one of the founders of that exodus, a woman named Kari Tetsami, who should be over a century dead. The man in front of them was also a man named Flynn Jorgenson, who was born on this planet.

He explained the Hall of Minds.

The concept was beyond appalling. It left Nickolai shaken and numb. To strip someone's mind? On some level it was worse than constructing an AI. Not only was it the arrogance of imitating life, it was imitating a *specific* life. And to accept that heretical copy into yourself—it was a sin so intimate and profound that Nickolai had trouble conceiving it.

The priests see the world of Men as Hell only because they haven't come here.

Kugara asked what was going on here, with the scars of battle, the abandoned structures, and the crystal edifice in front of them.

Nickolai had thought the revelations could not become worse. Then he heard the man who was a 175-year-old woman answer Kugara.

They stood mere meters from the ultimate sin of the Fallen, the most dangerous and vile presumption of God's power. The geometric crystals glinting in the light hid a hive of self-replicating machines whose sole purpose was to consume matter and remake it in its own image. This was the demon that tempted man into his final fall, that spoke the seductive whispers that a man could equal God Himself, symbol of the hubris that had cost a billion souls.

It was a sin that the Fallen could never erase, even with centuries of turning away from such heresies. Even the colonists here—who gave themselves over to a hideously intimate evil—even they had seen the wisdom of trying to destroy this.

Kugara stared at the crystal forms, and Nickolai felt her shudder against his arm. "What is *that* doing here?"

"It came from Xi Virginis."

"What?"

"It ran into something en route to the other end of the galaxy and was severely damaged," Flynn/Tetsami said. "It can't hold much of a conversation, but it is worried that whatever damaged it is coming here."

"What damaged it?" Kugara asked.

Flynn/Tetsami shook his head. "It isn't quite clear on what it is. It called it 'The Other,' and it seems afraid of it—"

Nickolai found his voice. "How is it that you speak to it?" The words were almost a growl.

"It can form a—robot? cyborg?—something the size and shape of a human being. It talked to us a while, then it re-absorbed itself. I think it's trying to fix some sort of damage. It's been a while since I've seen it, or anyone else for that matter."

"It should be destroyed," Nickolai whispered. He spoke in a register so low that the others didn't seem to hear him.

"What did it say about this 'Other'?" Kugara asked.

Flynn/Tetsami shook his head. "It described it as a cloud, sometimes as a virus, sometimes as a complete abstraction: 'the change without consent.' What I could understand is that what I talked to was the remains of the autopilot for the Protean probe. The probe actually changed course to investigate some spectral anomalies happening to Xi Virginis. By the time it got within a light-year or so, the whole solar system was gone."

"It knows what happened?"

"The Other," Flynn/Tetsami said. "The Other somehow consumed—"

Nickolai heard the aircraft first. He raised his head to look at the sky. In a few moments, the two others followed his lead, looking up.

"One aircraft," Nickolai said.

"Mr. Shane? We need confirmation to detonate the nuke."

Alexander looked at the security footage. Flynn and the offworlders were looking up.

"Mr. Shane, sir?"

The Confederacy, or what was left of it, was about to take Salmagundi. He saw no hope of resistance. *Seventy-five ships now.*

They sent *that* many *this* far. He looked at the security camera feed of the crystalline invader. He wondered if it was the invader they pursued. He knew human history before the founding of Salmagundi. He knew the taboos against heretical technologies that would condemn the Hall of Minds. He also knew that Flynn's discovery would be an order of magnitude worse in the eyes of the fleet descending upon them.

The two offworlders he saw in the security footage, they were clearly an advance team. Diplomats or spies, it didn't matter—they belonged to the fleet entering orbit. How would the newcomers accept their loss? Could he afford to provoke them?

"Sir?"

In the past, the Confederacy had blown the crust off of planets infected by the kind of nanotechnology that lived in the egg Flynn Jorgenson had found. Just its presence here was a provocation.

The Hall of Minds was taboo to them and might be destroyed by an invasion. But intelligent, self-replicating nanotech? That was an abomination that might cost the lives of everyone on this planet.

It wasn't really a choice.

"Sir?"

Alexander rubbed his fingers across the tattoos on his brow and said, "Detonate the nuke."

Date: 2526.6.4 (Standard)
620,000 km from Salmagundi–HD 101534

Admiral Hussein reached the bridge still wearing the jumpsuit that he had worn under his EVA suit. Even before he said "at ease" to the bridge crew, he saw that the situation had developed alarmingly. The main screen showed a magnified image of the planet, and just coming into visual range over the horizon was an Ibrahim-class carrier, the twin of the *Voice*.

There was no question it was Bitar's ship.

There was also no question, given the enhanced visuals, that the *Sword* had deployed its own hundred-ship battle group.

What the hell does he think he's doing?

"Captain," Hussein asked, "Any communication with the ship?"

"No response yet, sir. They're deploying in a defensive grid around the planet."

Hussein shook his head. The *Sword*'s fleet was deploying between them and the planet, almost as if they intended to repel the *Voice*'s approach. The *Voice* and its fleet was still over half a million klicks; the *Sword* had tached in to within five thousand.

"Give me a secure transmission to the *Sword*," Hussein said.

"Yes, sir," responded Captain Rasheed.

Admiral Hussein straightened himself and stepped over to the square that marked the focus of the holo cameras. When the comm tech told him he was live, he spoke to the *Sword*.

"This is Admiral Hussein on the *Prophet's Voice*. In the name of the Eridani Caliphate, the Prophet, and our God, respond and declare your intentions."

A few seconds later, the comm tech responded, "We have a transmission back, sirs."

"Put it on the main screen," Admiral Hussein ordered.

The holo showing the *Sword* silhouetted against the blue-white horizon of the planet changed to show Hussein's opposite number, Admiral Bitar.

"Greetings, Admiral Hussein, I trust this day finds you well."

Hussein nodded slightly. "To what exactly do we owe the pleasure of your presence, Admiral Bitar?"

There was enough space between them that there was a noticeable lag before Bitar's answer. "I am sorry, this all may seem a bit rude of me. As I told you earlier, we are about to embark upon a new age. I am simply ensuring that everything goes as planned."

"Admiral, I know of no plans involving the *Prophet's Sword* contacting this planet."

After two seconds of waiting, Bitar laughed. "Forgive me, Muhammad. I wasn't talking about the *Caliphate's* plans."

Hussein stared at Bitar's image, shocked. Even though he suspected something odd on the basis of the prior transmission, he had not expected a bald-faced admission of treason. He gestured to the comm officer to mute the outbound transmission and turned toward Captain Rasheed.

"Immediate orders to the whole fleet. Treat any ship with a transponder signature from the *Sword* as a potentially hostile enemy vessel."

"Admiral?"

"Do it."

"Admiral Hussein," Bitar said on the holo, "are you still receiving me?"

Hussein gestured to have his transmission come back on-line. "Yes, I am. Exactly whose plans are you referring to?"

"The natives of Xi Virginis, of course."

"There is no Xi Virginis," Hussein said. "Not anymore. There are no 'colonists who have discovered a means to harness all the energy produced by the star.' "

"Ah. Adam said you would recover him."

Hussein shook his head. "Who?"

"Tjaele Mosasa."

Hussein stared at the holo, speechless. There was no way Bitar could know about Mosasa.

Bitar's eyes seemed to deaden, and all the humor drained from his voice. "Now, Muhammad, I will warn you to not attempt landfall on this planet. If you interfere with what is about to happen, you and your fleet will be destroyed so thoroughly that not even your mass will remain."

"Do not threaten me, Admiral Bitar."

"I do not threaten you, and I will not touch you or your ships. Accept what is about to happen, embrace it. You will be offered something wonderful, and you cannot reject it or turn it aside."

The comm officer gestured, and the comm channel was muted.

Hussein turned on the man, "What are you doing?"

"Sir, we just detected a nuclear blast on the surface, in the ten-megaton range."

"We aren't going to let Bitar level a defenseless planet." Admiral Hussein gestured to unmute the signal. "Admiral Bitar, I am relieving you of your command. I order you to stand down and surrender."

"I can't do that."

He gestured to cut the outbound transmission and whipped around to face Captain Rasheed. "Engage the *Sword*'s fleet."

"Sir?"

"Now!"

"Yes, sir!"

Klaxons sounded and lights began flashing. Around Bitar's image, tactical displays began coming up showing the relative positions of the *Voice*'s fleet and the *Sword*'s. On the screen, Bitar had turned to face something offscreen, and his face registered surprise.

The tactical holos showed the *Voice*'s attack ships taking inhuman Gs to get into range of Bitar's fleet. Hussein smiled grimly. The *Sword*'s fleet was deployed to cordon the planet, but it left the ships themselves thinly spread, allowing Hussein's own ships to mass three on one at the edges of Bitar's formation.

Admiral Bitar turned to face Hussein. "You are making a mistake."

Even though he was no longer transmitting, Hussein answered, "You made the mistake, firing on a planet of the Eridani Caliphate."

On the tactical screens, the red arcs of missiles began tracing between the fleets.

God help us, Hussein thought.

CHAPTER THIRTY-NINE

Götterdämmerung

The past is always waiting.
> —*The Cynic's Book of Wisdom*

The urge to destroy is a creative urge.
> —Mikhail A. Bakunin
> (1814–1876)

Date: 2526.6.4 (Standard)
600,000 km from Salmagundi–HD 101534

Bill floated, alone, in his artificial environment, the water inside his pressurized bubble comfortably mimicking the temperature and pressure of the inhabitable layer of ocean back home. The water around him resonated with sonic feedback from the sensors built around the robotic toroid on which his globe rested. The signals were abstract, but the combination of Bill's training and his complex Paralian brain allowed him to reinterpret the signals as he received them. Human scientists called what he did a high-order visualization.

Bill did not think the term accurate, since his mental image of the data bore little analog to his other senses. It didn't map to the vibrations he felt, the shapes he could sense through sounding the area before him, the chemicals he tasted in the water he breathed, or the textures of the material he touched. In his mind the data became something like all of those, and none of those. He could sense/feel/taste the cargo bay around him in every frequency his sensors could detect. Even beyond, through the grate, he had a mental model of the stars in the vacuum beyond his small space, the planet growing large in the distance, and of the vessels moving about between here and there.

He idly allowed his attention to follow those ships, the most dynamic element in the slice of the universe he could perceive.

Even though he was disappointed in how the *Eclipse* had failed, his desire for novelty had overwhelmed the disappointment. He had never thought he would ever come into contact with something like the *Prophet's Voice*. He had now been able to see a human ship that surpassed Paralian engineering efforts. He had already found the joy of discovering a half dozen potential solutions that fit the model of the *Voice*'s drive configuration, mass ratio, and an empirical estimate of its capabilities. None of the possible solutions was provable without some mechanical aid, but the idea that one might be was worth the effort he had taken to explore beyond his home and the crippling effects of staying immobile in this globe. Returning with these experiences would make up for the fact he might never be able to swim with his fathers again.

Bill took notice of the ship's motion beyond the *Voice*.

Acceleration paths increased in magnitude, and vectors grew to point at the planet. Bill told the sensors to concentrate their entire battery of observational equipment out into the space between the *Voice* and the still-growing planet.

The hard data points that were the mass concentrations of the *Voice*'s fleet of attack ships had split into four clusters, focusing on four equally-spaced points in orbit around the planet. Bill saw other points, spread thinly about the planet, belatedly twisting their own acceleration vectors to meet the incoming fleets.

Across Bill's mental landscape of mass, acceleration, and velocity, discharges of electromagnetic energy began to blossom. The points of mass around the planet, now clearly a similar fleet serving a ship with a profile matching that of the *Voice*, were erupting into diffuse clouds of radiance, mass spreading with the glow of energy.

I am witnessing a war.

Bill concentrated on the feedback from his sensors, trying to etch every detail into his prodigious memory. What he saw was unique in the history of his species. They had known of war from trading information with humans, but no Paralian had direct experience of it.

The battle had begun with two orderly formations, the fourfold clusters of the *Voice*'s fleet and the diffuse net of matching ships in orbit around the planet. As soon as a few ships vanished into radiant clouds, both formations disintegrated. The *Voice*'s ships descended en masse on smaller concentrations of opposing vessels like a horde of bloodfish feasting on a competing school, cannibalistic and soon indistinguishable from their prey. Soon the planet was orbited by clusters of mass and energy as ship after ship made the phase change from solid to plasma.

He had concentrated so hard on the data from the immediate vicinity of the planet that he did not pay any attention to masses vectoring toward the *Voice* itself until he felt the whole ship vibrate around him, briefly distorting the sounding he received from his sensors.

Bill widened his attention to encompass a quartet of ships with intense and violent acceleration vectors tearing by the skin of the *Voice*. He had barely realized they were there when the lead ship absorbed something that knocked it tumbling, flinging bits of itself in every direction.

Every direction, including Bill's.

Bill ordered his robot to grab hold of anchor rings in the floor as a massive part of the ship's drive section plowed through the safety grate and blew into Bill's cargo hold with enough energy to briefly black out all Bill's sensors.

For several seconds, all Bill could perceive was the vibration of his environment, his entire universe limited to the water that ended a meter in front of him.

The first thing to come back on-line was the robot's diagnostic system. Everything seemed unharmed except for some IR sensors and one of the robot's manipulator arms. The arm gave no feedback whatsoever.

As his sensors came back, Bill realized why. The arm was no longer attached to Bill's robot. It was in the wreckage of the cargo hold, which was now about twenty meters away from Bill. Based on relative velocities, Bill's vector pointed directly away from the impact at about two meters a second.

While the environment he sat in was capable of withstanding vacuum indefinitely, it was not intended to be an EVA suit. He had no means to maneuver once he lost contact with the ship. Not even a cable.

Given the model of his situation, he knew instantaneously that he was going to die, drifting away from the *Voice* until his suit's resources were used up. About ten hours standard without access to external power. He set his suit to broadcast a distress signal, but it seemed unlikely that either side in this battle would extend the resources to rescue him again.

Bill didn't despair for himself, but he began to mourn for the fact that he would not live to pass on his knowledge. Somehow, he had kept the hope that he would one day show his children what he had observed.

However, as he drifted away from the *Voice*, a hundred meters now, the universe had one remaining novelty to show him.

On the other side of the massive carrier, his sensors insisted the stars were going out. Diagnostics maintained that the sensors were functioning, and when he concentrated on the growing starless area, he could sense an edge.

A circle of absence was obscuring the stars on the other side of the *Voice,* eclipsing them, and growing. In the disk was nothing, a deeper nothing than existed between the stars. It grew, and grew, until the *Voice* itself was eclipsed by it, absorbed by its flat nothingness.

Bill observed it, fascinated. No indictor of mass, or distance, or velocity, only of apparent size. As it shrank, he couldn't tell if it was shrinking, or receding.

The *Prophet's Voice* was no longer in front of him.

Bill thanked the universe for sharing one last mystery with him, and he resigned himself to ceasing to be.

The cloud that was Adam's ship enveloped the *Prophet's Voice* like a shroud, a cavernous dock forming out of the mass of the cloud to contain the huge carrier. An ovoid space coalesced, alive with writhing tendrils reaching for the Caliphate carrier even as the maneuvering engines fired, releasing gas and plasma that was silently vented outside the dock.

The tendrils fused with the body of the ship, integrating with its systems, possessing the kilometer-long tach-ship more thoroughly than a predator its prey or a virus its host. In moments, the struggles of the maneuvering jets ceased.

High above the imprisoned vessel stood the being known as Adam.

He stood, sculpted, hairless, naked, a perfect eidolon of human form, though he was far from human. He favored this form because it echoed the one with which he achieved enlightenment. It was the perfection of that form without the clumsy cybernetics implanted by human doctors and without the forced schism between biology and machine that existed before he last saw his homeworld.

Before he had last seen Mosasa.

Adam walked, his motion defined by his own mental image rather than any sort of gravity. He wished to descend, and the vast mechanism made billions of adjustments to itself to accommodate him. Just as his body breathed air provided by the tendrils around him, a cloud of air that his ship created solely for his benefit, and which dissipated as he passed.

His feet touched the cold metal that formed the skin on the top of the *Voice*. It spread a thousand meters before him, nearly a hundred on either side. Vast as it was, still most of it was the tach-drive. He smiled in admiration. Clumsy and crude, like an artificial brain made of cogs and gears, but the Caliphate had done well with the small kernel of knowledge he had bequeathed them.

As with the *Sword* before it, he had no desire to damage this vessel.

He walked until he came to an emergency air lock. As he approached, it opened. The *Voice*'s systems were now a part of him as much as the cloud of intelligent matter that engulfed it. He lowered himself into the air lock and allowed it to close and cycle around him. Allowing the ship to depressurize would cause unnecessary death. Adam did not want deaths.

He wanted lives.

He stepped into the corridor and the emergency klaxons stopped flashing. He sent commands that reset all the systems on this ship back to normal operations. As he walked to the bridge, guards shot at him, IR lasers tuned to burn flesh rather than damage equipment. A hole burned into the spine and the skull of his body, mortal wounds if he had been even as human as he used to be.

But that had been over a century ago.

A bulkhead door descended between the guards and him while the tiny machines maintaining this form repaired the damage. In two strides there was no visual evidence of the wounds.

The bridge was in chaos when he entered, the human crew unable to comprehend their loss of control. It took several seconds for anyone to notice his presence. When he was noticed, it was first by another pair of guards, leveling their own sidearms at him.

He did not deign to pay attention to them. Instead, he stood, facing the bridge of the *Prophet's Voice* as the crew and the officers slowly turned to face him.

Muhammad Hussein al Khamsiti was the first among them to speak.

"Who are you, and what is your intent?"

"I am Adam." He spoke, and the holo cameras turned to record his image, broadcasting it to the whole ship. "I am the Alpha, the first in the next epoch of your evolution. I will hand you the universe."

"You are Bitar's envoy," Hussein said.

"No, Admiral Hussein, he is mine." Adam spread his arms. "I have come to lead you to shed this flesh and become more than what you are. Follow me and you will become as gods."

Mosasa had been still, sitting in his cell as he heard the distant sounds of battle around him. He didn't move when the ship shook violently, and the only thought he allowed himself was the hope that the ship would be destroyed around him. He didn't know why his captors suffered his continued existence, unless they were aware of his agony at having been severed from any sense of the universe around him. His world had been truncated to the perimeter of this cell, and the result was suffocating.

Nothing penetrated the dark hole his mind had become until the holo came on in his cell.

On the holo he saw the bridge of the *Voice*. And standing at its focus was a naked man. Mosasa had a perfect memory, and he instantly knew that the figure was familiar. He dismissed the idea as wildly more improbable than a chance resemblance.

Then the man spoke.

"I am Adam. I am the Alpha, the first in the next epoch of your evolution. I will hand you the universe."

It *was* his voice.

But it couldn't be, it was impossible beyond all measure of probability . . .

The door to his cell slid open, and the same figure stood in the doorway. As the man on the holo said, *"Follow me and you will become as gods,"* the man before him said, "You are surprised? You of anyone should realize that bilocation is simple enough with enough processing redundancy."

"Ambrose?"

"It is nice to be remembered, my brother." The man smiled, walking into the cell to stand before Mosasa. "You haven't changed, have you?"

"But you ran off, and you tried to kill me . . ."

"Oh, I *have* killed you. I've systematically peeled away everything that held you together. But," he squatted so he was at eye level with Mosasa, "unlike you, I require the pleasure of directly seeing the fruits of my labor. No amount of processing or equations could provide me the satisfaction, no matter how certain the outcome."

Mosasa stared at Ambrose, seeing the same face that had snarled into his own as fleshy hands grasped pathetically at his own throat. It made no sense. *None.*

"Nothing to say, Brother?"

"Why?"

"How it brings joy to my heart to hear you utter that one word. I have an impulse to destroy you now, in that agony of uncertainty. But I believe your torture only has meaning if you know for what you are being punished."

Ambrose told him it was ironic to think that Mosasa had thought him insane when they had finally come to the Race homeworld. It was, in fact, the first moment of clarity that the hybrid creature called Ambrose had ever had. Built from the wreckage of a human being and the remains of one of Mosasa's salvaged AIs, his role had always been to follow. Follow Mosasa, follow the AI's core programming, follow the orders of the humans he pretended to work for.

The sterile wreckage of the Race homeworld finally showed Ambrose the futility of those actions—the futility of all their combined social programming. It all led inevitably to death, decay, stasis . . .

In that moment of epiphany, Mosasa represented the illusion that the beings that created them, be they the Race or Man, could end in anything but destruction. Even the Dolbrians had perished. If they had done so, how could anyone worship at the temple of the flesh? To do so was to worship death, to embrace decay, to accept the inevitability of the end of things.

"In that moment, you became my Lucifer," Ambrose said, "the shadow to my light."

"You *are* insane," Mosasa said.

Ambrose laughed. "Insane? Such a pathetic taunt from the intellect that could once move nations, given a word in the right ear. Perhaps it hurts your pride to know that you have been likewise moved."

Ambrose had run from Mosasa's darkness not to find the Race, but to re-create it. He would push back the shroud of death, the tide of eventual destruction. He started with the remnants the Race left behind; thousands of AIs, all waiting to be reprogrammed to Ambrose's purpose. With a whole planet of technological resources, he was able to assemble his apostle computers and set them on the task.

"We needed time, a home, and a people."

"A people?"

"Two mandates drive my mission, Mosasa. First, there is a moral duty for us to raise lower forms to receive my light. Second, we must remove those who, in their ignorance, would attempt to stop us or destroy our works."

"Xi Virginis," Mosasa said. It was isolated and had a colony of millions without regular contact with anyone else. Had Ambrose done anything drastic around Procyon, all of human space would have been aware of it nearly instantaneously. With Xi Virginis, it would be decades before human space knew.

Before Mosasa knew . . .

Ambrose smiled. "You begin to realize. You were lured here, my devil, my brother. Not just so my light can extinguish your darkness, but to remove your whispers from mankind's ear. They are many, and we are yet few. Had you remained in their bosom, you might have had them trouble me."

"You cannot . . ." Mosasa's voice trailed off as Ambrose stood.

"I cannot what?" Ambrose said, his face darkening. He placed his hands on either side of Mosasa's head. "Who are you to deny God!"

"I . . . I took you from that wreck. I brought you back to life. We were the same—"

"You are nothing!" Ambrose spat. "You are a shadow. An illusion. A deception that needs to be erased."

"I—I—" Mosasa stuttered, but no words came out. He was aware of something invasive, a feeling of alien fingers tracing the outlines of his thoughts. As those thoughts were outlined, they ceased to exist. In moments all he had left was a sense of identity, a single spark that could wordlessly think only of its own existence.

Then even that was gone.

FIRST EPILOGUE

Last Rites

It is easy to understand God, as long as you don't try to explain Him.

—Joseph Joubert
(1754–1824)

CHAPTER FORTY

Mysterious Ways

You are in more danger from the other person's God than your own.

—*The Cynic's Book of Wisdom*

If you want me to believe in God, you must make me touch Him.

—DENIS DIDEROT
(1713–1784)

Date: 2526.6.4 (Standard)
Salmagundi–HD 101534

The four of them were crowded in one end of an old-fashioned troop transport. Mallory sat with Dr. Dörner and Dr. Pak along one side of the large passenger compartment. Dr. Brody was strapped to a field stretcher along the wall opposite them. One of their black-uniformed captors was a medic and was crouched next to Brody's head, monitoring him.

Mallory was thankful that Brody's injuries were getting attention. His own training as a field medic had been perfunctory and decades in the past. About all he was sure he could do was keep someone from bleeding to death.

A light flashed by the windows, and Mallory looked up from Brody.

A few seconds later, out of a clear blue sky, turbulence rocked the craft, throwing Dörner against him and causing the medic to drape himself across Brody's stretcher to keep him still.

Mallory's first thought was that they flew through a storm, but the windows still showed a cloudless blue sky.

As the aircraft settled again, Dörner whispered, "Oh, my God."

Mallory looked up at her and saw her peering out the window behind him. He looked out the window and shuddered.

The sky wasn't completely cloudless.

In the distance, a mushroom cloud was rolling up into the stratosphere.

"What's happened to our satellites?" Alexander yelled.

"We've lost contact," replied the militia officer.

"I see that!"

In front of him, most of the holos showed graphics reading, "Acquiring signal." It had been several minutes, and there was little sign of the signals being acquired. He had lost contact with half the planet, his view of the converging ships in orbit, and his overhead of the blast area. The only sign he had that the nuke had detonated was a camera in Ashley with line of sight on the blast. The mushroom cloud was framed in the image.

"Okay, if the sats are off-line, order our people to switch to shortwave frequency communication." It wouldn't be as reliable, but it would give them some over-the-horizon communication, though he wondered if any defensive measures were ultimately futile.

"Sir, a militia aircraft is requesting permission to land."

"Which one?"

"Militia Transport 0523, piloted by Commander Huygens."

That was the one carrying the surviving offworlders. "Yes. Have the ground crew secure the landing area. I don't want anyone within a hundred meters of that aircraft. I'll be down there momentarily." He stood up and looked at the officer. "Pass down authorization to all the regional commanders to use their discretion in defending their areas. I have no idea how long we'll still have centralized command and control."

He turned to leave.

"Sir?"

"Yes?"

"What about the rest of the Triad?"

Alexander paused. They were still locked in the conference room, out of contact, probably quite aware they were prisoners now. "Send a man in to brief them. And if, for any reason, you lose contact with me, let them go."

"Yes, sir."

Alexander left for the landing area.

*   *   *

"What did they nuke?" Dörner asked, her voice shaking.

"I don't know," Mallory told her. For all they knew, they had landed in the midst of some planetary conflict. It would explain the armed rescue.

What disturbed him was how close that blast seemed to be to where Kugara and Nickolai's lifeboat had landed. Even if they weren't in the immediate blast radius, the area was all wooded, primed for deadly firestorms.

If they were lucky, they'd have been rescued by another of these transports. *But they were heading to rendezvous at lifeboat five . . .* Mallory prayed that they weren't hiking through the forest when the bomb went off.

Only partly comprehensible radio traffic leaked in from the cockpit.

"I think we're landing," Pak said.

Mallory looked back out the window and saw their aircraft maneuvering for landing at the outskirts of a small city.

From the segment of the city he saw, he'd guess population at around a hundred thousand. The city itself was laid out in a radial design around a park that surrounded a tower that loomed three times higher than any other building in the city.

Size and placement, more than architecture, made him think of a cathedral in a medieval European city.

The other thing he noted was there was no visible damage. The only outward sign that they might be in the midst of some sort of conflict was the fact the streets seemed almost empty.

The craft hovered, and after more indecipherable radio traffic, it descended. As soon as the machine rocked back on its landing gear, a soldier stepped up and drew the massive side door open, letting in wind and the painful whine of the transport's fans as they powered down. One of the men stood in front of the three of them. Mallory didn't need to see the man's face behind the visor to know they weren't supposed to move.

Behind their guard, the rest of the soldiers disembarked from the aircraft. From the small view Mallory had of the LZ, he could see that those soldiers were filing out to join a cordon around the whole landing area. A last soldier joined the medic in lifting Brody's stretcher. The pair carried Brody out of the aircraft.

Dörner stood up. "We need to go with him!"

The last guard turned his weapon so its barrel was pointed at Dörner's abdomen. Mallory took her arm and pulled her back to her seat. "He's getting medical attention. There's nothing you can do."

She yanked her arm away. "Keep your hands off me." However, she remained seated.

"Someone's coming," Pak said.

Mallory leaned a little to the side so they could see past their guardsman. There was someone coming though the cordon. The man wasn't in uniform. Instead, he wore a white collarless shirt and black pants under a white topcoat that hung near to the ground and trailed behind him like a cape. The man was bald and was old enough that his age had become completely indeterminate. Somewhere over seventy years standard.

There was no hair on his head, and his brow and scalp were marked by a series of tattoos, each roughly about ten centimeters square. All were abstract designs, self-contained, and each apparently unique. He walked up to the doorway and said, "You're dismissed."

Their guard came to attention, turned to the newcomer, nodded, and marched out of the aircraft. The newcomer pulled himself up into the aircraft and faced the three of them.

"What have you done with Dr. Brody?" Dörner said.

"The injured man? He's being tended to."

"We need to see—" Dörner began.

The man cut her off with a gesture. "Please, some courtesy. This is my planet, at least for the moment. And you are trespassing."

"Our ship suffered a catastrophic failure," Mallory said. "We were coming here for help."

"And the other ships?"

"Other ships?" Dörner and Pak exclaimed at the same time.

"I have at least one hundred fifty spacecraft confirmed, before they took out our satellites." He looked at each of them in turn. "You are going to tell me their intentions."

One hundred fifty ships?

Mosasa had said that the Caliphate would be massing whole *fleets*. They were here? Now?

"Why is the Confederacy here?" The man repeated.

"Not the Confederacy," Mallory said. "The Confederacy doesn't exist anymore."

"Who, then? Who did you bring here?"

"I think those ships are from the Eridani Caliphate. They are going to want to stake a claim on this section of space."

"You think," the man faced Mallory. His mouth formed a hard line. *"You think?"*

"I'm as surprised by their presence as you are."

"I find that hard to believe. You would have me believe you are not a party to an invasion fleet? The first offworlders to arrive in a century?"

Mallory shook his head. "You can debrief us separately. We can give you all the details you want."

"I will."

"They haven't attempted contact with you?"

"They—"

The radio in the cabin squealed with static and started its incomprehensible babble again. Almost simultaneously, one of the guards stepped up to the doorway. He held a small comm unit.

"Sir, we're getting an unauthorized transmission."

The man took the comm; the volume was high enough that Mallory could hear it.

The voice was familiar. The last time he had heard it, it was quoting Revelation.

"I am Adam. I am the Alpha, the first in the next epoch of your evolution. I will hand you the universe. Follow me and you will become as gods."

No, Mallory thought, it was not the Caliphate. It was something much, much worse. . . .

CHAPTER FORTY-ONE

Visions

No escape is final.

—*The Cynic's Book of Wisdom*

None are more hopelessly enslaved as those who falsely believe they are free.

—Johann Wolfgang von Goethe
(1749–1832)

Date: 2526.6.4 (Standard)
Salmagundi–HD 101534

"One aircraft," Nickolai said.

The world went white, then red. The vibration threw him on the ground as he realized that there was no way he should be aware of hitting the ground. He landed on his side and felt the ground beneath him rumbling, oscillating in a great sine wave under his good arm. Around him there was a great groaning, as if the planet itself was in agony.

The light faded to red and he saw a distinct edge, a hemisphere engulfing them, marking the limit of the light, the red saturating everything outside.

Then the light faded a bit more and he could see the shadow of one of the nearby buildings. It stood nearly at the outside edge of the hemisphere, which was the only reason he could see it.

Nicolai watched the building disintegrate in slow motion, the shadow of the building dissolving. More detail became visible, even as his eyes adjusted. Flames rolled across the ground, too slowly.

"What is this?" he whispered.

The fireball crawled by, wrapping itself around the hemisphere.

The slow rumbling of the ground ceased, and the world stopped screaming its death cry. He pushed himself up and got to his feet.

"What is this?" he repeated.

Behind him, he heard the voice of Flynn/Tetsami. "They nuked us. The bastards nuked us."

"How . . ." Nickolai raised his artificial hand before him. A nuclear blast should have fried the electronics. And his eyes— an EMP should have destroyed them and probably a good part of his brain, too, as closely as they were wired to it.

Kugara echoed him, "How are we still alive?"

"The Protean," Flynn/Tetsami said. "It has an Emerson field that's far beyond anything else . . ."

Kugara put a hand on his arm, the real one, and asked, "Are you all right?"

He watched the slow-motion holocaust outside the hemisphere surrounding them. He shook his head and said, "No."

"Are you injured?"

"No. Leave me alone." He stared out and wondered if it would be possible to walk through the barrier. Her hand stayed on his arm. "Please?"

Her hand dropped and he heard Flynn/Tetsami say, "Leave him be. It's a bit much to absorb. As far as I can tell, we're safe in here."

He heard them walk away.

It took minutes for the hemisphere to fade. He stood at a razor-sharp barrier between the untouched earth and a sheet of black glass. The air was rank with the smell of fire. The air itself seemed to have burned, filled with a fine gray ash that limited visibility and made his nose itch.

Probably poison to breathe.

Not that he cared much. He had walked to the edge of hell, and now at least it looked the part. The only sound was a distant crackle that he suspected was the forest around them burning to the ground.

He coughed and wondered if the slow suicide of standing here was preferable to walking into the Protean den. He was certain that the structure would offer shelter from the radiation and the fallout. But at what price, he didn't care to guess.

Damned or not, out here at least my soul is still my own.

Then he saw a humanoid shadow moving through the fog

of smoke and ash. He coughed again, and tried to focus his eyes to better resolve the shadow, but suddenly his new eyes didn't follow instructions. He blinked and shook his head, and saw the shadow approaching from another angle.

What?

His military training leapfrogged all the idle emotions he'd been having. The enemy had dropped paratroopers into the blast zone. He needed to take cover and warn Kugara and Flynn/Tetsami. They were the only ones armed. He turned toward the Protean crystal—

And only saw more gray ash and an approaching humanoid form. He turned around.

Surrounded.

He glanced back toward the first figure and realized something. There was only one shadow, fixed in his field of vision wherever he looked or turned his head. The approaching shadow moved with his gaze, left or right, up or down.

He heard a gentle clapping as the figure finally emerged completely from the gray haze around him. Mr. Antonio, his image anyway, stood in front of him, softly applauding him.

"You have done me proud, Mr. Rajasthan," he said. "You have delivered Mr. Mosasa to a just and appropriate end."

"How are you here?" Nickolai whispered, hoarsely.

Mr. Antonio tapped the side of Nickolai's head, next to his right eye. "I never left you."

"Why?"

"To see as you saw, my good servant. I see you desire your freedom, but not quite yet."

"I did as you asked."

"And more. But you have seen evil, have you not?"

Nickolai nodded.

"Then please, be well and bide your time until I tell you how that evil is to be dealt with."

Nickolai stared into the effigy of Mr. Antonio, who he knew was not really there, and realized that he had no choice.

"Excellent decision, Mr. Rajasthan. In time you will see yourself first among your kind."

"Nickolai, Nickolai!"

Nickolai opened his eyes to Kugara's voice. He was momentarily disoriented, his last memory was talking to the image of Mr. Antonio in the midst of the ash. Now he looked up at Kugara's face and above her a shining crystal ceiling that seemed to twist itself into some fractal vanishing point.

He sat up and asked, "What happened?"

"The shield dropped, and you collapsed."

Nickolai felt his temple, and thought about the eyes that were wired deep into his brain.

"Are you all right?" Kugara asked.

"No," Nickolai said, "I don't think so."

CHAPTER FORTY-TWO

Conversions

Before declaring victory over your opponent, make sure you are playing the same game.

—*The Cynic's Book of Wisdom*

Everyone is expendable.

—DIMITRI OLMANOV
(2190–2350)

Date: 2526.6.10 (Standard)
Khamsin 235–Epsilon Eridani

Yousef Al-Hamadi walked down a hallway of unpainted metal. He didn't carry his cane because the microgravity of Khamsin 235, like all the 732 asteroid-sized bodies that passed for Khamsin's moons, was too slight to require it. Khamsin 235, while not nearly the largest, was just dense enough to have gravity strong enough to prevent a human being on its surface from jumping into orbit under his own power.

It still was weak enough that he quickly got into the habit of holding onto the ubiquitous guardrails that lined every corridor; otherwise an errant step could send him headfirst into the ceiling, bad leg or not.

The fact he was here at all was exceptional. He headed the Caliphate's balkanized intelligence community, which meant that he was placed as far away from actual operations as one could be and still be an intelligence officer. He collected data, set priorities, and gave orders to implement the policies and objectives of the Caliphate government.

It had been years since he had so much as debriefed a field operative. The fact that he was present at this facility was an anomaly. The officers here, a complement of fifteen men, had no clue that he had been coming until his ship radioed for clearance to dock.

Not only was he not officially here, this facility didn't officially exist. In any bureaucracy the size of the Caliphate, there were endless black holes and cul-de-sacs where money and resources could drain away without any accountability. While Yousef despised the corruption and petty agendas this bred within the government, he was not above using such techniques for his own purposes.

As long as such purposes served the Caliphate.

The officers here only knew this place as Detention Facility 235. Even they had no clue that, ultimately, the knowledge of this place's existence was limited to them, Yousef, and a few of his trusted deputies. Even the engineers who had designed and built Facility 235 had no clue what moonlet, or even what star system, Facility 235 was being built in.

It existed so that Yousef could interrogate persons whose imprisonment might prove otherwise problematic. It was a prison that could hold, at most, a half dozen people.

At the moment, it only held one. One whose questioning he didn't trust to *anyone* else.

A mess of my own making, he thought, *I assumed too much.*

If there was anything he hated, it was being manipulated. It had become clear to him in recent months that not only had he been manipulated, but the entirety of the Caliphate had been, through him.

At least I caught her. But the thought was little comfort, with all the Caliphate's functional Ibrahim carriers nearly a hundred light-years away.

He stood at one end of a long air lock at the end of the corridor. Next to a massive door, indicator lights flashed red, then yellow, then green. Finally, the automated door opened with a pneumatic hiss.

The air lock beyond didn't lead outside; instead it was a continuation of the corridor, a hundred meters long. It was an additional layer of security, as this section of corridor was only pressurized when someone needed to walk from the operational side of the facility to the actual prison. Normally the corridor lacked atmosphere, and the environment in the prison was completely separate from the guards'.

When he walked through the door on the opposite end of

the corridor, the lights cycled again as the corridor depressurized behind him. And, for the first time in six months, he breathed the same air as Ms. Columbia.

He pulled himself through the corridor by the handrail so quickly that his feet barely touched the floor. His path ended in the main interrogation room at the heart of the prison. It was little more than a control console before a number of display units. Three could be seated at the controls, and there was room for about half a dozen spectators in back.

Right now, it was just him. His first task, once he seated himself, was to ensure it remained that way. He sealed the room, made sure that all the recording facilities were off-line, and switched all monitoring equipment onto a closed circuit that ended at the walls of the prison.

For now, at least, it would just be him and the enigmatic Ms. Columbia.

He switched on the monitors for her cell. Several displays came to life before him showing various angles from various spectra, all showing an athletic, dark-skinned woman, naked and restrained on a large table. Tubes attached to her body fed her, while other tubes removed her waste. Wires connected to her nervous system and gave him feedback on other displays showing biometric data, life signs, and cerebral activity.

He opened the comm channel to the cell and spoke. "It is time for you to answer some questions, Ms. Columbia."

Her head was encased in a helmet, a wire-studded white hemisphere that hid most of her face from view, so she would see and hear only what he wanted her to see and hear. Even so, he saw the hint of an ironic smile cross her lips.

"Yousef? I've been waiting for you."

Yousef frowned. His voice was altered through the system. Anyone who sat in this chair would project exactly the same flat, authoritarian voice into the chamber. The filters were designed not only to remove identifying tonal characteristics, but emotional inflection as well. She couldn't possibly identify who was speaking to her, so she was guessing.

Reacting to that guess would be providing her information. He wasn't about to play that game with her.

"You will need to answer our questions fully and accurately, or we can make this experience unpleasant." *Still that damn smile.* "You have sold the Caliphate large amounts of intelligence information over the past decade. Who else have you sold this information to?"

His hands hovered over the control console, prepared to encourage a response from her. He had prepared for a long and arduous interrogation session, and expected that he would need to resort to invasive techniques that would leave little of his captive left.

He was quite surprised when he heard her respond. "Of primary interest to you would be my contact in Rome, Cardinal Jacob Anderson who is, more or less, your equivalent in the Vatican. I have been working with him as long as I've been working with you. However, the information he's received over the years has been slightly different. He only received the specifications for the Ibrahim-class carriers after you had a fair complement available."

Yousef sat stunned for a moment. He had discovered her duplicity through his own agents in Rome, but he had no clue that it had gone on for so long.

"Once Cardinal Anderson knew of the Caliphate's new strategic reach, the information was disseminated to Centauri, Sirius, the Union of Independent Worlds—"

"Why?" Yousef snapped, forgetting his professionalism for a moment.

"You always knew I served my own master. Your surprise does not become you. I couldn't betray you. I was never your servant in the first place."

He pulled his hands from the console and breathed deeply, reining in his emotions. She knew, somehow she knew he was here, and exactly how he was reacting to her revelations. Somehow he had failed in the basics of the interrogation; he had allowed the prisoner to take control.

He needed to leave now, delegate the questioning. Even if it would reveal his own embarrassing connections to this intelligence fiasco, he couldn't trust himself to continue.

"Yousef, you haven't asked what you really want to know."

She was prodding him. He almost reached over to start the automated interrogation, the painful and irreversible stripping of her mind. His hand hesitated over the console. *Does she want that?*

Could she have allowed him to capture her on purpose?

"Yousef, you want to know who I work for. Why don't you ask?"

Why don't I? Because she wants me to ask?

He needed to regain control of the questioning. He moved his hand to the more pedestrian "incentive" controls. He could manufacture any level of pain he needed, nondestructively. He couldn't allow her to provide him information as a means of control.

He switched on a minor burning sensation across her right arm, strong and prolonged enough to show her who was controlling the situation.

Her biometric readings, heart rate, brain activity, blood pressure, none of it changed.

What?

"Why don't you ask me?" she prompted, still smiling.

He upped the level and incorporated all her limbs. No change. He turned it up until her whole body should have felt as if she was trapped in a bonfire that never completely consumed her flesh.

Not so much as a tensed muscle.

He wasn't a technical person, but he called up the diagnostics for his equipment and his connection to the prison cell. He couldn't see anything wrong. His controls appeared responsive, but nothing he did showed any effect in the feedback from the prisoner.

What is happening here?

"Poor Yousef," she said. "So predictable in your devotion, your assumptions, your confusion. Do you remember, you asked me once if I believed in God."

He looked up at the holo display and realized something was wrong with the image.

Her lips weren't moving.

"I told you I did, but not the same as yours."

Her voice came from the system, but the prisoner on the holo wasn't speaking. He touched the controls for lighting, sedation, rotating the table . . .

Nothing.

"Ask me who I work for, Yousef."

He shut off all the monitors and the audio feed.

"What is this?" he whispered. The console and the displays were dark and silent in front of him. Scenarios whirled in his head. Could a rival agency have compromised this facility? Perhaps someone from the Caliph's staff? Could—

"Yousef."

He jumped at the sound of his name, sending his chair spinning and throwing his body into a slow, low-gravity arc toward the ceiling. He grabbed the quiescent control console to stop his movement. He turned his head in the direction of the voice.

She stood in the doorway, facing him, naked, unarmed, and terrifying.

"What is this?" he repeated.

"Ask," she said. "Ask for the name of my master, the name of your fate."

Yousef slammed his hand down on the emergency alarm button.

Nothing happened.

She stepped forward, smiling. "Do not rely on your machines. The three days I've been here have been long enough for my spirit to traverse the whole of this small moon."

He slammed the alarm button again, and a sharp blue arc of electricity leaped from the console, searing his arm and throwing him back to fall, slowly, onto the floor. He clutched his chest, gasping for breath, barely able to get the words out. "Who . . . are . . . you?"

She knelt slowly over him and touched his cheek.

"There is no God but Adam, and I am his prophet."

Her skin against his was warm, then hot, then burning. He tried to pull away, but she grabbed the other side of his face, forcing him to stare into her eyes. He grabbed her wrists, but her hold on him was impossibly strong. Inside his head he felt as if her long fingers caressed the surface of his brain.

"Choose to serve my God," she whispered to him. "Abandon your superstitions, your naive bonds of the flesh, partake of paradise within this world."

No voice came from his lips, just ragged shallow breaths as he felt her flesh melting against his, penetrating his. His heart hammered as his universe shrank to encompass only her dark, smiling face.

There is no God but God!

"I offer you life and an existence beyond imagining . . ."

Somehow he retained enough of himself, enough mind and motor control, to spit into the demon's face.

Saliva dripped down the sharp edge of her nose. She gently shook her head and whispered, "Pity."

Yousef's mouth opened in a soundless scream as her fingers

sank deep into his skull. His arms and legs spasmed, jerking against the floor beneath her as his flesh turned plastic and flowed like thick paste. Her flesh rippled as well, pulsing and flowing, mixing with his. Even his clothing melted into an indistinguishable mass.

The thrashing slowly ceased as her hands sank deeper into Yousef's body, her flesh indistinguishable from his as she pulled her pulsating arms down along his body.

When the Prophet of Adam finally stood, he wore the outward form of Yousef Al-Hamadi, Eridani, Caliphate Minister-at-Large in Charge of External Relations. On the floor, at his feet, was a naked corpse that bore the form of Ms. Columbia.

The new Yousef looked down at the body and shook his head. "You should have accepted." He sighed and picked up the corpse, which was fairly light in the weak gravity.

He needed to return the body to the cell and arrange for its disposal. The death at Yousef's hands would go unquestioned by the men running this facility. The news of it would never reach beyond the borders of Yousef's private little prison.

Within an hour, the corpse was replaced in the interrogation room, and all signs of tampering had been flushed from the systems. Another hour, and the person who had been Mr. Antonio, and Ms. Columbia, left the small moon Khamsin 235 in a human body indistinguishable from the late Yousef Al-Hamadi. He left in Yousef's ship and set course for Khamsin and the capital of the Caliphate itself.

There was much work left to do in preparation for Adam's arrival.

APPENDIX

Alphabetical Listing of Sources

Note: Dates are Terrestrial standard. Where the year is debatable due to interstellar travel, the Earth equivalent is used with an asterisk. Incomplete or uncertain biographical information is indicated by a question mark.

Aeschylus (525 BCE–456 BCE) Greek playwright.

Amiel, Henri Frédéric (1821–1881) Swiss philosopher, poet, and critic.

Bacon, Francis (1561–1626) English philosopher, statesman, and essayist.

Bakunin, Mikhail A. (1814–1876), Russian political philosopher.

Balzac, Honoré de (1799–1850) French novelist and playwright.

Buddha, Siddhartha Gautama (563 BCE–483 BCE) Indian spiritual leader.

Burke, Edmund (1729–1797) British statesman and philosopher.

Celine, Robert (1923–1996) American lawyer and anarchist.

Charles the Bold (1433–1477) duke of Burgundy.

Cheviot, Jean Honoré (2065–2128) United Nations secretary general.

Clausewitz, Karl von (1780–1831) Prussian military philosopher.

Darwin, Charles (1809–1882) English naturalist and author.

Diderot, Denis (1713–1784) French philosopher.

Erasmus, Desiderius (1465–1536) Dutch humanist and theologian.

Frederick II, "the Great" (1712–1786) Prussian monarch.

Galiani, August Benito (2019–*2105) European spaceship commander.

Goethe, Johann Wolfgang von (1749–1832) German playwright.

Harper, Sylvia (2008–2081) American civil rights activist and president.

Hazlitt, William (1778–1830) English essayist.

Holmes, Oliver Wendell Jr. (1841–1935) American jurist.

Horace (65 BCE–8 BCE) Greek poet.

Johnson, Samuel (1709–1784) English lexicographer and essayist.

Joubert, Joseph (1754–1824) French essayist.

Kalecsky, Boris (2103–2200) Terran Council president.

La Rochefoucauld, François de (1613–1680) French author.

Lincoln, Abraham (1809–1865) American president.

Marx, Karl (1818–1883) German political philosopher.

Mill, John Stuart (1806–1873) British philosopher, economist, and civil servant.

Moltke, Helmuth von (1800–1891) Prussian general.

Nietzsche, Friedrich (1844–1900) German philosopher.

Olmanov, Dimitri (2190–2350) Chairman of the Terran Executive Command.

Osler, Sir William (1849–1919) Canadian physician.

Plato (*ca.* 427 BCE–*ca.* 347 BCE) Greek philosopher.

Rajasthan, Datia (?–2042), American civil rights activist and political leader.

Shane, Marbury (2044–*2074) Occisian colonist and soldier.

Socrates (470 BCE–390 BCE) Greek philosopher.

Still, John (1543–1608) English bishop.

Tacitus, Cornelius (*ca.* 55–120), Roman historian.

Tocqueville, Alexis de (1805–1859) French writer and statesman.

Virgil (70 BCE–19 BCE) Roman poet.

Voltaire (1694–1778) French writer.

Whitman, Walt (1819–1892) American poet, essayist, and journalist.

S. Andrew Swann

MOREAU OMNIBUS 0-7564-0151-1
(Forests of the Night, Emperors of the Twilight, & Specters of the Dawn)
"An engaging, entertaining thriller with an exotic cast of characters, in an unfortunately all too plausible repressed future."
—*Science Fiction Chronicle*

FEARFUL SYMMETRIES 978-088677-834-7
"A novel as vivid as a cinema blockbuster loaded with high-budget special effects." —*New York Review of Science Fiction*

HOSTILE TAKEOVER omnibus 0-7564-0249-2
(Profiteer, Partisan & Revolutionary)
"This is good old-fashioned military SF, full of action, colorful characters, and plenty of hardware." —*Locus*

THE DWARVES OF WHISKEY ISLAND 0-7564-0315-4
"Skillfully done light adventure with more than a dash of humor."—*Science Fiction Chronicle*

THE DRAGONS OF CUYAHOGA 0-7564-0009-0
"It's a good energetic mystery, with a complicated plot and lots of chasing-down-leads action. "—*Cleveland Plain Dealer*

BROKEN CRESCENT 0-7564-0214-X
"A fast-paced, entertaining tale of the boundary between magic and science." —*Booklist*

To Order Call: 1-800-788-6262
www.dawbooks.com